Teacups and Temptations

by

Kate Ellington

The Wild Rose Press, Inc.
PO Box 708
Adams Basin, NY 14410-0708
Visit us at www.thewildrosepress.com

Publishing History
First Edition, 2025
Trade Paperback ISBN 978-1-5092-5869-7
Digital ISBN 978-1-5092-5870-3

Published in the United States of America

Dedication

A heartfelt thanks to my wonderful friend Nancy,
who supported and encouraged me from day one
while I was writing *Teacups And Temptations*.

~

Next I'd like to express my deep gratitude
to Julie, Crista, Christina, Cat and Nancy.
Their insight and feedback
helped me write a better story.

~

Thank you to Brian,
who helps me keep things in perspective
and always keeps me laughing.

~

I must take a moment to acknowledge my parents
and sisters for their love and encouragement,
which means the world.

~

Special thanks to Nan Swanson and the rest of the team
at Wild Rose Press.

~

Finally, I'd like to thank
my husband Tom and our children,
whose love and support make my writing possible.

Chapter One

Molly Merriwether combed through her wardrobe, searching for the best gowns to pack for her trip. At long last, a chance to see the countryside, visit Rochester and, most importantly, escape her mother's constant chatter about suitors, balls, and the upcoming Season.

"You should have chosen your dresses last night," said her friend Caroline Darby, behind her.

"I know, but I've been busy." Molly turned, a cornflower-blue gown held up to her chin. "What about this one?"

"One of your most becoming. Yes, bring it."

Molly threw the gown onto the bed and continued rummaging.

As Rochester was two days away, they'd be spending tonight at an inn. With any luck, Molly could convince Caroline to sneak out while their chaperone slept and visit the common room or, better yet, a tavern. Molly had heard enough about taverns from her three brothers to be curious, but her mother had heard enough about them to forbid Molly ever stepping foot in one. She'd even hinted that Molly shouldn't *think* about taverns, which made them all the more intriguing.

Caroline walked over to the bed. "You really shouldn't leave these things to the last minute. We were supposed to leave two hours ago." She sighed and flopped down on Molly's chosen dresses, arms spread wide.

"Get, up, Caroline. You just told me we need to leave." Molly tugged at a gown under her friend's head.

Caroline looked up at her, unmoving. "Do you think I'm doing the right thing, going to meet Mr. Clarke? Perhaps I should wait a while longer."

Molly bit back a tiny groan. They'd been over this topic more times than she could count. "Of course you should go meet him. You've been corresponding with him for almost a year and he's the closest thing to a suitor you have. Moreover, if not Mr. Clarke, what's the alternative?"

Caroline sat up. "I suppose if I don't like him I'd have to hope my father has another friend with an eligible son."

"Right. Or go through a Season with me and meet somebody that way." Molly shuddered at the thought. Many young ladies reveled in the idea of new gowns, balls, suitors and the like, but Molly had always dreaded it; one would either be snapped up immediately or go through the humiliation of being passed over time and time again. If she ever fell in love, she hoped it would come about more naturally. Perhaps she'd be out riding and lock eyes with a passing gentleman, or brush hands with a man as they reached for the same novel at a bookshop.

"You're right," Caroline said. "I'm glad you convinced your mother to let you accompany me to Rochester. I don't know how I'd go through it without you."

Molly retrieved a pile of gloves from the dressing table and set them on the bed with her gowns. "You'd be just fine. Your aunt will be with you, after all."

"But Aunt Hazel's a chaperone, not my best friend."

"Fortunately, my mother did say yes, and we'll have a grand time." Molly glanced at the clock on her writing desk. "We'd better get downstairs."

Once Molly's trunk was packed, she and Caroline made their way to the parlor.

Aunt Hazel sat on the sofa, sipping tea. She was dressed in her customary high-necked gown—peach today—and her black hair was pulled back into a bun. Though not Molly's true aunt, Hazel had allowed her to address her as such all her life.

Mrs. Merriwether and Mrs. Darby stood beside the pianoforte, supposedly discussing the journey. From the way they whispered to each other, Molly suspected they were in fact having a good gossip. Their daughters going off to Rochester wouldn't bring such color to their cheeks or light to their eyes.

Molly and Caroline joined Aunt Hazel on the sofa. While Caroline chatted with her aunt, Molly helped herself to a cup of tea and looked out the window. Lilac bushes burst with flowers and beyond them the sky was a cloudless blue. In the distance four gray horses were being led to the carriage. Molly smiled as she stirred her tea. It wouldn't be long now.

Molly chose a scone and slathered it with strawberry jam but before she could take a bite her mother addressed her. "Packing your trunk took much longer than I expected. It should have been done last night."

Caroline gave Molly a pointed look. "As I told you."

Molly gave her a playful shove, spilling her tea in the process.

"Molly!" Mrs. Merriwether snapped. "You must control such childish antics while at Waverly Hall."

Aunt Hazel set her teacup down with a clatter, cutting Molly's answer off. "You may depend upon me keeping her firmly in line. She will certainly *not* behave so in front of the Clarkes."

"Of course I won't," Molly said, mopping the tea up with a napkin. After spending three weeks cajoling her mother into allowing her to accompany Caroline, she wouldn't allow anything to jeopardize her ability to stay for the whole visit.

Aunt Hazel looked skeptical as she turned to Caroline. "What do we know about this young man we're going to see?"

"His name in Benedict Clarke, and he lives with his family in Rochester, at Waverly Hall. Our fathers went to school together," Caroline said.

"And?" Aunt Hazel asked.

Molly chimed in with what Caroline had read to her from his letters. "He has a brother, he's well educated, and he enjoys long walks."

"He's the heir, and I met him once, when we went to Rochester last summer," Caroline said.

"Not much to go on," Mrs. Merriwether said. "But maybe that's for the better."

Caroline's mother waved a hand. "Oh, more than enough. We encouraged this exchange of letters between them so they could become acquainted."

"Exchanging letters!" Aunt Hazel's hand flew to her chest.

Mrs. Darby turned to her sister. "We've read all the letters, Hazel. I assure you nothing untoward has been going on."

"I'm glad you're taking proper precautions. But corresponding with a man at Caroline's age…" Aunt

Hazel shook her head, clearly doubting her sister's wisdom in this decision.

Molly met Caroline's gaze and had to stifle her laughter. Mr. Clarke wasn't what Molly would call verbose, and most of the letters had been more like notes. She hoped for Caroline's sake he was more engaging in person.

"When are we leaving?" Molly asked. She drank the only bit of tea that hadn't spilled and picked up her scone.

Mrs. Merriwether checked the clock. "As soon as your trunks are stowed."

Aunt Hazel rose and addressed the room at large. "Do the young ladies have clear expectations as to their behavior once we arrive at Waverly Hall?"

Since nobody looked quite sure who should answer, Molly did. "We're to act with the utmost decorum, not laugh, nor sing, nor draw unnecessary attention to ourselves. Caroline will meet with Mr. Clarke as his schedule allows, and otherwise the two of us will amuse ourselves."

Mrs. Merriwether widened her eyes at Molly, her usual way of reminding her she was talking too much. Molly set to eating her scone.

"Make yourselves available to Mrs. Clarke," Mrs. Darby said. "She'll no doubt enjoy having two young ladies to look after. And of course she'll appreciate another woman in the house, Hazel."

Aunt Hazel inclined her head just as a footman entered the room to announce that the carriage was ready.

Molly put her half eaten scone back on the tea tray and reached for Caroline's hand, smiling. "Finally," she mouthed silently.

Hours later, Molly slumped in her seat as the carriage trundled down the road. The beginning of the journey had been full of laughter, talk and excitement, but now all three women resembled wilted flowers. Caroline rested her chin in her hand, staring blankly out the window; Aunt Hazel had fallen asleep three villages ago.

Molly smiled as she watched the countryside speed by. She'd been yearning to get away from home for two reasons. The first was her mother. The older Molly got, the more critical her mother became. Or had she always acted thus but Molly hadn't noticed? She'd taken to muttering about any perceived fault of Molly's she could find—commenting on her clothes, her decorum, her hobbies—or lack thereof. It would be refreshing to be away from that for at least a little while. The second reason was that going with Caroline allowed her to delay her Season for another year. Going into town for the Season would have been almost bearable with Caroline to share it with, but alone? She didn't want to think about it.

Molly shifted in her seat, vainly attempting to stretch properly without standing up. She caught sight of torchlight up ahead and prodded Caroline's foot with hers. "Look. I think we're coming to the village."

Caroline turned away from the window. "Should we wake Auntie?"

Aunt Hazel had sunk down into her seat, arms crossed and hat askew.

"Not yet. We'll make sure we're stopping first."

Before long the carriage slowed and they pulled into the courtyard of The Blue Swan Inn. There was no need to wake Aunt Hazel, for the carriage lurched to a halt, knocking their bags to the floor.

Aunt Hazel's eyes flew open as both hands went to her hat. "Oh!"

"We're here, Auntie," Caroline said unnecessarily.

Aunt Hazel rubbed the sleep from her eyes, grimacing.

Within moments the coachman opened the door. Molly gratefully accepted his hand and jumped to the ground, followed by Caroline. Ignoring Aunt Hazel's reprimand, Molly walked in a circle, stretching her legs. Aunt Hazel exited the carriage and marched inside, the young ladies in her wake.

In the entryway they were greeted by the scent of a warm supper and a jaunty tune coming from the common room. Molly started toward the door, but Aunt Hazel grabbed her sleeve, peering into the room as though it might be full of vipers. "We'll settle into our chamber and have supper in our own parlor. There's no need to fraternize with other travelers."

"But Aunt Hazel—" Molly began, but was silenced by a stern look. Her shoulders sagged. The first night of their journey and they'd be holed up in the bedchamber with Aunt Hazel? But then again, she *would* have to sleep eventually. There was no reason why she and Caroline shouldn't sneak down here on their own later.

Aunt Hazel spoke to the innkeeper, Mr. Plant, who escorted them to their suite of rooms.

"Here we are," he said, holding the door open.

A fire burned in the grate of a comfortable sitting room furnished with a brown sofa, desk, and an oak dining set. Two open doors on opposite sides of the room offered glimpses into the bedchambers.

"See to our luggage and bring our supper in, please," Aunt Hazel said. "We will be retiring early."

"Yes, ma'am," Mr. Plant said and ducked out.

Molly strolled about the sitting room and peeked into the bedchamber she'd be sharing with Caroline. "It's a nice inn. Have you stayed here before, Aunt Hazel?"

"Yes, a number of times. It's a reputable establishment, and they always save me one of their best rooms if they know I'm coming."

"I didn't know you travel often enough to have a favorite inn, Auntie," Caroline said.

Aunt Hazel removed her hat and gloves. "One does need to get around from time to time."

A rap came on the door, and two young men came in carrying their luggage. After they deposited the trunks, Aunt Hazel went into her bedchamber.

Molly followed Caroline to their room. Two beds, draped with patchwork quilts, sat beneath windows overlooking the stables. She pulled the curtains closed. "I hoped to go to the common room for supper. Did you hear the music?"

Caroline opened her trunk. "Yes, and I knew you'd want to go, but we hardly can without a chaperone."

Molly sat in a chair beside her bed, mulling over the best way to suggest sneaking down. She looked up, about to speak, but Caroline was watching her with arms crossed, shaking her head.

"Oh, Caroline, it would be such fun! Your aunt won't even know we're gone."

Caroline pulled her nightgown out of the trunk and put it next to her pillow. "Certainly not. We'll stay here and retire early, as Auntie said. We're supposed to leave tomorrow right after breakfast."

"We needn't stay downstairs for long. We'll go down after she's asleep, have a glass of wine, and come right back."

"No." She sighed heavily. "The truth is, Molly, I'm so nervous about tomorrow, and I can't bear the thought of sneaking around the inn tonight and all it entails. I need to rest and settle my nerves."

Molly's plans were forgotten at once. She crossed the room and put an arm about Caroline's shoulders. "There's no need to feel nervous. He'll love you."

"I don't want to think about Mr. Clarke tonight. I want to eat supper, perhaps play cards, and go to sleep early."

"Then that's what we'll do. I'm sure we'll have plenty of adventures during our trip. Come, let's go see if supper's arrived. After we've eaten I'll read to you from that book of poetry you like."

Caroline gave Molly's hand a squeeze. "Thank you for understanding."

After supper Molly read to Caroline until she fell asleep, but it was a long time before she could settle her own thoughts. She wondered what Waverly was like and if the Clarkes would be pleasant company. What acquaintances might they make in Rochester, and would they be close enough to walk into town to visit the shops? Molly sat beside the moonlit window and pondered the trip until she could barely keep her eyes open. She climbed into bed with her book, but fell asleep before finishing one page.

Chapter Two

When Molly woke the next morning, she rose and crossed the room to look out the window. The sun, higher in the sky than she'd expected, shined over the grass and dandelions surrounding the stable.

After brushing her wavy, dark brown hair and changing into a deep blue traveling dress that matched her eyes almost perfectly, she shook Caroline awake. "I hope your aunt ordered breakfast. I'm famished."

"Not yet, Molly. It's so early." Caroline buried her face in the pillow.

"It's almost eight. I thought Aunt Hazel would have woken us by now."

"Perhaps she changed her mind about when to leave," came Caroline's muffled reply. "Waverly is only two hours from here."

Molly nudged Caroline over and sat on the bed. "Good, I had enough of the carriage yesterday. We could have made it last night if we'd pressed on."

Caroline rolled over and propped herself up on one elbow. "I wouldn't have wanted to arrive after hours on the road. I'd have looked a fright. What would Mr. Clarke have thought?"

"He would have been happy to see you, no matter what you looked like. Is he handsome?"

"It's hard to recall. We met a year ago, and he'll have changed. I know I have," Caroline said.

"A shame you don't have a miniature of him."

"It wouldn't have been appropriate unless we were betrothed."

Molly tilted her head. "But it's all arranged, isn't it?"

"Not exactly. Father said he thinks we'll 'get on,' but nothing's settled."

"He must like the Clarkes if he wants you to visit their son before you even have a chance to meet other gentlemen."

"Since he and Mr. Clarke's father are old friends, I suppose it seemed a logical conclusion when they realized they had children of a marriageable age. But if it doesn't work out with Mr. Clarke, at least I can go into town with you for the Season." Caroline threw back the covers and stretched her arms over her head, yawning.

"That would be wonderful," Molly said wistfully. "But for your sake, I hope you *do* like Mr. Clarke."

"So do I." Caroline prodded Molly off the bed and crossed the room to her trunk.

Molly checked her watch. "You'd better dress quickly. Aunt Hazel is probably pacing the parlor, waiting for us."

But she wasn't.

"Auntie?" Caroline called, looking around the dark room.

"She must be asleep. Or packing?" Molly pulled back the curtains and sunlight flooded the empty parlor.

"It's unlike her to be late for anything. She's usually up at dawn."

"Perhaps she went to the common room and we should meet her there," Molly suggested hopefully, already starting for the door.

11

"No. She must be asleep. We'll have to go in."
Caroline knocked on Aunt Hazel's door. "Auntie?"

No answer.

Caroline pushed the door open quietly, Molly right
behind her. As soon as they entered the pitch-black
room, Molly tripped over a trunk and bumped into
Caroline, who squealed.

Aunt Hazel's feeble voice came out of the darkness.
"Who is it?"

"It's us. You've overslept. Oh, I can't see a thing!"
Molly said as Caroline drew the curtains.

"Oh," Aunt Hazel whispered, covering her eyes.
"Oh, it's too bright. Too bright."

"Auntie!" Caroline cried.

Aunt Hazel put her hands over her ears.

Molly approached the bed. "What's wrong?"

"I feel most unwell." Aunt Hazel's complexion
matched the white nightgown buttoned up to her chin.

Caroline sat on the edge of the bed, took her hand,
and felt her forehead. "You aren't feverish."

"Perhaps you ate something that didn't agree with
you," Molly said.

Aunt Hazel closed her eyes and nodded.

"But we all ate the same thing," Caroline said.

"Did you feel unwell yesterday?" Molly asked.

Aunt Hazel slowly turned her head to face Molly. "I
thought it was from being in the carriage."

"The first thing is to summon the innkeeper," Molly
said. "He must know of a doctor in town who can help."

"I don't need a doctor." She pushed her blankets
away but made no attempt to get up.

"At the very least, we should order breakfast. You
might feel better after you've eaten," Caroline said.

Aunt Hazel placed her hands protectively over her stomach. "I don't think I could."

"Tea?" Molly suggested.

"I'd like tea," Aunt Hazel whispered, pulling the blankets up to her nose.

Molly went into the parlor to ring for the maid, who arrived within moments.

"Good morning," the maid said.

"Good morning. My friend's aunt isn't feeling well. We'd like a tea tray, and breakfast. Is there a doctor in town?"

"Oh, yes, he's right down the road. I'll go to the kitchen and order your food, then send Tommy off for the doctor." Without another word she hurried down the hall.

Molly went back to Aunt Hazel's room and leaned against the doorframe while Caroline sat beside the bed, wiping her aunt's forehead with a cloth. This was a conundrum. Should Molly send a message to Waverly Hall to say they weren't coming? Get a message to Mrs. Darby or her own mother? Speak to the innkeeper about staying on another few days? Caroline wouldn't want to delay the trip, but there wasn't much else they could do. The best course of action might be to bundle Aunt Hazel up, get her into the carriage, and go home. But then Caroline wouldn't meet Mr. Clarke, and any hope of forming an attachment would be lost. She let out a heavy sigh.

Aunt Hazel looked up at the sound. "Tea?" she whispered.

"Soon, Aunt Hazel. We'll be back in a few moments." Molly gestured to Caroline, and they went into the parlor. "This is a fine kettle of fish."

13

"What are we to do?" Caroline asked, twisting the top button of her blouse as she paced in circles around the coffee table.

Molly sat on the sofa. "We'll know more after the doctor's seen her. Poor Aunt Hazel."

"I hope it's nothing serious."

"I'm sure it isn't. She'll feel better after tea, and then we'll help her get dressed."

A moan came from Aunt Hazel's bedchamber.

Caroline fell into the seat beside Molly. "Oh, what will Mr. Clarke and his parents think when we don't arrive this morning? I'll appear inconsiderate and unpunctual."

Molly patted Caroline's shoulder. "Everyone knows travel is full of delays. They'll assume something happened to the carriage."

"I hope you're right. This won't make a good first impression, which Mother tells me is most important."

"They'll understand, especially once they get a look at your aunt."

Caroline glanced at the open bedchamber door and leaned in closer. "Do you think we should still bring her to Waverly?"

"What else can we do?" Molly asked. "If we don't go, you can't meet Mr. Clarke."

"I want to meet him, but I don't know if Auntie can travel. Perhaps after a rest? We could stay here one more night."

"That's what I was thinking. Tomorrow, if she's feeling better, we'll continue. If not…" Molly raised her hands.

Caroline sank deeper into the sofa cushions. "If not, we go home."

"No," a voice croaked. Aunt Hazel stood just inside the parlor, clinging to the doorframe. "Must get to Waverly Hall. You must meet Ben—Ben—" She sneezed. "Benedict."

Molly and Caroline leapt to their feet.

"Auntie!" Caroline cried, putting an arm around her.

Molly rushed over and took Aunt Hazel's arm. "You should be in bed."

She shook her head weakly. "Must pack…"

Caroline and Molly exchanged exasperated looks and helped her back to bed just as a knock came on the door.

"I'll get it," Molly said and left Caroline to tuck Aunt Hazel in.

She opened the door and the maid came in with the tea, followed by a young man carrying a heavily laden breakfast tray. As they left, a gray-haired man who could only be the doctor strode in.

"I'm Doctor Kellow. I hear you're feeling unwell?"

"I'm Miss Merriwether. I'm not ill, it's my friend's aunt." She poured out a cup of tea for Aunt Hazel and led Doctor Kellow to the bedchamber.

When Aunt Hazel saw him, she tugged the blankets up to her ears and tried to tuck her curls into her sleeping cap.

The doctor set his bag down and peered at Aunt Hazel. "What are your complaints?"

Aunt Hazel looked to Caroline, who addressed the doctor. "She has a headache and is fatigued. She's been sneezing a bit."

"Her stomach is bothering her," Molly said as she handed Aunt Hazel the tea.

"I see. Well, why don't you young ladies wait in the

next room while I examine her." As they left he added, "Oh, what's my patient's name?"

Aunt Hazel coughed.

"Miss Hazel Osgood," Caroline said.

"Very good. I'll call you when we're finished," the doctor said.

Aunt Hazel gestured to the door.

"Of course, we'll leave it open," Molly assured her.

She followed Caroline into the parlor, where breakfast awaited. They didn't speak for some time, instead giving their attention to the porridge, bacon, coffee, and rolls with fresh butter.

"Should we send a message to Waverly?" Molly asked, refreshed and fortified after eating.

"Yes, but first we'll see what the doctor says. We'll either be arriving tomorrow or not at all."

Molly reached for Caroline's hand. "Whatever happens, Mr. Clarke will understand. And perhaps we could come back here soon."

"It's a shame my parents couldn't have come with us, but Father's busy with the estate and Mother insists she can't travel until Mary's had her baby."

"When will that be?" It seemed to Molly that one of Caroline's four sisters was always recovering from a birth, about to give birth or caring for a newborn. It was a wonder Mrs. Darby had left home at all in the last seven years. Molly had seen her own mother gazing longingly at the babies and knew she hoped for a gaggle of grandchildren one day. It was lucky for Molly that her brothers were older and Michael was already married, otherwise Mrs. Merriwether probably would have tried to marry her off at the ripe age of fifteen.

"Mary's due next week, but it's her first, so I expect

the baby will be late."

"Perhaps your mother will come after the baby's born." Molly finished the last of her coffee and set the cup down.

"She'll want to stay with Mary for at least a month. My father would have come if possible, to keep an eye on the situation." Caroline lowered her voice though they were alone in the room. "He's heard unsavory rumors about Mr. Clarke's brother."

Molly leaned toward her, eyes alight. "What sort of rumors?"

"Oh, the usual sort. No maiden safe when he's in the vicinity."

Molly gasped. "You mean he's a rogue?"

"No! If he were, my father wouldn't even consider allowing me to marry into the family. Let's just say, as Father hears it, no lady is immune to his charms."

Molly was now more anxious than ever to reach Rochester. She'd like to see this brother of Mr. Clarke's with her own eyes. She didn't admit this to Caroline, however. "Well," she said, "we'll be quite safe from whatever charm he casts on us. You're there to meet his brother, and I've been explicitly told not to 'entangle' myself with any gentlemen until my Season starts. I have no idea who my mother thinks I could become entangled with, though. We're only going for a visit, not a house party or a ball."

"I'll give Mr. Clarke's brother a wide berth, and of course we'll have chaperones to see that he behaves. Three, I hope." Caroline cast her eyes toward Aunt Hazel's bedchamber.

They sat in silence, trying to make out the doctor's words in the next room, but it was impossible. Finally, he came out.

Caroline rose. "How is she, Doctor? What do you think is wrong?"

"Not to worry," Doctor Kellow said with a smile. "Your aunt is suffering from a cold and has a touch of a delicate stomach."

"What can we do for her? When will she feel better?" Molly asked.

"It's hard to say. A week, if she takes good care. She'll need rest and the usual remedies for such an ailment."

Molly's stomach sank as she met Caroline's eyes. A week!

Caroline stepped forward. "We're on our way to Rochester. Is it possible for us to take her home?"

"Where do you live?" Doctor Kellow asked.

"Hartford," Molly said.

"Oh, that's too far for Miss Osgood just now. I wouldn't even suggest taking her to Rochester in her condition. In my experience, it will get worse before it gets better."

"Thank you, Doctor," Caroline said. "We'll discuss our plans and decide what's best to be done."

"If I might make a suggestion—You could stay here for another few days, and I'd be happy to check on Miss Osgood daily."

"That may be our only choice." Molly glanced at Caroline, who had her eyes on the floor. Oh, dear. She knew that expression. Molly hurried Doctor Kellow to the door. "Thank you. We'll send word of our plans."

Caroline looked up as soon as the door closed behind him. "Oh, Molly! How long we've waited, and now…now…" She burst into tears.

Molly took her arm and led her to the sofa. "Here, have some tea." She poured out a cup and added Caroline's three sugars.

Caroline took one sip and set the cup on a side table. "To get so far, and now this. I don't blame Auntie, but, oh, how vexing!"

"I have an idea." Molly met Caroline's teary eyes.

Caroline raised her hands and let them fall into her lap. "Oh, *Molly*. Not another one of your schemes."

"Just listen. We'll stay for the week, if the room is available, and send a message for Mr. Clarke to visit you here at the inn."

Caroline wiped her eyes, sniffling. "That—that might work. It won't be the same as staying at Waverly, but I can see him and speak to him."

"It will all work out, you'll see," Molly said, patting Caroline's knee.

They went into Aunt Hazel's room to tell her their plan.

Aunt Hazel's eyes swam with tears. "I'm so sorry, my darling." Molly and Caroline exchanged a glance. Darling? Aunt Hazel hadn't called Caroline that for fifteen years.

"Don't be sorry, Auntie. You can't help being sick. I'll still be able to meet Mr. Clarke."

Aunt Hazel nodded and blew her nose.

Molly took her hand. "We'll take good care of you, Aunt Hazel. I'll read to you and make tea for you, and when you're feeling better we'll take a stroll around the village."

Aunt Hazel wiped her eyes. "Oh, you are a sweet girl, little Molly."

Molly put a hand over her mouth to hold back a

giggle. Just then a knock came on the door.

Caroline went to answer and returned in a moment with Doctor Kellow and Mrs. Plant, the innkeeper's wife.

Mrs. Plant stood at the end of Aunt Hazel's bed, looking like a round red hen fussing over her clutch of eggs. "Oh, Miss Osgood, the doctor's told me you're feeling poorly and need to change your plans. But I've an idea that will help the young ladies continue on to Rochester."

Molly's spirits lifted. Could there really be a way for them to go?

"What is it?" Caroline asked.

"Your aunt can stay here, and I'll keep a good eye on her, with my maids' assistance. We've known Miss Osgood for years and welcome the chance to care for her."

Aunt Hazel sniffled.

"I'll stop by twice a day to check on her," Doctor Kellow said. "No harm will come to her, you may rely on that."

Mrs. Plant nodded. "She'll be in good hands. Doctor Kellow's a wonder, he is."

"I'm not sure. I don't feel right leaving her alone in this state," Caroline said.

Aunt Hazel held out a hand to Caroline, who went to her side.

"Please go, dear Caroline. As I told you, I've been here before. Mrs. Plant and Doctor Kellow will look after me just as well as if I were back at home." She turned away to cough, covering her mouth with a handkerchief.

"You won't be lonely?" Caroline asked.

"Goodness, no," Mrs. Plant cut in. "Between me, the

maids, and the doctor, she'll hardly have a moment's peace."

"Would you be able to send us messages, updating us on Aunt Hazel's condition?" Molly asked Doctor Kellow.

"Yes, daily, if you'd like. When she's fit to travel, I'll escort her to Waverly Hall."

Caroline looked down at her aunt. "If you're certain…?"

"I am, sweetling. Don't worry. But do apologize to Mr. and Mrs. Clarke for your late arrival and tell them I'll be along when I can." Her eyelids began to droop.

On their way out of Aunt Hazel's room, Caroline turned to Mrs. Plant. "Thank you very much for helping."

"We appreciate it more than you know," Molly added.

"Oh, it's no bother, no bother at all," Mrs. Plant said. "I'll tell the stables to have your carriage made ready, and someone will be along to gather your luggage within the hour." She hurried from the room.

"Good day. I'll be in touch." Doctor Kellow tipped his hat to them and followed Mrs. Plant down the hall, whistling.

Molly closed the door and leaned her back against it. "What a morning!"

"Afternoon, now," Caroline said. "We'd better pack our things. Do you think we should send a message to Waverly?"

"No, we're only going to be a few hours late. But you should write to your mother. She'll want to know about Aunt Hazel."

"You're right." Caroline crossed the room to the

desk. "What should I say?"

"Assure her that Aunt Hazel will join us at Waverly Hall in a couple of days. Well, it might be more than a couple of days, but leave that part out."

Once their luggage had been taken away, Molly and Caroline went to Aunt Hazel's room to say goodbye.

"Auntie?" Caroline whispered.

Aunt Hazel's eyelids fluttered open.

"We're leaving now," Caroline said. "Let Mrs. Plant know if you need anything, and send word if you want us to come back."

"There'll be no need for that, my pet. Enjoy yourselves, and remem—" She broke off, coughing. After Molly helped her take a sip of tea she continued. "Remember what I've taught you about strange men. Don't speak to anyone you don't know."

Molly patted Aunt Hazel's hand. "Don't fret. We'll remember."

"Goodbye, my starlings," she whispered before drifting off to sleep.

Caroline and Molly tiptoed from the room.

"Sweetling, starlings? What's come over her?" Molly asked as she pulled her gloves on.

"I don't know, but it's sweet. It reminds me of when we were children and she played with us in the garden nearly every day. Well, shall we go?"

Molly didn't need to answer. After spending the morning thinking the journey wouldn't happen, she couldn't get back into that stuffy carriage fast enough.

Chapter Three

By midafternoon they'd made it to the outskirts of Rochester. They went at a snail's pace through the narrow streets, but Molly didn't mind. It gave her an opportunity to see the town that would be her home for the next month. Along the main thoroughfare she spotted two taverns, an inn, several intriguing shops, and an ancient church.

"I expect we'll be there soon," she said to Caroline.

"I know. But now that it comes to it, I can hardly stop shaking." She held her unsteady hand out for Molly to see.

"There's no need to be nervous."

Caroline gave her a that's-easy-for-you-to-say look. "What if he doesn't like me?"

"The question is if you like *him*. Of course he'll like you."

What man wouldn't? With her green eyes and golden curls, Caroline had that delicate, flowery look men seemed to love. And Molly had read Mr. Clarke's letters—It was clear he was more than a little interested in her.

Soon the busy street gave way to fields and meadows stretching to the horizon. After passing a number of quaint cottages the carriage turned onto a long, tree-lined lane. Every time they rounded a bend Molly expected to see the house, but it was some minutes before Waverly Hall finally came into view. With its intricate stonework, ivy-covered walls and multiple steep gables, the mansion should have been imposing. But it had a welcoming feel, like a cottage that had accidentally been built too big. As the carriage made its way up the drive, the front doors were flung open.

Molly expected a butler or a footman to step outside, but certainly not three gentlemen. They stood at the top of the stairs, two looking curiously toward the carriage while the third gave his attention to a dog sitting at his heels.

As the coachman pulled the horses to a stop, one of the men rushed down the stairs. A footman appeared and reached for the carriage door handle, but the gentleman waved him aside. Molly and Caroline exchanged a curious look just before the door opened and a hand reached in to help first Caroline and then Molly down the steps.

The man who greeted them was blond and had the friendliest face Molly had ever seen. It was open, as though ready to welcome in the whole world. He had a strong, robust look to him, as though he spent the majority of every day riding horses or taking long walks about the grounds. There was no denying he was unbelievably handsome. Was this Caroline's suitor?

His introduction quelled that hope at once. "Welcome to Waverly Hall. I'm Frederick Clarke."

Ah, the brother. He did indeed look perilous to young ladies. Molly flushed when he boldly met her eyes with a questioning look.

"I'm Miss Merriwether."

"Charmed," Mr. Clarke said with a smile, and kissed her hand.

He turned his gaze to Caroline. "Then you must be Miss Darby."

Caroline let out an almost imperceptible little gasp as he brought her hand to his lips. "Yes. Yes, I'm Miss Darby. How do you do?"

Mr. Clarke clasped his hands behind his back. "A pleasure to meet you both. I trust your journey was comfortable?"

"Yes, thank you," Molly said.

He nodded toward the carriage. "Were the roads bad? We expected you some time ago. Old Benedict was beginning to worry," he said with a glance behind him.

"I'm sorry to cause any distress," Caroline said. "We were delayed leaving the inn this morning."

Molly was about to explain about Aunt Hazel, but the other two men had reached the bottom of the stairs. They stood waiting to introduce themselves, but Mr. Clarke preempted them. He pointed to the slightly shorter of the men. "My brother, Mr. Benedict Clarke. It's far too confusing to have two Mr. Clarkes to contend with, so call us Fred and Benedict."

Benedict had blond hair like his brother and, though not of Fred's stature, had the same broad build. He gave Molly only a cursory nod before turning to Caroline.

Fred motioned to the other gentleman. "And this is my friend, Mr. Bailey."

"Good afternoon," Mr. Bailey said to the ladies. He had chestnut hair and dark eyes, but Molly couldn't tell if they were actually blue…or perhaps brown? The fit of his jacket suggested a muscular, if lean, frame. His complexion verged on pale, as if he rarely spent time out of doors.

Molly looked at Caroline to gauge her reaction to

Benedict, but she'd pasted a polite smile on her face and it was impossible to know what she was truly thinking.

Mr. Bailey rested his hand on the dog's head, staring at Caroline. Or was he glaring? When he noticed Molly watching him he cleared his expression.

"Miss Merriwether, is it?"

She smiled. "Yes. Mr. Bailey?"

He nodded.

The dog looked up at Molly, tongue lolling. It was reddish-brown, with a white blaze running from the crown of its head to the tip of its nose.

Mr. Bailey looked into the carriage. "Where's your chaperone? We were expecting three of you."

"Miss Darby's aunt was supposed to come, but she fell ill at the last moment."

"Did she?" Mr. Bailey stepped back as if frightened Molly might be contagious.

"Oh, nothing serious," Caroline cut in. "She'll be better soon but wasn't up for travel."

Benedict offered Caroline his arm. "Thank goodness. Shall we go inside?"

As Molly waited for one of the other men to escort her, she caught a number of short glances passing between them. Finally, Fred flared his nostrils at Mr. Bailey, who stepped forward and offered his arm.

"If you would allow me?"

She placed her hand lightly in the crook of his elbow. "Thank you."

As they walked up the stairs Mr. Bailey swayed, and Molly looked at him in alarm. His face was scarlet, but he said nothing. By the time they reached the sixth step Molly realized he was limping. Was he injured? She considered asking, but after a glance at his clenched jaw kept silent. She held his arm a little tighter as they climbed the stairs, the dog following.

Fred ran ahead and held the door open.

"Thank you," Molly said as she and Mr. Bailey stepped inside.

Windows at the top of the foyer's high, wood-beamed ceiling let in great shafts of light, illuminating paneled walls and giving Molly a view into rooms beyond. Ahead of them was a vast hall, where a long wooden table sat under four brass chandeliers. Tapestries adorned the walls, and at the end of the room was a monumental hearth that could have held an ox. A courtyard was just visible through multipaned windows. Immediately to their right was a parlor, and multiple doors led off corridors running down either side of the great hall.

"Up here," called Benedict from a balcony overlooking the entryway.

Beside her, Mr. Bailey shifted on his feet and Molly again wondered if he was hurt. She peered at his legs but saw no bandages or casts.

"Shall we?" he asked, following her gaze to his shoes.

Molly looked up, her cheeks pink. "Oh. Yes."

The dog bounded up the stairs ahead of them, then stopped on the balcony and stared at Mr. Bailey, whining.

"I'll be along, Penny." He smiled up at the dog, who barked.

"Penny?"

"Short for Penelope."

"That's a sweet name," Molly said as they continued up the stairs.

"My sister thought so."

When they reached the second-floor landing, Molly heard voices coming from a room across the hall. One was Caroline's, and the man's must be Benedict or Mr. Clarke.

Mr. Bailey gave Penny a pat and she trotted into the room ahead of them. As soon as they entered the drawing room, done up in various shades of yellow, Mr. Bailey dropped Molly's arm. He crossed the room to a bookshelf and picked up a thick volume. Penny curled up in front of an upholstered chair, obviously expecting him to sit there.

Molly crossed the room to where Caroline and Benedict stood in silence, staring out the window. She looked down at the ground but saw nothing of interest. The window overlooked a grove of trees and afforded a partial view of the front drive. "What are you looking at?"

"Benedict was pointing out that elm to me. Apparently, it's the oldest tree on the estate," Caroline said in a voice Molly had heard her use with her young nieces and nephews.

Molly stepped back from the window. "How interesting."

"Won't you sit down?" Benedict gestured to a buttercup-yellow sofa in the middle of the room.

"Thank you," Caroline said as she and Molly took their seats.

"Tea?" Benedict asked.

"That would be welcome," Molly said.

Fred strode into the room and sprawled in a chair opposite the sofa. "Tea? They'd like to wash up, more like."

Looking flummoxed, Benedict stared at Caroline and Molly. "Oh, would you? Want to wash up?"

"Actually, we'd hoped to pay our respects to your parents and explain to them about my aunt not coming with us. It's most unusual, and we want them to know it was beyond our control," Caroline said.

"Our *parents*?" Fred barely contained his mirth as he met Benedict's eyes. "Haven't you told them?"

"I hadn't gotten to that yet," Benedict murmured.

Caroline looked from Fred to Benedict. "What's this about your parents?"

Benedict turned back to her, attempting a nonchalant air. "Well, it *is* most unusual, as you said, but the fact of the matter is—"

"They aren't here," Fred said.

"Oh, have they gone on a call?" Molly smiled at Benedict, who looked like he needed encouragement or a strong drink.

Fred laughed. "In a manner of speaking."

Behind them, a book snapped shut.

"Fred, just tell them," Mr. Bailey said from across the room.

Molly swiveled in her seat to look at him. "Tell us what?"

"Mr. and Mrs. Clarke are gone for at least a month," he said without turning around.

"A month!" Molly and Caroline exclaimed together.

Benedict stepped forward, hands out as though trying to calm a skittish horse. "It wasn't planned, you see. It came up very suddenly, and as you'd have a chaperone, they decided it was entirely proper for them to go."

"But we don't have a chaperone!" Caroline said,

jumping to her feet.

Molly rose. "Do you mean to say we're alone, the five of us? For a month?"

"It isn't so scandalous as all that," Fred said. "The servants are here, and housekeeper and butler. We're upstanding gentlemen, so you have nothing to fear as far as your reputations."

From Mr. Bailey's chair came a cough that in no way disguised the laugh it was meant to conceal.

What was that supposed to mean? That he and his friends were *not* to be trusted? Molly almost wanted to laugh herself. Or cry. How could so many things go wrong in one morning? The obvious thing to do was leave at once, before their luggage was even brought inside. How could they stay here alone with three young gentlemen, especially one with a reputation? What would people say?

"Please, sit down," Benedict said. "I hope you'll accept my apologies."

After Molly and Caroline had retaken their seats, Benedict sat in the chair beside Fred's.

"Perhaps that tea, now," Molly said. She'd liked to have asked for a splash of sherry in it, but guessed Caroline would frown on the idea.

"Of course." Benedict rang a porcelain bell on the side table.

The butler arrived so quickly Molly guessed he'd been waiting just outside the room in case he was wanted.

"Tea, please, Mr. Dawson," Benedict said.

"Right away, sir." Mr. Dawson gave a slight bow and strode from the room.

Fred leaned forward and fixed his eyes on Molly.

"Where did you leave your chaperone?"

"She's at The Blue Swan Inn, in Hartford." Held by his striking blue eyes, Molly felt a flush in her cheeks.

"Ah, yes. I know it. They have good ale." Fred nodded approvingly and leaned back in his chair.

"I hope she isn't very ill," Benedict said.

"The doctor said it's only a mild ailment," Molly said, "but he didn't think she should be moved."

"It sounds like she's in good hands. When should we expect her?" Fred asked.

"Hopefully in a few days. I did hope to meet your parents," Caroline said, looking to Benedict.

Benedict fidgeted with his cuff links. "Well...they assumed—hoped—you could extend your visit by a week or so, in order to meet them when they return."

Caroline looked down at her hands folded in her lap. "I see."

The group lapsed into silence, the only sound coming from a clock on the mantel. At first glance the yellow tones of the room had felt like walking into an egg yolk, but the longer Molly sat here the more she enjoyed the brightness, as if they were drenched in sunshine. She rose and walked to the window, wondering what would happen next. Perhaps Aunt Hazel would arrive soon, or maybe Mr. and Mrs. Clarke would come home earlier than expected. Something nudged Molly's knee and she looked down to see Penny. She crouched to rub the dog's back, smiling when Penny leaned into her.

Mr. Bailey gave a short whistle and Penny looked at him but stayed beside Molly, who stood up. When Mr. Bailey patted his thigh, Penny still didn't move.

Guessing he didn't want to get up because of his injury, Molly led Penny back to his chair.

"Sit." Mr. Bailey pointed to the floor, and Penny stretched out in front of him.

"What kind of dog is she?" Molly asked.

Mr. Bailey opened his book, his eyes on the page. "Nothing in particular." He shifted so he was facing away from her and Molly returned to the sofa just as the tea cart was rolled in.

When the maid placed the cart in front of the sofa and turned to go, Molly had to remind herself not to stare. Though her features were not extraordinary, her countenance and poise suggested a lady rather than a maid. Her eyes were bright and the light brown hair peeking out from beneath a white cap was shiny and lustrous.

"This is Kitty," Fred said. "If you need anything while you're here, she's your girl."

Already halfway across the room, Kitty caught her foot on the edge of the carpet when she looked back at him.

Fred sprang to his feet and rushed to her side.

Kitty smoothed her apron. "I'm fine, Fre—Mr. Clarke. But thank you."

Fred touched her shoulder and whispered something in her ear. Kitty didn't answer but left the room with a smile on her face as Fred followed her with his eyes. With his handsome looks and friendly demeanor, Molly could see why he was popular with women. Still, Kitty was a maid. Was he *that* type of man, then?

Caroline poured out tea, handing cups around to the group. Mr. Bailey rose from his seat and accepted a cup, then limped back to his chair without a word.

Benedict addressed Molly and Caroline. "I'd be happy to put you up at an inn in town."

"I don't think that will be necessary," Molly said, glancing at Caroline.

"Unnecessary and ridiculous," Fred said before Caroline could reply. "Waverly's enormous. We could you give a wing to yourselves if it would set you at ease."

Molly couldn't tell if he was making light of the situation because he *did* find it ridiculous, or for some other reason. He didn't seem to understand the predicament she and Caroline found themselves in. It was one thing to arrive unchaperoned, it was quite another to remain unattended in their home. Though Caroline had corresponded with Benedict, they didn't truly know him, so they were essentially in a house full of "strange men," as Aunt Hazel would say. Molly could only imagine what she'd think if she knew what was going on.

Molly finished her tea and turned to Caroline. "Perhaps we should take some time to discuss our options. Alone."

"Yes, I think we'd better," Caroline said, setting her cup down.

Benedict rose. "We'll step out so you can talk."

Fred settled deeper into his chair as if hoping not to be noticed, but after a sharp look from Benedict stood and followed him out of the room. Mr. Bailey took Penny by the collar and left, closing the door behind him.

As soon as it clicked shut, Molly replenished their teacups. "Would you ever have dreamed we'd find ourselves in such a pickle?"

"Absolutely not. I imagine this means we need to leave." Caroline sighed a sigh that sounded like it had been waiting years to get out.

Molly lifted one shoulder. "I don't know…we're

already here and, as Fred said, it isn't as though we're alone in the house."

"I've the feeling Fred would say anything to get us to stay. He seems the type of man to enjoy bending the rules."

"I have the same feeling." After glancing at the door, Molly whispered, "What do you think of Benedict?"

Caroline shifted on the sofa so she was facing Molly. "It's too soon to say. I know he's embarrassed about his parents being gone. It doesn't appear to amuse him at all, unlike his brother."

"Do you think we should move to the inn?" Molly held her breath as she awaited Caroline's answer. She knew what *she* wanted, but it only seemed fair to let Caroline decide.

"I feel as though it's the right thing to do," Caroline finally answered.

"But do you want to?"

"No. Do you?"

"No. In fact, I think you'll get to know Benedict better without his parents here. I don't doubt they're all trustworthy gentlemen, despite Mr. Bailey's insinuations."

"So you feel we can stay here in good conscience?"

"Yes, I do." Molly grinned. "I think it will be marvelous. It will be the first time we're able to do whatever we like without our parents or teachers or your aunt watching over us. Think of it, Caroline. Waverly to explore, the estate, and Rochester. You'll have ample time to get to know Benedict, and *I'll* be your chaperone. I'm two months older than you, after all."

Caroline's eyes brightened. "Maybe you're right. We know how to behave appropriately; it isn't as though our parents have been letting us run amok all these years. When Auntie arrives, we'll tell her we followed all her rules and she'll be proud of us for rising to the occasion."

Molly finished stirring her tea and set the spoon down. "She will, indeed. Honestly, it couldn't be better. We must put any thoughts of impropriety from our minds and enjoy ourselves. In a way, this is exactly the scenario we've been preparing for all these years."

"But Molly—what if someone finds out? Our reputations would be ruined. I wonder that Benedict even wants me to stay, considering what would happen if anyone knew. People might get the wrong idea about me. About both of us."

Deflated, Molly reconsidered the whole affair. "That's true. If word got out, I most likely couldn't have a Season. Not many men would court me if I've been involved in a scandal. I do plan to marry someday, and this could hurt my chances of attracting a worthy husband."

"Perhaps we should leave. We must think of your future."

"And yours, if you decide you don't like Benedict."

Caroline put a hand to her cheek. "Oh, I hadn't thought of that. It could be that I'll need a Season too."

They lapsed into silence, both deep in their own thoughts.

In the quiet room, the tick-tock of the mantel clock sounded like the clang of church bells ringing, as though to remind Molly that her time at Waverly Hall was limited. But she didn't want it to be. She'd waited too long for this trip for it to end now. She sipped her tea, pondering the best action.

After ten minutes, Molly placed her cup back on the

tea tray. "No, we're being ridiculous. How would anyone find out? We won't tell anyone, and we'll ask Benedict to keep it a secret. Even if someone in the village knew we were here, they wouldn't know we arrived without a chaperone."

"Oh, I'm sure you're right." Caroline grasped her hand. "Benedict wouldn't do anything to jeopardize our reputations. After all, he wants us here just as much as we want to be here. And we can leave any time we want to. If Aunt Hazel doesn't arrive soon, we could go back to The Blue Swan."

"So we're staying?"

Caroline nodded, the joy on her face only slightly shadowed by trepidation.

Their eyes met, both realizing the enormity of their decision no matter how they tried to convince themselves remaining at Waverly Hall unchaperoned was of small consequence.

Chapter Four

"We should tell Benedict we're staying," Molly said, rising from the sofa.

Caroline crossed the room to peek into the hallway. She turned back to Molly, bewildered. "They aren't there."

"Really?" Molly joined her in the doorway and looked up and down the deserted corridor. No sign of anyone, not even the dog. "Hm. You'd have thought they'd stay to hear our plans."

Caroline stepped back into the room. "I suppose they wanted to give us enough time to discuss it in private. Very considerate, really."

"Yes. But what should we do? Stay here and wait until they come back?"

"No, there's no way to know when they'll return. I'll ring the bell."

Caroline did so, and soon a gray-haired woman wearing a black dress appeared.

"Good afternoon. I'm the housekeeper, Mrs. Lane."

Her pinched face and somber blue eyes reminded Molly of a governess, one who would never overlook notes passed in class, allow a spontaneous holiday, or forgive grammatical errors.

Caroline stepped forward. "I'm Miss Darby and this is my friend, Miss Merriwether. We're guests?"

Mrs. Lane kept her arms at her sides. "Mr. Clarke

told me you were debating about staying or moving to the inn."

"That's right," Molly said. "We want to tell him we've decided to stay."

Instead of going to find Benedict, directing them to a bedchamber, or asking if there was any way she could be of assistance, Mrs. Lane pursed her lips as she looked Molly and Caroline over. After an uncommonly long silence, she spoke. "Do you think it wise?"

Caroline looked too taken aback to answer, so Molly did. "I—We…yes. As long as nobody knows, it's fine if we stay. It's only for a day or so."

"Rochester isn't far away," Mrs. Lane said. "Word could get out."

This time Caroline found her voice. "Certainly nobody from the house would gossip?"

"Servants will always gossip," Mrs. Lane said in a voice that seemed to chill the room.

Caroline had paled and was clearly wavering.

Molly refused to be intimidated by the housekeeper. She stood up straight and looked Mrs. Lane in the eye. "We trust the servants of Waverly Hall to follow your example and be discreet."

Mrs. Lane looked like she wanted to comment further, but simply nodded. "I will relay your message to Mr. Clarke immediately after I show you to your rooms."

She set a brisk pace down the corridor, around a corner, up a short flight of steps, through another long hallway, and up a staircase. It was all Molly and Caroline could do to keep up with her, never mind noting how to get back to the drawing room.

At last Mrs. Lane stopped and opened a door. "These are your chambers. You have two connecting rooms. Mrs. Clarke thought you would appreciate being close to each other."

"That was thoughtful of her. Thank you," Caroline said.

Mrs. Lane said nothing but continued down the hall.

"What do you think of her?" Molly asked once Mrs. Lane turned a corner and was out of sight.

Caroline twisted a button on her coat. "Do you think she's right? Will everyone find out we're here unchaperoned?"

"I don't see how they could. I'm more concerned with Mrs. Lane treating us like women of ill repute. Of all the nerve!"

"She probably didn't mean anything by it. Perhaps she's truly concerned for our reputations."

"Somehow, I think she's more concerned with how it would reflect on the Clarkes. And she clearly has doubts about our propriety."

"She's only trying to be helpful. Let's unpack."

They strolled into the airy room. A canopied bed stood in the center of the bedchamber, while two plum-colored armchairs and a coordinating sofa made up a cozy seating area. Opposite the bed, a cushioned window seat overlooked a glade of trees just outside. Molly's trunks stood between the wardrobe and writing desk on the far side of the chamber.

"This must be mine," Molly said and climbed onto the bed. She lay back against the pillows, admiring the colorful vines and flowers embroidered into the blue canopy.

Caroline stood beside the bed, frowning as she unbuttoned her jacket.

"Caroline, what's wrong? Is it Mrs. Lane?"

"I didn't want to say this in front of Benedict, but I'm surprised Mr. and Mrs. Clarke didn't stay here to meet me."

Molly sat up. "I am, too. Leaving was an odd thing to do, but Benedict says they want to meet you when they get back."

"Yes, but we'll have to rearrange all our plans. It wasn't very polite."

"Perhaps they needed to go," Molly said, though she couldn't imagine what would take the Clarkes away at such an important time.

"Perhaps. Well, there's nothing to be done about it now. I don't think my parents would like it."

"Are you going to tell them?"

"I'll have to at some point, since we'll be coming home later than planned. I'll wait a while, though. It's possible they'd come here to fetch us right away if I told them now."

Molly hopped off the bed. "We wouldn't want that. It would defeat the whole purpose of the trip."

"Exactly. It's all so distressing. Well, I'm going to see my room," Caroline said and went through the connecting door.

Molly sat at the vanity and removed her hat. What a remarkable day. After all they'd been through, it felt like an accomplishment to have arrived and been given a room, a certain sign they'd stay for the duration of the trip. She wondered where Aunt Hazel would stay. The thought made her realize she should tell her they'd arrived safely, so she went over to the writing desk to pen a short note.

Caroline returned not long after. "My room is almost exactly the same as yours, but I have a corner window overlooking the forest. I've written a note for Auntie. I'll give it to Mr. Dawson when we go down."

Molly held up her note. "Shall we send both?"

Caroline tucked the notes into her pocket. "Yes, Auntie will appreciate it. I do hope she's feeling better."

"She will. If not today, then tomorrow." Molly rubbed her stomach. "I wonder what time dinner is. I was too distracted to have anything besides tea in the yellow room."

"I was too." Caroline sat in a floral easy chair beside the desk. "What do you think of the gentlemen?"

"I haven't had much time to consider them yet. But I'd say we'll be in for some fun with Fred, and Mr. Bailey probably won't spend much time with us. The real question is Benedict. What do you think of him? Love at first sight?"

"I hardly think so. All he really spoke to me about was a tree, and aside from that has spent most of our acquaintance apologizing to me for one thing or another."

"Do you think he's handsome?"

Caroline nodded, a slight smile on her face. "I do. Not like Fred, but in a pleasant, friendly way. He has nice eyes."

"I saw him watching you. I think he likes what he sees."

"I hope so, since our fathers have gone to great lengths to help us get acquainted."

"How extraordinary. Visiting someone you've only met in person once, and knowing your parents hope you'll want to court each other."

"Extraordinary indeed. It isn't as— Never mind. It's silly." Caroline looked down at her lap.

Molly leaned forward and touched her arm. "What?"

Caroline sighed. "It isn't as romantic as I'd like. It would be sweet to meet someone at a ball and be swept off my feet."

Molly raised a brow. "But you've been…shuffled off your feet?"

"My feet haven't gone anywhere. We met that one time, and we've written letters. It would be convenient to find someone without all the hassle of a Season, but as I said…"

"Not very romantic. Perhaps Benedict will surprise you. Maybe he *will* sweep you off your feet."

"You always know how to cheer me, Molly. One thing I think you're right about. Benedict will act more naturally without his parents at home."

"Yes, and hopefully Mrs. Lane won't hover over us too much."

"Oh, she won't," Caroline said. "She's just the housekeeper."

The soft sound of someone clearing their throat made Molly and Caroline jump as if a cannon had fired.

Mrs. Lane stood in the doorway. "Pardon me. The door was open. Dinner will be served in one hour." She left, closing the door behind her.

Molly and Caroline stared at each other in utter silence.

"We've made a good first impression on her, then," Molly said after a few moments.

Caroline threw a pillow at her.

An hour later, Kitty arrived to escort them to dinner. Molly tried to take note of how to get back to her room but had the feeling she'd need to do it two or three times before she'd truly know her way.

Upon entering the dining room, Molly immediately regretted her choice of gown. Every bit of the elegant furniture was either mahogany or upholstered in rich burgundy that matched the carpet—and Molly's dress. She'd blend into whatever chair she chose at the long, claw-footed table.

As soon as Fred noticed Molly and Caroline in the doorway he crossed the room to offer each of them an arm. "Good evening, ladies."

Molly declined. "Thank you, but I don't think we'd all make it through the door."

"Fair enough, Molly. That leaves you to Benedict. You don't mind if I call you Molly? We might as well do away with surnames."

Molly smiled. "I don't mind."

Benedict came over and offered his arm. "Right this way, Miss Merriwe—I mean, Molly."

A thumping noise came from the hallway, and they all turned toward the door.

"Ah, here you are, Roger," Fred said. "We were just discussing the pointlessness of surnames. Gets in the way of forming an acquaintance, don't you think?"

Mr. Bailey leaned on a cane, a slight grimace on his face. "I wouldn't say that, but I'm not one to go against the grain. The ladies may call me Roger, if I may call them Caroline and Molly."

"You may," Molly said, and Caroline nodded.

Once they were seated, Molly found herself sandwiched between Benedict and Caroline, which seemed counterproductive, but she could hardly insist on changing seats.

After dinner, Benedict and Fred gave them a quick

tour of the house, while Roger went off to the library. The house was so big they didn't have time to go over it all, but Benedict told them they should feel free to explore at their leisure. The tour ended at their bedchamber door, so Molly didn't need to worry about finding her way back.

When she woke late the next morning, Molly nestled into the comfortable bed, not wanting to get up. But the sun peeking through the windows told her it must be almost time for breakfast. She yawned, got out of bed, and plodded over to Caroline's room. "Wake up, Caroline."

"No."

Molly sat on the edge of the bed and tugged at the blankets Caroline had thrown over her head.

Caroline clung to them for dear life.

Molly tugged harder.

Finally, Caroline pulled them down to her chin. "Molly! I was in the middle of a dream."

"About Benedict?" Molly asked and stretched out beside her.

"That is none of your concern." She shoved her with her foot. "And get out. If you're pestering me to wake up, you can't make yourself at home in my bed."

Molly just burrowed deeper into the blankets. "I like your bed." Instead of blue hangings, Caroline's were green, embroidered with frolicking woodland animals. It was like lying in a forest glade.

"So do I." Caroline turned away and put the pillow over her head.

Molly folded her hands over her stomach. "What should we do today? Explore the house more? Take a ride? Go into town?"

Caroline flipped onto her back. "Benedict said we should feel free to look around the house. I wonder if we missed breakfast."

"I'd think they'd wait for us, or have a buffet, perhaps."

"I'm sure you're right. I hope we hear from Auntie today. I've been thinking about her."

"She's in good hands. Come on, let's get dressed." Molly jerked the covers back and Caroline said a word she wouldn't have uttered if her aunt *were* there.

Molly went back to her room and put on a lavender gown, brushed her hair, and pulled it into a loose bun. She nearly picked up her new novel to bring downstairs, but it would probably seem rude to read all through breakfast instead of talking to the gentlemen.

Caroline, who had decided on a yellow dress, came into her room. "Do you remember the way to the breakfast room?"

Molly tried to recall, but they'd seen so many rooms in so many wings last night it was impossible to know for certain. Fortunately, she did have an inkling. "I know it's downstairs."

"I'll ring for Kitty. She can show us."

After their encounter with Mrs. Lane the previous evening, Molly didn't want to risk her answering the summons. It was far too early in the day to deal with her. "We'll find it. On the way we can see more of the house."

They strolled up the corridor, down a flight of stairs, and through another hallway. Just outside was a wooded area that Molly was almost sure indicated they were on the opposite end of the house from the breakfast room. She stopped and turned in a circle on the landing. "Do you have any idea of where we are?"

Caroline glanced up the hall. "None whatsoever."

Molly put a hand on her chin. "Where are all the footmen? If we could find one, he'd be able to tell us which way to go. Perhaps we should go into a room and look for a bell pull?"

"We can't do that! We could end up in someone's private chamber."

"Then we keep looking."

They changed direction, walking up a long corridor that led to a small gallery. After admiring the paintings, they went through a doorway leading to a curved staircase. They followed it down to yet another hallway and found themselves in front of a window facing the stables.

"I think we're getting closer," Caroline said.

Molly blew a lock of hair out of her eyes. She was tired, hungrier than she'd been in days, and irritated. "I'm looking in one of these rooms. Either that or we go to the stables, saddle a horse, and ride to the front door. If we ring the bell, Mr. Dawson will lead us to the breakfast room."

Caroline gripped her elbow. "Molly, no. We might be barging in on someone."

"These can't be bedchambers, the family probably all sleep upstairs. Perhaps one of these is the billiard room, or the library." She pulled out of Caroline's grip and walked down the hall until she found a promising door. To Molly's immense relief, it was locked. Hopefully all of them were, because Caroline was right—it was rude to enter unknown rooms. But it would be worse to spend the day wandering aimlessly through Waverly Hall, so what was the alternative?

Molly tried two locked doors before one opened.

After a glance back at Caroline, they crept inside. A fire burned in the hearth of the wood paneled room. It wasn't large, and the book-lined shelves gave it a welcoming air.

Molly peered around, searching for a bell pull. It was then she noticed the thumping red tail.

And the chair in front of the fire, facing away from them.

And the hand resting on the arm of the chair.

And the cane propped against the wall.

She swallowed. Hard. Was this Roger's bedchamber?

"We'd better go," she whispered to Caroline. With any luck Roger hadn't noticed them enter.

"Oh, don't leave on my account," he said without turning around.

Molly closed her eyes, cringing.

Caroline pinched her arm.

"Ouch!"

"Are you hurt?" Roger called.

Molly ran a hand over her crimson forehead. "No, I'm not hurt. Please forgive the intrusion. We were looking for the breakfast room." Penny scampered over, tail wagging. Molly bent down to pet her, turned and nearly bumped into Caroline in her haste to leave.

Roger rose and faced them, holding his book as though loath to release it. "The breakfast room is in the south wing. You've come the long way around."

"Oh, I do apologize." Molly sensed that her face was still pink, if not red, with the warmth of embarrassment. "We've been wandering around for...for I don't know how long, trying to find someone to point us in the right direction. We never would have intentionally entered your bedchamber."

"This isn't my bedchamber. It's one of Mr. Clarke's offices."

Molly gave a short, tense laugh. "Oh, I'm glad to hear that. It's bad enough we barged in on you, but if it had been your bedchamber…"

She didn't finish the thought, or need to. They probably would have been asked to leave the house.

Roger appeared to be holding back a smile, and Molly realized she hadn't seen him smile once since they'd met. Granted, it was less than a day, but notable. Amusement brought a sparkle to his eyes, which she now saw were a rich, golden brown. A dimple on his right cheek almost made an appearance, but Roger cleared his throat and looked away. When he met Molly's eyes again, both the sparkle and dimple were gone. "I haven't had breakfast yet, so I'll show you the way."

He crossed the room and stood aside for Molly and Caroline to exit, then closed the door behind them.

Molly noticed Roger didn't bring his cane, yet he still limped. Perhaps his leg only bothered him enough to use it occasionally.

Penny trotted down the hall, casting frequent looks over her shoulder to be sure they were following.

"Were we very far off?" Caroline asked Roger.

"Yes. I'm not even sure how you managed to make it this far. Your bedchambers are in the same wing as the breakfast room."

"I'd tell you how we came to be here, but I'm not sure, either," Molly said. "I know there were multiple staircases involved. We looked for a maid or footman but couldn't find anybody."

Roger nodded but didn't turn to look at her. "You

must have been in the east wing. That isn't used very often unless the Clarkes throw a house party. Did you pass through a gallery?"

"A small one," Molly said.

"Yes, that was the east wing," he confirmed.

"I'll remember that," Molly said. "If I ever learn to navigate the manor."

"You will. For now, we'll cut through the quadrangle to the breakfast room." Roger went down a short hall and pushed a door open, Penny leading the way outside.

A fountain and benches sat in the center of the grassy courtyard, overlooked by windows from each of the four wings of the house. Though it looked like a perfect place to sit and read, Molly imagined it would be difficult to feel you had any privacy out here. She glanced up at the windows, trying to determine which was her wing. Apparently the one directly ahead of them, the south wing, as Roger didn't deviate from the straight cobblestone path. When they reached the other side, he knelt to pick up a stick, then threw it across the yard for Penny, who bolted after it.

Roger opened a set of French doors and ushered Molly and Caroline inside. They followed him down a corridor to the breakfast room, which was done up in pale blues and greens and caught all the light coming in from two bay windows overlooking a meadow. Both had cushioned window seats with a row of books upon the sill. A number of wingback chairs surrounded a hearth at the far end of the room.

At the dining table Fred read the newspaper while trying to scoop up fried eggs without looking at them, and Benedict sipped coffee, rifling through the mail.

"Good morning," Roger said as they walked in.

"Morning," Benedict replied, eyes on the envelope in his hand.

Fred said nothing.

Roger cleared his throat loudly. "Fred."

"What the blaz—" Fred looked up, eyes widening when he saw the ladies. He kicked Benedict under the table.

Benedict glared at him. "Ow! What th—"

Fred cut him off. "Roger's brought Caroline and Molly," he said loudly, rising.

Benedict leapt to his feet and crossed the room, his eyes on Caroline. "Good morning. I trust you slept well."

"Yes, the room was very comfortable," Caroline said.

Fred nodded to Molly as he straightened his tie.

Was this how gentlemen always behaved when they were by themselves? Paying no attention to each other and aggravated when interrupted? Molly would ask her brothers the next time she saw them.

"We serve ourselves in the morning," Roger said over his shoulder as he walked to the sideboard.

Molly and Caroline joined him, more than ready for breakfast after their trek through the house. There were eggs prepared in a variety of ways, bacon, sausage, and porridge, as well as toast and crumpets. After filling their plates, the women took their places at the table.

Roger finished breakfast first and settled into one of the window seats with a book.

Molly and Caroline sipped their coffee while Benedict and Fred described some features of the estate they might like to see. Molly was about to say she'd enjoy seeing the pond or the kennels when someone behind them spoke.

"Here you two are." Mrs. Lane, accompanied by a winded-looking Kitty, stood in the doorway.

"Good morning," Molly said.

Mrs. Lane looked right through her as she spoke. "We went to your rooms to escort you to breakfast, but you were gone. Kitty looked everywhere for you. To no avail." She cast Kitty a dark look.

Kitty seemed as though she'd like to say something, but instead stared at the ground. From the corner of her eye Molly saw Fred scowl and start to stand, then shake his head and keep his seat.

"We found breakfast on our own." Molly deemed it unnecessary to describe the whole ordeal.

"In future, if you would ring for Kitty she will make herself useful and bring you down." Her tone left no doubt that she currently thought Kitty far from useful.

"After today we'll find the breakfast room on our own, but I have no doubt Kitty would be of the utmost assistance, as she was yesterday." Molly hadn't said two words to Kitty yesterday, but couldn't bear to see her put down by Mrs. Lane for no fault of her own. How was she supposed to have found them while they traipsed around the manor, at least not without a bloodhound?

Benedict rose. "Thank you, Mrs. Lane."

She nodded and left the room.

"Thank you for looking after our guests, Kitty," Fred said before she turned to follow Mrs. Lane. "I've no doubt you did a splendid job chasing after the ladies."

Kitty gave Fred a grateful glance before hurrying down the hall, leaving an awkward silence in her wake.

Fred ran a hand over his mouth, jiggling his foot under the table.

"So," Benedict said to the room at large after a few moments. "What would you like to do today? Walk in the gardens? They're blooming at this time of year. There are some very tall trees on—"

Fred stood abruptly. "Excuse me. I feel I've left something in the...the library." He jogged across the room and went in the same direction as Kitty.

Chapter Five

Benedict stared at the door his brother had gone through as though hoping it would tell him what to say next.

Caroline set her napkin on the table. "You were saying about tall trees?"

Benedict looked relieved that she'd rescued him from explaining his brother's behavior. Not that it needed an explanation. Fred clearly had some sort of flirtation going on with Kitty and was concerned after Mrs. Lane chastised her.

Molly recalled what Mr. Darby had said about Fred's reputation. Chasing after maids would certainly put him in the category of a rogue. Kitty hadn't seemed displeased, though. Perhaps that explained Mrs. Lane's treatment of her. She wouldn't want any sort of indiscretion going on between a maid and a son of the house.

Benedict shook his head. "The trees most likely wouldn't interest you. I feel I should explain about Mrs. Lane."

"You don't owe us any explanation," Molly said, though after last night she'd like to hear what kind of explanation he *could* give about Mrs. Lane's behavior. It still rankled when she thought of it.

Benedict sighed. "If you're going to be with us for a few weeks, you should understand. Mrs. Lane has been here for years, even before my parents married. She's watched over me and Fred since birth. I've a feeling she intends to be a bit of a mother hen while our own mother is away."

"Isn't that somewhat..." Molly fumbled for the right—non-insulting—word.

"Presumptuous?" Roger offered from across the room.

Molly looked at him, but he was still reading his book.

Benedict shifted in his chair. "She doesn't mean it that way."

"But aren't you master of the house while your parents are away?" Caroline asked.

"I am. I'll remind Mrs. Lane to speak civilly to guests and not to scold the servants in front of you. I think since she's been here for so long she sometimes forgets what deference is due, and feels she needs to step in and help when our parents are away."

"Speaking of Mrs. Lane," Caroline said hesitantly, "Last night she implied she disapproves of our staying."

Benedict's brows creased. "Did she?"

"She said gossip about us is sure to reach Rochester, and she doesn't have a very high opinion of Caroline and me. She acted like we're wantons," Molly said.

Benedict turned red, and Caroline said, "Molly!"

Molly shrugged. "Well, it was obvious by the way she spoke to us."

"I'm sorry if she gave you that impression." Benedict said. "Don't worry about gossip. I'll make sure the servants know they aren't to tell anyone."

"After all, we're only here unchaperoned for a day or so," Caroline said, sounding more hopeful than confident.

Benedict let the subject drop and directed their attention to a tree just outside the window.

After ten minutes of listening to Benedict describe the foliage of the tree in different seasons, Molly spoke when he paused for breath. "Let's go see the kennels."

"Fred would like to go with us, I imagine, as he's raising a pack of hounds. He likes to show them off," Benedict said.

"He'll catch up," Roger said. "I'll tell him where you've gone."

"Won't you join us?" Benedict asked.

Roger flexed his ankle. "I'll stay here."

"Would you like me to ring for tea?" Molly asked, then blushed. Who was presumptuous now?

Roger gave her a blank look. "There's a teapot on the sideboard. I'll fetch some if I want any."

"Of course," Molly said. "Would it be all right if I brought Penny with us to the kennels?"

"She'd like that. You won't need a leash, she'll follow you." He flipped the page of his book and continued reading.

Benedict led Molly and Caroline to the quadrangle, where they found Penny sleeping beside the fountain. As soon as she saw them she leapt to her feet and ran over to Molly. They crossed the courtyard and passed through a stone passage to the back of the house. Once outside, Penny darted over a rise and disappeared.

"Penny!" Molly cried. First she'd intruded on Roger this morning, and now she'd lost his dog.

"Don't worry. She's heading for the kennels," Benedict said.

As they walked past manicured gardens and across

the lawn, Molly admired the acres of green fields and forest surrounding Waverly. Foals frolicked among spring flowers in a meadow off to her right, and horses grazed in a paddock beside impressive stables. In the distance, sunlight shimmered on a lake or river. She hung back from a silent Benedict and Caroline, hoping he'd have the good sense to start an interesting conversation.

She heard the kennel before she reached the crest of a hill and saw it standing close to the forest. It sounded like Fred had a pack of hundreds inside what looked like a small white barn.

Suddenly Penny whizzed by, paws tearing up the grass as she ran circles around Molly.

Molly laughed and patted her thigh. "Come here, Penny."

Penny leaned forward on her forelegs, tail wagging, then barked and bolted down the hill.

Up ahead, Benedict had finally drawn Caroline into a conversation. Molly held back as long as she could, but soon caught up with them as they reached the kennels. Inside, hounds bayed and barked.

"They're awfully loud," Caroline said.

"Yes, they are," Benedict half shouted.

Penny scratched the door.

"She wants to get inside." Molly was about to open the door when Fred appeared.

"Oh, Roger wouldn't want her to go in," he said. "Penny's been spending too much time with one of my bassets for his liking."

Penny whined when Molly stepped back from the door.

"Should we come back another time?" Caroline asked.

"No," Fred said. "I'll hold Penny's collar while you go in."

Molly opened the door and slipped inside, followed by Benedict and Caroline. Inside were a number of short, open stalls, each with one or two dogs lounging in them. There weren't as many as Molly had expected—twenty or so beagles and four basset hounds. The kennel smelled of fresh straw, and the howling ceased once they entered.

Fred came in behind Caroline and closed the door. "Here they are," he said proudly. "The finest hunting dogs in the county. Come closer, they won't bite." He opened one of the stall doors to reveal a basset hound lying on the ground, puppies scampering around her.

"Oh!" Molly and Caroline crooned.

"You've raised them yourself?" Molly reached down to pet the mother while Caroline scooped up a wriggling puppy.

Fred sat on the edge of a stall. "With our head groom's help. He knows all about dogs. We'll have a proper hunt while you're here."

Molly kept her grimace to herself. Though she loved to ride and liked dogs, she'd never taken to hunting. When her father organized hunts, she went along but usually managed to lag behind or wander off until it was all over.

Fred glanced at his watch. "Almost time for them to eat, and they'll make a racket. Might be a good time to sneak away." After Caroline set the puppy down, Fred opened the door for them. "I'll stay to help with the feeding. See you all later."

On their way back to the house, Benedict stopped abruptly, patting his waistcoat pockets. "I almost forgot. A letter came for you from The Blue Swan." He handed

Caroline an envelope.

"Thank you." She tore it open while Molly stood by waiting impatiently for news. "Aunt Hazel's worse. But Doctor Kellow says he'll write again tomorrow."

"Oh, no," Molly said.

"She'll be right as rain soon," Benedict reassured them.

"I hope so," Caroline said.

When they returned to the house, Molly and Caroline went up to their room.

"What do you think of our first morning at Waverly Hall?" Molly asked as she settled into the sofa.

"Which part? Getting lost this morning? The dogs? Kitty?" Caroline glanced at the door, lowering her voice. "Mrs. Lane? It's hard to believe we've only been here a day."

"It feels longer. Mrs. Lane is odd, but I suppose many housekeepers can be eccentric, especially if they've been long with the family."

Caroline took a seat beside Molly. "Perhaps you're right. Our housekeeper still calls me Caro, as she did when I was a baby. Still, Mrs. Lane was exceedingly rude to Kitty and to us. I do hope Benedict speaks to her. I'd like to know he's a man to take charge, not one to simply let his housekeeper walk all over him, no matter what sentimental attachment there may be."

"I think she had a hand in that seating arrangement last night," Molly said. "Did you see the way she walked through the dining room a few times? Mr. Dawson was managing dinner, so there was no need for Mrs. Lane to be there. Obviously she was keeping an eye on us."

"I wonder if she treats all the maids the same way she did Kitty?" Caroline asked.

"I hope not. I'd like to ask Fred about it."

"Don't go prying, Molly. They may not appreciate it, and things are already strained due to our lack of chaperones."

"I won't pry. But I *am* curious." She paused. "I'm also curious about Fred and Kitty. I think there's something going on between them."

Caroline tutted. "The maid? You really are a romantic."

"Don't you remember what your father said about Fred's reputation?" Molly asked as she slipped her shoes off.

"Oh, yes. Still, I don't think he'd be involved with a maid. That would be beyond scandalous."

"So do you find yourself helpless against his charms?" Molly asked with a grin.

"Of course not. Benedict already has a sort of…claim on me. You're in more danger than I am—you're free as a bird."

Molly laughed. "I think I'm safe from Fred."

"Don't you find him attractive? He's quite diverting."

"There's no question he's one of the most handsome men I've ever seen, not to mention amusing and…I don't know how to describe it, but he has a way of putting one at ease."

Caroline sat up straighter. "Aha! So, you do—"

Molly cut her off. "I'm not likely to be tempted by a man I've already been warned about, *and* who appears to be carrying on with a maid. Speaking of Kitty, if I'd seen her on the street I would never have guessed she's a maid. There's something elegant about her."

"I had the same thought. I only hope she welcomes

Fred's attentions and isn't forced to endure them because she works here."

Molly had the feeling this wasn't the case. Kitty had practically glowed when she looked at Fred this morning and seemed relaxed around him. But maybe Caroline was right and Molly was imagining something going on between them. Perhaps Fred cast warm glances at every pretty girl, and his racing out of the breakfast room this morning had nothing to do with Kitty.

On their fourth day at Waverly, Molly and Caroline managed to find the breakfast and dining rooms without getting lost.

Benedict had much more free time than Molly would have guessed and spent the majority of every day with Caroline. Though she stayed in the background, Molly had been able to get more of an idea of what he was like. Attentive, smart, considerate. He hadn't given any indication of his feelings yet, and Molly knew Caroline worried he wasn't taken with her. But it was obvious to Molly that he was. She suspected Benedict was either shy or waiting for a sign from Caroline that *she* liked *him*.

Every day brought a new intrusion from Mrs. Lane, be it her unwanted presence in the breakfast room, peering out the windows at Benedict and Caroline when they strolled around the grounds, or appearing suddenly in doorways while the young people gathered together to talk.

When Molly wasn't with Caroline and Benedict she spent her time in the library, exploring the estate or taking long walks with Penny. She was often thrown together with Fred for hours at a time while Caroline was otherwise engaged, and they usually visited the kennels.

For a reputed scoundrel, he was very well behaved. Though she'd told Caroline she was immune to his charms, Molly couldn't deny a certain swooping in her stomach every time he favored her with his most charming smile.

One day as she and Fred walked back to the manor, Molly noticed Mrs. Lane watching them from an upper-story window. "She certainly is keeping an eye on us, isn't she?" Molly asked.

"Who?"

Molly pointed to the window. "Mrs. Lane."

Fred looked up just as Mrs. Lane stepped back from the curtains. "Is Kitty with her?"

"I don't think so. Why would she be?"

He craned his neck to see into the window. "Mrs. Lane often pops up where Kitty is working. To check on her."

Molly ignored the voice in her head telling her not to pry. "I hope it isn't impertinent to ask, but is there a reason Mrs. Lane seems to dislike Kitty? I heard her chastising her the other day for not ironing a tablecloth properly. She doesn't take such notice with the other maids, from what I've seen."

"You're not impertinent. It would be difficult not to notice."

Since he didn't give her a straight answer, Molly assumed Fred was just as much in the dark about it as she was. "The way Mrs. Lane treats her, I'm surprised Kitty doesn't find work elsewhere."

Fred kicked at a tuft of grass. "I don't think Kitty has many options."

Molly didn't press for more information as she slowed to keep pace with a silent Fred on their way back to the house.

At the front door he turned to her with his customary smile. "I think it's time we had a go at the stables. Let's see if we can convince the others to go riding."

Only Molly and Fred wanted to go riding that day, so a plan was set for the following morning.

Chapter Six

On the way down to breakfast the next morning, Molly heard something she never had before—Kitty's voice raised in agitation. Poised to head back upstairs to avoid overhearing a private conversation, Molly froze when she heard her own name.

"What Miss Merriwether and Miss Darby do is none of your concern, Polly," Kitty said.

A woman replied, "But it's not right, them staying un—"

"Stop right there, Marietta," Kitty said. "I don't want to hear any gossip about that, do you understand me?"

"It isn't gossip. If anyone hears—" Polly began.

So she was speaking to two of the maids. Molly strained to hear Kitty's reply.

"Nobody will hear, not unless someone from the house spreads rumors, which will *not* happen. I don't want to hear you two chattering about this even here, never mind in town. The poor ladies had no idea Mr. and Mrs. Clarke weren't home."

Polly spoke again. "They could have left, though, couldn't they?"

"As I said, it's none of your concern. But it *will* be your concern if I hear you're telling tales."

Marietta said, somewhat loftily, "Mrs. Lane thinks they should have left."

"Just get back to work and don't let me hear you discussing this again," Kitty snapped. "If any whispers get out, I'll know who's behind it."

There were some disgruntled murmurs from the two women as they walked away.

Later, as Molly ate breakfast, she mulled over the conversation. She'd assumed only Mrs. Lane disapproved, but was the entire staff thinking the same thing? If Aunt Hazel didn't arrive soon, she and Caroline might have no choice but to go home early.

Molly put it out of her mind as everyone made their way to the stables. Since Fred had gone on ahead and Caroline walked with Benedict, Roger offered Molly his arm. Noticing he still favored his right ankle, she adjusted her gait to his. He gave her a sidelong glance but she looked away as if she hadn't noticed.

"Is Penny coming along?" Molly asked.

"No."

"Oh, is she afraid of horses?"

Roger just shrugged, putting an end to Molly's attempts at conversation. In future she'd be sure to keep up with Fred.

After a silent walk across the grounds, they reached the stables.

Fred met them at the entrance, rubbing his hands together. "Molly, I know just the horse for you. She's gentle, but strong and fast." He led her to a dapple-gray mare. "This is Opal."

Molly stroked Opal's muzzle. "She looks perfect."

"Excellent. I'll get Caroline settled with Pearl and we can go."

Before long they were all mounted and heading into the forest. Opal was a superb horse. She had a smooth, easy gait and responded to Molly's lightest touch. Caroline's horse, Pearl, was Opal's sister but closer to white than gray. Benedict, astride his bay horse, Falcon, rode beside Caroline while Fred led the way on a feisty black stallion named Birdie—short for Bluebird. Roger brought up the rear on Sparrow, a chestnut gelding.

They passed through a glade of trees to a trail wide enough for them to ride side by side. Birds sang in the trees overhead as sunlight sprinkled the dewy grass. The morning was fresh and sunny, a scent of spring in the air. Soon they came to a meadow and the group was able to spread out. Caroline stayed beside Benedict, and Roger trotted ahead to ride with Fred. Roger looked more relaxed than Molly had ever seen him, and sat his horse like he'd been born in the saddle. He talked and laughed with Fred, and Molly found herself wishing she was closer so she could hear what they were saying.

They rode through the countryside until the sun was high in the sky. By the time Rochester came into view, Molly was ready for a break.

Fred pulled up on Birdie. "Let's stop at the inn."

"Would you like to have lunch here in town?" Benedict asked Caroline.

"Yes, please," she said.

In the courtyard of the Trout And Mallard, they all dismounted. Molly removed her hat, letting the breeze ruffle her hair as she strolled out to the edge of the yard. In the distance the church steeple and a few houses were visible; a tavern stood a little way down the road. She wondered if anyone would accompany her there if she asked. Perhaps Fred?

Caroline joined her. "Aren't you hungry? Let's go in."

"Look. There's a tavern just over there." Molly pointed to the brown clapboard building.

"We are *not* going to a tavern."

"It's practically the same as an inn," Molly said and took an involuntary step toward the road.

"Practically. But not quite. We can't go in there in broad daylight. How would it look?"

Molly glanced at Benedict, Fred and Roger, who were talking just outside the inn's entrance. "I don't think anybody would notice, or care." A knot formed in her stomach. Or would they? She told Caroline what she'd heard between Kitty and the other maids that morning.

Caroline looked furtively around, fiddling with the buttons of her riding habit. "Perhaps we should go back to Waverly."

"No, I only told you so you'd know what they're saying up at the house and so we can avoid drawing any unnecessary attention to ourselves."

"Going to a tavern qualifies as unnecessary attention, so that settles that. I'm surprised the maids were gossiping. Benedict said he'd make it clear to the staff that us being here without a chaperone is a secret. I hope nobody in town hears about it."

"It looks like Kitty is also trying to keep it a secret. We needn't worry."

They lingered at the inn for longer than Molly had expected, but it was easy to do with the pleasant company and delicious food. She sat across from Caroline and Benedict, who were getting along well and chatted all through the meal. Perhaps that was because for the first time all week Mrs. Lane wasn't there to seat them at opposite ends of the table.

After lunch they made their leisurely way back to Waverly. Well, it was leisurely until Fred decided he wanted to race and bolted ahead, pursued by everyone else. Molly kept up until she lost sight of her friends, then slowed Opal to a walk. She came to a fork in the road and, though she'd only passed through here a few hours ago, couldn't remember which way to go. Opal stood patiently while Molly tried to decide which path looked familiar. She started down the left fork but hadn't gone far when hoofbeats came up the road behind her. Twisting in her saddle, she saw Roger approaching.

"It's the other way," he said, pulling Sparrow to a halt.

"Thank you for coming back. Where are the others?"

He gestured over his shoulder. "A good way ahead."

Molly turned Opal to follow Roger and they rode silently until the tall chimneys of Waverly Hall appeared in the distance. Off to the right Molly noticed a pond surrounded by wildflowers. It was too delightful a spot to pass. She turned Opal toward a break in the trees.

"Where are you going?" Roger called in a tight voice.

"This pond is charming. I'd like to take a closer look."

Roger followed, keeping Sparrow to a walk. "We should get back to the house."

"It won't take long."

When Molly reached the clearing she dismounted and tied Opal's reins to a branch. Towering conifer trees encircled the grassy meadow and flowers of every color swayed in the warm, earthy breeze.

Roger shifted in his saddle. "The others will be

waiting."

"Go on ahead if you'd prefer." Molly guessed he wanted to avoid walking because of his ankle and didn't want him to feel obligated. She wouldn't have minded if he left, as it was somewhat inappropriate to linger here alone with him.

He let out something between a groan and a sigh. "I'll wait. You might get lost again."

"I can see the house from here, so I doubt I'll get lost. But stay if you like." Molly clasped her hands behind her back and approached the pond. It was oval-shaped and probably twenty feet across at its widest. A narrow stream trickled into it, then slipped like a ribbon through the tall grass on the other side. Dragonflies flitted among the cattails, and Molly suspected if she stayed here long enough she'd hear crickets or see fireflies. But it was hard to relax when every so often an irritated sigh came from behind her.

Molly walked to the edge of the pond for a closer look. The grass fell away and a steep dirt embankment ran down to the gently rippling water, where lily pads and white and purple flowers floated on the surface. This was just the type of place she and Caroline could spend an afternoon. Perhaps they'd come back one day and bring a picnic. Turning her face to the sun, Molly smiled and took a deep breath of sweet smelling air.

It was then the earth shifted.

The ground beneath her feet seemed to sink and she started sliding down the bank. Molly looked for something to grab onto but found nothing but grass and cattails. She tried taking a step back, but the soil gave way and she ended up sliding farther down.

"Oh!" Unable to turn around, she called out. "Help!"

Roger didn't answer. Had he left?

Molly tried changing direction, but the loose soil wouldn't support her. As she slipped forward inch by inch, she braced herself for the inevitable. The next instant she was submerged in the pond, surrounded by lily pads.

"Ugh!" She scrambled to her feet, wiping cold water from her eyes.

Roger appeared at the edge of the pond, peering down at her. "What are you doing?"

"What am I *doing*?" She raised her hands and let them splash into the water. "I fell and I don't think I'll be able to get out. That bank is unstable."

"I did say we shouldn't stop."

"That's hardly the issue now," she ground out. "Will you help me?"

Roger gave a kind of grunt and stood, hands on hips, surveying the situation as water swirled about Molly's waist and her skirt billowed up around her. She was soaked from head to foot and her hat was nowhere to be seen.

"Do you think you could reach my hand?" Roger finally asked.

Shivering, Molly crept forward, mud sucking at her shoes with every step. She made it to the reedy bank and stretched her hand up to Roger. Their fingers were at least four feet away from each other. Molly let her arm drop.

He sighed again. "I'll have to come down."

"I think if you do we'll both be stuck." Truthfully, as much as she needed help, she didn't want him to re-injure his ankle.

"The bank on the other side is sturdier, I could help

you climb up."

She glanced at the far bank, which looked just as deceptively delightful as this side of the pond had. "You're certain?" she asked through chattering teeth.

"Yes, I fish here sometimes, and that's where I stand."

Molly hesitated but had to say it. "Why don't I meet you over there. I—I don't want you to hurt your ankle."

"How chivalrous of you."

She rolled her eyes. "Just meet me on the other side."

Roger didn't answer but stalked—as well as he could stalk while limping—around the pond, crossed his arms, and stood watching her slow progress. Molly's feet squelched in the mud and several times she nearly fell over, arms outstretched to keep her balance. Her riding habit was caked with muck from the waist down, but at least the sun was warming her shoulders. Finally, she made it across to where Roger stood.

"Will you allow me to come help?" he asked. "I'm certain we can both get back up from here. Look—those stones almost make a staircase."

She glanced to where he was pointing. He was right. If Molly weren't so tired from her exertions she'd have climbed up herself, but graciously accepted his offer of assistance. "Yes, thank you, but do be careful."

Roger climbed down and put an arm around her waist firmly. "You'll have to excuse the familiarity," he said as they started up the bank. Stepping slowly and cautiously over the slippery stones, they'd almost made it to the top when Roger pitched sideways and they toppled backward.

Molly slammed her fists in the water. "Blast!"

"Don't splash!" Roger, sitting in the pond beside her, wiped his face with his arm, only managing to make it muddy *and* wet.

"I can't help it. Look where we are!"

Roger rose and helped her to her feet.

As they stood there dripping, Molly glowered. "This pond should be filled in. It's a trap."

"Most people don't fall in."

"*Mr.* Bailey, if you please…" Molly was holding back tears at this point. From what, she wasn't sure. Frustration, embarrassment, soaked shoes? All she wanted was to escape this pond and this man.

"*Miss* Merriwether, if you would allow me."

Before Molly knew what was happening, he'd pushed her up the rocky bank in front of him, his hands on her hips to steer her like a horse. When they reached the crest of the hill, he placed both hands *on her backside* and shoved. She couldn't feel his hands through her soaked wool habit, and there was no way he'd felt any of her, but it was shocking nonetheless.

"Mr. Bailey!" Molly exclaimed, her face burning.

Roger climbed up after her, wiping his hands on his jacket. "You're up, now, aren't you?"

He limped away to Sparrow, and Molly limped after him. What had she done to herself? When she reached Opal, she needed help mounting, but after what they'd just been through Molly barely blinked when Roger grabbed her around the waist and practically threw her into the saddle. He mounted Sparrow and galloped off.

Keeping Opal to a walk, Molly spent the ride home pondering two things; How could she ever look Roger in the eye again, and how fast could she get a cup of tea once she reached Waverly?

An hour and a hot bath later, Molly was propped up in bed with a steaming cup of tea and a plate of biscuits. "And *then*, he galloped off and left me there!"

"How terrible," Caroline said. "Although, he did get you out of the pond."

"Yes, but I daresay I could have done better myself." Molly stretched her ankle, wincing. She'd twisted it when they'd fallen back down the bank. "Did you see Mr. Bailey when he came home?"

"Yes, he stormed through the hall and went upstairs. He was filthy."

"Not as filthy as me." Molly glanced at the dirty riding habit she'd thrown into a corner. "For him to stand there and ask me what was wrong! Was he mocking me or could he truly be that obtuse?"

"Roger doesn't strike me as the mocking type. Perhaps he didn't understand how dire the situation was."

Molly recalled him calling her chivalrous. If that wasn't mocking, she didn't know what was. She cast Caroline an incredulous look. "How could he not understand the gravity of a young lady up to her ears in pond water calling for help?"

"It's possible he didn't want to climb down but was embarrassed to say so."

"He could have told me that. It isn't as though we're complete strangers." Molly stirred her tea viciously, sending half of it sloshing down into the saucer.

"We haven't even known him a week, Molly. I'm certain he did the best he could."

Molly highly doubted that but didn't say so. As she'd wanted to escape him and the pond, she now wanted to escape talking or even thinking about Mr.

Bailey. She finished her tea, set the cup down, and turned back to Caroline. "How was your ride home with Benedict?"

Caroline smiled. "Invigorating! We cantered all the way home."

"And Fred?"

"He made it back before everyone else. I have a feeling he left us alone on purpose."

"I'm sure you're right." Molly shifted on her pillows. "I think tomorrow I'd like to do something *without* the men."

"Even Benedict?"

"I'll allow Benedict." Molly stroked her chin. "And possibly Fred."

"So when you say men, you mean Roger?"

Molly shrugged and they laughed as a soft knock came on the door.

"Come in," Caroline called.

Kitty entered the room, hands folded over her apron. "I came to see if there's anything else you need for your ankle."

"Oh, thank you," Molly said. "It's much better now that I'm not standing on it."

"Then I'll leave you to rest."

Just as Kitty put her hand on the doorknob, Molly said, "No, wait."

Kitty turned around. "Yes?"

"We fancy a little excursion, just the two of us," Molly said, gesturing to Caroline. "Could you recommend something in town?"

"Oh, yes. Shops, the inn, you could tour the church or go to the tea house."

"Tea house?" Caroline asked.

Kitty took a step back into the room. "Yes, it's the sweetest little establishment. My friend Violet's mother runs it."

"It sounds perfect," Molly said. "Could you tell us where it is?"

"It's easy to find. You—"

"Kitty!" Mrs. Lane marched into the room, glaring at her. "Why are you bothering the ladies with your yammering? Go on your way."

Kitty turned and left, chin held high.

"She wasn't bothering us," Molly said coolly. "She was telling us how to find the tea house."

Mrs. Lane's arms were stiff at her sides. "I'll write out the directions and give them to you in the morning. Will there be anything else?"

Molly wanted to tell her she could stop being mean to Kitty but held her tongue. Mrs. Lane left the room, leaving a ringing silence behind her.

Chapter Seven

The next morning, on the mail tray beside Doctor Kellow's daily missive, was a note written in tight script giving directions to the tea house.

Molly set the directions aside and opened the letter. "It isn't from the doctor. Your aunt wrote it herself. That must mean she's feeling better. She says she hardly coughed yesterday, and she took a walk in the garden with Mrs. Plant."

Smiling, Caroline buttered her toast. "She'll probably be here soon. I can hardly wait to see her."

Molly shook her head. "Doctor Kellow added a postscript that Aunt Hazel may be able to travel by the end of next week." She let the letter fall into her lap. "Another week?"

"Good gracious. And we thought it was a mild cold. Imagine if we'd stayed with her at The Blue Swan!"

"We'd be bored to tears. Although we may have gone home by now. Are you glad we stayed here?" Molly asked and scooped up the last of her porridge.

"Definitely."

"It was the right thing to do. Not having chaperones has made it all the more interesting." Molly glanced outside, where the men stood in a circle talking while Penny chewed a stick at Roger's feet.

"Auntie's going to be so upset when she finds out," Caroline said.

"Perhaps she never will."

Caroline clicked her tongue. "Of course she will. She'll arrive next week and find out Mr. and Mrs. Clarke have been gone the whole time. She'll tell our parents."

"Then we'd better enjoy ourselves while we still can."

About to sip her juice, Caroline set the glass down. "I know that look, Molly. What are you planning?"

"Oh, I just thought we might have a poke around while the gentlemen are otherwise occupied."

Outside, the men had set out across the field toward the kennels.

"We've done enough poking around," Caroline said. "We'll probably get lost again."

"No. We've done enough poking around that we *won't* get lost. And there's that arched door we saw in the east wing other day."

"It's most likely a broom closet."

Molly rose, leaving her napkin on the table. "It's in the corner of an empty room on the third floor. Who'd choose such a place for a broom closet? And with such an elaborate door? There were vines engraved on it."

"The room wasn't empty—it looked like an old sewing room. I'm sure it's nothing of interest."

"We won't know until we look."

Caroline looked at her watch. "We're supposed to go to the tea house today."

"We will." Molly picked up the directions and slid them into her pocket.

"You need to rest your ankle. We can't go traipsing off anywhere."

Molly stretched her ankle. "My ankle feels fine. I rested it last night." Fortunately, she'd only twisted it, not sprained or broken it like Roger's. She'd noticed with a twinge of remorse that his limp was more pronounced this morning and suspected it was because of their adventure the day before.

"You're doing this no matter what I say, aren't you?" Caroline asked.

"You don't have to come." Molly gave her an angelic smile as she backed toward the door.

Caroline let out an exaggerated groan as she crossed the room and took Molly's arm. "Let's go."

Even though the men were outside and nobody else was about, they tiptoed through the house to the east wing. When they reached the old sewing room they crept inside, trying to muffle their giggles.

The room still held a buzz of industry though it clearly hadn't been used as a sewing room in some time. Innumerable spools of colored thread lay scattered on a table just inside the door and mounds of old fabric filled a corner shelf. A basket of yellowed lace and a flat iron sat on the floor beneath the window.

"Sh!" Caroline said as they made their way across the room to the mysterious door. "We don't want Mrs. Lane to hear us."

"She won't." Molly turned the ornate brass knob, expecting the door to creak, or be locked, but it opened smoothly.

"Brooms?" Caroline asked hopefully from behind her.

"A staircase!"

Caroline took a step back. "We'd best leave it alone."

"Don't be silly. It probably goes to the attic." Molly started up the stairs, which went straight up for a time, then turned at a right angle. Some of the steps were worn in the middle, but others were crisp and straight, as though they'd been repaired not long ago.

"How high does this go?" Caroline asked, gripping the banister.

"We must be near the top."

Windows on the right lit their way and offered a view of the countryside for miles around. Molly shivered when she caught sight of the pond.

At last they reached a landing and stood in front of another door. Molly pushed it open to reveal a cavernous room as long as the corridor downstairs. They were greeted by the musty scent of old paper and aged wood, but sunshine streaming in through gabled windows gave the attic a welcoming air. Wooden beams ran along the peaked ceiling, and the walls on either end of the room suggested each wing of the house had its own entrance to the attic.

When they stepped inside, Molly felt a stab of disappointment. "It's empty."

"Not quite," Caroline said. "There are some trunks over there." She pointed to the far corner of the attic, where a deep recess sat between two shuttered windows. Just off the main chamber, it looked like a three-walled room.

They crossed to the alcove, which was filled with a jumble of mismatched furniture. A faded blue sofa long enough to sleep on, an ottoman, an ancient box bed, two green wingback chairs, and a low table. Assorted porcelain ewers and basins sat on a dressing table beside a gray chaise lounge. Five or six trunks stood against the wall, a pile of books stacked against them.

Molly picked one up. "*Maps of the Modern World*."

She leafed through it. "These maps have to be a hundred years old."

"Are the others old, too?" Caroline took a book from the pile. "*Recipes Every Woman Should Know*."

Molly set the map book down. "Are they recent?"

Caroline flipped to a random page. "No. There's a tonic in here for coughs that involves—Ugh! I won't even tell you."

Molly walked across the echoing attic to the large windows overlooking the grounds. Far below, the gentlemen were approaching the front doors with Penny and two bassets at their heels.

From behind Molly came the sound of a trunk being pried open. She turned. "What are you doing?"

Caroline's face shone. "I want to see what's in here. There could be more books or old clothes."

"Imagine if there are gowns," Molly said, going to help open the trunk. Just as she'd taken hold of the lid, she looked toward the attic door, sure she'd heard a creak. "Wait. We should go to our room or the parlor."

"You want to carry this downstairs?" Caroline asked skeptically.

"No, no. But I've just seen the gentlemen returning. Benedict might look for you."

"You're right. It wouldn't do to be found snooping."

Reluctantly, they let the heavy lid close.

"The men wouldn't come up here," Molly said, "but let's come back another day when we have more time to explore."

Their eyes met and they shared a smile, then headed for the stairs. When Molly opened the door to the staircase, she let out a piercing shriek, echoed by Caroline's and Kitty's. She put a hand to her wildly pounding heart and fell back against the wall. "Kitty!"

Kitty stared at Molly and Caroline as if trying to convince herself they were real. She put her hands to her face, shoulders heaving, and it was impossible to tell if she was laughing or crying.

Caroline reached out and grabbed Molly's arm. *She* was laughing. Molly started, too, and before long they were all grasping each other's hands, tears streaming down their cheeks.

"Oh," Kitty said, straightening. "Oh, I thought you were ghosts!"

"We thought you were!" Molly said. "What are you doing up here?"

Kitty sobered at once and adjusted her apron. "I saw the door open downstairs. I thought the wind blew it open."

"Wind?" Molly asked.

"From…from an open window."

Caroline, still wiping tears from her eyes, said, "But *this* door was closed. There couldn't have been wind."

"Yes, of course. How silly of me. Shall we go down?"

It occurred to Molly that Kitty must be wondering what *they* were doing in the attic. Perhaps she didn't think she should ask.

Molly mulled this over as they went downstairs. There was no way wind could have opened that door and, furthermore, she was almost positive she'd closed it. There must be some other reason Kitty had gone up. Come to think of it, the attic had been noticeably clean. Even the books and furniture hadn't been very dusty. Perhaps Kitty went there sometimes to read or have some time to herself when she wasn't working.

When they reached the bottom of the staircase, another surprise awaited them.

Roger stood, arms crossed, leaning against the wall. "Did I miss a party invitation?"

He may as well have asked the door itself to answer, for none of the women replied.

Kitty, now indeed pale as a ghost, nodded to him and scurried away.

Even from her place inside the sewing room, Molly heard Fred's delighted exclamation of, "Kitty!" She didn't hear Kitty's reply, but two sets of footsteps died away as Roger stared at Molly and Caroline.

"Kitty was just showing us the attic." Molly attempted a nonchalant tone, as if it was the most natural thing to do on a fine spring afternoon.

He raised a brow. "The attic?"

"Yes," Caroline said. "It was most interesting."

Molly sensed Roger had a flippant remark on the tip of his tongue but wouldn't utter it. Perhaps he was trying to restore his image after yesterday.

Roger pushed away from the wall. "I'm glad you enjoyed yourselves."

"How did you know we were up here?" Molly asked as she closed the attic door.

"I saw somebody in the window."

Molly flushed. "That was me."

"I know."

Caroline took Molly's arm and led her across the room. "You'll have to excuse us. We're going into town."

"I'll walk you downstairs," Roger said.

"No need. We know our way around," Molly said.

"Clearly." He looked pointedly at the attic door and

stood aside for them to exit.

Molly didn't bother with a smile or a nod, but hurried from the room with Caroline.

Once they reached their bedchamber, Molly sat on her bed. "What do you make of all that?"

"I don't know what to think. Why did Roger come up? And what was Fred doing there? Why was Kitty in the attic?"

"Roger said he saw me in the window. Although why it should matter to him what we're doing, I have no idea. I suppose Fred followed him."

"I wonder why Benedict didn't come up."

Molly grinned. "Why? Do you miss him?"

She slapped Molly's arm playfully. "I don't *miss* him."

"Have you fallen—"

"No, I haven't fallen in love with him." She paused, looking out the window. "I barely know him."

"I think he's half way to falling in love with you."

Caroline started pacing. "I don't know about that. I still think he sees courting me as a duty. He hasn't shown any sign of being romantic."

Molly would have liked to pull Benedict aside and encourage him to act the least bit like a besotted suitor. Caroline had already said she liked him, but what woman wanted to go into a relationship believing the man courted her out of obligation, not affection?

Molly would wait for love, another thing that aggravated her mother. When her Season inevitably came along, she and her mother would have different objectives. Her mother, a husband—Molly, a loving companion. She wouldn't settle for less than a man who could be her friend. Perhaps even a best friend, though that was hard to imagine. Was it even possible to confide in a man the way she did with Caroline? He would need to be special indeed.

"Don't give up on Benedict being romantic just yet. Men don't wear their hearts on their sleeves, but once he's sure of your feelings he'll warm up, no doubt."

"Do you think he isn't sure of my feelings?"

"I don't see how he could be when *you* aren't."

"It's all so awkward." Caroline perched on the edge of the sofa. "Not Benedict, he's fine. But coming here to be, as you say, swept off my feet. I feel as though everyone's watching us, waiting. I'm waiting, too. To feel that spark, or to see that certain something in his eyes you hear married ladies talk about."

"With Mrs. Lane lurking around to be sure you don't sit next to each other and turning up whenever you two are alone, it's no surprise you haven't fallen in love yet. Not that you have to."

Caroline let out a laugh. "Oh, Molly. In one breath you say I'll fall in love soon, and in the other say I don't have to."

"Just know that whatever does—or doesn't— happen with Benedict, life has a way of working out. You'll be happy one way or the other. And you'll always have me."

Caroline squeezed Molly's hand. "I know."

A knock came on the door and, after a pause, Kitty entered.

"Good afternoon," Caroline said.

"Good afternoon. Mrs. Lane sent me up to see if you found her directions to the tea house. Since you haven't left yet, she suspects I forgot to leave them on the mail tray."

Molly pulled them from her pocket. "Here they are. We were distracted because of our excursion to the attic."

"I thought so, Miss, but didn't think you'd want Mrs. Lane to know about that."

"You were right." Molly paused. "Close the door, if you please, Kitty. I want to discuss something with you."

Kitty did so, looking bewildered. She stood with her hands clasped in front of her, waiting.

The idea had come to Molly in a flash, and even as she opened her mouth to speak she wasn't sure if she should. "I overheard you talking to Marietta and Polly, and I wanted to thank you for helping us avoid gossip."

Kitty bobbed her head. "It only seemed the right thing to do. It isn't your fault you arrived without your chaperone, and you could never have known the Clarkes wouldn't be here. I'll keep the other maids from spreading rumors if I can."

"We truly can't thank you enough," Molly said.

Caroline nodded. "It was all so unexpected, and the last thing we want to do is put the Clarkes, or ourselves, in an awkward situation."

"I'm happy to help. Your aunt will arrive soon, no doubt, and this will all be forgotten. I'd best get downstairs to tell Mrs. Lane you have the directions but changed your plans."

"Thank you again. Oh, and I hope when we're alone you'll call me Molly instead of 'Miss.' Even if you can't look upon me as a friend, then at least an acquaintance."

"And call me Caroline."

Kitty smiled. "I don't mind calling you by your first names when we're alone. Good afternoon."

Caroline closed the door after her and turned to

Molly. "Do you think it's odd asking her to use our first names?"

"No. I can't say what, but there's something different about Kitty. She isn't like any maid I've ever met."

"I thought so too. And not just her looks, as we noted when we met her. After the way she helped us, she does feel more like a friend than a maid."

"That's what I thought." Molly glanced at the clock. "You know, there's really still time for tea."

"And the shops. If we hurry we can get to town before they close." Caroline went at once for her purse.

Chapter Eight

Inside Coddington's Haberdashery, Molly sniffed perfumes while Caroline debated which hairbrush to buy. They'd been in town all afternoon, and though Molly had enjoyed the teahouse, a walk through the park, a stop at the book shop and the milliner's, she was ready to go home.

But Caroline had an insatiable appetite for the little fripperies Coddington's stocked in plenty. In a basket on her arm were coils of colored ribbon, silk handkerchiefs, hairpins, a packet of buttons, and an embroidered purse.

Molly was about to sit down and read one of the novels she'd purchased when she happened to glance out the window. Fred and Benedict were just emerging from a brick building across the tree-lined street, apparently in the middle of an animated discussion.

"Caroline, come here," Molly called.

Caroline hurried over, glancing around expectantly as if hoping Molly had found a glove display she'd overlooked. "What is it?"

Molly pointed across the street just as Fred looked up and gave them a wave.

"Oh, they're coming over," Caroline said. "Let's meet them outside."

Molly took her arm before she could exit the shop. "You need to purchase your items."

"I won't be a moment." She dashed over to the sales

clerk.

Fred and Benedict crossed the street, stopping once or twice for carriages to pass by. As Molly turned to look for Caroline, a bell over the door jingled and the men stepped inside.

"Hello," Molly said.

"Good afternoon," Benedict replied, watching Caroline at the sales counter.

Fred removed his hat and spun it around in his hands. "Almost evening, now. Have you been enjoying yourselves?"

"Yes, there's so much to do here," Molly said. "We haven't even visited all the shops yet."

Caroline moved to Benedict's side, shuffling the packages in her arms.

"Allow me," Benedict said, taking the parcels.

"Oh, thank you."

Fred opened the door and they filed out to the sidewalk. "Where are you going next?"

"Back home, I suppose. I don't want to be late for dinner," Caroline said.

"Does the Trout and Mallard serve a good supper?" Molly asked as a harried-looking gentleman squeezed between her and the entrance to Coddington's.

"Yes, but not as good as the tavern. We're heading there now," Fred said, putting his hat back on.

Molly tried not to show her envy. "Perhaps we could all go?"

"Not this again, Molly." Caroline cast an apologetic look at Benedict. "She's been trying to get inside a tavern since we were thirteen."

Fred offered Molly his arm as they started down the street. "Is it that difficult for ladies to get inside?"

"It is for some," she said wryly.

Caroline took Benedict's proffered arm. "We should get our horses and other parcels from the inn. While we're there we can peek inside and see what they're serving tonight."

"We'll have supper with you there," Benedict said.

Caroline beamed. "That would be lovely."

Benedict, staring at her, tripped on a loose stone in his path. They both lost their footing and he put an arm around Caroline's waist to keep her from falling over.

"I don't think that's a good idea, Benedict," Fred said seriously as he picked up the packages Benedict had dropped.

Benedict removed his arm at once and Caroline stepped away.

Fred's eyes sparkled. "I'm not talking about *that*. I don't think we should eat at the inn. If Molly wants to go to the tavern, so she shall."

"Truly?" After all these years would she finally see what her brothers were hinting at? Brawls, tawdry songs, the best ale?

Fred smiled. "Truly."

"Where is it?" Molly tried to see around carriages as she peered up and down the street.

"Molly," Caroline hissed. "We are not going to the tavern."

She put a hand on her hip. "Why not?"

"Because it isn't appropriate."

"It isn't as if I'm suggesting going to a brothel." The moment the words were out of her mouth Molly covered her scarlet face.

Caroline blanched, Benedict spluttered, and Fred guffawed.

Molly lowered her hands, trying to remain composed. "Pardon me."

"You're pardoned," Fred said. "Now to the tavern. The Wayside, I think."

"But—" Benedict began.

"Oh, tosh, Benedict. I'll ask Brian to let us in the back way." Fred turned to Molly and Caroline. "My friend works at the tavern. He'll help us. We'll sit in a corner just long enough for Molly to have a glass of ale and a look around, and then we'll go home."

Molly wanted to clap but knew she would look ridiculous. "It will be so easy, Caroline, and just think— After today I'll no longer pester you to go to a tavern."

"I suppose that would be worth it." She leaned in close to Molly. "But what if someone sees us?"

Molly frowned. "That would be unnecessary attention, wouldn't it?" Had she gotten this close to a tavern only to have to pass up the opportunity? Oh, why couldn't Mr. and Mrs. Clarke have stayed home! Although if they had, Molly wouldn't have this chance.

"What's all this about?" Benedict asked, taking some of Caroline's parcels from Fred.

Caroline looked up at him. "We don't want to cause gossip that would reflect poorly on your family. You know, the chaperones. Mrs. Lane seems to think—"

Fred put a hand up. "Would you two forget Mrs. Lane? And never mind about gossip. There's nothing wrong with you popping in for a drink. We won't dance about in the middle of the room. Trust me, nobody will even notice you." He paused and cleared his throat. "Oh. Not that you aren't both lovely."

Molly went pink again. "Well, thank you for that, Fred. Perhaps you're right. After all, it will only be for a little while."

"Do you think it's all right?" Caroline asked Benedict. "I'll leave it for you to decide."

Molly was about to interject, as she didn't want Benedict deciding for *her*, but one look at his face told her she needn't worry.

"Yes, of course we should go in, if it makes you happy." Benedict stood up straighter as Caroline smiled at him and took his arm.

They made their way to The Wayside, a low building made of brick and age-darkened wood. It looked like it had been there as long as Rochester had. A painted wooden sign above the glowing front windows showed a fox dipping its muzzle into a pewter tankard. Fred went in to talk to his friend while the others waited outside. Intriguing murmurs and snatches of music came out every time someone opened the door, not to mention wafts of smoke.

After what felt like an hour, Fred came back and gave Molly a conspiratorial wink. "It's all arranged. Come on."

He took Molly's hand as they entered through the back door and walked down a twisting, narrow hallway to the main seating area. The entire ceiling was hidden by smoke, presumably from the kitchen because how could pipes and cigars make that much? Lanterns burned on every table and candles flickered in brass sconces on the walls. A minstrel played a lute in a far corner. It was hard to imagine a song being heard over the din of voices, but based on the number of men joining in, it was a well-known tune.

Molly felt a twinge of apprehension as Fred's fingers tightened around hers and he practically dragged her through the room to an alcove far from the hearth and most of the other tables. There were a number of other alcoves, some with curtains shielding them from view.

Molly sat in the chair Fred pulled out for her and beckoned to Caroline, who was still halfway across the room. Caroline held a lace handkerchief over her nose and mouth, her eyes darting from side to side as though expecting to be attacked by a wild boar. Benedict kept an arm around her, watching her with concern until they took their seats across from Molly.

Molly drummed her fingers on the table, looking around. There wasn't much to see. It was like a dark, loud, smoky inn. But perhaps the longer they stayed the more interesting things would become.

Fred sat in the chair beside her. "Ale?"

"Yes, please. You said they keep a good table?"

"So they do." He thumped the table, causing Molly and Caroline to jump.

A pretty woman with long black hair sauntered over, a round tray balanced on her hip. "Evening, Fred. What can I get you?"

"Ale all around, Rowena, and whatever's good to eat."

"I won't be a moment." Rowena left after a smile and nod at Benedict.

Fred rested his arm along the back of Molly's chair. "What do you think?"

Her eyes shone. "I like it. You must come here often to be on speaking terms with the barmaid."

"It's not so big a town. Benedict and I have been coming here for years."

Benedict looked like he wanted Fred to keep him out of it. He turned to Caroline. "The food here is very good.

That's why we come. The food."

Caroline just nodded, her eyes on the front door.

"My brothers have told me stories about the taverns they frequent back home," Molly said. "Now I think they were joking. I was so nervous to come in, but now I don't know what I expected to happen."

None of the other patrons glanced their way and Molly supposed it was because their table was set so far back. The alcove's low ceiling and wide, arched doorway gave their table a cozy feel, and Molly imagined it would be easy to sit here comfortably for a few hours.

Suddenly, across the room, two men stood and started shoving each other. A third joined in, followed by a fourth. In the next instant, almost every man in the room made a circle around them, shouting, but Molly couldn't tell if they were egging them on or trying to break it up. The volume in the tavern doubled and she caught snatches of curse words she'd never heard in her life. It was exhilarating.

Fred stood on his toes, trying to get a better view. "I'm going over there. Benedict?"

"No. No, I'll stay with the ladies," he said after a glance at Caroline, not quite masking his disappointment as he watched Fred sprint across the room.

Rowena, completely unperturbed, came back with a huge tray laden with food and four tankards of ale. As she unloaded the tray, she glanced at the ladies and jerked her head toward the scuffle. "It's rare, that. Don't go thinking you can't come in here without a fight breaking out," she said and strode toward the bar.

"Should we wait for Fred?" Molly asked.

Benedict looked wistfully across the room. "No, we

should eat before it gets cold. He won't mind."

Molly took a sip of ale, then chose food from the tray. Rowena had brought cheese, bread, sliced cucumbers, veal, partridge, and a fruit tart.

Caroline, eating as quickly as she could while maintaining her dignity, met Molly's eyes across the table and conveyed that she wanted to leave the moment the last bit of food had been consumed. Molly chewed her food slowly, earning her a scowl from her friend.

Fred returned not long after the food had been delivered. "That's all settled," he said and began eating as though they'd never been interrupted.

Around the room, men returned to their seats and the talking started up again. A few of them sported bloody noses, from which Molly averted her eyes.

It was while she was surveying the room that Molly noticed him. She leaned forward in her chair to peer at a man in the corner opposite their table. His chin rested in his palm while the other hand twirled an empty glass in circles. "Is that...Roger?"

Fred leapt to his feet, following Molly's gaze. "Roger?"

Benedict and Caroline twisted in their seats to look.

"Yes, that's him," Benedict confirmed.

"Should we invite him to our table?" Molly asked.

Fred and Benedict exchanged a glance.

"No," Fred said.

Benedict rose. "Let's go say hello, though, Fred."

Molly watched as they worked their way through the crowd and settled themselves at Roger's table. She couldn't hear what they were saying, but Roger shook his head more than once. Benedict and Fred returned before long.

"Is he coming over?" Molly asked.

"Perhaps later," Fred said without any real conviction.

Across the room, Roger accepted two more drinks from Rowena. He tossed the first one back and resumed twirling the empty glass, eyes boring a hole in the table.

After finishing her meal—which was indeed delicious—Molly relaxed in her chair while Fred alternated between singing tunes verging on the scandalous and sharing anecdotes about patrons in the tavern. Not long after he'd told a rambling tale about the time he and Benedict went fishing and lost their oars in a lake, Caroline checked her watch. "I'm so tired. I think we should go home."

Molly looked at *her* watch. "It's seven o'clock."

"I know, but I'm exhausted." Caroline faked a dainty yawn.

"I'd be happy to escort you home," Benedict said, rising from the table.

"Thank you, Benedict." Caroline gave him a bright smile before turning to Molly. "We'll be home well before dark. We could have a game of backgammon before bed."

Molly finished the last of her ale. After years of waiting to get inside a tavern, there was no way she was leaving now. "I think I'll stay a little while longer. But you go ahead."

Caroline looked at her as though she *had* suggested going to a brothel. "You can't stay here alone!"

"She isn't alone." Fred laughed and pointed to himself with both hands. "I'm right here."

"But—" Caroline began.

Fred cut her off, gesturing across the room. "And

Roger's just over there. Two gentlemen to look after her."

Benedict said nothing, but hastily collected Caroline's parcels.

"Molly, you really should come with us." Caroline narrowed her eyes at her over a tight smile.

Molly wrapped her hands around her tankard. "I won't stay much longer."

Caroline looked like she wanted to argue further, but couldn't or wouldn't in front of the men. "Don't dillydally. Come home soon."

"I will."

The look Caroline gave her before she walked away left no doubt she'd have much to say about this later. Molly could have pointed out that Caroline was now going out unchaperoned with a man. At least Molly was surrounded by others; Caroline and Benedict would be truly alone, riding through the night. It might be good for them, come to think of it.

Fred tapped her arm. "What do you think of our tavern?"

"It's…interesting. Thank you again for bringing me."

"It was my pleasure."

Molly gestured to Roger, who was slouched down in his chair, staring at the ceiling. "Should we go sit with him?"

"I do think he wants to be alone."

Fully aware it was none of her business, Molly inquired anyway. "Is something troubling him?"

Fred brought his head close to hers, his voice low. "Can you keep a secret?"

"Yes, of course." Molly shifted closer to him.

He glanced across the room, then met Molly's eyes. "It's about Roger. You may have noticed he's melancholy at times."

"Actually, I didn't." She *had* noticed he was antisocial, grouchy, and occasionally insulting.

"Roger's nursing a broken heart."

"He is?" Molly looked over at Roger, curiosity piqued.

Fred lowered his voice even more. "He was jilted."

"No!" Her hand flew to her chest.

He leaned back against his chair, nodding. "Yes, not too long ago. It hit him hard. He's been staying with us for a time because it's too painful to be back home where it all happened."

"Oh, I can only imagine. Poor Roger. So…so he isn't always this quiet?"

Fred snorted. "Certainly not the word I'd use for Roger. But I daresay you haven't met him under the best of circumstances. Not for him, anyway."

"How sad."

"It is. Please don't mention it to him or to Caroline. It isn't exactly a secret, but it pains him to talk about it."

"I understand. I won't tell anyone."

Fred changed the subject and they chatted easily about Molly's home and what else they might do around Rochester in the coming weeks. An hour or so later, Rowena came over to refill their tankards, and just as Molly thought it might be time to leave, Roger rose from his chair and limped across the room.

When he reached their table, he gave Molly an exaggerated bow. "Good afternoon."

"Hello, Roger." She tried to keep any trace of pity from her voice and chose not to mention it was well past afternoon.

He grinned down at her. "Ah, back to Roger now? No more *Mr.* Bailey?"

"What's this about?" Fred asked, glancing between the two of them.

"It's to do with what happened at the pond." Roger eased himself into the chair next to Fred's and polished off a glass of what smelled like whiskey.

Molly blushed. "It's nothing." Good gracious. Had he told Fred everything about the pond, including where his hands had been?

Fred didn't look convinced. "If you say so."

Roger stared into the bottom of his empty glass, then swapped it with Fred's full one and drained it. He leaned back in his chair with his legs loosely crossed, his jacket un-buttoned and his chestnut hair tousled as though he'd been running his hands through it all night. There was no telling where his tie had gone.

"What are you looking at?" Roger asked, eyes slightly narrowed.

Not realizing she'd been staring at him, Molly looked away quickly. "Nothing."

"It's Molly's first time in a tavern," Fred said. "She's taking it all in."

"Just then she looked like she wanted to take *me* all in," Roger said with a sidelong glance at Fred.

"Roger!" Barely stifling his laughter, Fred jabbed him in the side.

Roger laughed, lazily rubbing his ribs. "That hurt."

Fred shook his head, eyes sparkling with mirth. "You'll have to excuse him, Molly."

"Yes, do," Roger said, still chuckling.

Molly nodded, not sure what they meant, but with

the distinct feeling she was the butt of a joke. She'd try to remember it so she could ask her brothers the next time she saw them.

Fred and Roger began discussing their plans for a hunt the next day, with Fred assuring a skeptical Roger that his hounds were ready. They went back and forth on the merits of their horses, which trails to take and whether to postpone if it rained.

"I think I'd like to leave soon," Molly said when there was a break in their talk.

"Certainly," Fred said.

Roger hailed Rowena for more ale. "Not me. I'm staying the night."

"No, you aren't," Fred said, concern for his friend evident in his tone.

Roger waved a hand over his head. "Rowena's ignoring me. Or can't see me? Or she's busy. I'll go find her." He pushed back from the table and staggered toward the bar.

Fred turned to Molly at once. "Look, Roger's a bit of a mess. I want to go back for the carriage so he doesn't ride into a ditch or fall off Sparrow on the way home. Is your horse at the Trout and Mallard?"

"Yes, is yours there, too?" She started to rise, but Fred put a hand on her arm.

"I want you to stay here with Roger."

She blinked. "Alone?"

"It won't take long. I'll take the horses back home and return with the carriage." Fred sighed, watching Roger on the other side of the room. "I don't want him to be alone in this state."

Molly drew her head back. "What state? How on earth could I be of any assistance?"

"You don't need to *do* anything. Just sit with him so he doesn't wallow in misery. You have brothers, you must have seen them come home, uh, tipsy before."

Molly couldn't deny that. Much as her parents tried to shield her from it, it wasn't easy when one of them lumbered home in the middle of the night, calling for toast and tea. If one of her brothers was in a situation like this, she'd want someone to help him. She nodded to Fred, who gave her a grateful look.

Roger resumed his seat, proudly displaying two silver tankards. Ale sloshed over the sides when he banged them on the table. "Found her."

Fred took the one nearest him.

"That's mine," Roger said, reaching for it.

Fred pushed his hand away. "You've had enough."

Roger sank lower into his chair and took a long drink, watching Molly over the brim of his tankard.

Not knowing what else to do, she smiled as though reassuring a nervous child.

He continued staring. "Molly Merriwether. Why did your parents call you that?"

"Why did your parents call you Roger Bailey?"

Fred rose from his seat. "I'll go get the carriage. You two continue with your conversation, and I'll be back before you know it." He put a hand on Molly's shoulder, whispered, "Thank you," and was gone.

Chapter Nine

After watching Fred weave his way through the crowd and out the front door, Molly and Roger sat in silence, avoiding each other's gaze.

Molly picked at the bread on the tray, eyeing Fred's half-finished ale.

"Where was Rowena?" she asked.

Roger didn't answer but whistled tunelessly, tracing the table's woodgrain with his finger.

Molly sighed. She should have gone with Caroline. Well, she'd wanted to try a tavern, and perhaps being stuck at a table with a drunk, sad, inattentive man gave her a taste of the true experience. She might as well enjoy herself, as she doubted she'd ever set foot in a tavern again, least of all this one.

The next time Rowena walked by, Molly ordered herself a glass of brandy, a slice of ginger cake, and food for Roger. Hopefully filling his stomach would offset whatever he'd been drinking since he arrived.

Molly expected the crowds to thin as evening wore on, but every time one party left another took its place.

When Rowena returned with their order, Roger ate like he hadn't seen food in three days, yet somehow managed to look like he was at an elegant dinner party.

Molly's first sip of brandy sent tendrils of tingling warmth rushing through her. She ate her cake and tapped her feet to the music of the minstrel, who hadn't stopped playing all night, even during the scuffle.

"Molly Merriwether."

She looked up to see Roger staring at her, his chin in his hand.

"Molly Merriwether. It reminds me of a character in a children's rhyme."

"What are you talking about, *Mr.* Bailey?" Molly asked, pushing her empty plate aside.

He slowly shook his head. "Alas, I've lost my first name privileges again. Not to worry. I'll gain them back by the end of the night."

"We can only hope."

"Molly Merriwether…had a feather." Roger looked up at the ceiling for a moment, then slapped his hand hard on the table. "Molly Merriwether had a feather, she found it floating in the heather, when we strolled along together. In the weather? In sunny weather."

Molly laughed; she couldn't help it. "Very creative. More creative than my parents' reason for choosing it. They simply liked it, so called me Molly. But it isn't my true name."

"It isn't?" Roger shouted, then looked around as if to be sure nobody was listening.

She pressed her lips together, shaking her head slowly.

Roger leaned forward and gripped her forearm. "You'll tell me your true name?" he whispered.

"Not now." She sipped her brandy. "Why are you called Roger?"

He fell back against his chair. "My father is Roger. And his father, and his, and his, and his." He rolled his hand in circles as he spoke. "There are many Rogers, but I'm the only Roger *Wolfgang* Bailey." He puffed his chest out, then laughed. "As a boy I hated that name. When Fred first heard it he took to calling me Wolfie."

Molly giggled, then covered her mouth with her hand.

"Go ahead and laugh," he said, taking another gulp of ale. "I'm not much of a wolf."

"It isn't that. It's Fred giving you a nickname you didn't want."

Roger shrugged. "That's Fred for you. Freddy. I don't call him that anymore but, really, I should."

"I think Wolfgang suits you."

"Do you? You may be the first. Well, besides my parents."

"You're strong, as demonstrated when you propelled me out of the pond, and you're independent. You spend a fair amount of time alone, yet clearly enjoy being with your friends. Even though we don't speak to each other often, I can tell you're clever, probably from all the reading you do. And Penny is like your pack."

Molly looked away toward the bar, her cheeks glowing. She was talking nonsense. It must be the brandy.

Roger leaned his elbows on the table. "I had no idea I was so well observed."

"I notice things, that's all," Molly said, still not looking at him.

He reached over and lightly touched her arm. "I notice you."

"You do?" She looked up, surprised. His brown eyes looked almost amber in this light.

"It's hard not to, with you falling in ponds, barging into my office, and sneaking up to the attic."

"We weren't *sneaking*. Only exploring."

"Did you find anything interesting?"

"Old books. Some furniture." She made an exaggerated pout. "Not what I'd hoped for."

"And what was that?" He lifted his tankard to take another drink, but instead set it aside.

"You have to ask? It—"

"No! Let me guess." He stroked his chin thoughtfully. "Treasure. Mounds of old ball gowns. Maybe a casket of jewelry?"

Molly laughed. "Why, Roger, are you a mind reader?"

"Ah, Roger again," he said, grinning. "I'm not a mind reader, but it's what my sister Penny would want to find if she wandered into someone else's attic."

"Isn't that your dog's name?"

A smile softened his face. "Yes, she named Penny after herself. But forgive her, she has red hair like the dog and was only ten when Penny was born."

Molly wrapped both hands around her glass. "I think it's sweet. I always wanted a sister. Well, besides Caroline. She feels like my sister."

"Do you have a brother?"

"Three."

"You're the youngest? Oldest?"

"Youngest."

"I'm surprised they let you come here on your own."

"I'm not *that* young. And don't forget, we do have a chaperone, she's simply indisposed." Indisposed, miles away and unlikely to appear for days, if at all.

Roger shifted his chair a little closer to hers. "I meant I'm surprised your brothers wouldn't want to come with you. I admit I'm a bit over protective of Penny."

"All brothers are like that. My oldest brother, Michael, moved away with his wife last year, but Albert and Tristan might have come if given the opportunity. I wouldn't have let them interfere, though. They know better." Her giggle sounded higher pitched than usual, and she tried to recall how much ale and brandy she'd had. Enough, most likely. "I've been looking forward to this trip for months."

"You were that eager to accompany Caroline and take a look at Benedict?" He reached for his drink and took another sip.

"That and I wanted to get away from home for a while. My mother has plans for me. She wants to take me to town and introduce me to people, and, if truth be known, she wants me to be more like her. She disapproves of me reading novels, riding out on my own so often, and gallivanting around the countryside without telling anyone where I've gone. She wants my embroidery stitches to be neater and for me to learn to properly make preserves, as mine never gels correctly. Oh, and she wouldn't mind it if I'd take up a hobby. A ladylike one."

Molly blushed. Why was she telling him this? Perhaps the unusual circumstances, the brandy and his surprisingly kind eyes. Molly had the feeling the drink was wearing off and Roger was returning to his usual self. He hadn't spoken to her this much since they'd met, and he was actually rather charming. Her cheeks went pinker even though he couldn't possibly know what she was thinking.

"You're a blusher," Roger said, meeting her eyes. "That I've noticed, too."

"I'm not. It's hot in here."

"Yes, and it was very hot in the pond, and in the east wing."

She wanted to cover her face to hide the inevitable flush, but didn't bother. Oh, why couldn't her cheeks be permanently pink and be done with it? People were said to wear their hearts on their sleeves, but hers was always in her cheeks. It had been like that for as long as she could remember.

Molly finished her brandy, then realized that was foolish since she was already letting her tongue run away with her. Seeking to change the subject, she asked the first thing that came to mind. "How did you hurt your ankle?"

Roger slid his tankard back and forth between his hands. "Not very interesting."

"Still, I'd like to know. Did you fall off your horse?"

"That I would *never* do."

"Fell down a flight of stairs?"

"A young lady fell on me when I tried to rescue her from a pond," Roger said with a grin.

Molly laughed. "How did you hurt it before you shoved me up the bank?"

"It isn't as chivalrous as the pond story. Six months ago I was chasing Penny—the dog, not my sister—through the garden and I slipped on some loose gravel. I fell at an odd angle and badly sprained my ankle. Satisfied?" A shadow appeared in his eyes. Apparently the memory of the accident still bothered him.

"Then you re-injured it when a young lady was too clumsy to climb up a wet, rocky slope by herself. I *am* sorry about that."

He smiled, a slight flush in his cheeks. "I didn't mind. But I do apologize for the shoving."

She recalled where his hands had been that day and knew a flush crept into her own cheeks. *Blusher*, indeed.

"How long will it take to heal?" Molly asked.

"Not much longer. I couldn't get out of bed for a week after it happened."

She glanced down at his foot. "I hope it isn't too painful."

"It isn't. But I appreciate your concern."

Looking up, Molly suddenly noticed the tavern crowd had thinned. The alcoves on either side of them were empty, the curtains pulled back. How long had they been sitting here? She leaned back in her chair and closed her eyes.

"Don't fall asleep. Freddy's here."

She sat up straight. "Is he?"

He pointed at the front door, where Fred stood waving at them. Molly felt a sense of relief, yet also regret. She liked this side of Roger. At home, off on his own all the time, she hadn't really gotten to know him. There was something about him that felt comforting or familiar somehow. Or perhaps it was the brandy and she'd feel this way about Mr. Dawson at the end of such a strange evening.

"Ready to go?" Fred asked as he approached their table.

Roger stood first and pulled Molly's chair out for her.

"Thank you," she said and smiled.

He returned the smile, but then sobered and looked away.

"Not too bored waiting, I hope," Fred said.

"Not at all," Roger replied. He swayed as they walked to the door and Molly wondered if he actually

106

was still drunk. Maybe she hadn't been getting to know the true Roger, but the drunk Roger. Of course, he could be wobbling because of his ankle.

As she stepped outside, Molly took her first breath of smoke-free air in hours. It was beyond refreshing. She gazed up at the cloudless, star-filled sky. "Beautiful."

Beside her, Roger sniffed and wiped his eyes. "It is."

"Are you all right? Are your eyes irritated from the smoke?"

He looked as if he'd forgotten she was standing there. "Something like that," he said in a sad voice.

"We'd better get you home." Fred gently took Roger's arm as a glance Molly couldn't understand passed between them.

When Roger started toward the carriage he almost fell over.

"Is it your ankle?" Molly asked, automatically reaching out to steady him.

Roger just looked away.

"That and more, I'd say." Fred put an arm around Roger's waist and helped him over to the carriage. He climbed inside and reached down for Roger's hand. "Molly, I'd usually help you in first, but—"

She waved a hand. "Please, think nothing of it."

"Stand behind him in case he falls over, will you?"

She obeyed, uncertain of how she could help if he did. Catch him? Be a soft place to land?

"I won't fall over," Roger insisted as Fred hauled him into the carriage.

Molly was tempted to push him on the backside, purely to see how he'd react.

After settling Roger, Fred hopped down and handed Molly into the carriage. He climbed into the driver's seat and moments later they pulled away from the tavern.

Roger, tucked into the corner opposite Molly, rocked slightly with the movement of the carriage, his eyes closed.

Molly didn't mind having some quiet time to herself after the noisy tavern and long conversation with Roger. Gazing out the window as they rolled through the night, she idly wondered how long it would take to get back to Waverly Hall.

The next thing she knew, Roger was gently shaking her shoulder to wake her up. She looked blearily at him in the dim light of the carriage's lanterns.

"We're almost home," he said.

Molly straightened in her seat. "I didn't mean to fall asleep. How silly of me."

"So did I. It's later than I realized." He stretched his arms, yawning. "Pardon me."

Stifling her own yawn, Molly just nodded.

They came to a stop in front of Waverly Hall and a moment later Fred opened the door and took Molly's hand to help her out. The grounds were quiet, the house mostly dark. Lights glowed in only a few windows and torches lit the long drive. There was something peaceful in the stillness of the night; a mild, sweet breeze reached Molly from unseen wooded hills beyond. She stayed beside the carriage while Fred assisted Roger. Or tried to.

"No need, Fred. I'll manage myself."

Fred held Roger's elbow as he climbed gingerly down the carriage steps. Once on the ground they all watched his ankle as he tried putting his weight on it.

Roger looked up at Molly and Fred, smiling. "Still standing." He offered Molly his arm. "May I?"

She took it and, as usual, fit her gait to his.

Mr. Dawson met them in the foyer. "Good evening. May I be of assistance?"

"Yes, Dawson," Fred said. "We're off to the library for rum."

"Are we?" Molly asked, taken aback.

"We need to discuss tomorrow's hunt," Fred said, practically bouncing on his heels.

Roger, squinting against the light of Mr. Dawson's lantern, held up a finger. "Not tomorrow, Freddy. The day after."

"Very well," Fred said with a pout.

"It's time I went upstairs," Molly said. "Thank you for a *most* interesting evening, gentlemen."

"Goodnight, Molly." Fred followed Mr. Dawson to the library.

Molly released Roger's arm and took a candle from a table beside the staircase. "I hope your ankle feels better in the morning."

"It will. Sleep well, and don't forget you owe me your true name, Molly Merriwether."

"Goodnight."

The next morning Molly woke to Caroline and Kitty standing over her, whispering. She kept her eyes closed, letting them think she was still asleep.

"Out very late, they were," Kitty said quietly.

"When did they get home?"

"Past midnight."

"Midnight!" Caroline cried, then lowered her voice. "We left them at the tavern at seven o'clock."

Kitty whispered something unintelligible, followed by Caroline's drawn out, "Oh," and then, "That explains it. I did wonder."

"What did you wonder?" Molly asked, opening her eyes.

Caroline gasped. "Molly! You startled me."

"And you *woke* me." She threw a pillow at Caroline, managing to hit Kitty as well.

Kitty handed the pillow back to her. "Would you like breakfast, Mis—Molly?"

"After Caroline tells me what she's wondering about."

"I'll go tell the kitchen." Kitty turned and left the room.

Caroline sat on the end of the bed. "I wondered why Fred came home late with the horses and went right back out again with the carriage. Kitty's just explained about Roger's condition last night."

"You saw him at the tavern. Are you that surprised?" Molly sat up and unbraided her hair, letting it fall loose around her shoulders.

"I knew he'd had some drinks, but didn't realize it was enough to make him incapable of riding a horse."

"I imagine Fred was being overprotective." Molly felt an unexpected desire to shield Roger from gossip or speculation, even from Caroline, and wasn't remotely tempted to tell her about Roger being jilted. She swung her legs over the side of the bed and went to the wardrobe to choose a dress.

Caroline followed her. "You were out very late."

"The tavern was so exciting!" Molly said over her shoulder.

"Parts of it were, yes. I could have stayed for half the time, though, and have no wish to go back."

Molly gave her a sheepish look. "To tell the truth, I don't either. I did enjoy myself, but I'll no longer wonder what I'm missing and will be happy to visit inns instead."

"Imagine what Auntie would say."

"She wouldn't approve of us going there at all, let alone with 'strange men.' Any word from her today?"

"Not yet, but it's early." Caroline walked over to the mirror to look at herself while Molly stepped behind a screen to change into a lilac-colored dress. Thankfully there would be no need for a habit today. She couldn't imagine how she'd have gone on a hunt this morning.

"Have you had breakfast yet?" Molly asked after she'd finished dressing.

"Yes, but I'll sit with you while you eat."

Molly took Caroline's arm and led her to the window seat. "After you tell me what happened with Benedict last night."

"Oh, nothing of consequence. We had a pleasant ride home, and afterwards went to the library to play chess. But Mrs. Lane came and sat in the corner, claiming she needed light from the fireplace to work on her knitting. I went to bed not long after."

"That woman! Before she arrived, did you and Benedict enjoy yourselves?"

"Yes. He's been trying to draw me out. Asking questions about my home, what types of things I like. It's sweet."

"It is. I'm glad you had some time alone." Molly glanced out the window. Outside, leaves danced in a stirring wind and gray clouds loomed in the distance.

Caroline shifted to face her. "Speaking of which, how was being alone with Roger?"

"Fine. He came over to our table and we talked."

"About what?"

There were too many details she wasn't supposed to

share, so she said evasively, "This and that. We spent most of the evening in silence, waiting for Fred to return."

Caroline patted her arm. "It sounds awkward. You should have come home with us."

"Probably. Let's get breakfast, I'm hungry." Curious to see if she'd be met by the friendly Roger of last night or the reclusive Roger, Molly led the way downstairs.

Chapter Ten

As she walked into the breakfast room, Molly was immediately aware of the absence of men's voices. Fred was usually chatty in the morning, but he and Benedict sat at the table, not speaking. Benedict turned when they entered and nudged Fred, who winced and put a hand to his head.

"Good morning." Molly walked over to the table and rested her hands on the back of a chair.

Fred covered his ears. "Not so loud if you please, Molly."

"That was loud?" Caroline asked.

"Don't mind him," Benedict said. "He was up all night drinking rum and making elaborate maps for the hunt."

"But don't the dogs find birds, or foxes or whatever it is you're hunting?" Molly asked.

"That's what I've been trying to tell him," Benedict said.

Fred rubbed his temples, his eyes on the full plate in front of him. "They need a spot of help."

Molly took a closer look at him. He was wearing the same clothes as last night and had dark circles under his eyes.

"Would you like some tea, Fred?" she whispered.

"Oh, yes, please. Thank you." He pushed the plate aside, folded his arms on the table, and rested his head in them.

Molly and Caroline went to the sideboard to fill their plates and afterwards Molly brought Fred a cup of tea. He didn't look up but gave a small snore, so she left it at his elbow.

"Should we wake him?" Molly asked Benedict.

He looked fondly at Fred. "No, let him sleep."

Molly took a seat opposite Fred and began her breakfast. As she looked about the room, she noticed Roger in a chair facing the fireplace. For once he wasn't reading but rested his head against the chair, his legs stretched out in front of him. Penny dozed at his feet. When Molly gave a whistle, Penny trotted over and licked her hand. Roger shifted in his seat when Molly laughed, but he didn't turn around.

While they ate, Molly, Caroline and Benedict discussed what they might do today. Molly whispered at first, but Benedict assured her their talk wouldn't wake Fred at this point. After the busy day yesterday Molly wasn't interested in much besides a day of reading in the garden or the library, but she'd go along with whatever Caroline and Benedict wanted to do. She could tell they were becoming better acquainted and didn't want to stand in the way. Ideally she'd leave them alone but felt certain Mrs. Lane would appear to act as chaperone if she didn't.

Almost on cue, Mrs. Lane walked into the room. She didn't greet anyone but handed Benedict the mail and looked like she wanted to produce a ruler to check how close he was sitting to Caroline.

Mrs. Lane peered at Fred. "What's the matter with Mr. Clarke?"

"Nothing," Benedict said. "He's sleeping."

"On the table?" She gripped her hands together. "That is most undignified. Especially with ladies present."

"We don't mind," Molly said and took a bite of her poached eggs.

Mrs. Lane stiffened and looked down her nose at Molly. "Perhaps you should. Though I hear you are not unaccustomed to undignified behavior."

"Excuse me?" Molly set her fork down and pushed her chair back from the table.

"Taverns are not the most private place to hold a tête-à-tête with a man," Mrs. Lane said.

Benedict rose. "Thank you, Mrs. Lane. That will be all."

"Now, wait just a moment," Molly said, wanting to defend herself.

"It was hardly a tête-à-tête," Roger said icily. "And I might remind you it isn't seemly for the housekeeper of Waverly Hall to indulge in village gossip. Miss Merriwether was good enough to assist me last night when I fell ill."

Molly, intent on Mrs. Lane, hadn't noticed him cross the room to stand behind her.

Mrs. Lane paled. "I—I did not realize…" She squared her shoulders and looked in Molly's general direction. "You must allow me to apologize, Miss Merriwether."

Molly just fixed her with a level stare and Mrs. Lane hurried from the room.

Penny crouched low to the ground, whining. Molly gave her a reassuring pat and the dog rested her head in her lap.

Roger closed the door after Mrs. Lane, then settled

into the chair beside Molly. He had the same rumpled, gray look as Fred, but with the addition of bloodshot eyes. When Penny jumped on him, he pushed her down with a groan.

Molly was about to thank him, but Caroline spoke first. "Really! Why is Mrs. Lane allowed to behave like that?"

"I'll…I'll speak to her again," Benedict said, taking his seat.

Roger drummed his fingers on the table. "That she would dare speak to a guest like that, or say such things about Fred… You should dismiss her."

"You know I can't. That would be for my father to do. I'll talk to him when they return."

"When will that be?" Roger asked.

"Two weeks," Benedict mumbled.

"That's not long," Caroline said in a cheery voice and drew Benedict into a conversation about the gardens.

Molly was fuming, but there was nothing to do about Mrs. Lane besides avoid her as much as possible. She finished her breakfast and soon had other things than Mrs. Lane to think about.

Roger shifted in his seat and briefly met Molly's eyes. "I don't clearly remember all of last night, but I have the feeling I owe you an apology. It wasn't my finest hour, and I fear I may have said some inappropriate things."

"Oh, it was nothing. But thank you all the same."

When Molly's cheeks colored, Roger nodded. "I see I *do* owe you an apology."

"You seem to have forgotten, I have brothers. I'm used to seeing men when they aren't at their finest."

"So, no hard feelings?"

Molly smiled. "None whatsoever." If anything, she'd enjoyed the way Roger had opened up to her. "How's your 'illness' today?"

He put a hand to his head, grimacing. "Regretful? I should know better."

"Would you like some tea?"

"That would be nice. In the quadrangle?"

"Yes, that sounds lovely." As Molly rose to fetch another cup, the clouds opened up and rain lashed against the windows.

"Here at the table is fine," Roger said with a grin.

Behind them, the clock let out a clang and Fred bolted upright, spilling tea all over the tablecloth. "What!"

"Nothing, Fred," Molly said. "Go back to sleep."

By the following afternoon the rain had cleared and the hunt was on. A cloudless blue sky awaited Molly as she walked to the kennels with Caroline.

Fred had been acting like a child all morning—fussing about the dogs, coaxing everyone to come on the hunt, and generally giving the day the feel of a long-awaited party. He'd gone to the kennels right after breakfast and hadn't returned for lunch. Benedict and Roger had gone down to join him not long ago, leaving Molly and Caroline to follow.

Molly's stomach twisted as they walked down the hill. This morning she'd coughed a few times and suggested staying home, but Caroline had taken one look at her and known she was only feigning illness to get out of the hunt. Molly's last hope had been unexpected thunderstorms, but the weather remained stubbornly perfect. It had been a long time since she'd been on a hunt, and she dearly hoped the dogs wouldn't find any animals. She'd have preferred a gallop across the countryside, but it was hard to say no to Fred.

Once in view of the kennels, Molly and Caroline stopped in their tracks. Ahead of them, Fred's pack milled about, howling, barking, and leaping over each other inside a square paddock. Roger and Benedict stood off to the side, watching Fred try to get some semblance of control over the animals. Penny quivered at Roger's feet.

Within a few minutes Benedict noticed them and strode over. "We'll be off soon," he said.

"Does Fred know how to handle them?" Molly asked, eyeing the swarming pack.

Benedict hesitated just a tad too long to sound convincing. "He's trained them well."

As they continued down the hill, conversation became impossible over the barking. Since the horses hadn't arrived yet, Molly stepped inside the mercifully quiet kennel to see the puppies. She knelt down to pet the mother, who wagged her tail as puppies toddled around trying to lick Molly's hands.

A little while later, someone spoke from behind her. "I've been sent by Fred to tell you we're leaving soon."

She turned to see Roger standing in the doorway, Penny at his side. The sun shining behind him brought out red highlights in his hair and Molly startled herself by realizing he was a good-looking man. Not so blatantly handsome as Fred, but in a more down-to-earth, comfortable way. His eyes, which she'd thought of as amber at times, today looked rich and dark. There was something alluring about him that she'd never noticed before. Perhaps because she knew him slightly better after their night at the tavern. Molly couldn't say exactly what it was that made him so attractive, but at that moment she felt she could have stared at him all day.

Roger smiled. "You're blushing again. Embarrassed to be caught fawning over the puppies?"

"I'm not blushing. It must be a trick of the light." She rose to her feet, wiping dirt off her skirt.

He stepped closer until he was mere inches away. "I'd say you *are* blushing. Even more, now."

Looking up into his face, Molly knew her cheeks were turning pink. Or worse, red. Before she could reply, a horn blast made them both jump.

Roger opened the door. "I believe that's Fred's subtle way of telling us the time has come."

"Is Penny coming along?" Molly asked as she followed him out of the kennel.

"It would break her heart to be left behind," Roger said in a soft voice, reaching down to scratch Penny's ears.

Molly smiled. "We wouldn't want to break Penny's heart."

"She'll stay with me. She's well trained."

They made their way to the paddock, where the horses waited.

Once everyone had mounted, Fred addressed them like a giddy general preparing his troops for certain victory. "Everything's ready. We'll follow the pack and no doubt find more than our share of game. On each of your saddles you will find a horn. If you see any foxes or rabbits, blow it and I'll come over with my rifle. If anyone should fall behind, have no fear, we'll find you on our way back to the house. If worse comes to worst, use your horn to let us know your location."

Caroline gave Molly a worried look, while Roger

and Benedict simultaneously rolled their eyes.

"Now," Fred continued, "on my signal, the groom will release the hounds and we'll be off."

Molly's hands tightened on the reins as Fred brought a horn to his lips and blew. The groom opened the pen and the dogs sprang out, scattering in every direction. Fred blew again, and the dogs picked up speed. Some fled toward the house, others to the forest, a few in the direction of the pond. Two of the beagles remained on the ground while one basset wandered back into the kennel. Penny leapt after the dogs sprinting into the woods.

"Penny!" Roger cried.

Fred's head swiveled from side to side, the horn hanging at his side. "Uh. Oh. Go after them!" He bolted after the dogs heading for the house, Caroline and Benedict galloped away in the direction of the pond, and Molly found herself close behind Roger, who'd spurred Sparrow toward the woods.

Opal flew over the grass, not slowing until they reached the trees. Just inside the forest Molly found Roger, turning Sparrow in a circle as he sought Penny. From all sides came the sound of baying hounds. Molly strained to hear Penny, but it was impossible to distinguish her bark from all the others. Everywhere she looked, Molly caught glimpses of white tails and brown, floppy ears disappearing under bushes or racing down narrow trails.

Roger spurred Sparrow on. "This way."

They trotted through the lush forest, every so often taking a different path in their quest for Penny. The beagles must have caught a scent, because they reformed into a pack and ran deeper into the woods.

Molly brought Opal to a halt and shouted to Roger, who was almost out of sight. "Any sign of her?"

He turned Sparrow and cantered back. "I don't think Penny's with them."

"How can you be sure?"

"She'd stand out with her red coat."

Molly peered into the undergrowth. "Maybe she went back to the house."

"Maybe. Let's go this way." He guided Sparrow toward a winding path roofed with tangled, leafy branches.

Molly looked warily down the dark trail. "What makes you think she's down here?"

"Just a hunch. I hope she's still in the woods, I don't want her finding her way into that pond."

Molly assumed a shocked voice. "You don't want to save another damsel in distress?"

Roger's laughter rang through the forest. "I wouldn't call Penny a damsel."

"She won't go into the pond. She's too smart for that."

He cocked an eyebrow. "As we know, intelligence has nothing to do with falling into a pond."

"Does it have anything to do with following someone else into a pond?"

"No. That only has to do with…what did we decide it was? Chivalry?"

She didn't have time to answer, because at that moment came the sound they'd been waiting for.

Molly and Roger looked at each other, smiling. "Penny," they said together.

Urging their horses to a trot, they soon came to a sheltered glade strewn with mossy boulders. Penny was on her forelegs, tail high in the air, yelping at a fox who sat on the other side of a narrow brook, unconcernedly cleaning its paws.

Roger was unable to hide his glee. "All the hounds ran off to who knows where, and my Penny finds the fox?"

Molly laughed. "Fred won't like this."

"No, he won't." Roger held out a brown-and-white hunting horn that was decorated with engraved silver bands. "Would you like to do the honors?"

"What do you mean?"

"If you blow the horn, Fred will come here with the rifle."

"Oh, no. You do it if you want to." Molly backed Opal up a few paces.

Roger followed her. "You probably don't hunt as often as I do. You should do it. I don't mind."

He tried to press the horn into her hands. Why was he being so persistent? Was he trying to continue with his chivalry nonsense? Looking at the fox, now curled up in the pine needles like a cat, Molly couldn't bear the thought of what would happen if she summoned Fred and the others. But if she admitted that to Roger, he'd think she was cowardly.

She leaned back as far as she could in the saddle. "You do it, and I'll go back to the house. It must be time for tea."

"Molly, it's nowhere near teatime. I insist."

She shoved the horn back at him. "No, *I* insist."

Roger let the horn drop to the ground. "Please, Molly. I don't want to. I can't." His voice held an unexpectedly pleading tone.

"You don't want to call Fred?"

"No."

"Why not?"

He let out a groan. "Why don't you want to?"

Fine, let him think she was a coward. "Because— because it's a sweet, innocent creature."

Roger broke out laughing.

Molly glared at him, turned Opal, and headed back down the path. She hadn't gone far when Roger caught up to her.

"Molly, wait!"

She didn't.

He trotted ahead of her, planting Sparrow in the center of the trail so Molly had no choice but to stop.

Still laughing, Roger wiped tears from his eyes. "I don't want to call Fred here either, for the same reason."

First he laughed at her, and now he mocked her? She let out a slow breath. "Roger, don't tease. Now let me pass."

"I'm entirely serious."

"Really?"

"Yes. I've always thought it was cruel, but try explaining that to Fred or my father, or any number of friends who invite me on hunts."

"You've hunted even though you don't like it?"

"Oh, yes, many times. But I thought if there was a chance to avoid it today, I would."

She put a hand on her hip. "So, you'd make me do it instead?"

"I thought you were enjoying yourself."

"I was. I am. Riding through the forest and exploring the countryside is one of my favorite pastimes. But not going after the fox. When I hunt with my father and brothers I usually make up a story that my horse refused to cross a river or I fell behind or some other such nonsense."

"I'll try that next time."

"Do you enjoy any hunting?" Molly asked, walking Opal up to meet him.

"I don't mind bird hunting. But generally, I'm not much for it." He leaned forward to rub Sparrow's mane.

"Because you like to spend most of your time indoors?"

Roger gave her a quizzical look. "What makes you say that?"

"Most days you're in the office or the library."

"That's because of my ankle. If I'd listened to my doctor and rested it more right after the accident, it would be completely healed by now. I only rested it for a week, but he would have liked a month."

She glanced down at his boot. "Does it hurt much today?"

"Riding doesn't bother it. It's almost back to normal."

"Take good care so you don't injure it again."

He met her gaze, a slow smile coming to his face. "I will."

The forest silence closed around them as they held each other's eyes and his smile faded into something else. Something soft, curious and warm. Something Molly wanted more of, even as her mind raced with such thoughts as, *Are you mad? This is* Roger. *Roger who barely speaks to you, Roger who finds you irritating, Roger who likes to be alone.* And then—*Roger who is nursing a broken heart.*

Molly breathed a small sigh of relief. That explained this unexpected warmth in her chest when she looked at him. She felt sorry for him. And who wouldn't? Jilted at the altar, and still recovering from an injury.

The moment was broken when Penny ran up the trail, stopping at Sparrow's feet.

"Some hunting dog you are," Roger said, looking down at her. "You've abandoned your quarry."

Penny barked and tried to put her paws on Roger's leg, but Sparrow sidestepped.

"She's done us a favor," Molly said. "Now we can honestly tell Fred the fox escaped. I wonder where the other dogs have gotten to." They'd been hearing howls and barks since they entered the forest, but at some distance away.

"Fred's going to have quite a job rounding them up. Do you want to go back to the house, or continue riding?"

In the back of her mind, Molly knew going off alone wasn't the most appropriate thing to do. Yet she had the feeling she and Roger were becoming something like friends and didn't want to lose an opportunity to get to know him better. There was no harm in it, not really.

"Let's go riding," she said. "If you're up to it."

Roger slapped his leg. "I am." He turned Sparrow back toward where they'd seen the fox. "I think you'll enjoy this route. We'll stop and pick up the horn on our way by." He whistled to Penny and they set off.

At first the horses kept to a walk and Molly was able to enjoy the flowers and shrubs that had almost overtaken the trail in some places, but the farther they went the more open spaces they encountered. It was here she would let Opal gallop over the turf. For most of the ride Molly and Roger didn't speak, but she found they didn't need to. She didn't feel pressed to make pointless conversation but was perfectly at ease riding beside him in silence until one of them had some observation to share, or when Roger pointed out interesting landmarks to her. They encountered no more foxes, but did find a few beagles, who ran along with Penny.

Halfway back to Waverly, Molly noticed what looked like a stone tower surrounded by trees. "What's that?"

Roger turned in his saddle. "Oh, that's part of the old hunting lodge."

"It looks like a castle." Molly shielded her eyes against the sun to get a better look.

"Fred told me it was part of the original Waverly Hall that burned down a few hundred years ago. Whoever it was that lived there thought it was bad luck to rebuild in the same spot, but Fred's great-grandfather used the turret as part of a hunting lodge. You can't see that part from here, but it's a comfortable enough house."

Molly wanted to gallop straight over. "You've stayed there?"

"Yes, but not for a few years. Mr. Clarke—Fred's father—closed it up."

"Let's go see it," she said, turning Opal in the direction of the lodge.

Roger glanced at his pocket watch. "We should get the dogs back to the kennel. But I'd be happy to show it to you another day. I'll need to ask Benedict for the key."

"You're right about the dogs." The beagles had all curled up in the grass when Molly pulled Opal to a stop and looked like they were ready to stay there for the rest of the day. "But let's come back here soon."

He gave her that soft grin again. "The day after tomorrow?"

Molly's stomach didn't swoop the way it did when Fred smiled at her, but it certainly took a little tumble. "That sounds perfect."

They looked at each other for a few moments before Roger handed Molly the horn and gestured to the dogs. "Ready to sound it now?"

"Definitely."

When the horn blasted the dogs leapt to their feet, running in circles.

Molly and Opal took off at a gallop, with Roger and Sparrow close behind. The dogs, led by Penny, raced all the way back to the house.

Chapter Eleven

The kennel was curiously quiet when they arrived and there was no sign of Fred, Benedict or Caroline.

"We can't be the first ones back," Molly said, dismounting. Penny ran over and licked her hand, then followed the beagles into the kennel.

Roger slid off Sparrow. "It appears we are."

"Where can they be?" She glanced toward the woods, but there was no sign of anyone approaching.

"They'll turn up. I'll close the kennel and we'll walk the horses back to the stable."

Once this was done, they went up to the house. Molly changed out of her riding habit, then met Roger in the yellow drawing room. After chatting over coffee for half an hour or so, Roger started casting glances toward the chair he usually occupied beside the fire. Following his gaze, Molly noticed his book sitting on a side table.

"Go read if you'd like to," she said.

"I'm halfway through the last chapter. You wouldn't mind?" He was already rising from his seat.

"Not at all. I have one I've just started. I'll go get it."

He retreated to his chair, and Molly went upstairs for her novel. She settled in the chair opposite Roger's and was so engrossed in her story she didn't notice Caroline calling her name until she was practically standing on top of her.

"Molly!"

Molly rose, regretfully closing her book and setting it on the chair. "You're back."

"Only just. Oh, what an afternoon!" Caroline's eyes gleamed as she looked at Molly. She removed her gloves and shook out her blonde hair, then took a seat on the sofa, where Benedict sat drinking coffee. He inched closer when she sat down.

Molly settled into a chair facing them. "Did Fred come back with you?"

"We didn't see him," Benedict said.

"Did you find any of the dogs?" Molly asked.

"A few," Caroline said. "They followed us home and we put them in the kennel. We saw some others in there, so Fred must have been here and gone back out to look."

"No, they followed us," Molly said, gesturing to Roger.

Benedict shook his head. "Those dogs need more training."

"Or a proper master of hounds," Caroline muttered.

Benedict gave half a nod, as though trying to agree with Caroline yet not be disloyal to Fred.

"It was a fine day, anyway," Caroline said. "But I'm a mess. I'm going upstairs." She gave Molly a pointed look.

"I'll join you."

As soon as they reached Caroline's room, she hugged Molly then flopped onto her bed, muddy boots and all.

"Did Benedict find something to talk about besides trees?"

"No." Caroline sat up, sighing happily. "But he

almost kissed me."

Molly sat beside her and gripped her hand. "Almost? What happened?"

"Well, we'd gotten off our horses to look at an oak tree—it's so tall, you should go see it one day—and I'd just said we should head back, but he took my hand and leaned toward me."

"And?"

"And a horn blasted. We thought that meant someone was coming our way. He didn't say anything, but looked very warmly at me. I'm certain he'll try again."

Molly felt a pang of regret. That had probably been when *she'd* sounded the horn. "So, love?"

"If not love, then…like very much?" Caroline unlaced her boots and dropped them on the floor. "I don't know if Benedict's the type to fall head over heels in love with someone, but after getting to know him better, I don't think he sees courting me as only a duty." She paused, smiling. "He likes me."

Molly knew that meant all the world to Caroline. What a difference from just a few days ago, and again she thought being here without chaperones was the best thing that could have happened.

Caroline began unbuttoning her jacket. "Were you with Roger all day?"

"Yes, we ended up looking for Penny in the woods. We found her."

"Then you came right home?"

"We took a ride first."

Caroline eyed Molly in that suspicious way only your best friend can. "First the tavern and now this. You two keep being thrown together. Alone."

"Yes, but not on purpose."

"At least not on your part."

Molly had to laugh. "Certainly not on *his*. It really has been accidental."

Though Roger finally seemed to be warming up to her a bit, it was a far cry from the romantic intrigue Caroline was suggesting. He was friendly at best.

Before Caroline could ask more, Molly said, "You'd better change."

"Yes, I suppose so."

As Molly glanced out the window she saw Fred striding up the lawn, looking exhausted and triumphant.

Caroline soon returned, tying the sash on her mauve gown. "Would you like to go the library and play cards?"

"It looks like Fred's home. Let's go see what the gentlemen are doing."

"All right. Earlier, Benedict said he'd like to play chess after dinner."

On the way to the drawing room, Molly and Caroline passed Mrs. Lane on the staircase. She gave them something that strongly resembled a smirk and Molly suspected she was going upstairs to harass Kitty. She had half a mind to follow her but thought better of it. Mrs. Lane might be even crueler to Kitty if she knew Molly had tried to befriend her.

In the drawing room, Fred sprawled on the sofa with a glass of whiskey in his hand. He was covered in dirt from head to foot but looked immensely satisfied. "Ah, here you are. I was just telling Roger and Benedict I've rounded up all the dogs. Plus one." He looked at Roger. "Penny's in the kennels, too."

Roger leapt from his chair. "Oh, no. I'd better get her before that basset—" He glanced at Molly and

131

Caroline, who watched him with interest. "I'd better get her so she can have some food."

"Before you go, I want to make some plans," Benedict said. "Why don't we go on a picnic tomorrow?"

"What a fun idea," Molly said.

Fred drained his glass, folded his hands over his stomach and closed his eyes. "As long as it's an afternoon picnic. Late afternoon. I'm sleeping in tomorrow."

Not long after, Roger went to the kennels. Molly almost accompanied him, but changed her mind at the last moment since she'd already spent basically the whole day with him. They'd have ample time to talk tomorrow at the picnic, and the day after that he was taking her to the hunting lodge.

After dinner, Molly took a long walk around the grounds while Caroline played chess with Benedict in the library. On her way out of the house she'd asked Mrs. Lane to speak to the cook about preparing a special dinner for the following evening. Since she needed a good reason for such a scheme, she told Mrs. Lane it was to celebrate Fred's first hunt with his dogs. Mrs. Lane had agreed tomorrow night would be perfect for an elaborate dinner and had almost smiled. Hopefully going down to the kitchens to chat with the cook would keep Mrs. Lane far enough from the library for Caroline and Benedict to finish their chess game for once.

Strolling through the garden, Molly recalled her time with Roger this afternoon. That was the second time this week they'd been alone together for a few hours. He seemed to be more comfortable with her now. Perhaps he wasn't as aloof as she'd assumed, but merely shy. The objective in coming to Rochester had been for Caroline to form the ultimate attachment, but maybe Molly had managed to find a friend for herself in the process.

Night was falling when she turned back to the house, serenaded by crickets as she walked along a graveled path. She'd just passed through an arched hedge when someone leapt out in front of her and cried, "Kitty!"

Molly screamed and took an inadvertent step backwards, nearly falling over.

Fred reached out to steady her. "Molly? Oh, no."

"Fred! What are you doing out here?"

"I...well..." He seemed at a loss to answer such a simple question.

"Why would Kitty be in the garden at this hour?" Understanding dawning, Molly's cheeks burned. Had she interrupted a lovers' tryst?

Fred wouldn't meet her eyes, but looked over her shoulder toward the gazebo. "She wouldn't be, of course. But in the dark, well, I thought you were her."

Molly and Kitty were roughly the same height, but other than that they looked nothing alike. It had to have been only wishful thinking on Fred's part.

Molly took a deep breath to steady her still fitful heart. "She must be inside."

"Yes, she must be. I don't know what I was thinking," he said with a forced laugh as he offered her his arm. "I'll walk you back to the house."

Early stars blinked in the twilight sky and the scent of roses swirled about them as they walked through the garden and onto the lawn. They'd almost made it to the drive when Fred abruptly stopped just outside a ring of torchlight and turned Molly to face him.

"Has anyone told you about Kitty yet?" he asked.

Molly gave him a bemused look. "I'm not sure I

know what you mean."

"I'll take that as a no." After seeming to deliberate for a moment, he went on. "Kitty came late to service. She's the parson's daughter, you see."

Molly couldn't mask her astonishment. "The parson's daughter! A maid?"

"Her parents died and left her with nothing. Before her father died, he asked my parents to take Kitty in. But she didn't want charity, as she called it, and asked to be given a job. My mother didn't like the idea, but both my parents could see how much it meant to Kitty not to feel like a burden."

"That's very brave of her."

"And proud. And ridiculous."

Interesting as this undoubtably was, Molly felt she was betraying Kitty's trust simply by listening to Fred. She let go of his arm. "Why are you telling me this? Isn't it a secret?"

"Kitty told me how kind you've been to her and I don't think she'd mind if you knew. I thought it would help you understand what's been going on between her and Mrs. Lane."

Molly put a hand up. "Wait. Doesn't this mean Kitty is actually Mrs. Lane's superior?"

"That's part of the problem. I don't think she can forget that Kitty has 'come down in the world,' as she'd call it. Mrs. Lane is harder on Kitty than all the other maids. She thinks since Kitty didn't grow up in service she'll get discouraged with the work and leave, but I doubt that will happen. She's already been here seven months."

"But that's terrible! Can't anything be done?"

Fred put his hands in his pockets and kicked a loose

stone at his feet. "Benedict will speak to our parents about it when they return. Mrs. Lane has been worse since they left."

Molly could see it all now. The impoverished parson's daughter coming to the house to work, clinging to whatever independence she had left. Fred and Kitty had grown up in the same town, socialized in the same circles, most likely attended the same functions and church over the years. Perhaps Fred had always liked Kitty. But now, as a maid in his own house, he couldn't court her.

Molly started walking again, Fred keeping pace.

"With Kitty's upbringing, I'm surprised she'd take a position as a maid," she said.

"The idea is that she'll be governess when the time comes. For Benedict's children. Kitty will work here as a maid for a time, get to know the house and its inhabitants, and then be a nurse to the baby. When the child is old enough she'll be the governess. She's very well educated."

"Perhaps she could have gotten a position elsewhere as a governess or even worked as a teacher at a school."

Fred looked away. "She didn't want to leave…Rochester."

They continued on in silence until they reached the house, where Fred bade her goodnight. As Molly climbed the stairs to her room, she wondered if it was only Rochester Kitty had not wanted to leave.

The next day at breakfast, Molly received the news she'd thought would never come. "Aunt Hazel's arriving tomorrow!" she exclaimed, entirely missing the saucer as she set her coffee down on the table.

Caroline looked up from her omelet. "Finally. Does

she say when?"

"No. Just tomorrow." Molly folded the letter and handed it to her. "But we'd better tell Kitty so she can get a room ready."

"Mrs. Lane will take care of it," Benedict said. "If I can find her. I haven't seen her today."

Fred liberally buttered his toast. "So, we finally get to meet Caroline's aunt. The chaperone arrives at long last."

Molly couldn't say why, but there was a new feeling in the room, as though they were all aware things wouldn't be the same after tomorrow. They'd be staying for at least two more weeks, but there would be no more flitting off to taverns, walks through the grounds or long evenings in the library. Possibly no visit to the hunting lodge. They'd have two people watching them now. Between Mrs. Lane and Aunt Hazel, they'd be chaperoned at all times, and Aunt Hazel was liable to instill a schedule to limit the time Molly and Caroline spent with the gentlemen.

"Good thing we're getting out today," Fred said, as though he'd read her mind. "We'd better make the most of it."

Benedict turned to him. "Did you already talk to Dawson about the picnic?"

"Last night. I told him not to bother setting up a table in the garden. We'll carry the food ourselves and sit on the ground."

Roger left his book on the window seat and approached the table. "Where do you propose we have this picnic?"

"The quadrangle?" Benedict suggested.

Fred shook his head. "No, let's get away from the

house and take the ladies to the waterfall."

"Oh, I'd love to see that." Caroline said. "Where is it?"

"Near the river," Benedict answered.

Molly chimed in that she'd love to go, while silently vowing to herself not to get too close to the water.

In the end it wasn't much of a waterfall but was delightful nonetheless. Water cascaded over a cliff, only ten feet high or so, into a deep pool that fed into a meandering river. They spread the picnic blanket in a meadow dotted with purple, pink, and yellow wildflowers.

"What's for lunch, Molly?" Fred asked. He lay on his side, a long blade of grass between his teeth.

Molly began unpacking the food. "Sandwiches, iced tea, meat pies and strawberry tarts."

They spent a leisurely hour eating and chatting about what to do for the rest of the visit. Clearly it would be different when Aunt Hazel arrived, but there was no reason they couldn't still enjoy themselves. There were shops in Rochester they hadn't visited yet, and though Molly had had enough of The Wayside, there was a smaller tavern in town that might be worth a visit if she could manage it without Aunt Hazel finding out. Fred suggested going to the next village, where a glassmaker had a studio. Everyone agreed it would be an interesting outing and they set a date for the following week.

After lunch, Molly and Caroline took a stroll around the meadow. They made their way to a shady spot beside the river, where Caroline sat on a large boulder and fanned herself with her hat.

"How are things with Benedict?" Molly asked.

Caroline smiled. "He's been especially attentive

today. I have the feeling he might try to kiss me again."

"I hope so." Molly once again regretted blowing that horn during the hunt yesterday.

"I do, too. It would be an indication that he has some romantic feelings toward me."

"We already know he likes you."

"Yes, but does he like me as a friend or something more? I wish he'd tell me."

Suddenly, someone behind them called Caroline's name and they turned to see Benedict standing not six feet away. Molly met Caroline's abashed gaze. Had he heard what they said?

He walked straight past Molly and took Caroline's arm. "Would you care to walk along the river?"

Caroline grinned. "That would be lovely."

Molly strolled back to the picnic blanket, where Roger and Fred were engrossed in conversation. They both gave her a nod when she settled on the opposite side of the blanket from Roger. Fred occasionally drew her into the conversation, but Roger had reverted to his old self and didn't say a word to her. This left Molly with time to consider the flowers, birds, trees, and Benedict and Caroline, who'd made their way over to the waterfall.

"Will you go take a look at the falls?" Fred asked, breaking into her musings.

Molly shook her head. "No, I wouldn't want to fall in."

"Fall in?" Fred asked. "That's unlikely."

Roger laughed, but before Molly could make eye contact he'd turned away.

"I suppose I can risk it." She glanced at Roger to see if he'd comment, but he'd lain down in the grass and closed his eyes.

Molly rose and called to Penny. They ran across the meadow to the river, taking care to leave Benedict and Caroline to themselves. Molly kept a generous distance between herself and the water, though the ground looked much firmer here than at the pond. Penny leapt into the river, barking at Molly to join her. The sun on the back of her neck made her wish she *could* join Penny. Perhaps she'd come back here with Caroline in a few days and they could at least put their feet in the water.

Molly jumped when she heard a shrill whistle, and spun around to see Roger walking toward her. Or rather, toward Penny. He slapped his leg and called to the dog, who scrambled up the bank and rolled in the grass at Molly's feet. Then she stood and shook, splattering Molly with water.

"Penny," Roger chastised.

Molly brushed droplets off the front of her dress. "It's all right."

Penny barked and wagged her tail.

Molly gave Roger an encouraging smile, but he took Penny by the collar and started back across the meadow.

Molly's shoulders fell as she watched Roger walk away. She couldn't understand it. They'd been getting on so well, and she'd begun to think of him as almost a friend. But aside from the occasional glance or polite word, he'd barely looked at her since yesterday. She sighed and turned around to look for Benedict and Caroline. They'd disappeared into the trees. That had to be a good sign.

Molly had just resigned herself to go talk to Fred when a stick soared over her head and Penny went charging after it.

Roger stood a few feet away, hands in his pockets. He shrugged. "She could use some exercise."

Before Molly could answer, Penny sprinted back and dropped the stick at her feet. Molly picked it up and threw it as far as she could. It landed on the other side of the river. Penny barreled after it, pacing along the bank as she sought a way across the water.

"Now you've done it," Roger said, unexpectedly close.

Molly turned around. "Oh, dear! I'm sorry. Should I—"

He laughed and pointed toward the river. Penny jumped in and swam across, then lay down to gnaw the stick.

"I needn't have worried," Molly said, laughing.

"No." Roger swung his arms lightly, watching Penny.

"It was such a nice day for the picnic. And I didn't fall in the river," she said with a smile.

Roger just nodded.

She shifted from foot to foot, waiting for him to speak or for Penny to return. After ten silent minutes, Molly wondered if she should just leave him alone. When she glanced at him, he was staring at the grass as though it held the answers to all of life's deepest secrets.

"What time is it?" she asked, simply to break the silence.

Roger pulled out his pocket watch. "Almost four."

"Time to go home soon, then."

"Yes."

Penny jumped into the river and swam back, but left the stick behind. She ran over to Molly and sat at her feet.

"We'd better go help Fred clean up," Roger said.

Molly glanced at Fred, who was lounging in the grass and showing no sign of imminent departure. But she wouldn't point that out. Roger most likely wanted to get away from her and this was the most polite way he could think of to do so.

Molly trailed behind Roger and Penny, but halfway across the meadow Roger stopped and waited for her.

"What are you doing later today?" he asked when she reached his side.

"I don't have any plans. Why?"

Roger met Molly's eyes with a warm gaze. "I thought you might like to join me in the quadrangle for tea. We weren't able to the other day because of the rain."

"Yes, I'd love to," Molly said with a smile.

Roger grinned and they continued on.

When they reached Fred, Penny jumped on him and he leapt to his feet with much cursing, followed by much apologizing to Molly. Just as they'd finished packing up the picnic, Caroline and Benedict emerged from the woods. Not holding hands. Not beaming. When they drew closer, Molly cast Caroline a questioning look. She just shook her head.

Before long, the picnic was packed away and they started for home. As they rode, Molly kept an eye on Roger, who was ahead of her, and wondered why he'd suddenly decided to ask her for tea. Most likely it didn't mean anything. He must know by now she liked tea, and offered because he incidentally wanted to have some, too. She reminded herself not to read too much into it, at the same time wondering if her lavender gown or her pink one was more becoming. After all, she'd need to change out of her riding habit when she got home.

The sun was low in the sky as they rode through the woods, mostly quiet but for an unintelligible conversation happening between Benedict and Caroline, who rode side by side behind everyone else. Perhaps to avoid overhearing them, Fred belted out a song Molly recalled from the tavern. He was about to start a second tune when they emerged from the woods and Waverly came into view.

Fred reined in hard and Birdie reared, throwing dirt up with his hooves. Behind him, everyone either halted or swerved to avoid the person in front of them.

"Fred!" Benedict called angrily. "What's all this?"

Fred turned Birdie to face them all. His voice was low, but the words carried as if he'd shouted. "They're home, Benedict. It's Mother and Father."

Chapter Twelve

Molly twisted in her saddle to look at Benedict, who was alarmingly pale.

Beside him, Caroline's wide eyes fixed on Molly's. They simultaneously put their hands to their heads, adjusting their hats. Molly knew she must look a fright from lounging in the grass all day. It didn't matter so much for her, but she could tell Caroline was mortified— about to meet Benedict's parents with no notice and no time at all to make herself presentable.

"Who's that with them?" Roger asked, standing in his stirrups to look at the front steps, where Mr. and Mrs. Clarke stood.

"Mrs. Lane," Molly said flatly.

Roger met her eyes. They had the least to worry about from the sudden appearance of the Clarkes, but both understood what was at stake for Fred, Benedict and Caroline. They'd most likely be angry with their sons, and staying here without a chaperone would not raise Caroline high in their esteem. Or Molly, for that matter. Oh, what would they say when they realized Aunt Hazel wasn't here?

"She must relish being the one to tell our parents what's been going on," Fred said bitterly.

"Nothing's been 'going on,' " Roger said. "You have company, there was a problem with the chaperone, and you were hospitable enough to make the ladies welcome under unusual and unforeseen circumstances. That's all. Don't look so guilty."

"That's right," Molly said, regaining her composure. "We haven't been doing anything we wouldn't have done if Caroline's aunt had been here." Except the tavern and a number of other things, but that was hardly the point. "We'll help explain to your parents."

"Yes, we'll tell them you've all been perfect gentlemen the whole time," Caroline said.

Benedict stared at her for a moment before spurring Falcon forward. "I'll deal with it. I'm the oldest, so it's my responsibility."

Molly was reminded of a funeral procession as they rode sedately and silently toward the house. Benedict and Fred rode side by side, followed by Molly and Caroline, with Roger and Penny bringing up the rear.

As they approached Waverly, Benedict turned Falcon toward the stables, but his father gestured that they should come to the front of the house.

Mr. Clarke was taller than his sons, and his position at the head of the stairs combined with the grave expression on his face made him look larger than life. Mrs. Clarke, from whom Fred and Benedict had inherited their fair hair, stood with both hands covering her mouth as though about to be sick.

Standing beside Mrs. Clarke, Mrs. Lane looked happy for the first time since Molly had met her. Mr. Dawson's head was just visible behind her. Molly wondered if more servants were gathered out of sight, waiting to hear firsthand what was sure to become fantastic gossip.

Caroline kept swallowing and trying to tuck her hair

up into her hat. Molly wanted to reach out and take her hand, but instead caught her eye and gave her a reassuring smile. Caroline managed a kind of turned-up grimace.

When they reached the front steps, they dismounted and grooms came to take the horses away. Molly stood with her hands folded in front of her, unsure of what to do. Introduce herself, hang her head in shame, smile? Fleeing into the woods seemed the best idea.

From the top of the stairs, the Clarkes looked down at them, frowning. Mrs. Lane whispered in Mrs. Clarke's ear and pointed at Molly. Mrs. Clarke's eyes grew round and she said something to her husband, who bristled.

Molly's cheeks burned.

"Mother, Father," Benedict said in a strained voice as he climbed the stairs. At the last moment he went back and offered Caroline his arm. Together they went to meet his parents, followed by Fred.

Roger offered Molly his arm, and she subtly gestured toward the Clarkes with a questioning look. He gave her hand a reassuring squeeze and nodded in a way that implied everything would be fine.

But the raised voices coming from the head of the stairs suggested everything was *not* fine.

As she and Roger reached the landing, Molly tried not to hear what Mrs. Clarke was saying to her sons, but it was impossible.

"…and as if that wasn't enough, Lane tells me you took these ladies to the tavern? You spent whole days with them away from the house?" Benedict tried to answer, but his mother turned her back on him and addressed Molly and Caroline. She clasped her hands together tightly in front of her. "You must allow me to apologize for my sons' abominable behavior."

Mr. Clarke gave them a slight bow. "You should have been escorted home at once. At once."

Fred looked at his father. "We were perfectly hospitable, well mannered, and did nothing untoward."

Behind him, Mrs. Lane cleared her throat pointedly. Mr. Dawson hovered in the doorway, listening raptly to every word.

Caroline gave a little cough, then addressed Mr. and Mrs. Clarke. "We've had a grand time. The ride home would have been so far, you see, and my aunt was sick, and it seemed staying here was the best thing to do, and…and we apologize for upsetting you."

Mrs. Clarke threw her hands up. "My dear, we aren't upset with *you.*" She gave Benedict a stormy look, then turned to Molly. "Or you. Oh! We haven't even been introduced!" She put a hand to her chest, and Mr. Clarke wrapped an arm around her waist.

Roger stepped forward. "May I present Miss Molly Merriwether."

"It's nice to meet you," Molly said.

The sudden shift to formalities upset Mrs. Clarke even more, and she collapsed against her husband. "Oh, good afternoon. A pleasure."

"I believe it's time we went inside," Mr. Clarke said, tightening an arm around his wife.

They all filed into the house, but once inside the foyer, Caroline stopped. "If you'll excuse Molly and me."

All four Clarkes looked at her with expressions ranging from gratitude to dread.

"Of course, Miss Darby," Mrs. Clarke said. "You must be tired from your—from the—whatever it is you were doing."

"We had a picnic," Molly said.

"Beside the waterfall," Roger added.

Mrs. Clarke clutched her chest as if she'd heard something scandalous. "I'll send Lane up with tea."

"Please don't put her to any trouble," Molly said. "Kitty's been taking wonderful care of us."

Over Mrs. Clarke's shoulder, Mrs. Lane glared at Molly.

"Kitty, then," Mrs. Clarke said, and darted into the parlor.

"Benedict! Fred!" Mr. Clarke snapped, and they followed their mother.

Mr. Clarke bowed to Molly, Roger, and Caroline and strode into the parlor, slamming the door behind him.

Upstairs in their room, Caroline paced to and fro, wringing her hands. Occasionally she muttered, "What are we to do?" and, "What a disaster!" or, "Will they even let him court me now?"

"They'll let him court you. That's the whole purpose of the visit." After a glance outside, Molly closed the window. Gray clouds gathered around Waverly Hall as if mimicking the mood of its residents. Thunder and lightning would have been more apt.

Caroline buttoned and unbuttoned her top collar button. "What must the Clarkes think of me? Oh! They'll tell our parents what happened."

"Our parents would have found out sooner or later."

"I was hoping for later," Caroline said. "Much later. Perhaps in ten years or so."

Molly crossed the room and put a hand on her shoulder. "Once your parents get over their surprise, they'll be happy to hear how well you got on with Benedict. This will all be forgotten."

"Do you really think so?" Caroline asked, grabbing Molly's sleeve.

Molly gave Caroline's back a reassuring pat. "I do. Now, go change before Kitty arrives with the tea. Perhaps she'll have news of what's going on downstairs."

Once she was alone, Molly changed into a dark green gown and brushed her hair, already mentally packing her trunk. There was no way they could remain in Rochester now. She crossed to the window, the forgotten hairbrush held loosely in her hand. Raindrops spattered the panes as she tried to catch a glimpse of the hunting lodge. She couldn't see it from here. Molly turned away, sighing. She wouldn't see it with Roger tomorrow, either. Of course, with the way he'd ignored her for most of today, she didn't know if he actually would have taken her to the lodge. And with the household thrown into a tumult over the Clarkes' sudden arrival, Roger definitely wouldn't be joining her for tea in the quadrangle later today. She wondered if she'd ever see Roger again. He was only visiting Waverly, after all, and somehow they'd never gotten around to talking about where he lived, or much else about his life.

When Caroline returned, one look at her face told Molly they'd both come to the same conclusion.

"We'll need to go home," Molly said, setting her brush on the vanity.

Caroline went to the writing desk and fell into the chair. "I know, but I don't want to. I want to stay."

"So do I. We'll have to turn right around with your aunt tomorrow and go home." Molly checked the watch pinned to her dress. "I wonder if it's too late in the day to send her a message."

Caroline pulled a pen and paper out of the drawer. "Not if we send it soon. It's only two hours to The Blue Swan, and she could have it by morning. I'll write. I'll tell her—" She looked to Molly for a suggestion.

"Tell her there's been a change of plans and we'll explain when we see her. Tell her to wait at The Blue Swan and make arrangements for the journey home."

Just as Caroline finished writing, Kitty arrived with tea.

"Could you send this to The Blue Swan?" Caroline asked, rising.

Kitty took the note. "Certainly."

"We want to make sure it arrives tonight," Molly said, "so please send it off now and come back up."

Kitty checked the tea tray. "Do you need something else?"

"News." Molly sank into the sofa, rubbing her forehead.

Kitty nodded in understanding and left the room.

Molly and Caroline sat in silence on the sofa, drinking tea.

"The message is on its way," Kitty said when she returned.

"What's going on downstairs?" Molly asked.

Kitty peeked outside the room, glancing up and down the hall before closing the door and lowering her voice. "I saw Fred just after he left his parents. They're livid. They think Benedict should have taken you home or sent a message for them to come back at once."

"They can't blame Benedict for everything," Molly said. "We had a hand in it, too."

"Fred says Benedict insisted on taking all the blame." Kitty gave Caroline a significant look. "He's trying to protect you from his parents' anger."

Caroline put her hands over her face as the tears began to flow.

Molly rubbed her back, looking up at Kitty. "Did Fred find out why Mr. and Mrs. Clarke came home early?"

Kitty drew herself up, planted her hands on her hips and lost any semblance of a maid. "Mrs. Lane. Mrs. Lane wrote to them and told them to come home straight away. I haven't seen her letter, of course, but she told them everything that's been happening and, to hear Fred tell it, embellished her reports for good measure."

Caroline wiped her eyes on the heel of her hand, sniffling. "Why would she do such a thing?"

"That vile woman!" Molly exclaimed. She could think of two reasons why Mrs. Lane would do it. To give Mr. and Mrs. Clarke a report ahead of time to get in their good graces, and to make trouble for Benedict, who she must suspect wanted her dismissed.

"She did it because she's cruel," Kitty said. "There's no reason. No reason at all. But she's trying to act humble, as if she was trying to protect your reputations."

"Our reputations?" Molly asked incredulously. "I think she's trying to protect her job."

"I don't doubt it," Kitty said.

Caroline pushed the hair out of her eyes and looked at Kitty. "How's Benedict? Did you see him?"

"No, he was still in the parlor."

"What will happen now?" Molly asked.

"There's to be a dinner, and then I suppose everyone will retire for the evening."

Caroline dabbed fresh tears with a handkerchief. "Molly and I will need to pack our things afterwards."

Kitty cocked her head. "Pack?"

Molly rose, smoothing down her dress. "We're going home tomorrow. We'll need to tell the Clarkes and prepare to leave in the morning."

"You needn't go!" Kitty took a hasty step toward the sofa, then seemed to remember herself and stopped.

Caroline sighed. "It doesn't feel right to stay now, and I need to get home to explain to my parents."

"The Clarkes probably don't feel they can ask us to leave, but they must want us to," Molly said.

Kitty shook her head. "Fred and Benedict don't."

"I doubt that will mean much to their parents," Molly said. "We have to go."

"It must be almost time for dinner," Caroline said, rising.

Kitty looked at the clock. "Yes. Do you want me to ask Mr. Dawson to have your trunks sent up? Or do you want to speak to the Clarkes first?"

"We don't need to speak to them," Molly said. "We've already made our decision."

"But you can ask Mr. Dawson to bring our trunks," Caroline said.

"I'll be sorry to see you go. Waverly Hall has been much…brighter since you two arrived," Kitty said and left the room.

After closing the door behind her, Molly resumed her seat and drank a cup of lukewarm tea.

Caroline sat on the arm of the sofa. "When we decided to stay, it made so much sense. But now I don't know what we were thinking."

Molly looked up at her. "I do. We were thinking you

151

needed to get to know Benedict, and we know how to behave without chaperones present."

"I don't see why we need chaperones at our age."

"The way of the world," Molly said with a one-shouldered shrug. "But it doesn't seem as scandalous as Mrs. Lane and the Clarkes are making it out to be."

Caroline slid onto the seat beside her. "And as my parents will, and Auntie."

"And my parents. But if they'd seen us together, they'd know everything was right and proper, all through the visit."

"Except perhaps The Wayside."

"And the hunt."

Caroline looked off into the distance. "And those quiet walks, just Benedict and I."

"And Roger's way of helping me out of the pond."

Their eyes met. It most definitely hadn't *all* been right and proper, but the motive behind it had been innocent. There'd been opportunity for true mischief, but that hadn't happened. At the end of the visit the ladies had their virtue, their integrity and—hopefully—their reputations intact.

Dinner was a quiet affair. No more raucous laughter, long conversations and lingering at the table after the meal was over. Everyone was subdued, except Fred, who entertained his parents with tales of yesterday's hunt and peppered them with questions about their visit to the coast.

After the meal, they all retired to the parlor, where Molly and Caroline shared the news that they'd be leaving in the morning.

"But that's ridiculous," Benedict exclaimed, springing from his chair.

Caroline kept her eyes on the floor. "We feel it's best under the circumstances," she said quietly.

"You're supposed to stay for two more weeks," Benedict said, taking a step toward her.

Mrs. Clarke spoke before Caroline could answer. "She's made up her mind, Benedict."

"But—" he began, staring at Caroline.

His mother fixed him with a look that brooked no argument, and he silently took his seat. Fred opened his mouth to speak, but Benedict put a hand on his arm and shook his head.

Mr. Clarke then drew Caroline into a conversation about her father and the rest of her family.

As Molly sipped her port, she had the distinct feeling she was being watched. She looked up to find Roger staring at her from across the room. When she met his eyes, he put his hand on Penny's head and pointed toward the quadrangle. Molly gave him a quizzical look, not sure how they could both slip out unnoticed.

Aside from Mr. and Mrs. Clarke, Mrs. Lane had been lurking close by all evening, and Molly had the feeling she'd been assigned to keep an eye on them. Roger subtly motioned to the door behind Molly, which led to the library. She nodded in understanding.

Roger bent to whisper something to Penny, who began wagging her tail and barking, drawing the attention of everyone in the room.

"Excuse me," Roger said, "Penny needs to—"

Mr. Clarke cut him off. "Of course."

Roger rose, Penny at his heels, and strode from the room.

Molly waited for ten minutes, until the conversation was reestablished, then stood. "Pardon me. I'm afraid I left my book in the library and I should get it now so I don't forget it in the morning."

Mrs. Clarke reached for a porcelain bell on the side table. "Kitty can find it for you."

"Oh, don't bother ringing. I'm not sure she'd know which one it is."

"Kitty *can* read," Fred said testily. "Tell her the name of the book."

"I…I'm not certain of the title. I only bought it last week, you see."

Fred looked from Molly to Roger's empty chair and understanding dawned on his face. "If it's lost, it's lost. Better go find it."

"Yes, I will." As she left the room, Molly wondered how long it would be before anyone noticed she wasn't coming back. She walked toward the library in case anyone was paying the slightest attention to where she was going, then veered off to the left, down a short hallway and out a side door to the quadrangle.

Penny ran over the moment she stepped outside. Roger followed, albeit more slowly. He leaned against the wall. "What a to-do."

"I could hardly believe it when we saw Mr. and Mrs. Clarke on the steps." Molly crossed her arms over her chest. "And to think Mrs. Lane did this."

Roger scowled. "Did she?"

"According to Kitty, who heard it from Fred."

He stuffed his hands into his jacket pockets. "Probably because she knows Benedict was going to try to have her dismissed."

"I thought that, too," Molly said, leaning beside him.

After a few silent moments watching Penny roll in the grass, Roger spoke. "You're really leaving?"

"It seems the right thing to do."

He shifted so he was facing her. "Do you *want* to leave?"

"No." Looking into his warm, brown eyes, Molly's heart gave an unexpected little flutter.

"Couldn't you stay?"

"It's too late. Didn't you see how relieved Mr. and Mrs. Clarke looked when we told them?"

"I did. But they should have insisted you stay instead of allowing you to skulk off as if you've done something wrong. You didn't ask to be in this situation, and behaved beyond reproach the entire time. Even with, I could say, not the most responsible hosts."

Molly put a hand to her chest and batted her lashes, doing her best imitation of a damsel in distress. "Why, Mr. Bailey, are you defending us? How chivalrous."

"Ah, back to Mr. Bailey. But I don't mind, Miss Merriwether."

He studied her face for a few moments and the look in his eyes added a sharp pang of regret to the misery of Molly's sudden departure.

"Where do you live?" Roger asked, taking a step closer.

Molly grinned. "I was going to ask you the same question, but was afraid you'd think me impertinent."

"After all we've been through together? You almost broke my ankle, lost my dog and sat beside me through a drunken stupor. You've earned confidences few of my friends have."

"Does this mean you'll tell me all your secrets?"

"If I had any."

Hardly aware that she'd moved, Molly found herself within only an inch or two of him. "Everyone has secrets."

A shadow flickered in his eyes. "Not me."

"Oh, Roger, you must."

He looked off into the distance as if trying hard to recall. "I've been up to that attic, but I never told anyone."

"Oh! Did you find any treasure?"

Roger made an exaggerated frown, shaking his head. "No, no treasures for me."

"What would your treasure be? I have a feeling you wouldn't have been disappointed to find a pile of old books up there."

"I have other treasures in mind." He gazed into her eyes for so long Molly felt her cheeks growing warm. Roger abruptly looked away. "But, no, I wouldn't mind books."

Molly had the urge to take his hand or meet his eyes again, but he pushed himself away from the wall and took a few paces back.

She looked toward the door. "Speaking of books, I told everyone in the parlor I was going to the library to find mine. They'll be wondering where I am."

"And it only takes Penny so long to do…whatever it is they all believe she's doing." He offered his arm, and she wrapped both hands around it.

Molly fit her steps to his as they crossed the quadrangle, Penny following. "Are you going back to the parlor?"

"No. I'll go to the office with Penny. I have a feeling the Clarkes want time to themselves."

"They'll have their fair share tomorrow, after we're gone."

He looked down into her face. "What time are you

leaving?"

"I don't know exactly. Early, I think."

When they reached the door to the north wing, Roger held the door for Molly to go ahead of him. Once inside, he walked her over to the staircase. "Well. I suppose this is goodbye."

As they stood in the quiet hallway, Molly wasn't sure what to say. Was this really goodbye? Forever? "Perhaps we'll meet again one day." She knew it was bold, but it was the closest she could come to saying she *hoped* she'd see him again.

"Perhaps. Goodnight, Molly Merriwether."

"Goodnight, Roger."

"Oh, and don't think I've forgotten you haven't told me your real name yet. Now that would be a treasure." He kissed her hand and walked down the hall with Penny.

Molly slowly climbed the stairs, her mind swirling with questions she hadn't had yesterday, her heart pattering when she recalled Roger's words and the look in his eyes as they'd stood in the quadrangle.

Chapter Thirteen

The next morning was a flurry of packing, locating missing items, saying their goodbyes and, for Molly, comforting Caroline as well as she could.

Caroline hadn't seen Benedict alone since his parents' arrival, and there was much left unsaid between them. "I don't understand why they won't give us any time together," she said for the fourth time that day.

Molly paused in bustling about the room gathering her things. "Perhaps they think there's been sufficient time already."

Halfway through folding a gown, Caroline sat on the edge of the bed. "Is he interested in me at all as more than just a friend? Are we officially courting? How will I know if we don't have a chance to talk?"

"Didn't you discuss it at the picnic yesterday?"

"No." Caroline's shoulders fell as she looked at Molly. "Benedict hasn't told me how he feels or spoken about the future at all. One thing I've learned about him; he takes his time. With everything. Even when we're chatting he sometimes mulls over his next comment for much longer than necessary."

Molly placed a pile of books in the last trunk. "Perhaps he wants to impress you."

"I suspect he thought we had more time and didn't want to do anything rash."

"I'd hardly call it rash, as both families approve."

Caroline tossed the gown on the floor. "Oh! Why did I bother with any of this? I should have insisted on a Season with you next year."

"No, you're better off with someone you already know rather than hoping to meet a man at a ball. You do *like* Benedict?"

A line appeared between Caroline's troubled green eyes as she looked up. "Yes, but there's this business of him not dealing with Mrs. Lane and, I know it sounds selfish, but I would have liked him to stand up for me more with his parents. Last night I was surprised he didn't insist that I stay."

"But we'd already told everyone we want to leave."

"I know, but I would have appreciated the gesture. And really, Molly, if he'd asked me to stay, I would have."

"He did imply—strongly—that he wants you to stay."

"Yes, but that isn't the same as *asking* me to stay and telling his parents he refused to let me leave."

"So, you would have liked a grand, sweeping gesture leaving no doubt of his feelings for you, and proving he's willing to face anything to make you happy?"

Caroline raised her chin a touch. "Well, yes. It doesn't seem too much to ask of the man who supposedly wants to court me. But it all makes me wonder. Does he want that? Or does he simply do whatever his parents tell him to do? Would he have courted you if they'd told him to? Does he lack the courage to stand up for me, or to deal with unruly servants, or tell me how he feels? If that's the case, I'm not sure I want to be with him."

Molly wanted to quash this line of thinking, and fast.

But, on the other hand, Caroline had a point. This visit had been meant to allow her to get to know Benedict, and she had, but as of now that knowledge was not to his advantage. She sat beside Caroline and put an arm about her shoulders. "Now isn't the time to decide anything. We'll go home and, after a few days away from here, you'll have a new perspective."

"Yes, perhaps this is just what we need. It will give me a chance to really think about Benedict, which might be easier if I'm not seeing him every day."

"We'll sit in the garden and drink tea and talk about Benedict to your heart's content."

Caroline leaned against her shoulder. "You are a comfort, Molly."

Before long, the trunks were packed and stowed. Their bedchambers looked like they'd never been there at all.

Molly stood beside the window, pulling on her gloves. "It feels like much longer than two weeks since we arrived."

"It could be a month for all that's happened, or a day for all that didn't," Caroline said. She turned her back on the room as if she couldn't bear to look at it anymore and hastened out the door.

Downstairs in the parlor, Fred, Benedict and their parents waited.

Benedict was pale and haggard, his eyes on Caroline as she spoke to Mr. and Mrs. Clarke.

Fred took Molly's arm and led her to the corner, out of earshot of everyone else. "I'm sorry it's turned out this way. You've been a pleasure and I'm glad you stayed, even though it was somewhat unconventional. I hope Benedict's able to work things out with Caroline."

Molly followed Fred's gaze to Benedict and Caroline, who now stood whispering to each other under the watchful eyes of Mrs. Clarke.

"I hope so, too. If you ever find yourself near Hartford, please stop to visit. I'm at Walsingham Manor, and Caroline's at Norbury Hall.

"I'll do that. Have a good journey."

"Thank you, Fred. Where's Roger?"

He shrugged. "Probably off with Penny somewhere."

"Please tell him I said goodbye and give Penny a pat for me."

"I will."

Mr. Dawson came in to announce that the carriage was ready, and they all filed outside. The day was sunny and dry; they'd make good time to The Blue Swan.

As Fred walked Molly down the stairs, he lurched sideways. "Gah! Molly, I hate to insult you, but you're walking like a sailor who hasn't got his land legs."

"Oh, I'm sorry, Fred," Molly said, heat flooding her cheeks. "I'm used to accommodating Roger's ankle."

He gave her a sharp look. "Are you?"

"Well, it seems only polite when we walk together."

When Molly turned for a last look at Waverly Hall, she caught sight of a movement in an upper window. Shielding her eyes to look, she saw Roger, who pointed to a book in his hand. So he'd gone back to the attic for his treasure. Molly waved and climbed into the carriage. It was only later she realized she'd never found out where he lived.

The next afternoon Molly sat beside her bedroom window, looking across the fields to Norbury Hall. Caroline was in disgrace, and Molly not much better off.

If she'd thought the ride to Rochester was tedious, it was nothing to the ride home *from* Rochester, with Aunt Hazel chastising them throughout the hours-long journey.

When they'd arrived home late last night, both sets of parents were waiting to greet them at Caroline's house. This immediately dispelled Molly's hope that she and Caroline would arrive before Mrs. Clarke's letter explaining what had happened.

Aunt Hazel entered the parlor first and spoke to the parents, with many hand gesticulations and peeks over her shoulder at Molly and Caroline, who lingered in the doorway. But there was only so long they could put off what was bound to be a tedious lecture. Especially once Aunt Hazel finished her explanation and snapped her fingers at them as one would a small dog who refuses to get off the bed.

Mr. Merriwether and Mr. Darby poured themselves drinks and greeted their daughters before sitting on the sofa, where they lit their pipes and settled in for a long chat as though they were at a dinner party. Molly and Caroline bypassed them and presented themselves to their mothers, who stood in grim silence in front of the empty hearth.

There was no, "How was your journey?" Or, "Are you tired?"

Mrs. Merriwether jumped right in with, "Molly! I thought I'd raised you better. Gallivanting around with three—*three!*—young men unchaperoned."

Molly rubbed a hand over her temple. "Mother, there was no gallivanting. It was simply a visit. I'm sorry if you were worried."

"Simply a visit! Yes, I *am* worried. You might have

thought of worrying me before you stayed at Waverly Hall. We can only hope nobody finds out about this. If word gets out, we won't be invited to any balls when the Season starts," Mrs. Merriwether said, bringing a lace handkerchief to her eyes. "Not one!"

Mrs. Darby glared at her daughter. "Caroline, what on earth were you thinking?"

"Can't we discuss this tomorrow?" Caroline asked.

"You had little thought of 'tomorrow' when you decided to abandon your sick aunt and traipse off to Rochester by yourselves," Mrs. Darby said.

"We didn't abandon her. We discussed the whole thing and Aunt Hazel agreed we should go," Caroline said.

Aunt Hazel spoke then. "It's true, I did." She looked around at the other adults as though hoping they would relieve her of her shame. When nobody did, she went on. "But it was with the understanding that Mr. and Mrs. Clarke would be in attendance. I never dreamed I would be ill for so long and would certainly not have sent the young ladies if I'd known they would be alone with the gentlemen."

"We weren't alone," Molly said. "There was a butler, and a housekeeper who barely left us alone."

Mrs. Merriwether pounced. "I can tell from your tone that you *wanted* to be left alone. What were you doing with these men?"

Molly's blush did not help her insistence that nothing out of the ordinary had happened. "I only meant we weren't unattended. The Clarkes and their friend were perfect gentlemen."

Mr. Darby crossed the room and put an arm around Caroline's shoulders. "It seems to me no harm was done.

Caroline went to meet Mr. Clarke and she did so, even if the circumstances weren't ideal."

"Not ideal?" his wife echoed. "What will people say?"

"Most likely nothing," Mr. Merriwether said from the sofa. "I doubt anybody knows, or will know, unless the two of you continue talking about it."

Molly wasn't sure if he referred to herself and Caroline or to their mothers, but replied anyway. "That's right. It isn't as scandalous as all that. You must trust that Caroline and I behaved with decorum."

"We did," Caroline said. "Please stop treating us like children and acting as if we'd do anything to put ourselves or our reputations in jeopardy." She paused for breath, and Molly was sure she saw tears standing in her eyes. "Furthermore, the gentlemen took great pains to see that we enjoyed ourselves and didn't suggest anything untoward."

Recalling the tavern, Molly wondered if Caroline crossed her fingers as she uttered that last sentence. She turned to her mother. "I'm exhausted. Could we go home now?"

Mrs. Merriwether and Mrs. Darby shared a glance and nodded to each other in some kind of timeless mother-to-mother signal.

"Yes, we'll go home," Mrs. Merriwether said. "But you're not to visit Caroline for at least a week."

Molly put her hands on her hips. "Why not?"

"Don't use that tone, Molly," her mother warned.

Caroline looked at Mrs. Darby. "I don't see how us visiting each other does any harm."

"Nevertheless," her mother said, and that was all.

Molly and Caroline exchanged their own look, both

knowing they'd see each other tomorrow.

Molly had gone home with her parents after that. The silence of her bedchamber was heavenly after the chaos of the last few days. She undressed and fell into bed, welcoming the familiar scent and feel of her own blankets and pillows. Extinguishing the lanterns, Molly gazed out the window at the full moon until she fell asleep.

This morning she'd woken to her brother Albert bursting into her room with a breakfast tray. "Wake up, Moll."

Albert was just shy of a year older than Molly and had the same blue eyes and dark brown hair as the rest of the family. Well, besides Tristan, who'd inherited blond hair and hazel eyes from some long-forgotten relation.

"What time is it?" Molly asked, rubbing her eyes.

"Breakfast time," he said, setting the tray on her desk. "Looks like you're in trouble. I heard Mother and Father talking about you."

She pushed aside her blankets and sat up. "What did they say?"

"Just what you'd expect."

"I'm surprised Mother has any more to say about it after last night."

Albert raised a brow. "Really?"

"No," she said, and they laughed together.

Molly hopped out of bed. "Is Tristan here?"

"No, he's out. Mother sent a message to Michael, so I expect he and Lydia will come visit in the next week or so. Let's go riding when I get home."

"Oh, I'd love to. We should invite Tristan and Caroline."

Albert started for the door. "If Mother will allow

you out. I hear you aren't to go to Norbury."

Molly smirked. "We'll see about that."

"Good to have you back," Albert said, laughing, and left the room.

Molly pulled her floral dressing gown on and ate breakfast, wondering what type of speech she could expect from her parents. After eating, she slipped into a raspberry-colored gown and went downstairs.

She found her mother pacing around the library, but her father was nowhere to be seen.

Molly sat in a brown armchair facing the sofa. "Good morning."

Mrs. Merriwether came to a halt in front of Molly. "Did you sleep well?" The question came out as an accusation, as though she had no right to sleep well.

Molly rested her elbows on the arms of the chair and folded her hands across her stomach. "Very. It's always nice to get home."

"I'm glad to hear you like being home, because you're going to be spending a great deal of time here."

"Am I?"

"Yes. Your father and I have decided that after what happened, you should devote more time to preparing for your Season."

Molly sat up in surprise. "That isn't for another year."

"It's sooner than you think."

"I'm already old for a first Season. Most women have had one or two by now. I'm not sure it's necessary."

"Don't be ridiculous. How else will you find a husband?"

Molly had no answer for this. "I have plenty to do without preparing for a Season. Caroline and I are hoping to go back to Waverly since our visit was cut short."

"If you're invited back after what happened," Mrs. Merriwether said and pursed her lips.

Molly tutted. "Will you please stop acting as if I stormed into Waverly Hall, smashed the china, set fire to the curtains, and stole the jewelry? Through no fault of our own, we found ourselves there unchaperoned. If we'd come home, Caroline wouldn't now be on the cusp of becoming engaged. We had to stay." There was no indication that Caroline was any closer to getting engaged than Molly was, but it seemed a good argument.

Her mother must have agreed, for she sat on the sofa across from her. "I never thought you set fire to the curtains."

"I know. You can trust me to behave myself."

"I hope so, Molly," she said with a doubtful shake of her head. "I'll agree to putting off preparations for your Season, but only until Michael and Lydia go home. I'll have so much to do while they're here, but once they leave, you and I will be very busy. You'll need new gowns, and probably dancing lessons, and who knows what else. We've never had a girl who had a Season before. I'll ask Gwen all about it, as Caroline's her fifth daughter."

It was all clear to Molly now. Her mother was so excited to be involved in the Season that she couldn't wait to get started. She'd sent her sons off to ball after ball, but a daughter was a whole other matter. Her mother started rattling off a list of things they'd need. Molly just nodded along.

Chapter Fourteen

Later that day Molly made her way to a grove of willow trees on the border of Walsingham's grounds. The sweeping branches of six ancient willows brushed the grass, giving the glade the feel of a green, leafy cave. When Molly stepped through the branches she was immediately embraced by that old favorite hideaway.

As expected, Caroline was already there, lying among the wildflowers.

Molly stretched out beside her, an arm behind her head. "How was it?"

"Between my parents doubting if Benedict would make a good husband, despairing over my abandonment of Auntie, and practically accusing me of lecherous behavior?"

"They didn't accuse you of that!"

"They may as well have. What do they think we did there? My parents should know I wouldn't do whatever it is they think I was doing, and if they thought Benedict was the type of man, well—they'd be wrong. He's kind, isn't he? You like him. He didn't even attempt to kiss me for almost two weeks, and it didn't even happen, and that isn't lecherous, it's—"

"You're rambling."

"I know. All of this has me rattled. And…"

Molly propped herself up on one elbow, facing Caroline. "Go on."

"I miss him. Benedict. I miss Benedict."

"It's only been two days."

She sighed. "Almost three."

"Does this mean…?" Molly gripped her hand.

Caroline positively glowed. "Yes. I think I love him."

They sat up and embraced.

"Oh, Caroline! What changed? At Waverly you weren't sure."

Caroline adjusted the folds of her skirt and kneeled in the grass. "My parents have been talking all day about how they wonder if he's responsible enough, and what does this say about his character, and they've even been wondering if the family is respectable. So I of course had to defend Benedict, and the more I told them, the more I realized I hadn't been seeing Benedict clearly before. He isn't weak by not firing Mrs. Lane—he knows he can't overstep his father's authority. Isn't that a good thing?"

"Yes, I suppose so," Molly said.

"By not trying to talk me into staying, that shows he respects my feelings. Many men would have thought it was their place to force me to stay. But Benedict listened, and let me have my own way even though he wanted me there. He's thoughtful, and conscious of his position."

Molly was almost reeling with the complete change of Caroline's opinions about Benedict. Everything she'd thought questionable about him two days ago she now saw as indications of a flawless character. But perhaps that was what falling in love was like. Caroline understood Benedict now, and that must have opened her heart. It was sweet, really. But it would have been convenient if it had happened three days ago. "What will you do now? Will you write to Benedict?"

"Yes, we'd planned to write. But I can't tell him how I feel in a letter. I'll have to hope he invites me back," Caroline said.

"I'm sure he will."

"I have that feeling, too." Caroline paused and looked up at the willow leaves for a moment, then turned back to Molly. "Were your parents very angry?"

Molly told her about this morning's interview, and Caroline insisted that Molly accompany her to Waverly Hall if she was lucky enough to go back.

"You won't need a Season," Caroline said. "I'm sure Benedict has nice friends, and if I marry him we'll throw balls to find you a husband."

"My mother would be very disappointed. She's already planning my gowns. I get the feeling she's been waiting for this day since I was born, after three boys."

"We'll invite her to the balls. Believe me, after watching my sisters go through it, I hope I don't need to."

"You won't. Benedict will write soon and invite you back to Rochester," Molly reassured her.

Caroline fidgeted with the top button of her blouse. "If his parents will have me. Auntie seems to think I've done something unforgivable."

"No, they weren't angry with us, only with Fred and Benedict. Speaking of Hazel, how is she? She looked so upset last night."

"She feels she let Mother down. But I assured her it was the right thing to do."

"There wasn't much else she could have done, in the circumstances."

"That's what I told her." Caroline rose. "I'd better get back to the house before my mother realizes I'm not in my bedchamber. Same time tomorrow?"

"Yes. I'm going riding with my brothers later. Would you like to join us?" Molly asked, standing up.

"If I can escape again."

Molly gave Caroline a hug. "I'm happy for you about Benedict. You're right. He's a good man."

"He is. I only hope he feels the same way about me."

Molly had no doubt that he did.

It took a few days for the excitement of their return to die down, but once it did, Molly settled back into her old routine. She and Caroline continued to meet under the willow trees daily until their parents decided they were allowed to see each other again. They took long walks around the grounds discussing Benedict, resumed their thrice-weekly tea parties, and spent hours in one or other of their bedchambers—discussing Benedict. It wasn't long before Molly wished she had a beau to talk about, simply to add some variety to their conversations.

They went into Hartford to visit the shops regularly, and every time Molly passed the Plainfield Tavern she wondered how it compared to The Wayside. Molly rode with one or more of her brothers every day, depending on who was available. When none of them were, she was happy enough to go out on her own, much to her mother's chagrin.

Despite Mrs. Merriwether saying they wouldn't worry about Molly's Season just yet, she'd been taken to the dressmaker four times and had been given more dancing lessons. Her mother took to offering tidbits of household management advice whenever a chance presented itself and strongly hinted that Molly should spend extra time on making preserves once blackberries were in season.

One thing Molly made sure to do was corner her brothers and tell them about her trip to the tavern— sworn to secrecy, of course—and they both agreed it sounded like a typical experience. She left out the part about Roger being drunk, and when she recounted the joke about Molly wanting to "take Roger in," they looked shocked and wouldn't tell her what it meant.

Three weeks after her return, Molly went out to the willows alone. She lay in the middle of the glade, watching branches sway in a light breeze. Given the warmth of the day, the softness of the grass and the low humming of bees, she should have known she would fall asleep. Having no idea how much time had passed, she woke to someone nudging her. Or some*thing*. Something soft, making whining sounds. Molly opened her eyes.

"Penny?" Certain she was dreaming, she closed her eyes again. When she opened them, Penny was still there, standing over her. If Penny was here, that had to mean— But no. It was impossible. Heart hammering, Molly sat up just as Roger burst into the glade.

He skidded to a halt when he saw Molly sitting in the grass, and a slow smile came to his face. "Molly Merriwether."

"Roger! What are you doing here?" Molly started to get up but thought better of it, as her knees were inexplicably shaky. Probably the shock of seeing him so suddenly.

He just stared down at her as Penny ran in circles around both of them, barking.

Molly reached out to pat the dog, partially to gather herself before trying to speak. "What are you doing here?" she asked again.

He looked at her as if it was obvious. "I came to see

you."

"You did? But why?"

"I'm on my way home and Fred told me this is where you live. I couldn't pass by without saying hello."

"Did you go to the house?"

"I was heading there, but Penny shot off toward these trees. I thought she might be chasing another fox, but somehow she knew you were here."

"Maybe she remembered my perfume, but I don't know how she would have caught the scent from the road."

"She must have. That mix of orange and vanilla has a sweet, distinctive aroma." Roger looked away, but not before Molly saw the flush creep into his cheeks.

"When did you leave Rochester?" she asked as Penny lay down and leaned against her.

Roger sat beside Molly and stretched his legs out in front of him. "Two days ago."

"I thought you were staying through the summer."

"I was, but I had the feeling the Clarkes need some time alone."

Molly could only imagine how true that was. When she and Caroline had left, everyone was in a turmoil. Frankly, she was surprised Roger had stood the stress at the house for this long, although from what she'd seen, he was regarded as one of the family. "How are they all doing?" she asked.

Roger stared at the tips of his riding boots. "It depends which one you're asking about. Mr. and Mrs. Clarke are fine, though they still chastise Benedict at least once a day. He's more depressed than I've ever seen him. Fred's up to his usual antics."

"Poor Benedict," Molly said, rubbing Penny's silky

ears.

Roger met her eyes briefly, then looked away. "How have you been since you came home? Have you been enjoying yourself?"

"Mostly. For the first week Caroline and I were forbidden to visit each other, so I had to sneak out here to see her. But we've been doing that for years, so it was no trouble."

"How is Caroline?"

"She's doing as well as she can under the circumstances. She'll be better once she hears from Benedict. So, where do you live?"

He pointed east. "Concord. Two hours' ride, so it was easy to stop here on my way home."

"That's so close. I never asked, how do you know Fred?"

"We went to The Lombard School together."

"I can't picture Fred at school. Benedict, yes. But not Fred."

"He did get into his share of trouble."

Molly raised a brow. "And did you share in that trouble?"

Roger looked at her out of the corner of his eye, grinning. "I tried not to get drawn into it, but you know how Fred is."

"I certainly do."

It felt surreal to be talking to Roger in the shade of the willows as if not a day had gone by. Molly hadn't realized until she'd seen his face how much she'd missed him. She'd been so distracted by everything going on at home it hadn't really occurred to her until now how many times a day she'd wondered what he was doing, recalled things he'd said, or remembered things they'd done together.

A heavy silence filled the willow glade as their eyes met and held. Molly felt the inevitable heat in her cheeks, and when Roger smirked she looked away, wiping her suddenly moist palms on her skirt.

"I saw you in the attic the day I left," she said to break the silence.

Roger didn't answer, but she felt his eyes on her. Had he shifted closer?

"Did you find your treasure up there?" Molly asked.

"If you consider old books a treasure." His voice in her ear was much closer than she'd expected, and he laughed lightly when she jumped.

Were these actually goosebumps? Because of Roger? What had come over her? When she turned her head, his brown eyes were only inches away. Molly had never noticed how striking they were, or how soft his lips looked.

"Books are nice. So many people enjoy them. Books." And now she was speaking nonsense.

His brow creased but the grin remained. "What?"

"You asked if books could be considered a treasure and they could, really."

Before Roger could answer, the sound of voices came from just outside the willows. Something like ice cold water rushed through Molly's veins.

"Is she in there?" a man asked.

"She knew I was arriving today, I thought she'd be up at the house."

"Whose horse is that?"

Molly blanched and covered her face. Roger tried to pull her hands away, but she scrambled to her feet, straightening her clothes. "It's my brothers!" she hissed.

Roger stood up, acting for all the world as if they were in the drawing room and he'd just arrived for a prearranged meeting.

Albert came first, stopped short, and was almost knocked over by Tristan, who was right behind him. Michael came last, eyes narrowing when he saw Molly wasn't alone.

They all spoke at once.

"This is Mr. Bailey."

"Who is this?"

"What's going on?"

"It's nice to meet you."

"Who are you?"

Penny barked at Albert, Michael and Tristan, inviting them to play.

Molly put her hands up for quiet, and everyone besides Penny obeyed.

"May I introduce Mr. Bailey," she said as calmly as she could.

Roger extended his hand to Albert. "It's nice to—"

"From the tavern?" Albert asked and crossed his arms.

Roger looked at Molly. "What did you tell them?"

"She told us you took her to a tavern and weren't the most well behaved," Tristan replied.

Molly stomped her foot. "Tristan, I never said that!"

"You basically did," Albert argued.

Molly let out a huff and turned to Roger. "Please forgive my brothers. I didn't say anything of the sort. All I told them is that Fred took me there and I stayed with you while he fetched the carriage."

"Why would you stay there alone with Molly?" Michael demanded.

"Mol—Miss Merri—your sister helped me because I was under the weather."

"I can imagine," Tristan said dryly.

Molly glared at her brothers. "Have you gotten that out of your systems? Are you ready to be polite and meet my friend?"

Tristan, Michael and Albert stepped outside the willow glade and Molly heard them whispering.

"I do apologize," she said to Roger. "I didn't imply that you were anything but a gentleman."

"You lied to your own brothers?" he asked, eyes sparkling.

Molly lightly hit his arm, unable to hold back a grin. "*No.*"

"I was too far gone to be much of a gentleman, but thank you for saying I was."

"You were sweet and funny. I liked that side of you." She reddened. Had she really just said that?

"Blushing. You'd better hide that before your brothers come back."

This made her blush all the more. She turned away to pet Penny and didn't look at Roger again until her brothers returned.

"Albert Merriwether." He extended his hand, and Roger shook it. "And my brother, Tristan."

Tristan shook Roger's hand.

Michael made a slight bow. "I'm Michael."

"This is Mr. Roger Bailey," Molly said. "What were you three muttering about out there?"

"We've decided no harm came of you going to the tavern," Tristan said. "In fact, Mr. Bailey did us a favor because now you'll stop badgering us to take you."

"Not necessarily. I've only been to that one."

"I don't remember the whole evening clearly, but I didn't have the impression you liked it enough to want to try another one," Roger said.

"You're probably right," she said. "At least not any time soon. Well, shall we go in for tea?"

As they walked to the house Molly noticed Roger wasn't limping at all anymore. He walked ahead with Albert, leading Sparrow by the reins. Tristan, chased by Penny, ran to inform their mother that company was coming.

Molly was left to accompany Michael, who talked about the new house he and his wife Lydia had just moved into and apologized for her not accompanying him on the visit. He talked at length about the joy and security of matrimony, and Molly suspected Mrs. Merriwether had invited him to stay purely to convince her that she'd be happier once she was married. Molly tried to pay attention, but spent most of the walk wondering what Roger and Albert were laughing about.

Chapter Fifteen

As soon as Mrs. Merriwether met Roger she insisted he stay for dinner, not tea, and after the meal it had been surprisingly easy for Molly's brothers to persuade him to stay the night.

When everyone retired to the parlor after dinner, Molly assumed she'd have a chance to talk to Roger alone, but her whole family seemed to have decided he needed to be questioned thoroughly about everything he knew about the Clarkes and how Molly had spent her time at Waverly. She had to hand it to him, he answered every question honestly without divulging much at all.

After Mr. and Mrs. Merriwether went to bed, Molly's brothers whisked Roger away to the billiard room, making it clear she wasn't invited. The closest she'd come to communicating with him all night was a few smiles.

So now she sat beside the library fire, reading a book of sonnets while Penny lay at her feet. Close to eleven Molly tiptoed out of the room, trying not to wake the sleeping dog. Backing out of the doorway, she collided with someone on their way in. "Oh!"

"Ouch!"

It was Roger, looking a bit ruffled with his jacket unbuttoned and collar loosened.

Penny leapt to her feet and ran to greet him. He kneeled down to pet her, his eyes on Molly. "I'm sorry I left her with you so long, but she didn't want to leave your side when I went with your brothers."

"That's all right. I liked having her with me."

He rose, taking hold of Penny's collar. "I'll take her up to my room."

"You know the way?" Molly asked on their way out of the library.

"Yes, thank you. Are you going upstairs?"

Molly nodded, barely stifling a yawn as they walked down the hall to the staircase. "Did you enjoy your evening?"

"Yes. Your family is very hospitable."

His voice was low, as if he was bored or tired. She hoped it was the latter.

As they mounted the stairs, Molly trailed behind so Roger could go ahead with Penny. "I was surprised you decided to stay. Aren't you eager to get home?"

"Yes, but it's only two hours away. I'll leave first thing in the morning," he answered over his shoulder. "So I'll say goodbye now."

Molly pushed Penny's wagging tail out of her face as she addressed Roger's back. "Won't you stay for breakfast?" She'd planned to take him on a tour of the gardens.

When they reached the second-floor landing, Roger stopped. "No, I asked the groom to have Sparrow ready at first light."

"I see," Molly said, trying not to show her disappointment. "Well, Goodnight."

"Goodnight." The look on his face made her wonder if he regretted staying over.

As Molly walked down the hall she thought she felt his eyes on her, but when she turned back he was looking the other way.

When Molly went down for breakfast the next day, Roger was already gone. Albert and Tristan raved about him, and Mrs. Merriwether wanted to know all about him. Molly was surprised at how few facts she actually knew about Roger—only what he'd told them all at dinner the night before.

Molly had a sense of Roger that the others didn't, but it wasn't the type of thing she could describe or explain. She knew how it felt to be with him, and if someone pointed out a certain item, she'd be able to say, "Oh, yes, Roger would like that," or, "He'd detest that." Even though she had a good sense of him he often surprised her, which only made her want to understand him better. His quiet, strong presence set her at ease. Most of the time. At others she wondered if he'd rather be elsewhere. But then there were those *other* times, when she caught a certain gleam in his eye or a lilt in his voice. She had the feeling he was fond of her, or at least liked to tease her. But frustratingly, whenever they seemed on the brink of growing closer he pulled back. It was as though there was a line he wouldn't cross, but Molly didn't even know where it was.

Later that day Molly rode to Norbury Hall to tell Caroline about Roger's visit and get her opinion about his sometimes odd behavior.

She found Caroline with her aunt in the garden, facing each other like fencers at the end of a match.

Molly hesitated. "Am I interrupting something?"

"No, you aren't interrupting," Caroline said, gesturing for her to come over. "We were through."

"We're discussing Rochester," Aunt Hazel said.

Molly passed under the rose arch and moved to

Caroline's side. "I came over to ask if you've heard from Benedict."

Caroline twisted a button on her blouse. "No, and it's been three weeks since we left."

"I'm sure—" Molly began, but Aunt Hazel cut her off.

"Caroline, stop fiddling with your buttons! I've been telling you that since you were a girl. You'll only need to mend them later."

Caroline pressed her arms to her sides as if she was a wooden nutcracker. "Better?"

"Much," Aunt Hazel said. "Mr. Clarke will no doubt write when he has something to say. Perhaps he's keeping his distance in order to give both of you time to think about your actions and consider what you should have done differently."

"Auntie, *please* don't lecture me about that anymore."

"Lecture? It isn't a lecture. I'm merely pointing out that you both have some maturing to do."

Caroline crossed her arms. "Benedict is twenty-four years old. I'd say he's mature."

"His age has nothing to do with his maturity." Aunt Hazel clasped her hands in front of her and put on that expression Molly knew meant she wasn't going to argue about it.

"Benedict is very nice," Molly said. "Thoughtful, kind, responsible. You'd like him, Aunt Hazel."

"We'll see. I'm going in. Would you girls like to join me in the library?"

Molly answered before Caroline could. "No, we'll stay out here."

Aunt Hazel turned on her heel and walked away.

Caroline's shoes crunched on the gravel as she paced along the garden path. "I hope we don't hear one more word about Waverly Hall from Auntie or our parents. You'd think they'd had their say."

"Speaking of Waverly, you'll never guess who came to my house yesterday."

Caroline came to an abrupt halt. "Your house? Who?"

"Roger. He was on his way home and stopped in to say hello, then accepted my brothers' invitation to stay the night."

"How extraordinary! Did he say anything about Benedict?"

Molly debated about how much to tell her. It sounded as though Benedict wasn't doing very well, which might upset her. On the other hand, not knowing anything at all could be worse.

"Roger said he's depressed. I'm sure he must miss you."

"Then why doesn't he write?" Caroline held her hands up in front of her. "No—don't answer that. I'm tired of talking about Benedict. Tell me about Roger's visit. What did you do?"

"Had dinner with the family, then my brothers took him away and I didn't see him until it was time for bed. He left before I woke up so I didn't see much of him, really." Molly looked down, sighing. "We didn't have any time alone."

"You wanted to be *alone* with him? Why are you blushing?"

"I'm not." She was.

"Hm. He came all this way to see you, but not me, even though I'm right next door. You'd think he would visit both of us. Why would that be?"

Molly hadn't considered it until this moment. Did the visit mean more than she'd realized? He'd looked so happy to see her in the willows. But then she thought of his manner last night. Not cold, but certainly not friendly. "I don't know."

Caroline gripped her hands. "Molly, is there something between you and Roger that I don't know about?"

"Not unless it's something I don't know about, either."

"What does that mean?"

"It means there's nothing between Roger and me." Molly walked over to a bench under the vine-covered trellis and sat down. "Sometimes, during our time in Rochester, I thought Roger and I were becoming friends. But the next thing I knew, he'd be virtually ignoring me."

Caroline took a seat beside her. "He did have that way about him, didn't he?"

"You noticed it, too?" It would be a relief to know it wasn't something personal he only did with Molly.

"I noticed him doing it to you. He and I didn't spend much time together, so he didn't have the chance to warm up to me and then act like I wasn't there. But I'd say, in a way, he did it to the whole group at times. I assumed he likes to be alone."

"I thought that, too. But at other times he could be almost…charming."

Caroline scrunched up her nose. "Roger, charming? Really?"

"He has a way about him sometimes," Molly said, twirling a lock of hair around her finger.

"When will you see him again?"

"I'm not sure. We didn't make any plans."

"Well, I do wish he'd stopped to visit. I would have liked to ask him about Benedict. Did he say if he'd be back?"

"He didn't mention it. But he only lives in Concord, so I suppose he could come back at any time."

The next moment, the door opened and a footman walked down the path. "There's a gentleman here for you, Miss Darby. A Mr.—"

"Oh, he's come back!" Caroline exclaimed, interrupting him. "Please show him out to the garden."

The footman bowed and went back into the house.

"What a surprise," Molly said. "And so thoughtful. Perhaps he'll stay for tea. We could take him on a ride around town if he has time."

They both rose, eyes on the door.

Molly clasped her hands in front of her, trying to maintain a relaxed expression. She would never have expected Roger to return so soon. He must not have made it halfway home before deciding to call on Caroline.

The door opened and a gentleman hurried down the path, his eyes on Caroline. She fell back onto the bench. "Benedict!"

He stopped a few feet from her and stared. "Caroline," he whispered.

Molly glanced at the door to see if Roger was with him, but he was alone. She stepped off to the side as Caroline and Benedict looked at each other, feeling as though she'd intruded on a private conversation, though they didn't speak.

Molly coughed twice before Caroline looked up. "I'll go get your aunt. Or your mother? Or we could all go inside."

It was Benedict who answered, though he didn't take his eyes off Caroline. "Not just yet, if you please, Molly."

Caroline flushed prettily. "Molly, would you please stand over by the door, behind the rhododendrons? You can war—tell us if anyone is on their way out."

"Yes, I'd be happy to. But I won't be able to avoid hearing what you say."

"It's all right if you do," Benedict said. "Everyone will know of it soon enough." He paused and added, his voice cracking, "I hope."

Caroline gazed at Benedict as he approached the bench and kneeled in front of her.

Molly hurried over to her place behind the rhododendrons. It wasn't long before she heard what she'd been expecting the moment Benedict walked through the door. A heartfelt proposal, a squeal, and "Yes!" followed by a longer than anticipated silence. She was just about to go inside when Caroline called for her to come back.

On the bench, Benedict and Caroline sat with their arms around each other, beaming.

"Look." Caroline extended her hand to show Molly a diamond ring. "We're betrothed!"

"Congratulations!" Molly said, smiling. "Should I get your mother now?"

The next day Benedict went home with a promise to meet Caroline at the altar, three weeks hence. Caroline was perpetually walking on a cloud and couldn't say or hear enough of Benedict. She asked Molly to be her maid of honor, as they'd planned since they were children, and they spent hours discussing the wedding.

The only damper on the happy time was Mrs. Merriwether's abrupt change of heart about Molly staying with Caroline in Rochester. All the talk of weddings and trousseaus had apparently made her desperate to see her own daughter settled.

"But you said if Caroline went back to Waverly I could accompany her," Molly said, standing in front of her mother's desk.

Mrs. Merriwether, arranging flowers in a porcelain vase, didn't even look up. "Of course we'll go to the wedding, but we'll come home straightaway after the reception."

"Caroline wants me to wait for her while she's on her honeymoon. We thought I might help her settle in once she gets back."

Mrs. Merriwether removed her spectacles and looked up at Molly. "Caroline will need to devote her time to Mr. Clarke, so there's no reason for you to stay. Furthermore," she went on, "I see no reason why you shouldn't have your Season this year."

Molly blanched. "It's three months away! I'll never be ready in time."

"Oh, fiddlesticks. There's nothing to prepare. You already have your gowns, and I don't think you'll grow anymore talented between now and next year. I mean no offense, my dear, I only mean to say you're already accomplished."

Molly ran her fingers along the edge of the desk. "But what about Caroline?"

"Trust me, Molly, Caroline will be just fine without you. She doesn't yet understand how…preoccupied she and Mr. Clarke will be with each other. We'll go to the wedding and afterwards stop at home for a few days before going to town. With any luck, it will be you getting married this time next year." She stared dreamily at the ceiling, probably picturing Molly walking down the aisle.

Molly plucked a peony off her mother's pile of discarded blooms. "What does Father say to all this?"

"He says he'll leave it up to me." Her mother carried the vase to the windowsill. "I've spoken to Mrs. Darby, and she's been most helpful. She's connected me to all the right people and said she'll come stay with us for a time in town. She has been through four Seasons, after all."

Molly followed her and reunited the peony with its fellows. "I always imagined going through this with Caroline."

Mrs. Merriwether patted her shoulder. "I know. But she doesn't need it, and you do. Albert and Tristan are going to come along, so they'll attend balls with you when I can't. They'll look after you and might even meet someone while they're there."

Molly couldn't see how she'd find a suitor with her brothers shadowing her all night, but she didn't bother mentioning this to her mother.

Caroline was sympathetic when Molly told her of her mother's plans. "Didn't you tell her I need you with me?"

"Yes, but she's convinced you and Benedict will be, well…busy with each other."

"I suppose." Caroline blushed. "But that won't take all day. Do you think there's a chance she'll change her mind?"

"I doubt it. She's already spoken to your mother and made arrangements to travel to town shortly after the wedding."

Caroline gave Molly an obviously forced smile. "You'll enjoy it. I know you will. You only need to allow yourself to. We've both been talking about how dreadful the Season would be for years, but really, there are worse things than going to balls and meeting new people. If I wasn't about to marry Benedict, I imagine we'd be looking forward to it."

Skeptical, Molly just nodded.

The following weeks were a jumble of visits to the shops, dress fittings, long talks about Benedict, and whispered guesses about the wedding night. Caroline had asked her married sisters what to expect, but they refused to tell her anything.

Molly looked forward to the wedding for a number of reasons, one of which was that she knew Roger had been invited. She hadn't spoken to Caroline about him since that day in the garden, but that was understandable considering Caroline had become betrothed not half an hour after the conversation. Molly wasn't sure what she'd say, at any rate. She couldn't deny she found Roger intriguing, but he didn't make it easy to get close to him.

The night before they left for Rochester, Molly slept at Norbury so she and Caroline could have "one last night as girls," as Caroline said. They spent the night reminiscing about their girlhood days. Even though they planned to write, visit, and stay in touch, they both knew things wouldn't be the same after Caroline became Mrs. Benedict Clarke.

Chapter Sixteen

With three carriages and multiple people on horseback, Molly and Caroline's arrival at Waverly Hall couldn't have been more different from last time. They rode ahead of their families; there was no need for a chaperone now. The Clarkes stood at the foot of the stairs, waiting to welcome them. The moment Caroline stepped out of the carriage, she was swept into Benedict's arms.

Fred offered Molly his arm. "Good to see you, Molly."

"It's nice to see you, too." It seemed rude to immediately ask if Roger was there, so she instead asked after his health.

"Fine, fine. We've been busy getting ready for the wedding. I'm the best man."

"I thought you might be. I'm the maid of honor."

"Then I'll be walking you down the aisle." He gave Molly a brilliant smile, with no ill effects whatsoever to her stomach. Apparently, she was now immune to Fred's beauty.

When they reached the crowded parlor, Molly automatically looked to the corner where Roger usually sat, but it was empty. She supposed he would be arriving later in the week.

"Will all these people be staying over for the wedding?" Molly asked.

Fred didn't answer, as he was staring at Kitty.

Molly nudged his arm. "Fred?"

He shook his head as if recollecting the question. "Yes, they've been coming in droves. Most of them aren't local and will be sleeping here, like the entourage from Hartford. Where's your family?"

Molly pointed to her parents and brothers, who'd just walked into the room. "There they are."

"Let's go say hello," Fred said.

After introductions, Albert craned his neck to look around the parlor. "Is Mr. Bailey here? We'd hoped to see him again."

"Again?" Fred asked. "You know Roger?"

"He stopped by to see me on his way home and met my family," Molly said, trying to keep her tone matter-of-fact and her cheeks pale.

"Did he, now?" Fred asked.

Molly nodded, avoiding his inquisitive stare.

"Is he here?" Tristan asked, drawing Fred's attention.

Seemingly reluctant to take his eyes off Molly, Fred turned to Tristan. "Yes, but his dog is sick and he's fussing over her. You'll see him later."

Molly pressed Fred's arm. "Penny's sick? What's wrong?"

"I have no idea. Probably nothing serious. My beagles often look a bit under the weather, but they perk up soon enough."

Molly doubted they simply "perked up." She knew the head groom kept a close eye on the dogs and probably called in the veterinarian at the first sign of trouble.

"You have beagles?" Tristan asked.

"A whole pack," Fred said proudly. "And some

bassets."

"Wha—" Mr. Merriwether started to ask, but Molly interrupted him, drawing a glare from her mother.

"Where's Penny?" Molly asked Fred.

"The kennel? The quadrangle? I don't know." Fred released her arm as he began an animated discussion with Albert, Tristan and Molly's father.

Mrs. Merriwether and Molly left the men to discuss the dogs. Her mother took a seat on the settee and helped herself to a cup of coffee, motioning for Molly to join her. Molly tried to slip past but hadn't gone two steps before she felt a tug on the back of her gown.

Pulling free, she turned around. "Please excuse me, Mother. I'll be back soon."

"A word, Molly." Mrs. Merriwether gave her a stern look, crooking a finger.

Barely resisting running away or flopping theatrically onto the settee, Molly sat and posed herself as though ready to have her portrait painted, complete with faux smile. "Yes?"

Her mother leaned in close, stirring her coffee. "You aren't going in search of Mr. Bailey, are you? That would be *most* forward."

"I want to ask him about his dog. There might be something I can do to help the poor girl."

Mrs. Merriwether lowered her voice to a whisper. "Surely that can wait. I could plainly see how happy you were to hear that Mr. Bailey is here."

Molly flushed. "He's my friend, Mother. I'll be pleased to see him."

"Is that all?" Her mother narrowed her eyes at Molly's cheeks.

"What do you mean?"

After searching her eyes for a moment, Mrs. Merriwether straightened. "Never mind. But don't go chasing after him. Perhaps Caroline could tell you about the dog."

"Maybe. I think I'll get some air."

Molly grabbed a plate of food on her way out to the quadrangle. It was peaceful and quiet after the parlor, but there was no sign of Penny or Roger. She started for the kennel, then stopped. Roger wouldn't take his sick dog there. If he'd brought Penny to his room, there was no way she'd find him. Since the house was so crowded, the most likely place was the office. She crossed the quadrangle and opened the door Roger had led them through all those weeks ago. When she reached the office, she stood outside for a moment, debating whether to knock or just go in.

As Molly stood there, she heard a low whine. Penny was definitely inside. She opened the door and went in, where she found Penny lying on the floor in front of the hearth. Sitting beside her, Roger looked so worried Molly had to fight the urge to go over and hug him. His face was drawn and there were dark shadows under his eyes. Fear gripped her. How sick *was* Penny?

"Roger?"

Her quiet greeting made him jump and he looked up quickly, a hand to his chest. "You startled me." When he gave Penny a pat and stood up, the dog didn't stir. Roger stretched, and Molly guessed he'd been sitting there for a long time. He rubbed his eyes. "When did you get here?"

"Would you like me to fetch some tea?" It was the first thing she thought of, and it brought a small smile to his face.

"No, thank you."

She held out the plate of food she'd brought—an assortment of fruit, sandwiches and savory tarts. "Would you like something to eat?"

"That I will say yes to. Maybe we can persuade Penny to eat something."

"What's the matter with her? Fred said she's sick."

Roger resumed his place on the floor. "I wish I knew."

Molly sat beside him and they offered food to Penny, but she turned away. They shared it between themselves, and after a time Molly leaned forward to scratch Penny's ears. "How long has she been like this?"

"Her condition varies from day to day. She isn't always interested in food and the other day she snapped at Fred. She's never done that. She's been sleeping often and, as you can see, not acting like herself. Have you ever walked into a room without her running over to greet you? When she whined earlier, it must have been because she knew you were outside the door. That may be a good sign."

He looked into Molly's blue eyes as if for reassurance. Without thinking, she took Roger's hand. He immediately entwined his fingers with hers and she suspected he, too, had acted without thinking.

Fortunately, Molly had an idea of what was troubling Penny. "Has she been chewing things lately?"

He looked surprised. "Yes. A blanket from my bed and three ties. How did you know?"

"Have you spoken to the head groom about her?"

"No. I hoped it would pass. What do you think is wrong with her?" His grip on her hand tightened.

Molly ran a hand over Penny's stomach, and her

suspicions were confirmed. "Nothing's wrong, Roger. She's going to have puppies."

"Puppies!" He looked at Penny as though he'd never even considered the possibility. "You're certain?"

"Yes. I've seen it before, with our dogs at home. Haven't you?"

Roger's whole body visibly relaxed. "Yes, but it never occurred to me. I thought Penny ate something odd or had an internal injury."

"Apparently not."

Roger laughed and raked a hand through his untidy hair. "Molly, I'd already been hoping you'd arrive sooner, but now I wish I'd gone to your house to bring you here days ago. What a lot of worry I could have been saved."

Molly blushed at his comments, but he seemed not to notice.

He looked at Penny in wonder, shaking his head.

"I'm surprised nobody else thought of it," Molly said. "Fred, for instance. One of his bassets had puppies not long ago."

"Oh, those bassets. I'd wager one of them is responsible for this."

"I doubt either one of you would have been able to keep the dogs apart if they'd really wanted to…"

"Be together?" he suggested, apparently amused by her embarrassment.

"Yes. Do you mind about it?"

Roger rubbed Penny's back. "Oh, no. But I wouldn't have chosen one of Fred's unruly bassets for a father."

"With Penny as their mother, the puppies are bound to be sweet."

He smiled. "I'm sure you're right."

Roger released Molly's hand and crossed to a desk in the corner of the room, where glasses and a number of crystal decanters stood on a silver tray. He returned a moment later and offered his hand to help Molly up, then gave her a glass of sherry.

As they stood facing each other, he clinked his glass against hers. "To Penny."

"Penny," Molly said and grinned.

The tension had melted away from Roger's face and he looked like he could barely stop smiling. "Is your family here?"

"Most of them. Michael and Lydia couldn't come. Is yours?"

"Not yet. Penny has a cold, so they aren't certain they'll make it."

"I hope they do. I've looked forward to meeting Penny's namesake. Or is Penny Penny's namesake?" she asked and sipped her sherry.

"Either way, you'll meet her eventually. She says you sound interesting and she wants to meet you."

Roger put his empty glass on the side table.

"She does?" Molly asked.

"Yes. Well, I did tell her all about you. You and Caroline." Was it her imagination, or was Roger blushing?

Roger kneeled down to pat Penny. "I wonder how long until the pups are born."

"A few weeks? It's hard to tell." Molly finished her drink and set her glass beside Roger's.

He rose, took her hands and stepped closer. "I should have told you sooner. I'm glad to see you, Molly Merriwether."

Why did his handsome looks always surprise her?

And what was that soft tone in his voice?

"I'm glad to see you, too," she said.

They stood gazing at each other for a few minutes until Roger looked away and released her hands. "What about that tea now?" he asked.

She had the feeling that wasn't what he'd been about to say, but smiled up at him. "Yes. Yes, that sounds perfect."

Chapter Seventeen

"Three days," Caroline said, gazing at her wedding gown. The high-necked bodice and puffed sleeves were covered in fine lace, but the long, flowing skirt was smooth satin.

"Does it seem so long to you?" Molly stood beside her, sipping a cup of tea.

"An eternity."

Molly smiled. "It will pass quickly. More guests are arriving every day, we're going riding tomorrow, and there's the banquet the day after that. And then, of course, the wedding the next day."

"I'd like to skip all of it and marry Benedict today."

Kitty, who was helping them unpack, said, "It's so romantic. Not all brides are as anxious as you to say their vows."

"Who wouldn't be?" Caroline asked, turning to face her.

"Women who aren't marrying for love," Kitty said.

Caroline clasped her hands together. "I am."

"We know," Molly said, smiling. "Here, sit down and have some tea. You've hardly eaten anything all afternoon."

When Caroline sat on the sofa, Kitty handed her a cup of tea and a plate of sandwiches.

"Your dress is perfect," Caroline said to Molly.

Molly ran her hand over the blue gown hanging

beside Caroline's. It had a wide neckline that showed off Molly's shoulders, and a tiered skirt decorated with pink roses. "Thank you. You did choose it."

"The color will bring out your eyes," Caroline went on. "Perhaps you'll meet someone at the wedding and won't need your Season after all."

Molly joined her on the sofa. "I doubt that. Isn't it mainly your cousins and other gentlemen I've known for years?"

"No. Benedict is inviting people we've never met." Caroline gave her a sly look. "And some we *have* met."

Molly prayed she wouldn't mention anything about Roger in front of Kitty.

And she didn't.

Caroline said something even more surprising. "Fred will be there."

"Fred!" Molly exclaimed.

Across the room, a vase slipped from Kitty's hands and crashed to the floor.

Molly and Caroline jumped to their feet.

"Are you all right?" Molly asked.

Kitty, flustered, nodded. "I'm so sorry. I'll clean this up right away."

"Don't worry, Kitty. Benedict will send more tomorrow," Caroline said.

After Kitty gathered the broken pieces and hurried from the room, Molly and Caroline resumed their places on the sofa.

"Well. That was unlike her," Caroline said, reaching for her half-eaten sandwich.

"It must have been wet and she couldn't keep hold of it. Caroline, don't try to play matchmaker between me and Fred."

"But he's so pleasant and funny. *Very* handsome."

"No."

"We could be sisters!" Caroline said, grabbing Molly's hand.

Molly laughed. "We practically already are. I love you like one, so there's no reason for me to marry Fred."

"I suppose you're right."

"More importantly," Molly said hesitantly, "Kitty likes him."

Caroline let out a small gasp. "No!"

Molly clicked her tonge. "You knew that, but Benedict's driven everything else from your mind."

"I wouldn't have forgotten something like that."

Molly now tried to recall if she'd actually come right out and told Caroline of her suspicions. She knew she hadn't told her what she'd heard about Kitty's upbringing.

"Caroline, has Benedict told you anything about Kitty? About her past?"

"Her past?" Caroline paused in the middle of choosing a petit-four from the tea tray. "No, not that I recall."

Molly recounted everything she'd learned about Kitty, including her suspicions about Fred's feelings for her.

Caroline put a hand to her cheek. "The poor dear! And Mrs. Lane being so terrible to her. But do you really think there's something romantic going on between her and Fred?"

"I'm almost positive," Molly said and helped herself to a mini sponge cake.

After apparently ruminating over this new development for a time, Caroline clapped her hands together. "I should invite Kitty to the wedding! They could dance."

Molly shook her head. "It wouldn't be allowed."

"It's *my* wedding."

"The Clarkes would allow you to invite their maid?"

"She isn't a typical maid, but I suspect you're right."

"You're sweet to want to help her."

"If Kitty and Fred have a chance at love, we should help them. You do think he loves her? He isn't merely amusing himself with her?"

Molly remembered the look in Fred's eyes when he saw Kitty sometimes, and his anger at her being mistreated. Even if he wasn't in love with her, he genuinely cared for her. Who was to say it couldn't grow into more? "I believe he might."

They sat in silence, eating pastries that had been brought up with the tea tray.

Suddenly an idea—a simple, maybe impossible idea—came to Molly. "Caroline…"

"Oh! You've thought up a scheme."

"What if we disguised Kitty for the ball?"

Caroline fell back against the sofa cushions as if sorely disappointed in Molly's efforts. "That would never work."

"Why not?"

"Everyone here knows Kitty. Anyone who lives in Rochester will recognize her."

"Not necessarily. We'll lend her a gown, and perhaps rouge." Molly looked ready to go buy Kitty a new dress that moment. "Oh, let's try."

"All right. We'll ask her." Caroline rose and tugged the bell pull, then rejoined Molly on the sofa.

Kitty arrived within minutes. "What can I do for

you?"

"Come sit with us," Molly said. "We want to talk to you."

"I can hear you well enough from here." Kitty stood in front of them, arms at her sides.

Knowing there was no delicate way to put it, Molly began. "Kitty, I've heard about your upbringing and what happened to your parents. I'm sorry you're in this situation. I know it can't make things any easier, but I hope you'll look on me as a friend. If not for your circumstances, we'd probably have met at a ball or through the Clarkes."

Kitty opened her mouth to speak, but Caroline broke in before she could try to reply. "We don't want to make you feel awkward by broaching the subject, but just know we think you're very brave and if we could avoid treating you like a maid, we would. It doesn't seem fair that you're working here instead of visiting as a guest."

Fiddling with her apron strings, Kitty cleared her throat. "You're too kind. Both of you. I—" Her chin came up a notch. "It isn't for life to be fair, and I chose my lot. I came here knowing, mostly, what to expect. It was either work here or move away and become a companion to my great-aunt, but I couldn't bear to leave…Rochester."

She looked down at the floor, and Molly could tell she was about to take her leave. Before she could, Molly plowed ahead. "There's something else, Kitty. We know you like Fred, and we want you to come to Caroline's wedding so you can dance with him."

Then Kitty did sit down. Her voiced quivered. "Who told you that?"

"Nobody," Caroline said. "Molly suspected it, and

from the look on your face she's right."

Kitty put her face in her hands and wept.

"Oh, dear." Molly poured a cup of tea and placed it on the table next to Kitty.

Once Kitty had taken a few sips and composed herself, she wiped her eyes. "You're right. I do like Fred. I always have."

"Does he know?" Caroline asked.

"Oh, yes. We were friendly with each other…before."

Molly leaned forward. "But not courting?"

"No. It hadn't gotten to that point yet."

"How are things now?" Caroline asked.

"Impossible." Kitty shook her head. "We live in the same house but we might as well be a hundred miles apart."

"Have you ever talked about your feelings for each other?" Molly asked.

"Not exactly, but…"

"You don't need to," Caroline said. "Because it's clear to you both."

Kitty nodded. "Yes, but it doesn't matter. Nothing can come of it."

"Of course it matters!" Molly said.

"I have nothing to offer him. He can't marry me—his parents would never allow it." Kitty sighed. "I should leave, really, but I can't bear to. I'd rather stay here and be near Fred than move away and never see him again."

They were all silent, Kitty's words hanging in the air.

Caroline was the first to speak. "You're coming to my wedding ball."

"I can't. The Clarkes wouldn't approve."

"One Clarke would," Molly said. "Imagine the look on Fred's face when he sees you at the ball, not covered by an apron but in a gown, with your hair done and a fan strategically placed to disguise you from everyone else. Fred would recognize you, wouldn't he?"

"He would." Kitty laughed. "He'd better."

"It's settled," Caroline said. "The night of my wedding ball, you'll come up here and change into one of my gowns."

"We'll tell Mrs. Lane you're ill and not to be disturbed. Once the ballroom is full, you'll slip in unnoticed and find Fred," Molly said.

Kitty's eyes glistened with tears. "Thank you. If I could have even one dance with him…one night where he sees me as I used to be, before all this…to be in his arms…" She wiped her cheeks with the corner of her apron.

"Do you have a gown, or will you borrow one of ours?" Molly asked.

"I brought one with me from the parsonage. I wore it to a ball a few years ago. It isn't the latest fashion, but it will do. If Fred was paying any attention to me that night, he'll recognize it."

"Bring it to our room later to air it out," Caroline said.

Molly glanced at the clock. "It's time we all went downstairs for dinner. We'll work out the details of the ball later."

Before she opened the door, Kitty paused. "I cannot thank you enough. This means more to me than you know."

Molly put a hand on her arm. "We're happy to do it. We haven't forgotten how you tried to keep our being here unchaperoned a secret."

"That's right," Caroline said. "You've been so kind from the moment we arrived, not looking askance at us like some other people I won't mention."

"This is the very least we can do to thank you," Molly said.

Kitty gave them a watery smile, wiped her eyes and led the way downstairs.

Dinner was a long, boisterous affair in the great hall. Molly was seated between Aunt Hazel and Benedict's school friend Lou. He was very handsome and Molly suspected Caroline had seated her next to him on purpose. They kept up a steady conversation through most of the meal, with Aunt Hazel breaking into their talk when she could. Roger was on the other side of the table, sandwiched between two talkative women. Molly tried to catch his eye once or twice, but he didn't appear to notice.

Caroline sat with Benedict at the head of the table, happier than Molly had ever seen her. As Molly watched them she felt an unexpected twinge of jealousy. After the wedding it would no longer be Molly but Benedict who came first in Caroline's life. This was as it should be, and Molly wished Caroline nothing but joy. Still, the marriage would change the relationship she'd depended on all her life.

When the meal ended, everyone retired to the library and parlor. The doors to the quadrangle had been thrown open, and some guests found their way out to the moonlit courtyard. After mingling and chatting for an hour, Molly found Roger standing beside the library window, holding a glass of wine.

She greeted him with a smile. "Good evening."

"Good evening," he said, staring straight ahead.

"How's Penny?"

"Fine, thank you."

When he didn't elaborate, Molly inquired further. "Is she still in the office?"

He nodded and drained his glass.

"Are you enjoying yourself?" she asked.

Roger took a step away from her. "Yes, thank you. Are you?"

She didn't answer. Why was he acting this way? Was he worried about Penny? Was he tired? Molly tried to catch his eye, but he steadfastly looked away. Well, she didn't know if Roger was tired, but she was. Tired of his cold shoulder. She'd never known anyone to have such mercurial moods from hour to hour. This afternoon Molly had thought Roger was glad to see her and that they were on friendly terms again, but apparently she'd been wrong.

"I'll say goodnight," Molly said, and walked away before he could nod at her again.

The next morning, most of the wedding guests assembled for a ride through the forest. Molly relished the fresh air and time away from the crowded house. She positioned herself close to Caroline and Benedict at the head of the large group, but the fast pace didn't provide an opportunity for conversation.

At midday, they reached a clearing that had been set up for luncheon. With rows of tables and abundant food, it was a far cry from the riverside picnic they'd had the day Mr. and Mrs. Clarke returned.

Molly dismounted and settled Opal with the other horses, then helped herself to lunch and wandered over to a stand of trees. She removed her hat and tossed it on the ground next to her. Caroline gestured for Molly to join her, but she shook her head. The glade was too peaceful to give up for a packed table.

After her meal, Molly noticed Roger having an animated discussion with Fred, Tristan and Albert. She was tempted to join them, but had the feeling it was the sort of talk that stopped when ladies appeared. Since the picnic showed no signs of ending anytime soon, Molly set her plate and glass aside, closed her eyes and leaned against a tree.

Not long after, she heard footsteps approaching.

"You have a bad habit of sleeping on trees." It was Albert.

She kept her eyes closed. "I'm not sleeping."

"It looks like you are," Tristan said.

"How many times have we come across Moll asleep in the willows?" Albert asked.

"Too many to count."

Molly opened her eyes. "I'm relaxing and listening to the leaves rustle."

"Why listen to that when you could talk with us?" Albert asked, stretching out on the grass.

"I talk to you all the time," Molly said. "Or do you have something particular you'd like to say to me?"

"No." Tristan sat beside her, leaned against the tree and closed his eyes.

Molly wanted to ask what they'd discussed with Roger but it would be nosy, and if they suspected she liked him she'd never hear the end of it. Anyway, she didn't like him. Not that way. A tiny voice inside called her a liar. But really, how *could* she like him? Whenever she thought they were growing close he started ignoring her. Like today. They'd ridden all morning and had been at the picnic for over an hour, yet he hadn't sought her out once or even looked her way. If she was going to have feelings for someone, it should preferably be someone who paid attention to her. And if she was going to be honest, at least with herself, then fine—She did find him fascinating. And handsome. And he could be amusing. Well, yes, he was clever and smart and interesting to talk to. At times, the affection he held for Penny melted Molly's heart. But aside from those things, what was to like about Roger? He teased her and called her a blusher. Nobody else had ever called her out on her inexplicably flush-prone cheeks. So add rude to what was *not* to like about him. She folded her arms across her chest, glowering.

"What's the matter?" Albert asked.

"What?" she snapped.

Albert pretended to back away as though she were a poisonous snake.

Tristan shifted to look into her face. "You look…angry."

"I'm not angry." She glanced toward the table, where luncheon was lasting forever. "When are we leaving?"

"What's wrong, Moll?" Albert asked.

"Nothing."

Tristan put an arm around her. "Come, you can tell us. Is it Caroline?"

"What are you talking about?" she asked.

"Mother thinks you're sulking because Caroline's getting all the attention," Albert said.

"Why would I be sulking?" She looked him in the eyes. "Wait. Are you joking?"

"She said you wish you were the one getting

married, and that's why you want your Season this year," Tristan added.

Molly was almost speechless. "I'm not sulking, and I *don't* want my Season this year. Why would Mother tell you that?"

Molly caught an irritated glance pass between her brothers.

"Perhaps to convince us we need to travel to town with you next month," Albert said and groaned.

"You should have heard her, Molly," Tristan said. "Mother said you're depressed and want to find a husband as soon as possible, and the only way you'd have your Season is if we're there to support you. She said that. *Support* you."

Molly's laughter bubbled up and soon her brothers joined in.

"She's diabolical," Molly said when she could speak again.

Tristan wiped his eyes. "She wants you to be a bride, Molly."

"Don't look so smug. She also wants the two of you to *find* brides."

"No," Albert said. "She merely wants to fuss over you."

"I wouldn't be so sure. I think she'd like more daughters to fuss over," Molly said.

"Maybe we should tell her we can't make it to town," Tristan suggested.

"I already tried putting it off for a year, but she said no," Molly said. "If I'm going, you're going with me."

"Ah, well. We'll make the most of it," Albert said.

Molly grinned. "If you two are with me, it will at least be amusing."

Across the clearing, people were finally standing up from the table.

"Looks like it's time to go," Tristan said.

"Will you ride back with us, Moll, or do you want to sulk over Caroline on the way home?" Albert asked.

Molly pretended to deliberate before answering. "I've done enough sulking for one day. I'll ride with you."

"Good," Tristan said. "Roger and Fred are joining us."

If Molly had known that ahead of time, she would have declined their invitation. She wasn't in the mood for Roger's indifference today.

The men raced home at a full gallop, Opal easily holding her own against them. Whenever the trail forced them to slow, Molly chatted with her brothers and Fred. Roger occasionally offered comments to the group in general, but was quiet for the most part and didn't make any attempt to engage Molly in conversation. She supposed this was just his way and would try not to take it personally. But in future she wouldn't assume Roger was her friend simply because they sometimes passed a pleasant half hour together.

Chapter Eighteen

As soon as she returned from the ride, Molly went to her bedchamber. After changing into a cream-colored gown with a blue sash, she picked up her book and went downstairs. She'd intended to read in the library, but it was full of chatting ladies. As were the parlor, the drawing room, and the garden.

The quadrangle, too, was replete with wedding guests. Greeting people as she passed, Molly crossed the courtyard to the north wing. She hesitated before knocking on the office door. What if Roger was in there? He clearly didn't want to talk to her today. Well, she could always leave. She knocked and, when there was no answer, went inside. Penny was sitting beside Roger's empty chair.

"Hello, girl," Molly said, kneeling beside her.

Penny gave a wag of her tail and leaned against Molly's legs. After petting her for a time and seeing that her food and water dishes were full, Molly left. She'd have liked to stay with Penny, but there was too great a chance of encountering Roger. She stood in the hall, tapping her book against her thigh. Where could she go? The dining room? The forest? And then it hit her. Humming, she headed to the east wing.

The attic was exactly what she needed—empty and quiet. Molly made her way to the alcove and went straight to that old trunk she'd seen the day she came upstairs with Caroline. She lifted the heavy lid, holding her breath as she waited for silk gowns or sparkling gems to appear. Molly laughed at herself as she ran her hands over yellowed linens monogrammed with an elegant "C" for Clarke.

She let the lid close and considered stretching out in the box bed but opted for the sofa. After the busy morning and crowded house, settling in for a long read was the utmost luxury. The only thing that could have made it better was if she'd brought herself a drink. It was awfully warm up here. Molly rose and opened the window nearest to her. Cool, fresh air rushed in, ruffling the bed curtains. She kicked off her shoes and sat on the sofa, her back against the armrest. Glancing at the watch pinned to her blouse, she was pleased to see there were hours before dinner.

Three hours later, Molly was stretched out fully on the sofa, an arm behind her head, wiggling her toes in the breeze coming through the open window. She'd just started the next chapter when she heard a click. Looking up, she saw nothing amiss; only dust swirling in shafts of sunlight. Assuming the noise had come from outside, she brought her attention back to her book.

Lost in the story again, she didn't hear the footsteps on the stairs, or the attic door opening, or someone tiptoeing across the room. But she did notice the shadow that fell across her page. Annoyed, she shifted her position to make the shadow disappear. When this didn't work, she rose to adjust the window shutters. That was how Molly ended up nose-to-nose—or rather, nose-to-chest—with Roger.

Molly's breath came out in a whoosh. She dropped her book and would have stumbled backwards if Roger hadn't caught her in his arms. His own book thumped to the floor after hers. Molly wanted to ask what he was doing here, but she'd never been this close to his velvety brown eyes. They looked lighter today, and sunshine streaming through the windows picked up tiny hints of gold she'd never noticed before. His breath was sweet and seemed fast under the circumstances. Perhaps he'd been startled, too. When he'd caught her, Molly's hands automatically latched onto his upper arms, her fingers pressing into harder-than-expected muscles. Not thinking why, she spread her hands out over them, feeling the heat through the thin fabric of his shirt. His chest brushed her bodice and she craned her neck to look into his face. When he swallowed, the muscles moving in his throat were oddly mesmerizing. Molly's cheeks reddened, but for once Roger didn't mention it. She would have stepped out of his embrace but she had nowhere to go, and besides, his arms were still tight around her. They stood like that for what could have been a moment or an hour.

When Molly finally broke the silence, her voice came out in a whisper. "What…what are you doing here?"

Roger looked into her eyes as he took what looked like a reluctant step back, and their hands fell away from each other.

"I was looking for someplace quiet," he said.

"So was I."

Roger bent to pick up his jacket, which Molly hadn't even noticed he'd dropped, and both their books. "Am I interrupting?" he asked.

The answer was yes, of course.

He must have read her eyes, because he started

backing away. "I'll leave if you'd rather be alone."

"No, you don't need to go. As long as—"

Roger cocked a brow. "As long as I'm quiet?"

"Yes," she said lightly. "I couldn't find anywhere downstairs that isn't full of people."

"Neither could I, even the office. Mr. Clarke is hiding in there."

"Hiding?"

"Looking for a quiet spot. He's keeping Penny company."

"Oh, good. I checked on her earlier and she seemed lonely. I stayed with her for a while before I came up here."

"Did you?" He smiled softly. "Thank you."

Molly's heart fluttered but she wished it wouldn't. She held out her hand. "My book?"

Roger looked puzzled for a moment, as if he'd forgotten he was holding it. "Oh, right. Here it is," he said and gave it back to her.

"Thank you."

As they settled on opposite ends of the sofa, Roger draped his jacket over the back cushion. "It was hot in the stairwell," he said, even though she hadn't asked why he'd taken it off.

"Yes, it was getting hot up here, too," Molly said and opened her book.

After staring blankly at the pages for ten minutes or so, Molly began to wonder if Roger was able to focus on reading, because she certainly wasn't. She replayed that moment when he'd held her in his arms. There hadn't been anything romantic about it, but it was the closest she'd ever been to a man when not in a ballroom. His chest pressing against her bodice had been firm and solid, and his muscular arms suggested he was quite strong. And his shoulders… She'd never noticed how broad they were. His warm hands on her waist had aroused a curious feeling of safety mixed with exhilaration. Then there was his scent…

Molly rose abruptly. "I think I'll go downstairs."

"Oh, no. I will. You were here first," Roger said, getting to his feet.

"I've been up here for hours. I should check on Caroline, anyway."

"If you insist."

She started backing away. "I do."

"Then I'll see you at dinner." Roger resumed his seat and continued reading.

When Molly reached the bottom of the stairs, she closed the door and leaned against it, reminding herself that under no circumstances was she to think Roger liked her. He was polite at best and was only friendly under unusual circumstances, like the tavern. After the wedding she'd most likely never see him again. True, what had just happened in the attic was intriguing, but Molly suspected most men would have acted the same way, and she'd have had the same reaction to them. Knowing Roger as she did now, she expected he'd most likely ignore her all through dinner tonight.

Molly was mostly right. At dinner she was seated between Caroline's cousin, Thomas, and Roger. She'd known Thomas for years and had an easy rapport with him, so the meal passed pleasantly enough.

Roger spent the meal alternating between nodding at statements Thomas or Molly made and chatting with the woman seated on his other side, Benedict's great-aunt Jean. It was hard to tell if he was enjoying himself, as he wore a bored expression all night. When Molly inquired after Penny, he told her she was sleeping in his room and seemed comfortable. That was the extent of their interaction for the evening.

After dinner, Molly followed Caroline to the parlor. Over the course of the day, a weight had settled on her heart as she'd realized this was the beginning of the end of their time together. Caroline would stay here in Rochester while Molly went back to Hartford, without the company of her best friend for the first time in her life. She'd been so happy for Caroline that until this moment, watching her laugh with Benedict over a joke, she hadn't recognized how lonely she was going to be. Tears started in her eyes. She blinked them back, but for the rest of the night felt they could burst forth at any moment.

When it was time for bed Molly was pleased to be alone with Caroline even though they were both exhausted.

"What a perfect evening," Caroline said after she'd changed into her nightgown and come back to Molly's room. She sat on the sofa, twirling her engagement ring around her finger.

Molly was at the vanity, brushing her hair. "It was. I'm glad we have some time together tonight."

"So am I. And don't worry, we'll be able to visit all the time, even after I'm married. I'll write to you every week."

It was as though Caroline had read her thoughts.

"Hartford isn't so far," Molly said.

"No, and when your Season is over—unless you marry—you'll come stay with us."

Molly joined Caroline on the sofa. "Will you and

Benedict live here at Waverly?"

"Yes, and I'm going to ask Kitty to be my lady's maid. Then she needn't deal with Mrs. Lane."

"That's a splendid idea," Molly said and took her hand. "You're so thoughtful, Caroline. I want to thank you for being my best friend over the years. You've always been supportive, and funny, and…and you're such a special person. Benedict is lucky to have you, and I hope he knows that."

"You're sweet to say so, but don't act as if it's goodbye."

Molly's tears started then. "But it is goodbye. You won't live next door, we won't go walking every Saturday or have tea parties or meet under the willow trees." She sniffed and looked away. "Don't pay me any mind, I'm being ridiculous."

"Oh, Molly, your ridiculous side is what I love best about you." Laughing, Caroline reached out to her and they embraced.

"You'll have a happy life with Benedict, and I'm so, so happy for you. I love you and I'll always be here for you." She paused. "I hope soon I'll be *Auntie* Molly."

They pulled away, wiping their tears.

"Speaking of that, I'm still not sure what to expect…you know…on the wedding night."

"Didn't your mother tell you anything?"

Caroline rolled her eyes. "She gave me a scientific lecture, but she didn't tell me anything you and I don't already know."

"What were you hoping to find out?"

"I'm not sure. Maybe what it feels like? After my sisters married, it was if they'd been let in on a secret."

"They wouldn't tell you what it was?"

"No. They said I'll find out myself in due course."

Molly shrugged. "That isn't very helpful, but if they looked happy, it must be nice."

"I assume so. But Mary didn't look so pleased as Anna."

"Did she tell you why?" Molly crossed her legs, one foot poking out from beneath her nightgown.

"No, but her 'You'll find out' sounded much more ominous."

"Perhaps some women like it and some don't, just like with anything."

"One thing I promise you," Caroline said, taking her hand. "When I get home from the honeymoon, I'll tell you *everything*."

Molly laughed. "I should hope so."

A soft knock came on the door.

"Who could that be?" Molly asked.

"Maybe it's Benedict!" Caroline jumped up and answered the door.

Kitty stood in the doorway, carrying a tray with the chocolate pot, cups, and a pile of biscuits. "I saw the light under your door and thought you might enjoy a treat."

"Oh, thank you," Caroline said.

"You're welcome." She set the tray down on the table and turned to go.

Molly leaned toward Caroline and whispered a question. Caroline colored, but nodded.

Before Kitty could leave the room, Molly called, "Wait a moment, please."

"Do you need something else?" Kitty asked, her hand on the doorknob.

"Um. Yes. Have a seat," Molly said, not sure if this was merely strange or bordering on inappropriate.

"I must warn you," Caroline said. "This is incredibly awkward."

Molly simply blushed.

Kitty looked like she was preparing for the worst as she took a seat in the chair opposite the sofa. "What's wrong? Is it the ball? You've changed your mind about me coming."

"No!" Molly said.

"Of course not. You're going to the ball. It's something else," Caroline said.

Clearly relieved, Kitty looked from Molly to Caroline. "Then what is it?"

Molly poured out the hot chocolate and handed biscuits around, unsure if she should ask, or Caroline. After all, it wasn't Molly who needed this information. She raised her brows at Caroline, who took a deep breath.

"Well, Kitty. You know I'm going to be married."

Kitty nodded.

"The day after tomorrow," Caroline added.

"Yes, we all know that," Kitty said with a laugh.

"Then there will be the wedding night," Molly said and drained her hot chocolate.

"Yes…" Kitty looked puzzled, still not understanding.

They all sat in silence for a moment until Molly blurted out, "We're trying to understand why women, some women, look so happy after the wedding night and what exactly happens with—with the man."

Kitty shot out of her chair. "*I* don't know that!"

"We didn't think you did," Molly assured her. "But we've run out of people to ask, and we wondered if you have a married sister or a friend who might know?"

Kitty sat down and covered her cheeks. "I was afraid

you thought that because I have a soft spot for Fred, we would have—"

"Certainly not," Caroline said. She leaned back in her seat and took a sip of hot chocolate. "The wedding is in two days. I do understand the basics of how things work, but no more than that. I know what…what happens, physically, but I want to know what it's *like*. That's what nobody will tell me."

Molly poured a cup of hot chocolate and handed it to Kitty, trying to recall anything she'd overheard in the past about honeymoons.

Finally, Kitty set her cup down. "Well, I do have one friend—Violet. She married two years ago. I asked her what it's like, and at first she said it was too hard to explain. She said it's what we always thought it would be. As you said, Caroline, the basics. But then—I'll never forget this—she smiled and said it made her feel closer to her husband than she'd ever been before, and after it happened once, she knew she wanted it to happen often."

For a few minutes they ate biscuits and glanced at one another, alternating between dreaming looks and nervous giggles.

Molly's face hadn't been its natural color for over an hour.

"Well. It sounds as if I have nothing to fear," Caroline said.

"No, not at all," Molly agreed. "Thank you for telling us, Kitty."

"Is Violet still happy with her husband?" Caroline asked.

"Oh, yes. They have a child and another one on the way."

As if by some unspoken agreement, the three women rose at the same time. Kitty carried the tray out of the room, while Caroline and Molly went off to their beds.

Molly lay awake for a long time, going over what they'd heard from Kitty. She hoped, when her time came, she'd have an experience more like Violet's than Mary's. And she would hold Caroline to her promise of a detailed explanation when she returned from her honeymoon.

Chapter Nineteen

The next day Molly met her parents and brothers for breakfast, after which they all walked down to the kennels with Fred to see the dogs. There was much talk of bloodlines and training regimens, but Molly and her mother ignored this and spent all their time playing with the puppies.

In any case, Mrs. Merriwether had her own agenda. As they watched the pups tumbling over each other, she said, "I had a list from Mrs. Darby today."

"A list of what?"

"A list of gentlemen who will be at your first ball. We'll read it later and decide who you might be interested in meeting first." Her mother smiled indulgently; the same smile she'd worn when she'd presented Molly with the rose-print tea set she'd pleaded for when she was seven.

Molly picked up one of the puppies. It rested its head against her shoulder and promptly fell asleep. "Isn't the point to meet as many gentlemen as possible? It would be hard to choose who I want to meet *first*."

"There might be someone who particularly catches your eye."

"I think that would be difficult to do on paper." Molly paused. It was worth a try. "Mother, do you think it's necessary for me to have a Season?"

Mrs. Merriwether's shoulders stiffened. "We've

been over this, Molly. Of course you need one. What else would you do? Stay home all the time and hope fate sends a husband your way?"

"No, but I don't see why I need to rush into anything."

"You aren't rushing. Look at Caroline—She's so happy to be settled." Her mother's eyes glistened with tears. "I want that for you, too."

Molly knew that no matter how vexing her mother might be, she did have her best interests at heart. There was no harm in going into town and attending a few balls. Perhaps she *would* meet someone. A man she could talk to and feel comfortable with. Molly had always known she'd get married one day, but hadn't given much thought to her husband or where she'd find him. Somehow the idea of wandering through ballrooms searching for him didn't feel right. She'd like the meeting to come about more naturally, like when her brother Michael accidentally got into the wrong carriage and met Lydia. They'd married four months later. But since this was unlikely, she'd have to allow her mother to whisk her off for the Season.

Molly gently set the puppy beside its littermates and took her mother's hand. "Very well. We'll go to town and have a grand time."

Mrs. Merriwether cheered considerably, all trace of tears gone, and recited a list of names and titles Molly was sure she'd never remember.

Molly stayed with her family through lunch, then went in search of Caroline, who was nowhere to be found. When she went to the stables to get Opal, Benedict's and Caroline's horses weren't in their stalls. She kept an eye out for them on her ride through the forest, but saw only a few other guests.

After her ride, she went upstairs to change, then aimlessly wandered her room trying to think of what to do with the rest of her day. There was no telling how long Caroline would be out with Benedict. Well, there was one thing she could do to amuse herself for the afternoon. She went to the bell pull and gave it a tug, then headed for her bed.

Molly was rifling through the bedclothes when Kitty knocked and came in.

"What are you doing?" Kitty asked.

Molly reached under the pillows. "Looking for the book I was reading last night."

"Would you like me to help?"

"No, but could you bring up a tea tray for me?" Molly asked, pausing to look at Kitty. "With two cups."

"Of course," Kitty said and left the room.

Molly got up and circled the bed, finally finding her novel stuck between the mattress and footboard. Alas, the bookmark was nowhere to be seen.

Kitty arrived soon after with the tea.

"While you're here, Kitty, I wanted to ask about your gown for tomorrow. Is it ready?"

"Yes, it's in my room, but I'm going to bring it up here later while everyone's at dinner."

"Tomorrow night you should be able to get down to the ball without being seen."

"I can hardly wait. I've told Mrs. Lane I'm tired today, and made sure to cough a few times."

Molly smiled. "An excellent idea."

After Kitty left, Molly put her book on the tea tray and made her way to the east wing. When she reached the attic, she half expected to see Roger already on the sofa, but it was empty. Molly set the tray on the table and opened the windows, then poured herself a cup of tea and picked up her book. Before long she was immersed in her novel, every so often eating a cucumber sandwich or a jam-laden scone.

The tea was half gone when the door opened and Roger came in carrying a basket.

"Good afternoon," he said.

Molly set her book down and rose. "Hello."

He sniffed the air. "It smells better in here than it did yesterday."

"It's the tea. It mixes well with the scent of old books."

"I hope it also mixes well with brandy." Roger pulled a bottle from his basket. "And cheese." He withdrew a block of cheese, wrapped in cloth, and a loaf of bread.

"I didn't realize we were having a picnic."

Roger looked at the tea tray. "Neither did I."

Molly grinned. "I was thirsty up here yesterday and I thought there was a chance you'd come today. Hence the two cups."

"Hence two glasses." He placed his basket on the table and proceeded to fill the glasses with brandy.

The brandy smelled delicious, but it would be unseemly to drink it alone with a man in the middle of the day. In an attic. Molly recalled the silly things she'd said to Roger at the tavern, and she hadn't even had much to drink that night. Not to mention her cheeks would go pink, whether she was embarrassed or not, once she drank brandy.

Molly took her seat. "I'll only have tea."

"Whatever you like." After offering the bread and

cheese, he settled into the other corner of the sofa and took up his volume.

Molly didn't find him distracting at all today. Perhaps because she'd had a feeling he'd come to the attic, or because the encounter hadn't begun with her wrapped in his arms. They sat in silence, both absorbed in their books, only moving when, from time to time, one of them took food from the table or refilled their cup.

Dark clouds moved fast across the sky, occasionally blocking out the sun. Molly glanced at the lantern on the table, wondering if it would light. Probably not, since there was barely any oil in the base. She squinted at the pages, drinking in the words when light allowed her to.

She'd made it to the second-to-last chapter when Roger closed his book and let out a contented sigh.

Molly marked her place and looked over at him. He was leaning against the back of the sofa, eyes closed, the book clutched to his chest.

Molly smiled. "Good ending?"

"Very," he said, opening his eyes.

Reaching for the teapot and finding it empty, she gave the brandy bottle a sideways glance. It must be close to dinnertime. Why not have some?

Roger, apparently a mind reader, filled her teacup with brandy, then tipped the bottle into his glass.

At the first sip, Molly shivered slightly. "What was yours about? Your book?"

"I don't think I'll tell you."

She arched her brows at him.

Roger laughed. "It was a mystery, and you may want to read it one day. How would it be if you already know what's going to happen?"

"Fair enough. But you did enjoy it?"

"Oh, yes." Roger set his book on the table. "I guessed the answer a few chapters ago, but it's gratifying to find out I was right."

"Perhaps I'll read it after I've finished mine."

Roger shifted so he was facing her, one arm draped over the back of the sofa. "What's yours about?"

"It's a novel."

"Enjoyable?"

Molly leaned forward. "Oh, yes. A young woman goes to a castle, and there's an old man there. Well, she thinks he's old, but he isn't. She finds a secret room, and it isn't a room at all, but a crumbling passage leading outside, and—" She flushed and took a sip of brandy.

His eyes shone as he pointed his empty glass at her. "Go on."

"No. What if you want to read it yourself?" She spread her hands over the cover.

Roger laughed that deep, throaty laugh she'd heard a few times before. "When you're finished, give it to me, and I'll lend you mine."

"I will. I'll be done in the next day or so. I'd say tomorrow, but with the wedding I might not have time to read…" Her voice trailed off as she finished the sentence, and to her horror those tears from last night returned. She finished her brandy and looked away, blinking furiously.

"Molly?" Roger's voice shifted to the smooth, quiet tone she'd heard him use when soothing Penny.

She turned all the way around to face the window, her back to him, and tried to wipe the tears away. Oh! Why was this happening now? She'd thought the tears had disappeared last night, not lain in wait for the most inopportune moment imaginable.

His hand came over her shoulder, holding a handkerchief. She took it, sniffling.

"Molly? Should I call someone? Your mother?"

She laughed through her tears. "Imagine going to my mother and telling her she's needed in the attic, where she'll find her daughter sitting in the half dark after spending the afternoon drinking brandy with a man."

Roger rubbed her shoulder. "You only had half a glass. You mostly drank tea. What about your brothers?"

"They'd respond even worse than my mother."

"Caroline?"

"You…you wouldn't be able to find her." The tears began in earnest, there was no hiding them now. Molly folded her arms on the arm of the sofa, buried her face in them, and wept. It was some time before they slowed, and even longer before they stopped, leaving her with a wet face, hiccups, and deep mortification. To think Roger had seen all this! If only she could crawl out the window or, better yet, if only he'd run from the room and left her to her misery. But he'd stayed all through her weeping, his warm hand rubbing her back. She wiped her face with the handkerchief, took a shuddering breath and turned to face him. "I must seem so foolish."

"What's wrong?"

She dabbed her eyes. "You'll think I'm ridiculous."

"No, I won't," he said gently.

Molly wanted to look away from him, but something in his voice made it impossible. Certain she was a soggy mess, she met his gaze. "Caroline's getting married tomorrow."

"Yes. I know."

"I didn't see her today. I'd hoped to have more time

together, just the two of us. I thought we'd talk and…and just be together. I thought we had one more day, but now it's too late. She'll be busy tonight, and *married* tomorrow, and then she'll be off on her honeymoon."

"You like Benedict, don't you? Are you worried she won't be happy?"

"I know she will be. I just—I thought I'd gotten used to the idea, but it suddenly hit me afresh. I don't know why. I've already gone through this twice." She lifted her hands and let them fall into her lap.

Roger put a hand to his chin, and Molly guessed he was trying to think of the right thing to say.

"Perhaps some things take more adjustment than others," he said after a moment.

"Perhaps. I know I'm acting like a ninny. I truly am happy for Caroline and Benedict. It's just that I'll miss her." She sniffed again and wiped her eyes.

"I understand."

Molly poured herself a bit more brandy. "You do?"

"Yes. Last year my cousin Neville married and moved to his wife's estate on the other side of the country. I'm happy for him, but I still miss him. We've always been close, and it was difficult right after he left, because we'd usually see each other every day. We had routines like our Saturday morning walks and weekly visits to the tavern."

Molly's eyes widened. "Are you fabricating this to comfort me? It sounds just the way I feel about Caroline."

Roger let out a soft laugh. "I assure you, Neville is real. I could show you his letters, if you like. Or you can ask Penny. My sister, not the dog."

"Your sister! She's here?" Molly found it odd he'd

have spent all afternoon in the attic if his family had arrived.

"She'll be here with my parents in the morning."

Molly wiped her eyes a final time and folded the handkerchief. "I hope I'll be able to meet her."

"You will, tomorrow. Don't worry about losing Caroline. She and Benedict will get married and settle down, and you can visit her whenever you want."

"That's just what she said. Please don't mention this to anyone. I wouldn't want Caroline to hear about it."

"I won't. You can trust me." Roger took her hand. Now that she wasn't crying, it felt more intimate.

Molly's stomach did a little flip and she hoped it was the brandy. She did trust Roger, but why she didn't know. What was it about him that made her want to open up to him? Even though they'd known each other for some time, it wasn't as though they'd become close friends. Or had they? Had friendship sprung up between their strange interludes like this one and the times he acted like he barely knew her?

She returned his handkerchief. "Thank you for listening to me. And to think you came up here for quiet."

"That wasn't the only reason I came up." Roger brushed a hair away from her forehead. He was sitting so close she could smell the spicy, musky cologne he wore.

Molly's heart raced as his eyes met hers. She swallowed. "It wasn't?"

Roger shook his head but didn't speak.

As the seconds ticked by Molly held her breath, waiting for him to answer.

Something in his eyes shifted and he leaned back, releasing her hand. "I needed somewhere to finish my book where I wouldn't be disturbed."

Molly was almost certain that wasn't what he'd been about to say. Simply for a reason to look away, she glanced out the window. The sky was that light, dusky blue just before twilight and the first twinkling stars were beginning to emerge. "Oh, the stars look beautiful from up here."

Stars? Molly had been so distracted by her emotions, so intent on Roger's words, she hadn't noticed the room growing darker or the sky outside moving from light to dusk.

They stared at each other, mouths agape.

"The banquet!" Molly cried.

Roger looked at his pocket watch. "Oh, Molly." He put a hand to his stomach, laughing. "We're very late."

She winced. "How late?"

"They're most likely beginning dessert right about now."

"Oh!" She put a hand to her mouth, unsuccessfully trying to stifle her giggles.

They bolted off the sofa, scrambling around gathering books and dirty dishes. After filling the basket with any evidence that they'd been there, they rushed across the ever-darkening attic.

Molly stopped laughing when she opened the door to the stairwell. It was pitch black. "Oh, no."

"Don't worry," Roger said, taking her hand. "Just hold tight and go slowly."

"All right, but next time I'm bringing a candle or a fresh lantern."

With one hand Molly gripped the railing. With the other, she clung to Roger's hand. There was an odd, surreal quality about descending stairs she couldn't see.

Halfway down, he put an arm around her waist and pulled her close. Roger's heat and steady presence seemed like the only real thing in the world. Molly caught the scent of brandy mixed with his cologne, and something woodsy she couldn't place. She imagined it was simply…Roger. They didn't speak but she was as aware of the sound of his breaths as she was of the beats of her own heart. The walk took twice as long as the journey up, but with Roger at her side Molly didn't mind.

Once they turned the corner, light from under the door illuminated the staircase. When they reached the bottom, she pushed the door open. Roger removed his arm from her waist as they stepped into the sewing room.

Molly turned to face him. "How do I look?" she asked, then wished she could take it back. "Forget I said that."

"You look blushing," Roger said and smiled mischievously.

She clicked her tongue. "I forgot I wasn't talking to Caroline for a moment."

"Do I look like Caroline?" He folded his arms, the basket dangling off one hand.

"Certainly not."

He considered her for a moment. "Now you look…rosy. Like a red rose."

"Roger, would you stop?" She crossed the room and peeked into the empty corridor. "I only meant whether I look a mess. You know, from all the crying and creeping downstairs in the dark? Am I fit to go straight down to the great hall?"

He gave her an apologetic look. "I'm afraid not, Molly Merriwether."

Her heart pattered. Oh, *no*. She'd begun to like it

much too much when he called her that.

"I thank you for your honesty, Mr. Bailey."

"My pleasure, as always." He held the door open for her. "We'll stop by your room so you can fix your hair before we go downstairs."

Molly looked him up and down. "You might need to tidy up a bit, as well."

"Do I?" he asked, looking down at himself.

"Your tie has come loose and your hair is messy. Your jacket's picked up some dust."

He ran a hand over his head. "Right. We'll stop at my room, too. With any luck we can slip into the great hall during coffee and nobody will notice us."

Molly blushed. "Together?"

Roger looked at her as if she was the silliest creature in the world. "If anybody happened to notice, which I doubt, we'll tell them we were looking after Penny. I'll bring her down to the office. Meet me there."

"Don't move her if it would make her uncomfortable."

He smiled. "I won't."

They continued in silence to Molly's room.

"Don't be long," Roger said when they reached her door.

"I won't."

They looked at each other for a moment then parted without another word. As he strolled down the hall, Molly saw Roger slip the handkerchief she'd borrowed into his waistcoat pocket, and it almost looked like he brought it to his face before tucking it away.

Chapter Twenty

Half an hour later, Molly waited at the office door. She'd changed into a pink gown and brushed her dark hair, letting it flow over her shoulders. After telling her not to be late, Roger was taking an awfully long time. How would he treat her now? If history was any indication, he'd come down and talk to her as if they'd just met yesterday. But maybe not. She recalled his words upstairs, and that look in his eyes.

More alarming still, Molly recalled her heart's fluttery antics whenever he was near. Apparently, without meaning to, she'd developed what Kitty called a "soft spot" for Roger. The question was, should she try to stop it, or hope he'd develop one for her, too? There'd been more than one time, especially today, when Molly suspected he fancied her. But this was Roger, who, since the day she'd met him, had proved almost impossible to read.

What she'd really like to do was talk to Caroline about it, but she had her own romance to occupy her thoughts. For the time being, she'd do her best to act normally around Roger and not give him any indication that a part of her was always hoping he'd take her hand or call her Molly Merriwether.

A moment later Roger strolled down the hall with Penny. "I apologize for the delay."

"How is she?" Molly knelt to pet Penny, who

wagged her tail.

"I think she's tired, but the food I left out for her was gone."

"Oh, that's good."

When Roger opened the door to the office, Penny went right in and curled up in front of the hearth.

"She's so big," Molly said. "It can't be long before she has her puppies."

"I hope so. She's carried two more of my blankets under the bed. I'm down to one." Roger offered his arm as they left the office.

Crossing the quadrangle, it was easy to see into the great hall. Benedict and Caroline sat at the head of the main table, completely absorbed with each other. Everyone at the banquet appeared to be at their ease, chatting and sipping drinks.

Molly had hoped they'd have dispersed to other rooms, as it was hard to imagine walking in unnoticed. "What's the best way to enter? The side door?"

Roger seemed to consider. "I don't think we should go in. Look at the tables—there's nowhere for us to sit. We'd be standing there awkwardly until Dawson noticed us and found us seats, and then everyone else would notice us, too."

"What about your plan to tell everyone we were with Penny?"

His eyes swept slowly over her. "I don't think anyone will believe you've been playing nursemaid to a dog. You're too elegant, and too clean."

"So are you, aside from your trouser leg that's half orange from Penny walking beside you."

Roger had obviously lingered in his room to do some freshening up of his own. His hair was combed, and he'd changed into a perfectly fitted black suit. He looked like he'd just stepped off a ballroom floor, not spent the afternoon in an attic.

"Still." Roger took a step closer. "You look—I don't know how to describe it. Fresh. Radiant. Angelic?"

"Angels don't wear pink."

"Perhaps they should. You should wear it more often. It almost disguises your cheeks."

Molly put a hand on her hip and looked up into his face. "*Mr.* Bailey, when will you cease noticing every time I blush?"

"I can't help it. It's obvious, and adorable, and by now I've come to expect it. I'd be disappointed if you didn't."

She covered her crimson face with her hands. Had he just called her adorable?

"No, you don't," Roger said, trying to pull her hands away.

Molly lowered them, smiling, and as she tried to think of a clever retort a movement caught her eye. "Oh. Oh, Roger."

His brow furrowed. "What is it?"

"Turn around."

He did, and let out a low whistle.

The crowd in the great hall had risen, and Caroline, Benedict, and Fred stood at a window, staring at Molly and Roger.

Roger offered his arm. "Shall we?"

She took it, trying in vain to hold back a laugh.

They walked through the quadrangle and entered the house through a door in the west wing.

"Where are we going?" Molly asked as they meandered down the hall.

"To the parlor, I think. I'm assuming that's where we'll find our friends."

"Perhaps they're all going to bed."

Roger covered her hand with his. "No, they'll be up for hours."

"You're probably right. We'll just slip inside and hope nobody notices."

As it turned out, slipping unnoticed into a small room crowded with people who were looking for them wasn't as easy as it sounded. As soon as they walked in, Molly received a glare from her mother, a curious look from Caroline and a wink from Fred. Instead of going over to talk to any of them, she followed Roger to two chairs beside the fire, where they received glasses of champagne from a footman.

"Caroline's itching to talk to me," she whispered.

Roger casually crossed his legs. "Fred will be here any moment."

"To making a spectacle of ourselves," Molly said and held up her glass.

"I like to think we can make more of a spectacle than that." He clinked his glass on hers. "Perhaps during the ball tomorrow."

They broke into laughter just as Fred strode over and stood in front of them, hands behind his back. "Where have you two been?"

"With the dog," Molly said, as Roger answered, "Upstairs."

Molly nodded. "Upstairs with the dog."

"Penny. We were with Penny," Roger said.

"Not his sister," Molly said. "The dog." She sipped her champagne and tried to look innocent, but Roger gave her a quick glance and they both broke into grins.

"For *six* hours?" Fred asked.

Molly feigned shock. "We weren't together for that long! I spent most of the afternoon reading. I can't speak for Mr. Bailey."

"I was also reading," Roger said. "I lost track of time."

Fred glanced at Molly, then back at Roger. "I imagine you did."

Molly knew what Fred was insinuating, but didn't know what to say. She supposed she should be offended, but after some of the things that had happened this afternoon…well, Fred wasn't exactly wrong if he suspected they were growing closer. But was he implying something more risqué?

Roger looked up at Fred. "Did you need me for something?"

"No. Only, when it came time to eat, nobody could find either of you."

"That's odd," Molly said.

"Very," Roger agreed, sipping his champagne.

Fred gave them what was apparently supposed to be a stern look, but his eyes twinkled as he perched himself on the arm of Roger's chair. "You missed a good meal. But never mind, the real party will start later."

"Will it?" Molly asked. "I thought this was the party."

"For the men," Fred said. "At least some of us. Roger and I have something special planned for Benedict."

Molly leaned forward. "What is it?"

"I can't tell you that," Fred said, and pressed his lips together.

Roger met her eyes. "It would make you blu—"

"Don't say it." She held up a hand.

He watched her cheek for a moment, then whispered, "I told you so."

Molly finished her champagne and rose, setting her glass on the table. "Take my seat, Fred. I think I'll go find Caroline."

Before she'd gotten anywhere near Caroline, Mrs. Merriwether found *her*. "Molly!"

Molly cringed, knowing what was coming. She turned to face her mother. "Good evening."

"Good evening? Is that all you have to say for yourself? Where have you been, and why did you arrive with Mr. Bailey?"

Molly glanced around to be sure they weren't being overheard. "We were looking after his dog."

Mrs. Merriwether's penetrating stare implied she suspected Molly of far more than that. Fortunately, there was no way she could know what had happened upstairs with Roger. If she did, she'd most likely faint.

"You're spending too much time with him, Molly." Her mother took her elbow and led her into a corner. "You might think I don't notice, but I do. And so does your father."

Molly put on as innocent a tone as she could. "Why shouldn't I spend time with him? He's my friend. I also spend time with Fred, Benedict, and Caroline. We all became close when I was here before."

Mrs. Merriwether linked her arm through Molly's as though fearful she might try to flee. "You know perfectly well what I mean. You have the Season to look forward to, and I don't want you becoming entangled with anyone before then."

"Entangled! Mother, it isn't like that between Roger

and me."

Her mother gave her a skeptical look. "Don't spend any more time alone with him. I don't want anyone getting the wrong idea."

"I'm sure nobody would." Molly pulled out of her mother's grasp. "I'm going to find Caroline."

"Very well. But do try to be a bit more discreet."

She turned away so Mrs. Merriwether couldn't see her scowl. "I will."

It wasn't for her mother to say who she could or couldn't spend time alone with, but Caroline's wedding banquet wasn't the place to have that discussion.

As she looked around for Caroline, Molly couldn't keep the smile off her face. Roger hadn't ignored her the way she'd feared he would this evening, in fact he was even friendlier than he'd been this afternoon. They'd shared something close to intimacy upstairs when he'd comforted her. Did that mean he'd finally decided he could trust her, or gotten over whatever had been holding him back before? Would he continue being friendly, even flirtatious, instead of shutting her out? Molly shook her head to clear it. Was she really going to get excited just because Roger hadn't been aloof tonight? That was a far cry from a sign that he liked her.

Molly caught up with Caroline just as she was heading out of the parlor.

"Here you are, Molly! You missed the banquet."

"I'm sorry." Molly took her arm as they continued down the corridor. "I was with Penny."

Caroline leaned into her shoulder. "*And* Roger."

Molly flushed. "Yes. Well. Isn't it time to go upstairs? You don't want to be tired tomorrow."

"That's where I'm going. Benedict insisted. He said

the sooner we go to sleep, the sooner tomorrow comes, and the sooner we'll be married."

The sounds from the parlor grew fainter as they climbed the stairs.

"It isn't as though he's going to sleep. Fred has plans for him," Molly said.

"I heard. Well, let them have their fun. I'll never be able to sleep tonight, but I'm ready for some quiet time." She met Molly's eyes. "Besides, it appears you and I have much to discuss."

"All we're discussing tonight is you and the wedding."

"We'll see."

After changing into their nightgowns, Molly and Caroline sat on the settee in Caroline's room, watching flames dance in the hearth.

"Tomorrow," Caroline said with a sigh.

Molly kicked her slippers off and drew her feet up onto the settee. "You must be so excited."

"You'd think so, but I feel calm. Like I'm about to open a door and I have no doubt I'll like what I'm going to find." Caroline paused. "I'm sure that sounds silly."

"No, it sounds just as you should feel the night before your wedding. You're sure about Benedict and you're ready to begin a life with him."

"Can you believe how well it's all turned out? After that unusual start we had here, and at first I wasn't even sure if he liked me."

Molly tucked her nightgown around her knees. "I can believe it. He's perfect for you."

"He is." Caroline leaned her head back and began listing Benedict's best qualities.

Molly was more than happy to listen. She was

241

grateful she'd been able to deal with her sorrow earlier, because now she was able to truly enjoy this time with Caroline. She'd ceased thinking about it as their last night because, really, it wasn't. Things would change, but that was the way of life. Molly looked at it as a new chapter. A new chapter of Caroline's life, a new chapter of their friendship.

When Molly glanced at the clock on the mantel, she almost started. "Oh! It's time for bed."

"Stay in here tonight, Molly. Like when we were girls," Caroline said, standing up.

"All right. We'll stay up late and share secrets."

"We already know each other's secrets."

Molly thought of at least one Caroline didn't know but said nothing of it.

After climbing into Caroline's bed, Molly gazed out the window. The inky blue sky was clear and starless, unlike this evening.

"Molly."

"Why are you whispering?"

"It seems like we should. Tell me about Roger."

"What about him?"

Caroline nudged her shoulder. "You know. Where were you two this afternoon, and what was going on in the quadrangle?"

Molly told her about the attic, leaving out the part where she cried about the wedding, but didn't really know how to explain about the quadrangle. She was still trying to understand it herself.

"I think he likes you," Caroline said.

"Do you?" She was glad of the half-dark so Caroline couldn't see the hope that sprung into her eyes.

"Yes. He talks to you more than anyone, save Fred.

He lets you help with Penny, and sometimes when you aren't in the room I've noticed he keeps a close eye on the door, like he's waiting. Or hoping."

Molly's chest felt suddenly light. "Does he?"

"Do you have feelings for him?"

Molly hesitated, unsure of what to say. It was all a bit confusing. "Yes, but I'm not sure if I should."

Caroline laughed. "I don't think it's something you can help."

"What I mean is, sometimes I think he might like me. But at others, he hardly looks at me. It's so hard to tell what he's thinking, never mind feeling. I'm afraid I'm reading too much into his behavior when he's kind to me." Molly flipped onto her stomach, her head resting in her folded arms on the pillow.

"Would you say he's been more friendly lately, or more standoffish?"

A dreamy look came to Molly's face. "Today, definitely friendly."

"I don't think you're reading too much into his behavior. When you were in the quadrangle, he looked outright flirtatious."

"He did, didn't he?" Molly said with a smile.

Caroline grasped her hand. "Oh, Molly, it would be wonderful if you marry Roger!"

"It's too soon to speak of that." She paused. "There's one other thing."

"What?"

Molly propped herself up on her elbow. "I'm...scared to let myself like Roger. What if he rejects me again? When I didn't care about him, it didn't matter as much that he's so hot and cold. Rude, yes. Strange, yes. But it didn't bother me. But now, if I embrace my romantic feelings and he still acts that way, it would be heartbreaking."

Caroline nodded. "You want to be able to trust him."

"Yes, and I want him to trust *me*. I wish he wouldn't ignore me sometimes."

"For all we know, he's like this with everybody. Moody and likes his time alone."

"Maybe I'm the only one he shuts out. I haven't noticed him doing it to you."

"That's because he hasn't let me get close enough for it to be an issue. Let's forget about his odd behavior for a moment. If he didn't act like that, and was always friendly…would you like him?"

"Oh, yes. He's smart, and interesting, and so sweet with Penny, and handsome. Also—Why are you laughing?"

"You remind me of myself, talking about Benedict. I don't think there's a question of you letting yourself like Roger. It's too late."

Molly flipped onto her back, hands folded over her heart. "You're right. Oh, I do care for him. How foolish of me! Why couldn't I have liked someone like Fred? I'd never have any doubt about what he's feeling."

"Perhaps Roger *is* letting you know how he feels. You said he was different today. Those days of him ignoring you might be over."

Molly smiled. "Oh, I hope you're right. I'll know more tomorrow. Speaking of which, it's time we were asleep."

"This time tomorrow I'll be with Benedict."

"And the day after that you'll be telling me everything."

Caroline laughed. "No, you'll have to wait until we

get back from the honeymoon."

"Well, at least my mother decided to let me wait here for you. I wouldn't have wanted to hear about it in a letter."

"There's no way you would have, because I certainly wouldn't have told you about *that* in a letter. You'll just need to be patient."

Molly sighed. "Not my strong suit."

"I know," Caroline said, smiling. "Goodnight, Molly."

"Goodnight." Molly blew out the bedside candle.

The next morning at breakfast, Caroline was bright, beautiful, and fidgety. Molly, sitting beside her, had her toes stepped on more than once by Caroline's tapping feet. A constant hum of voices hung over the breakfast room and the anticipation in the air was palpable.

Afterwards Molly and Caroline went upstairs to dress for the ceremony. They hadn't been in their room long when Mrs. Lane brought up the chocolate pot and a covered tray, grumbling about Kitty being sick today of all days.

"We've just had breakfast, but thank you for the hot chocolate," Caroline said.

"Mr. Clarke—the younger—sent this," Mrs. Lane said, lifting the cover off the tray.

Caroline clasped her hands under her chin. "Oh! How sweet and thoughtful he is."

Mrs. Lane's face was oddly transformed by the smile that came to it. "He always has been. I know you'll be happy here, Miss, and I look forward to us getting to know one another better." She left the room, leaving Molly and Caroline to stare at one another in disbelief.

"Is that the first time she's smiled at you?" Molly

asked.

"I believe so. There could be hope for us having an amicable relationship after all." Caroline went over to the tray Benedict had sent. "Look at this!"

Molly looked down at the tray, where a pile of heart-shaped scones sat beside a red rose. "How romantic."

Caroline nodded, pressing her lips together.

"Don't start crying yet, Caroline. You have all day for that."

Caroline flapped her hands in front of her eyes as if to fan the tears back inside. "I won't."

Molly hugged her. "Let's get you ready to marry your Benedict."

Chapter Twenty-One

They couldn't have asked for a more beautiful day for the wedding. During the ceremony Molly stood off to the side with Fred, holding the bouquet as Caroline and Benedict exchanged their vows. From her vantage point at the front of the church Molly had a clear view of the guests.

As subtly as she could, she scanned the crowd for Roger. Molly found him sitting in the second row, just behind the Clarkes. He must have been looking in her direction, because as soon as she saw him he met her eyes and pointed to the young girl sitting next to him. Penny waved at her and Molly nodded, as she couldn't really wave to the whole congregation. She turned back to the ceremony, trying to pay attention but with the distinct feeling Roger's eyes were on her the whole time.

Back at Waverly Hall, a sumptuous luncheon awaited the wedding guests. Molly looked for Caroline, but couldn't find her among the chattering people mingling in the great hall. The long dining table was now surrounded by a number of smaller ones, each set for four to six people. Flowers decorated the windowsills and tables, their fragrance mingling with the aroma of delicious food.

As Molly weaved between the tables on the way to her seat, Roger approached her, his family in tow. "Good afternoon," Molly said, trying to include them all in her greeting.

Roger smiled. "Good afternoon. I'd like you to meet my family." He kept his eyes on hers as he addressed his parents. "May I introduce Miss Molly Merriwether."

Molly pulled her gaze away from his and turned to Mr. and Mrs. Bailey. "A pleasure to meet you."

"It's nice to meet you, too," Mrs. Bailey said. "We've heard so much about you."

Had they? Molly thought she caught a quick, significant glance pass between Mr. and Mrs. Bailey.

Roger put his arm around Penny. "And this delightful young lady is my sister, Penelope."

She held a hand out to Molly, glowering at Roger. "I'm *Penny*, and Roger's right, you're pretty."

Molly was not the only person in the group to color at this statement. Roger looked down at his feet. Blusher, indeed.

"Oh," Molly said, shaking Penny's hand after she'd recovered her voice. "Thank you. You're pretty, too. Your hair is lovely."

"Thank you. I'm the only one in the family with red hair, though my grandmother's once was. Roger's looks red sometimes in the sun. Will you join us for luncheon?"

In the distance, Molly saw Caroline and Benedict enter the room as a string quartet in the next room began playing. "I need to sit with the wedding party. Caroline's my best friend, and I'm her maid of honor."

"We'll see you at the ball, then. I'll be allowed to stay up late and dance." Penny twirled her dress, nearly bumping into a footman carrying glasses of champagne. She skipped away, her mother close on her heels.

Molly said goodbye to Roger and his father, then

went to join Caroline. Her head swam as she made her way through the room. She stopped now and then to say hello to people, but her mind was full of what she'd heard from Roger's family. He'd talked about her at home? He'd called her pretty? Hope stirred in her chest as she recalled the look in his eyes back at the church. It no longer appeared to be a question of if he liked her, but of how much he liked her. And, most importantly, how much she liked him.

Later that afternoon Molly went up to her bedchamber. She picked a novel off the bookcase and removed her shoes, then lay on the bed. The book remained untouched as Molly recalled the wedding, the luncheon, and Roger's words. And Roger's glances. A number of times during the meal she'd looked up to find him watching her from across the room. Molly could hardly wait for tonight, when she'd have another chance to be in his arms. Unlike that day in the attic, this time she'd be expecting it and would appreciate every second.

Close to dinnertime, Caroline strolled into the bedchamber.

"Caroline! I didn't expect to see you until the ball." Molly started to ask if she was enjoying her day, but based on the rapturous look on her face there was no need.

Caroline leaned against the bedpost and slipped her shoes off, letting them fall to the floor. "I have to change. Benedict's gone to his room to do the same, and we're meeting downstairs shortly."

Molly hopped off the bed. "I'll help with your gown."

"Oh, thank you." Caroline crossed to the other side of the room and peeked into the mirror.

"You needn't bother checking," Molly said. "You're glowing."

Caroline stood on tiptoes and spun around. "I feel like I am. Oh, Molly, I'm so happy!"

Molly had to hold back tears, not from sorrow this time. "I couldn't be happier for you, but you've got to stand still. A fine thing it would be to have the bride sprain an ankle on her wedding day. Here. Turn around and I'll undo your buttons."

Caroline did so, leaning her neck forward so Molly could reach the top buttons. "I won't sprain anything. Even if I did, it couldn't spoil my mood."

"Besides, it isn't as though you'll be on your feet much during the honeymoon."

"Molly!"

Caroline tried to spin around, but Molly held her firmly by the shoulders. "I'm not through yet."

She reached behind to slap Molly's arm but only managed to get tangled in her veil. "I suppose you're right. But you make it sound as though that's all we'll be doing. We'll go on walks, and have picnics on the beach, and all sorts of things."

"Then we know you'll need your ankle for part of the time, at least. There," Molly said, taking a step back. "Finished."

Caroline stepped out of the gown and held it to her chest as she walked into her own room, Molly following with the veil.

As Caroline rifled through her wardrobe, Molly sat in the wingback chair. "So. The wedding night. Are you nervous?"

"Not at all. In fact, I wish Benedict and I could skip the ball and retire now." Caroline sounded almost giddy.

"Really?"

"Yes. We had some time alone recently and, well, did some things that give me an idea of what to expect tonight." Caroline slipped into a carnation-pink gown. "I feel quite sure I'll enjoy myself."

This statement brought so many questions to mind that Molly was speechless for a moment. What had they done? Unfortunately, there wasn't time to ask, as the ball started shortly. She had to curb her curiosity for now. "I'm glad you aren't nervous. You're leaving for the honeymoon first thing tomorrow?"

"Yes. We'll spend tonight in the bridal chamber and leave for the coast in the morning." Caroline went to the dressing table to brush her hair. "Why don't you change, too, and we can go down together."

"All right. I won't be a moment."

Molly mulled over Caroline's words as she donned a midnight blue gown. She'd planned on pink, to look 'angelic' for Roger, but it didn't seem right to match the bride. In any case, the blue hugged her in all the right places and brought out the color of her eyes. Molly sat at the vanity to fix her hair and had just added an amber comb when Caroline came in, looking ready to start spinning again.

"Let's go. Benedict will wonder what's become of me." She took Molly's arm and they left the room.

The moment they stepped into the ballroom, Benedict swooped down to claim his bride. Watching Caroline dance with Benedict, gazing at him with love, Molly no longer felt jealous at all, only beyond happy for her friend. She let out a small sigh. Suddenly the idea of having a partner to go through life with, someone to share her dreams and make a home with, filled her with warmth and unexpected longing.

Walking along the perimeter of the room, Molly barely had time to take in the hundreds of glittering candles and ascertain what piece the orchestra was playing before Roger appeared at her side.

"Good evening," he said. As he bent to give her a low bow, Molly caught what could only be described as tenderness in his eyes. She almost gasped. Had she imagined that? When he straightened the expression was gone and he was watching her expectantly.

It took a moment for Molly to realize her lips had parted slightly and she was staring at him. "Oh. Good evening, Roger."

"I wanted to get to you before the other men claimed all your dances," he said, brown eyes twinkling.

Molly lifted her arm to show an empty dance card dangling from her wrist. "They wouldn't have, I planned on saving one for you."

He took a step closer. "Only one?"

"Well. Yes. Isn't that customary?"

"Do we need to adhere to custom?" Roger reached for her dance card, but she held it at arm's length.

"What are you doing?" She stepped back, almost colliding with Fred and his partner, who swept past after a look of indignation on the lady's part, and amusement on Fred's.

Roger drew a pencil from inside his waistcoat pocket. "If you must know, I'd planned to write 'Roger Bailey' on every line."

She hid the dance card behind her back, holding it with both hands. "Really, Mr. Bailey."

"Really, *Miss* Merriwether."

When Molly broke out in tinkling laughter, several

couples turned their way. Unfortunately, her parents were among those couples. Her mother looked like she was about to sprint over, but after a cold look at Molly, Mr. Merriwether steered his wife away. It could only be because he didn't want her to cause a scene.

"Perhaps it's time to join the dance?" Molly asked, casting a look over her shoulder to see which way her parents had gone so she could head in the opposite direction.

"By all means." Roger took her arm while they waited for a new song to begin.

Molly assumed a serious expression as she removed the pale yellow dance card from her wrist. "You may have my card and claim your one dance. Don't you usually adhere to custom, especially on a night like this?"

"I do when it pleases me. But tonight? Tonight I might rather snap my fingers at custom and dance with you as many times as you'll allow." He took her dance card, tucked it into his jacket pocket, and slid an arm around her waist.

A warm, tingly shiver flowed through Molly. He'd skipped friendly, touched on flirtatious and now bordered on scandalous. Delighted, she rose to the occasion. "In that case, I'll allow as many as you care to take."

Roger tightened his grip on her waist, the heat of his hand searing through her dress. "To the dance floor, then, Molly Merriwether."

They took their place among the other couples, and when the music began he swept her around the room in his strong arms. While they danced, they continued their banter and Molly had to remind herself this was the same Roger who in the past had gone for hours, sometimes days, without acknowledging her. What had gotten into him? Fred had once told her Roger wasn't acting like himself when she'd met him. Perhaps this was the *real* Roger Fred had referred to.

They danced two dances, and though they'd joked about dancing all night, both knew they couldn't do that without causing a stir. Roger signed her dance card and handed it back somewhat reluctantly. She slipped it onto her wrist without checking to see how many more dances he'd claimed. Hopefully more than one. Since she hadn't even talked to any other gentlemen tonight, perhaps he'd get his wish of having him to herself. And, she must admit, that was her wish, too.

But just as she'd begun to imagine what her parents would say to that, Fred sauntered over. "If you'll have me, Molly?"

"That would be lovely, Fred."

Fred went to take her arm, but Roger shooed him out of the way and kissed Molly's hand. Twice. "I'll be back to claim my other dances later."

"I look forward to it." Molly had an absurd notion to bring the spot he'd kissed to her cheek, or even her lips.

Roger held her gaze, walking backwards, then turned on his heel and was lost in the sea of colorful gowns.

When Molly turned back to Fred he was watching her with more interest than he ever had before. She put a hand up to adjust her hair, willing herself not to scan the room for Roger.

After a moment Fred seemed to recall himself. "Are you hot? You look flushed. Would you like some lemonade?"

Molly touched her cheek, which was indeed warm—but not from exertion. "That would be nice, thank you."

Fred offered his arm and they went in search of refreshment.

The punch room's windows were wide open, welcoming in the cool night air and heady scent of roses. Just stepping inside rejuvenated Molly, and if Roger weren't waiting in the ballroom she would have stayed in here for the rest of the night. Three silver punch bowls and a row of crystal glasses sat on a round table in the middle of the room.

Fred handed Molly a full glass of lemonade and took one for himself.

"Are you enjoying yourself?" she asked after a tart sip.

Fred looked vaguely around the room, tapping his fingers against his glass. "It was a nice wedding. Benedict's happy."

"So is Caroline. I'm happy for them." Molly held out her glass to make a toast, but Fred seemed not to notice.

A few moments later he turned his head in Molly's direction, his eyes barely flitting over her face before settling on a potted fern beside the door. "Mm. So am I. Happy for them."

The musicians in the next room struck up a brisk tune, followed by the sound of heels flying over the ballroom floor. Molly sipped her lemonade while listening to crickets just outside the window, as Fred showed no sign of speaking again all night.

Other wedding guests came and went, but none stayed for long. Molly hoped Roger would appear, but so far the only people she'd recognized were Caroline's sisters. She was about to ask Fred if he wanted to dance when he wandered over to the grandfather clock and stared up into its face, his drink untouched.

Molly set her empty glass down and moved to his side. "Fred, is everything all right?"

He kept his eyes on the clock. "Weddings. They make you think, don't they? About—about love, and what's important, and…and life. Your whole life, and what will you do with it?"

"Yes, I suppose so. They have a way of making you think of beginnings, and the future."

"Yes! The future. It won't wait forever."

Clapping emanated from the ballroom as the musicians finished with a flourish and immediately began a slow tune.

Fred crossed the room to the table and set his full glass down as thirsty dancers trickled into the punch room, laughing and chatting.

Molly pushed through the crowd and placed a hand on Fred's arm. "What's the matter?"

He looked down at her, his blue eyes not as bright as usual. "Are you ready to dance, Molly?"

"Yes, but do you want to?"

"Of course we should dance. Let's go."

Fred led Molly to the middle of the ballroom and took her stiffly into his arms, moving a pace slower than the music as if not aware of the tune. Possibly not even aware of her.

After some minutes of this, Molly stopped. "Fred?"

Looking over her head, he started talking as though they'd been in the middle of a conversation all along. "I shouldn't tell you. I shouldn't tell anybody. But I have to. And I think you might already know. Here, keep dancing."

"What are you talking about?" Molly asked, shifting slowly from foot to foot.

Fred looked surprised she had to ask. "Kitty. I'm talking about Kitty."

"What about her?"

He leaned close to whisper in her ear. "Kitty is the most amazing woman I've ever met. We were friendly before she came here, but I didn't court her when I had the chance—and now it's too late. I should have done…something." Fred pulled away, looking into Molly's face. "I can't stand living like this anymore. I'm going away."

"But that would break Kitty's heart," Molly blurted without thinking.

"You do know something," he said urgently. "What did Kitty tell you?"

A man approached to cut in but Fred waved him away, then looked at Molly apologetically. "Oh. Was he on your dance card?"

"Nobody's on my dance card." Except Roger Bailey.

"What did Kitty tell you?" Fred asked again.

"Only what you did." Not wanting to accidentally betray Kitty's confidence, Molly didn't quote her word for word. "That you never courted, but were close in the past."

His eyes lit up and he came to a halt. "Close? She said that?"

"In so many words. But you must know that already."

Fred ran a hand through his hair. "We don't speak

of it. It's too painful."

"What if you did court her?"

"How can I court a maid? How would it look? Like I'm a philanderer taking advantage of a woman in my family's employ. No. That would create a scandal, and I won't do that to Kitty."

They moved through the steps in silence until the song was almost over.

"What will you do now?" Molly asked.

Fred sighed heavily. "I don't know. I usually have no problem thumbing my nose at the world. What do I care how I look to people? But I suppose I'm scared. What if Kitty leaves Waverly so I can court her, but it doesn't work out? I'd upset my parents and uproot Kitty's life for nothing."

"But you care for her."

"I do. I care about her more than she knows. But couples don't always stay together. Look at Roger. Is it worth the risk to Kitty, to both our hearts?"

Molly wanted, first of all, to ask for more details about Roger, and second of all, to give Fred a hug. But she did neither of those things. "Perhaps the right thing to do will become clear in time. Maybe Kitty will leave and get another position close by. Who knows what life has in store for you two? If there's a chance for love, why not take it? It's best to accept that precious gift when it comes your way. If, as you say, it doesn't work out, at least you know you tried. It seems to me a big part of your troubles right now is regret that you didn't take a chance with Kitty sooner."

"You're a wise woman, Molly. I'll think about what you said. In a few weeks, when all the wedding dust has settled, I'll talk to Kitty."

When their dance ended, Fred escorted Molly to her brothers. She'd hoped for another dance with Roger, but he was nowhere to be seen. After dancing with Albert, Tristan, and three other men, Molly made her way back to the punch room. She strolled over to the clock to see what Fred had found so interesting. Apparently nothing. It looked like any other clock.

"What are you looking at?"

The back of Molly's neck tingled as she recognized Roger's voice. When she turned around, her skirt swept over his shoes and he took a step back. Not a large one.

"Oh, nothing," Molly said. "I was in here with Fred earlier and he was staring at the clock. I thought I'd missed something."

Roger glanced at the clock. "It seems quite ordinary."

His sister Penny, wearing a lavender frock swimming in flounces and bows, stood on her toes to peer at the face. "I don't see anything. Let's get a drink. Dancing does make one so thirsty."

"Have you been dancing all night?" Molly asked her as they walked to the punchbowl.

"Almost. I danced with Roger, Fred, Father, and some boys whose names I don't know." Penny bent down to rub her toes. "There were so many of them!"

Roger handed Penny a glass of lemonade. "You must be ready for bed."

"Oh, no. I don't mind dancing with all of them again." She drank her lemonade in one gulp and chose another glass, then ambled back over to the clock.

The orchestra's song ended and once again the room was inundated with guests who brought the heat of the ballroom with them. Fans fluttered, skirts swished, and

259

ties were subtly loosened as couples milled about the room.

Roger took a step closer to Molly, presumably because the room had grown more crowded, but she couldn't help noticing there was nobody else in their immediate vicinity.

"Have you been enjoying yourself this evening?" he asked.

Molly tipped back the very last of her punch, feeling that she couldn't or shouldn't look Roger in the eye. His tone reminded her of their time upstairs yesterday. Intimate, she'd thought it then.

Roger's fingers brushed Molly's as he took her empty glass and set it on the table.

"I've been enjoying the ball very much. Have you?" Molly clasped her hands behind her back to keep them from trembling. This was ridiculous. It was only Roger, not a crown prince.

"Yes, but the evening would have been even more enjoyable with a different partner."

When Molly's cheeks grew rosy, Roger smiled.

He glanced around the room, apparently looking for something, but Molly couldn't imagine what. The chamber was sparsely furnished, with only a floral settee and a few armchairs. Landscape paintings adorned the walls, but nothing of note.

Roger leaned in close as though about to impart a fabulous secret. "Have you seen the moon tonight?"

"The moon? I can't say that I have."

"Come with me to the window." Roger kept a hand on her lower back as they crossed the room. It did not help with the trembling.

Molly made sure to steady her breath before

attempting to speak. "What about Penny? Your sister."

"She'll be fine. See? She's made a friend." He gestured to Penny, who was deep in conversation with one of Caroline's young cousins. It looked like they were comparing the ribbons in each other's hair.

When they reached the window Molly leaned out, expecting an especially breathtaking moon. It was lopsided, gray, and partially obscured by clouds.

"Would you look at that?" Roger asked, gazing up at it in wonder.

"Roger! It's…it's just the moon. The same as yesterday but, I'd say, much less pleasing." Heavy clouds drifted over to completely block it from view, reinforcing Molly's point.

He gave her a roguish grin she'd had no idea he was capable of. "I admit I was looking for an excuse to get you alone."

"We aren't alone," she said, suddenly light as air.

Roger took her hand and drew her toward him, lowering his voice. "Well, nobody can hear us. I want to see your dance card."

She straightened and pulled her hand away. "Again? Why are you so interested in my dance card? I must say, no other gentleman has ever expressed such an interest in it as you."

"Good." The look on his face as he held out his hand set Molly's pulse racing. When she gave him the card he opened it, a satisfied smile coming to his face as his eyes trailed down the empty lines. "I see I had no need of my pencil, after all."

"Between you and Fred, I never had time to fill it out." She moved to take the card back, but he held it fast.

"I don't think you'll be needing this, Molly," he

said, his eyes locked on hers.

She swallowed. "No? You think I'll be retiring early?"

Roger ran his hand lightly from her wrist to her elbow. "No. I think you'll be dancing with me for the rest of the ball."

Molly inched closer, a wave coming in to shore. "Haven't we already determined it wouldn't be appropriate?"

The roguish grin changed to a sweet, soft smile. "Nothing could be more so. You're the only—"

"Roger!" Penny skipped across the room, skidding to a halt beside them.

Molly jumped back as if she'd been about to fall off a cliff. And perhaps she had.

Roger tore his eyes away from Molly and looked at his sister. "What is it, Penny?"

"I'd like another drink." Penny took Roger's hand and led him to the refreshment table, Molly trailing behind.

After Roger served drinks for all of them, Penny drew Molly into a long conversation about being allowed to stay up late, her frock, her horse, the journey from Concord, and most of all about Penny's puppies. Though Molly and Roger both listened to Penny, he cast Molly so many warm glances and significant looks they might as well have been alone.

A little while later Penny set down her fourth empty glass and straightened her frock. "It's almost time for more dancing."

"Well," Roger said with a peek at his pocket watch, "I'd say it's time for me to escort you back to Mother and Father."

Penny took a step back as though Roger meant to drag her away by force. "I'd rather stay with you and Molly."

"We'll be dancing. You won't miss anything," Roger said.

Penny wagged a finger at him. "As long as you don't discuss anything interesting without me."

"We wouldn't dream of it."

"Definitely not," Molly assured her.

"All right. Perhaps I can convince Mother to let me stay up until midnight," Penny said.

Roger offered Penny and Molly each an arm. "Shall we?"

Molly held back. "I think I'll wait here. I...I want to get another drink."

"I'll come back for you soon," Roger said with a smile.

As she watched him walk away with Penny, Molly tried to understand what Roger's new behavior meant. It seemed it could only mean one thing. But what would happen now? Would he call on her when she went back home? Court her here at Waverly Hall? Or was she seeing things that weren't there, and he was simply in a good mood, back to his usual self? Whatever was going on with Roger, she liked it. Perhaps after the wedding excitement died down they'd spend more time together. They'd have the house virtually to themselves after the other guests left. Molly had grown to like him already, but this new side of him was even more appealing and she wanted more of it. More talking, more flirting, more...Roger.

Chapter Twenty-Two

Molly and Roger strolled around the edge of the ballroom, waiting for the music to begin. The fragrance of innumerable flowers combined with a dizzying array of women's perfumes and men's colognes suggested an apothecary or an overgrown garden.

But in truth, Molly hardly noticed. Of all those scents, Roger's stood out to her the most. He held her arm close against him and perhaps because of the heat in the room, or his nearness, his cologne was even more tantalizing than usual. She would have leaned in to sniff his jacket if she could have done it without him noticing.

"Penny likes you," Roger said suddenly as they completed another circle of the room.

"I like her. She's sweet. She's your only sibling?"

"Yes, but she'd like it if there were more of us."

"Why?"

"I'm afraid she doesn't always find me the best companion. She wants a sister, and one closer to her own age."

Molly wanted to ask exactly what their age difference was, but it seemed rude. She'd guess at least ten years, but perhaps Roger was younger than he looked. As they waited for the dancing to recommence, Molly watched Roger out of the corner of her eye. He looked relaxed and from time to time smiled to himself. She could hardly wait to be in his arms again, when she'd be able to touch his shoulder and feel his hand on her waist. Perhaps she'd try getting a little closer to him during the next dance, or let her hand drift to his back instead of his shoulder. Or would that be too forward? More than dancing she wanted to hear him talk about himself. There was still so much she didn't know.

She looked up to find him gazing at her and realized her mind had wandered in the middle of their conversation. That happened often lately when she was with Roger. She scrambled to recall what they'd been talking about.

"Does Penny have friends her own age?" Molly asked.

"Oh, yes, a fair few. She can't wait to go home to tell them all about tonight. Brag, I should say." Roger stopped walking but kept Molly's arm pressed close to his side.

"When will she go home?"

"Tomorrow. We're leaving after lunch."

Leaving? Something cold settled in her chest as Molly looked down at the floor to give herself a moment to compose her features. "I didn't realize you were going with them."

"I'm accompanying my family to Concord, but I'll only stay a few days and come back. I hope you'll keep an eye on Penny for me."

The tightness in Molly's shoulders vanished. "I'd be happy to. Perhaps the puppies will be here by the time you return."

"I hope so."

They lapsed into silence, and as Molly looked around the room she saw Kitty slip in through a door on the other side of the ballroom. At least, a woman who

265

vaguely resembled Kitty. If Molly hadn't known what her dress looked like, she never would have recognized her. Kitty's hair was done up elaborately and her gown accentuated her delicate neck and shoulders. More than the gown and hair, the confidence and air of grace had transformed Kitty. There was no hint of a maid. Nobody else in the room gave Kitty a second glance, but Molly saw Fred hurrying across the ballroom toward her, transfixed.

Molly smiled broadly as she watched them.

Roger squeezed her arm gently. "What are you smiling about?"

"Oh, I'm excited for the dancing to start," she said to avoid divulging Kitty's secret.

"Why wait?" He swept her into his arms and spun her around.

"Roger, not yet!" Molly said, laughing.

Just then the music started and he gave her a smug look. "Yet."

He kept an arm around her as they walked out onto the dance floor, where Molly saw Kitty and Fred dancing, eyes locked on each other. A smile lit up her face.

Roger took her hand as his other encircled her waist. "You're happy tonight, Molly Merriwether."

"I am. Weddings are happy occasions."

He twirled her around. "Then we should attend weddings all the time."

We?

"Weddings don't happen every day," she said. "Fortunately, many other things make me happy."

"Such as?"

Molly's mind went blank. She couldn't think of

what else existed, never mind what made her happy as she looked into his eyes. His smile faltered, replaced by an expression that made her knees weak. She fervently wished they were alone, somewhere quiet and dark. Perhaps the garden or the attic. They could dance, or—Molly went pink just imagining it.

Roger's arm around her waist tightened, holding her closer than the dance warranted. "Your eyes are blue," he whispered.

Molly's brow furrowed. "Excuse me?"

"Your eyes are blue."

She laughed. "I'm aware of that."

He smiled, and she was pleased to see some pink in *his* face for once.

Roger brushed her cheek lightly, but it felt like a bolt of lightning. "What I meant is, they're very blue. Like a lake, or an ocean. They're so dark. But sometimes, like now, when you're happy, they look brighter. Like the sky."

"Maybe it's the light from the candles," Molly said, her voice unexpectedly hoarse.

He continued to stare into her eyes. "Maybe."

They were the only people standing still on the dance floor as waltzing couples veered around them. Something from the corner of Molly's eye caught her attention and she blinked, then reluctantly turned her eyes away from Roger.

Fred and Kitty were dancing, oblivious to Mrs. Lane, who was peering at Kitty as she barreled across the ballroom.

What was she doing here? If Mrs. Lane exposed her, Kitty would lose her position, not to mention being humiliated in front of scores of people. Molly had to do something, but what? It came to her in a flash.

"Roger!"

"What's wrong?" He looked down as if to be sure he hadn't trodden on her foot.

"I need you to do something that won't make any sense. We're going to have to make a spectacle of ourselves again." She looked over her shoulder, where Mrs. Lane was being held up by a cluster of ancient couples who'd decided to do a quadrille.

Roger looked amused but puzzled. "Why?"

Not thinking, she put a hand on his chest as they started dancing again. "I'll explain later. But trust me, I'm doing this because it's the only way I can help someone in this room right now."

He covered her hand with his. "What do you need me to do?"

"I'm going to faint and you'll have to catch me."

Roger froze. "You're what?"

"I'm only pretending."

Across the room Mrs. Lane was only two couples away from Fred and Kitty, a triumphant look on her face.

"Ready?" Molly asked.

"I'm always ready to do anything for you."

His fervent tone almost made her forget what she was doing. She leaned in close. "I'm going to swoon. Catch me."

Roger didn't have time to answer, because Molly fell sideways, apparently lifeless. He swept her into his arms, one arm under her knees, the other supporting her back, her head pressed against his chest. She remained motionless as people cried out, clustering around to see what had happened. When Mrs. Lane's voice was among those asking what the trouble was, Molly breathed a silent sigh of relief.

Mrs. Merriwether broke through the crowd and put a hand to her forehead. "Oh, Molly! What's wrong?"

Roger played his part perfectly. "She must be tired from all the dancing. Perhaps it's the heat."

"She needs a drink." Caroline took her hand and patted it.

Oh, not Caroline! If only Molly could tell her this was all an act.

"She needs to get to her room," Mrs. Merriwether said.

"What happened? Did she fall asleep? Is she hurt?" That was Penny.

Roger started walking. "I'll bring her to the parlor."

"Do you want me to take her?" Albert asked in a worried tone.

Roger tightened his hold on her. "It's probably easier if I carry her."

Molly was glad. Even with all the commotion, she was not unaware of how divine it felt to be cradled in his arms.

Roger made his way to the parlor, a small crowd trailing behind. He laid Molly on the velvet chaise and smoothed down her hair, then his hands were replaced by smaller, softer ones. Caroline.

Since Kitty must have had time to get away by now, Molly let her eyes flicker open. "What…what happened?"

"You fainted!" Penny shouted, looking down at her from behind the chaise. "Roger carried you. Don't you remember? Are you ill?"

Caroline, perched on the edge of the chaise, gave Molly a glass of wine with a shaking hand.

"Oh, Caroline. Go back to Benedict," Molly said, putting a hand on her shoulder.

She watched Molly closely as though worried she might faint again. "As soon as I know you're well."

Molly could have cried. She propped herself up. "I *am* well. I promise. It must have been the heat."

"If you're sure?"

"Yes." She leaned in and whispered, "I did it on purpose. For Kitty. I'll explain later."

Caroline looked at her like she was mad, but the worry drained from her face. "Oh, Molly." She kissed her forehead and left.

Mrs. Merriwether immediately took Caroline's place, smelling salts in hand. "Do you need anything else? I hope you didn't overexert yourself." She sent a chilly glance in Roger's direction.

Molly swung her feet around and set them on the floor. "No, Mother, I'll be fine once I've caught my breath."

"You need to lie down for a while longer," her mother said, pressing on her shoulder.

Mrs. Merriwether, Mrs. Clarke, Mrs. Bailey, Penny, and Aunt Hazel stayed with Molly, offering drinks, shawls, cold compresses, books, and advice. Penny brought cake, certain it was the only thing that would help. When Molly was finally allowed to stand up, Roger was gone.

The next morning Molly slept in. After her stunt at the ball last night, her mother had insisted she go upstairs early. Molly hadn't minded getting away from the clutch of fussing women but regretted not being able to dance with Roger again and thank him for his help.

Molly climbed out of bed. She shouldn't tarry

upstairs. After all, her family was leaving today. But it wouldn't be long before they came back to take her home for the Season. Well, she'd enjoy every moment she could while she was still here.

Remembering last night, Molly smiled. There could be no doubt now that Roger fancied her. She glanced at the clock. He must be downstairs by now. She dressed hurriedly and went to the breakfast room, where a buffet was set up. Extra tables had been erected outside and some people, the Baileys included, sat in the quadrangle. Molly filled a plate and went out to join them.

Dewy grass left watermarks on her shoes as she approached their table beside the fountain. The water glistened and splashed in the sun, reminding Molly of the waterfall they'd visited during the picnic. It felt like a lifetime ago, especially when she considered how much closer she and Roger had grown since then. "Good morning," she said.

Roger rose when he saw her, and she had the feeling he'd been waiting for her to arrive. The thought made the morning even brighter.

He pulled the chair beside him out. "Good morning."

"Roger, I want her to sit next to me," Penny said from the other side of the table.

"Now, Penny," Mrs. Bailey said, "Roger and Miss Merriwether probably want to chat."

Molly stepped back from the chair, unsure of where to sit. She wanted to sit beside Roger but it seemed churlish to say no to a child.

"They had all that time for talking last night while they danced," Penny said. Penny, the dog, lay dozing at her feet.

271

Roger pulled out the chair next to Penny. "It's true, I do have Miss Merriwether to myself most of the time."

Something in his tone made it sound much more intimate than it was, and Molly's cheeks reddened. She took a deep breath of crisp morning air, but apparently it didn't help.

Mr. Bailey looked at her. "Would you like a drink? You look flushed."

"Yes, thank you," Molly said, fanning herself with her hand. "It's so warm out this morning."

"Indeed." Roger cast her a glance that was much more than warm.

Mr. Bailey poured a glass of juice for Molly and they all continued their meal. Everyone but Molly, who could hardly eat because her heart was taking up the space where her stomach usually resided. She nibbled at a blueberry scone, taking covert glances at Roger while he chatted with his parents. She'd rarely seen him so at ease, except in the tavern or when he was with Fred.

Her heart skipped a beat when she realized where else she'd seen him like this before. With her. In the attic, and last night at the ball. Roger was so different from what she'd supposed when she first met him. She'd thought him distant, cold, and unfriendly. Now that she understood what he was really like, she regretted those first few weeks before they'd become acquainted. Why hadn't she tried to draw him out? It felt like time wasted.

Penny tapped her arm. "Molly!"

Molly set her drink down, aware of Roger's amused eyes resting on her. "Yes?"

"You'll watch Penny while we're gone?" Penny asked, sliding off her chair to sit in the grass beside her dog.

Molly swiveled in her seat to look down at her. "I'll keep a very close eye on her, and if she has the puppies I'll send a message."

Penny reached up for the toast she'd left on the table. "To Roger?"

"No, to you. I'll let you know how she is and how many puppies there are." Molly leaned down to scratch the dog's head.

"I hope she has at least six," Penny said.

Roger folded his napkin and set it beside his plate. "What on earth would we do with six more dogs?"

"We have space for them," Penny said. "Perhaps they could be hunters, like Fred's dogs." She finished her toast in one bite and wiped her hands on her skirt. Mrs. Bailey held out a napkin, pursing her lips.

Roger scoffed. "I wouldn't call those dogs hunters."

"Perhaps Penny's puppies *will* be hunters. She did capture that fox," Molly reminded him. He met her eyes as they shared a laugh.

Penny rose and walked over to Roger. "What happened?"

"I'll tell you on the way home."

"I'd rather hear about it now," Penny said, draping an arm around his shoulder.

"We'll have plenty of time for stories in the carriage," Mrs. Bailey said before Roger could answer. She turned to Molly. "Are you going home today, Miss Merriwether?"

"No, I'm staying until Caroline returns."

"It's unfortunate you aren't coming home today," Penny said. "Roger says your house isn't far from ours. You could have ridden with us."

Just the idea of two days in a carriage with Roger

made Molly wish she *was* leaving today.

"Speaking of which, we'd better finish packing," Mr. Bailey said, rising from the table.

While the family went upstairs, Molly and Roger followed behind the dog. Penny looked like a barrel with short legs as she made her slow way back inside, tail wagging as she stopped to sniff almost every flower patch or tuft of grass.

When Molly glanced at Roger she was surprised to find him watching her. He didn't say anything, but casually took her hand as though he did it every day.

"Are you looking forward to going home?" she asked.

He entwined his fingers with hers. "Actually…I'd stay here if I could."

"You would?" Molly asked, unable to stop the grin that came to her face.

Roger met her eyes. "I would."

Molly tried not to read too much into that warm gaze. "You won't be gone long, will you?"

"No, not long. Did you find time to finish your book?"

Molly hardly knew how to answer, as it was difficult to form words at the moment. He'd never held her hand like this, not out where anyone could see them. "Not yet. But I'll have plenty of time to read now that everyone's leaving. I expect I'll be bored."

"I'll leave my book behind for you to read, if you like. When I come back we can go up to the attic to discuss it."

"Thank you. I've been curious about it since you liked it so much. I doubt we'll need to meet upstairs, though, now that everyone's leaving."

"I wouldn't want to give up our visits to the attic. That book will always remind me of you now, since—"

"Since what?"

Roger looked away. "Oh, since I read it when we were together."

The word *together* had never sounded so sweet. Molly tightened her grip on his hand.

They walked in silence for a few moments before Roger turned back to her. "Why aren't you going home if you think you'll be bored here?"

"Caroline and I thought it would be nice if I'm here to welcome her when she returns. My mother will come fetch me not long after, though, to go to town for the Season." She held back her grimace so she wouldn't look childish.

Roger's steps faltered. "The Season?"

"Yes, Mrs. Darby helped my mother secure invitations to all the best balls." Molly smiled, recalling her mother's excitement over the stack of invitations she'd received.

"I see." He paused for a long moment. "Will you be attending the balls with anyone in particular?"

"My mother may have arranged something. She's eager for me to form new acquaintances. I'll be very busy, but I suppose that's the whole purpose of the Season."

Roger looked down at the ground. "I hope you enjoy yourself."

"Thank you. I think I'll see you before I leave Rochester. When will you be back?" She hoped it wasn't presumptuous to ask, but it was bad enough he was leaving, and not knowing when he'd return made it worse.

"In a week or so. As far as I know, I don't have any business that will detain me, but one never knows." He pulled his hand away, leaving Molly's quite empty and cold.

"No, one never does. But you *will* be back?" She tried to smile at him, but couldn't catch his eye.

"Most likely." He didn't speak again or look at Molly as they followed Penny back to the house.

When they parted ways, Molly watched Roger as he walked down the hall, shoulders slumped. Perhaps he didn't want to go home or was worried about Penny. She considered following him so she could ask but didn't want to appear meddlesome.

Molly went to her mother's room for tea, and later they spent a happy hour at the kennels with Fred, Tristan, and Albert while the family's luggage was taken to their carriage. As she and Mrs. Merriwether walked back to the house, Molly kept at an eye out for Roger on the grounds. She'd hoped he might join them at the kennels.

"Who are you looking for?" her mother asked. "Tristan and Albert are probably in the house by now."

"I thought Roger might come out to say hello before you all left." She shielded her eyes against the sun, looking up at the attic windows.

"Mr. Bailey, you mean."

"Yes, of course."

Her mother stopped walking and peered into Molly's eyes as though trying to read her thoughts. "I hope you aren't becoming too attached to that young man."

"Not at all. He's only a friend." This was true, as, even though he'd been especially attentive at the ball, this morning he was as hard to read as ever. Holding her hand one moment, practically ignoring her the next.

"Good," her mother said with a satisfied look. "See that it stays that way."

Molly narrowed her eyes. "Do you mean to say that even if I came to care for him, you wouldn't approve?"

"You just said he's only your friend." Her mother's fingers whitened as she gripped the handle of her purse.

"I know what I said. It isn't about Rog—Mr. Bailey, in particular. But it doesn't seem to be your place to tell me who I should or shouldn't get attached to."

"Not my place! I'm your mother. We have a whole Season ahead of us, and who knows who you might meet or fall in love with? You'd be doing yourself a grave disservice by becoming infatuated with Mr. Bailey." She pulled a fan out of her bag and started furiously flapping it in front of her face.

"I'm not infatuated with Mr. Bailey. But when I do find someone to love, it's my decision, not yours."

"You can't make a decision like that without speaking to your father and me first. Oh!" Her mother rubbed her temple. "This is what comes of you being here unchaperoned all those weeks!"

"Mother, it has nothing to do with that."

Mrs. Merriwether stared at Molly for several long moments, tapping her folded fan on her palm. When she tucked it back into her bag and squared her shoulders, Molly knew she wouldn't like what was coming.

"I know your father and I had decided to let you stay here a bit longer, but it's now clear to me that you should come home with us today," her mother said. "How long will it take you to pack?"

Molly gasped. "I'm not coming home! It's all arranged. I'm waiting here for Caroline." She started up the hill but her mother caught her arm.

"I cannot leave you here with that man, now that I know you like him. Whether you admit it or not, Molly, I know you do."

"*That man* is leaving today." Molly pulled out of her mother's grasp. Even if Roger wasn't leaving, Molly knew how to conduct herself around gentlemen. How had her mother come to distrust her so much after the unchaperoned fiasco? It was as if she didn't know her own daughter.

Mrs. Merriwether visibly relaxed. "Mr. Bailey's leaving?"

"Yes, and I don't know when he'll be back. So you needn't worry about it."

"In that case, you may stay. But don't become embroiled with Mr. Clarke's brother, or any other man you might meet. You have your—"

"Season to think of. *Yes, I know.*" You'd think any woman would be happy if her daughter fell in love with a man she already knew and liked. But not her mother. She wouldn't be content until Molly had gone to every ball and met every eligible man in the country.

Her mother stared thoughtfully at the house. "I could leave one of your brothers here. I daresay Albert wouldn't mind."

"Mother, I'm not a child. You don't need to leave Albert behind to keep an eye on me. I'm perfectly capable of staying here by myself. I've done it before, and without Mr. and Mrs. Clarke here."

"And look what happened! But yes, I'd forgotten the Clarkes will be here. I'll have a word with Mrs. Clarke before I go."

Molly's jaw dropped. "You're going to ask Mrs.

Clarke to make sure I don't talk to any of the men? That will make me look foolish, Mother."

Mrs. Merriwether laughed. "Of course you can talk to them."

"But not get *entangled* with them?" Molly asked through gritted teeth.

"That's right. Now, I can't argue with you about this anymore. It's almost time for the carriage to leave. Will you come say goodbye?"

The last thing she wanted was to go anywhere with her mother right now, but she didn't want to part ways with hard feelings between them. "Yes. I'm sorry for being irritable, Mother. Perhaps I'm tired after the wedding." Molly knew very well she wasn't arguing with her mother because she was tired.

"We all are." Her mother patted her arm and they continued to the house.

A few hours later, Molly was reading in the yellow drawing room when Roger knocked on the doorframe. She set her book aside and rose, smiling. "Hello, Roger."

He stayed in the open doorway, hand on the knob. "We're about to leave and Penny wants to say goodbye. Could you come out to the drive?"

"I'd be happy to."

"Thank you." He stood aside so she could pass and walked beside her as they went down the empty corridor, hands behind his back. The house already felt quieter, hollow somehow, now that so many guests had departed. It would be even emptier after Roger left.

"I didn't have a chance to thank you for helping me last night," Molly said as they walked down the stairs.

"It was my pleasure."

Molly considered taking his hand, but decided it

would be too forward. And besides, he'd now thrust both hands into his jacket pockets. "I wish I could tell you why I acted that way, but it isn't my secret to divulge."

"You don't need to. Fred told me about Kitty. That was kind of you."

She trailed her hand along the banister. "You must have thought I was quite odd. But now you understand why."

"When it comes to you, Molly, I've come to expect the unexpected."

Not sure if it was a compliment or merely an observation, Molly didn't reply. He hadn't met her eyes once since this morning, and something about his demeanor reminded her of the Roger of old. Not precisely cold, but she could hardly believe this was the same man who'd wanted to claim her whole dance card last night.

They continued in silence to the front of the house, where they found the Baileys waiting beside their carriage.

"Goodbye, it was a pleasure to meet all of you," Molly said.

Mr. and Mrs. Bailey bade her farewell and climbed into the carriage.

Penny looked up into Molly's face. "Do write and tell me about the puppies, and if you like you could write to me afterwards, to stay in touch. I'd write back. You live so close to us, we could meet for tea one day."

"I'd love that. Have a safe journey." She extended a hand but instead of shaking it, Penny wrapped her arms around Molly's waist. Molly smiled and hugged her back.

"Goodbye. Enjoy your Season." Penny climbed into

the carriage and poked her head out the open window. "Write to me about your balls. I'll want to hear all about them, and be sure to describe your gowns." She disappeared into the carriage and pulled the curtains closed before Molly could answer.

Then it was only Molly and Roger.

He looked at his watch and made to leave without bidding her farewell. Something was wrong, but what? There was no way she could ask, as his family was waiting to leave, not to mention the other carriages lined up behind them.

"I'll see you in a week or so?" Molly asked before he could open the carriage door.

"Most likely. Here's our address, if you need to write to Penny." Roger handed her a piece of paper and she barely resisted unfolding it right away to see his handwriting.

"Thank you." She slipped it into her pocket even though her bodice seemed a more suitable place. "I'll let you know if Penny has the puppies, or if there's a change in her health."

They stood in front of each other, Molly staring at Roger's face while he stared at the sky. At a time like this Molly would expect him to take her hand or embrace her, but he didn't.

One of the horses hitched to the Baileys' carriage whinnied suddenly, breaking Roger out of whatever reverie he'd been in. He gave her a quick nod. "Goodbye."

"Goodbye, Roger."

He got into the carriage without even a backwards glance. The horses pulled away immediately, and Molly's heart leapt when a hand reached out of the window to wave. But no. The hand was small and wearing a bracelet. She waved back to Penny, then went into the house, where she stood at a window, watching until the carriage was out of sight. There was an uncomfortable feeling in her stomach, or perhaps it was her heart. Why had Roger's goodbye felt like an ending, not merely a temporary parting? She thought back over the morning. He'd held her hand and seemed happy in her company, at least for a while. But then his mood had shifted, and Molly wished she knew why.

There'd been more than one moment during the ball when she'd thought he might kiss her, but he certainly wasn't acting that way now. Maybe he was tired since he'd stayed up late with Fred. Moreover, he could hardly flirt with her or embrace her when his family had been sitting right there in the carriage. Molly pulled out the paper he'd written his address on and ran her fingers over the words, already anxious for Roger's return.

Chapter Twenty-Three

Waverly Hall felt like a vast palace now that most of the wedding guests were gone. All over the manor, rooms were being cleaned, furniture put back in place, and a feeling of peace restored.

Four days after the wedding, Molly went up to the attic. Not because she needed to avoid anyone, but simply because she liked it. And, to be honest, it reminded her of Roger. She'd started looking forward to his return but hadn't asked Fred when he'd be back because she suspected he already knew she liked Roger. She wouldn't have minded talking about him, but not to Fred. Molly missed talking to Caroline more than she'd imagined she would. It had been years since she couldn't just walk over to Norbury to speak with her, and even longer since she'd had anything so important to discuss.

When Molly reached the attic, she crossed the room to the sofa. To her surprise, Roger's book was waiting for her, a piece of paper poking out of the top. Smiling, she opened it and saw his now familiar handwriting.

I hope you enjoy this as much as I did.
Roger

A simple enough note, but Molly held it to her chest as if it were a love letter. Roger had only been gone a few days but it felt like longer, and it surprised Molly to realize how aware she'd been of his presence. She didn't think the same could be said for him, however. More often than not she'd thought she was disturbing him if she came upon him in the library or office. He seemed tolerant of the intrusions, but not as though he welcomed them. That had changed since the ball, or she hoped it had. After that day in the attic, things had been different between them. She could hardly wait for his return, and was daydreaming about simple things like being in the same room with him, sitting together and reading or playing with Penny. It couldn't be long now before she'd be looking into his eyes and hearing him laugh. Molly smiled to herself, running her fingers over his note before settling in to start the book he'd left for her.

A few days later, Molly was in the attic when she heard the unmistakable sounds of arrival. She set her book aside and went to the window in time to see Fred running down the front steps to greet Roger, who'd just dismounted. They shook hands, and Roger looked up at the house as he followed Fred inside.

Molly ran across the attic and down to her bedchamber. After changing into her pink dress, she brushed her hair and headed to the parlor. Then the drawing room. Then the breakfast room, the dining room, the billiard room and finally the library. She wondered where to look next. Perhaps the kennels?

Molly put a hand to her forehead. Of course. Roger would go straight to Penny. She made her way to the north wing and knocked on the office door.

"Come in."

Oh, his voice. She took a deep breath and pushed the door open.

When Molly saw Roger sitting on the floor beside Penny, it was like not a day had passed—aside from the fact he looked even more handsome than when he'd left.

Had his lips always been so tempting? His eyes so beautiful, his hair curling in that adorable way at the nape of his neck?

Roger got to his feet and rested a hand on the back of the chair. "Hello."

"Hello." She could hardly hear the word over her thumping heart. Molly stepped forward, but he didn't come any closer or reach for her hand, as she'd hoped he would.

His grip on the chair tightened as his eyes drank her in.

"Good afternoon, Molly," Fred said from the corner.

Molly jumped and, of course, reddened. "Oh, Fred! I didn't see you there."

Fred cast a knowing look over his shoulder. "I gathered. Roger and I are having a drink. Join us?"

"Yes, please."

"Have a seat," Fred said and turned back to the decanters.

Roger stepped aside so Molly could sit in the chair. He hadn't taken his eyes off her since she'd arrived, but they weren't shining as they'd been the first moment they'd seen each other. They were guarded, presumably due to Fred's presence.

"How was your journey?" she asked, trying to clear her expression of the obvious fondness she felt for him.

He stood stiffly with his hands behind his back, looking down at her. "Nice, thank you."

"How's Penny?"

Roger looked at the dog.

"I meant your sister," Molly said with a grin.

"Happy to get home. She invited her friends over and told them all about the wedding and the ball." Was he avoiding her eyes now?

"She must have enjoyed that." Molly smiled again but he simply nodded. She gave him a moment to answer, but when he didn't, she went on. "I haven't finished the book you left me yet, but when I do we can discuss it." She glanced over at Fred, whose back was to them, and whispered, "In the attic."

He just nodded again and stared at the rhododendrons outside the window.

Fred came over and handed each of them a glass of wine, then drew Roger into a discussion about an old school friend.

Molly was happy enough to just sit and listen, petting Penny and hearing Roger's voice. She'd missed him. Truly missed him. She hadn't realized how much until now. But had he missed her at all? He certainly wasn't acting like it, but perhaps his cool demeanor was because of Fred.

After a time, the men remembered Molly was there and started talking about people she knew. Soon after, it was time for dinner. They went to the dining room, where they ate with Mr. and Mrs. Clarke and the few remaining houseguests. Roger sat on the other side of the table, and though Molly tried to catch his eye several times she was not successful.

Afterwards, she joined Roger and Fred in the parlor. She and Fred sat on the sofa, but Roger chose a book from the shelf and settled himself in a chair beside the window. Molly tried her best to follow Fred's conversation, but it wasn't easy when her eyes were constantly drawn to the far corner of the room. After an hour or so, Fred excused himself and Molly was finally able to approach Roger.

Surely he'd be more friendly now that they were alone. That was always his way, after all. Perhaps he was shy of her in front of others because he didn't want to betray his feelings. Feelings that, until today in the office, Molly had been almost certain of. She crossed the room, admiring his profile as he bent over a book. "Good story?"

Roger jumped as if he hadn't heard her approach. "Yes, it is." He gave her a quick glance but kept the book open.

"Are you tired from your journey?" Molly expected him to rise, but he sat rigidly, as though fused to the cushions.

Roger turned back to his book. "It was a long day."

The crackling fire and ticking clock sounded loud as drums as Molly waited for Roger to say something else. From down the hall came peals of laughter; it sounded like Fred and Kitty.

Molly waited for a few moments, not wanting to leave but with the distinct feeling she wasn't welcome. "I'll say goodnight."

He didn't look up. "Goodnight."

Molly took a few steps but halfway across the room she paused. After waiting all this time to see him, she simply couldn't leave things as they were. She walked back, coming to a halt in front of his chair. "Roger?"

"Hm?" He looked up at her face but didn't meet her eyes.

She put her hands behind her back so he couldn't see her wringing them. "Is…is everything all right?"

"Why, yes, of course," he said with a thin smile. He crossed his legs and resumed reading.

"You seem…upset. Or tired?"

"Tired. Goodnight." Since it was stated as a dismissal, she took it as such.

Molly trudged upstairs and collapsed onto her bed. "That did not go well," she muttered to herself.

The next day at breakfast, Roger was polite but distant. Over the course of the next few days Molly came to realize that was Roger's new personality—polite but distant. To her, at any rate. She often heard him laughing with Fred or talking animatedly to Mr. and Mrs. Clarke, but when Molly tried to engage him, he treated her like an acquaintance.

It wasn't only the conversation that was stilted. Whenever he entered a room and found himself alone with Molly, he promptly left. If one of the Clarkes suggested an outing and Molly agreed to come along, Roger bowed out at the last moment. If they were the last two people at a meal, he'd bolt his food down and practically run from the room.

Molly tried making eye contact with him daily, but he avoided it. Sometimes she felt his eyes on her, but when she looked at him he'd be gazing in the other direction.

The first day or so, Molly assumed Roger was tired or distracted or busy, but by the third day it was abundantly clear he was snubbing her. At first she'd been sad. Had she offended Roger somehow? Had he gone back to his old ways because of something that happened while he was home in Concord? Had he met someone?

It wasn't until the fifth day that Molly's sadness turned to annoyance. She went to see Penny that afternoon, as she always did. Molly rubbed the dog's ears the way she liked and offered her bits of food. Based on Penny's size, Molly expected the puppies to be born any day and had taken to visiting her more often than usual. She wouldn't be surprised if one day when she stopped by Penny would be gone, having located a secret spot to have her puppies. Molly was contemplating likely places when the office door opened and Roger bounded in, smiling, with an exuberant, "Hello, Penny!"

As soon as he saw Molly the smile evaporated, and he straightened. "Good afternoon."

Molly wasn't sure why this, of all things, was the last straw. But it was. "Good afternoon?" she asked coldly.

"I'm sorry I disturbed you. I'll come back later."

"Penny is *your* dog. I'll leave." Molly rose, but instead of marching out the door as she'd intended, she planted herself in front of him, fists on her hips. "But before I go, might I ask, what is the matter with you? Why are you ignoring me?"

Roger lowered his brows slightly. "I'm not. I speak to you every day."

"You speak to me?" Molly crossed her arms tightly over her chest.

He looked at her as though wondering why she couldn't comprehend his simple answer. "Yes, I do."

"You speak *at* me, but you don't talk *to* me, you don't smile at me, you act like you barely know me." It was all she could do to keep her tone civil.

Roger looked off to the side. "I don't know what you mean."

"Oh, stop, *Mr.* Bailey. You know very well the last few days you've been either ignoring me or avoiding me." Molly took a step closer.

Roger took a step back.

She glared at him. "Aren't you even going to say

something?"

"I don't know what you expect me to say."

"An apology? An explanation? Anything?" Molly cleared her throat to rid it of the pleading tone.

"I'm sorry?" He lifted his hands helplessly. "For…for not doing what you want?"

Molly let her arms drop to her sides, suddenly weary. "You truly don't understand why I'm upset?"

"No." He finally met her eyes but there was no sign of friendliness, let alone affection. That veil she'd hoped was gone forever had returned.

"Well, Mr. Bailey, I'm upset because"—Oh, not now, tears!—"because I thought we were friends. But you come back and act as if you hardly know me, even after…after the ball." She didn't say exactly what had happened at the ball, because she didn't need to. Roger was no doubt aware their relationship had changed that night. Or Molly had thought it had. "And now you stand here and pretend nothing's wrong. What do I need to do? Take you back to the tavern, or up to the attic, or some other unusual place? Is that the only way you'll be nice to me? Maybe you don't think I'm worthy of your attention when we're around other people, is that it? You like to talk to me and…and flirt with me when we're alone, but you don't consider me your friend?" She stood there, chest heaving, staring at him, begging him with her eyes to tell her she was wrong, that he did care, that he *was* her friend.

But Roger Bailey said nothing.

Molly took a deep, shuddering breath and wiped away her tears. "Goodbye, Mr. Bailey." She strode past him without another glance and ran down the hall.

Roger's cry of, "Molly, wait!" came much, much

too late.

In her bedchamber, Molly sat at the desk drinking cold tea still here from this morning. After a moment she jumped to her feet and set the cup back in its saucer with a trembling hand. As she paced back and forth between her room and Caroline's, Molly knew she had to get out of here.

There was no way she was staying another night under this roof with Roger. Well, one or two, only because she must. But she'd stay in her room or the attic—no, not the attic, she thought with a pang—or anywhere *he* wasn't while travel arrangements were made. Maybe she'd take a room at an inn. The Blue Swan, perhaps. Yes. She'd go there tomorrow and hire a carriage to take her back home.

Her mother would be pleased she didn't need to come back for her, and they'd go to town early for the Season. Mrs. Merriwether's worries about Molly getting too attached to Roger had been utterly pointless, as Roger himself made it impossible.

Molly would write to Caroline from Hartford and explain why she'd had to leave early. She'd understand. After that, Molly could forget all about Roger.

She need never see him again.

The thought didn't make her feel strong, it made her want to throw herself on the floor and weep. Molly sat on the edge of her bed, sniffling. What had gone wrong? She'd never know. She wiped away a solitary tear, swearing to herself it would be the last one she ever shed over Roger.

Molly forced down a few sips of tea, ate a stale sandwich, and changed into her blue riding habit. Striding toward the stable, she veered onto the forest path instead. She needed to walk. Just walk.

An hour or so later, Molly's pace finally slowed. The heavy afternoon sky warned her that she should turn back, but she didn't want to. Not yet. As she walked, she recalled the words she'd exchanged with Roger, and the look on his face. Was he truly so indifferent to her? Molly wiped a hand across her cheek. Wait. That wasn't a tear. When she looked up, light rain sprinkled her face. She trudged along, not minding the drops. It was a bit refreshing, really.

When Molly came to a small stream, she sat on a fallen log beside it, remembering the day Roger helped her out of the pond. She'd barely known him then. He was so quiet, kept so much to himself, she'd never considered growing close to him. But somehow it had happened. At least she'd thought so, but whatever bond she'd imagined they forged had evaporated.

The rain came harder and it was time to head back, whether she wanted to or not. Molly would go straight to her room and have a hot bath, then pack her things. After that, she'd retire early and leave first thing tomorrow for The Blue Swan.

As Molly walked, she realized she didn't recognize the trail she was on. She paused and turned in a circle. Was this the way she'd come? After a few tentative steps down the path she stopped and went back. The forest appeared the same whichever direction she looked. She'd been so deep in thought on her way here she hadn't paid any attention to landmarks at all. "Fool," she said aloud.

Molly made her best guess as to the direction and started walking. And walking. And walking. The rain was steady and there was no denying the sky was growing darker. Thunder rumbled and, not long after, the first bolt of lightning illuminated the forest. Suspecting she wasn't going the right way, Molly changed course. Shivering, she wrapped her arms around herself, her sodden riding habit clinging to her legs as icy water seeped into her clothes.

The longer she walked, the more often thunder roared through the sky like the constant growl of some monstrous beast. Dark clouds roiled and churned high above as rain poured down. There was no sign of a trail. Molly half ran through the woods, hoping to find something recognizable. She'd even be happy to see the pond at this point. At least she'd know where she was.

As she squeezed between two trees, the long veil of her riding hat caught in thick branches and stuck. After giving it a few fruitless tugs, she abandoned it. All Molly wanted was to get back to Waverly and stay there. Oh, why had she come out! There was no way to know how long she'd been walking, but it felt like all her life. The rain and semi-darkness made it impossible to check the time on her watch. It could be twilight or midnight.

Suddenly Molly screamed as thunder cracked directly overhead and lightning plunged into a tall oak just ahead of her, splitting it in two. Sparks from the burning tree rained down on the forest, hissing when they reached the ground. Pungent smoke crept through the underbrush and, heedless of where she was going, Molly just ran. Arms over her head, she couldn't stop the tears as she stumbled through the night, praying to see the lights of Waverly Hall.

At long last, Molly's heart leapt when she recognized the glade where she and Roger had found Penny the day of the hunt. But then it plummeted just as fast. In place of the quaint brook she'd seen weeks ago was a wide, fast, overflowing stream. Molly pushed the sheet of wet hair out of her eyes. There was nothing for it. It was either ford the stream or go back to…where?

She picked up her skirts and stepped cautiously from one stone to the next until she was almost across. Already considering which direction she should take when she reached the other side, Molly's foot slipped off a wet, mossy boulder. She landed hard in the water with a thud, with no Roger in sight to help her out. Spluttering, she half crawled, half swam through the frigid water to the far bank.

When she reached the other side she lay down in the dirt, gasping for breath as rain pelted her. After a few minutes she rose to her feet and tried to wring out her waterlogged, heavy skirts. Molly set her shoulders and kept walking, heartened to know she was in the right part of the woods.

Lightning was now coming so fast the forest appeared to flash between night and day every few minutes. Remembering the burning tree, Molly quickened her pace. After emerging from a stand of towering maples, she gasped. A light! She hurried toward it. It must be a lantern, but who would be out on a night like this? Whoever it was would be able to lead her home.

Molly panicked when she lost sight of the light for a moment, but then it returned, brighter than before. Perhaps she'd finally come to Waverly's grounds! Just the thought made her forget how cold and wet she was. Molly lifted her skirts and ran. As she drew closer she realized it wasn't the manor or a lantern, but a windowpane that must have reflected a lightning flash.

Barely visible in the falling darkness was the hunting lodge she'd seen with Roger weeks ago. She ducked onto the porch to escape the rain and tried the door. Locked. Molly huddled against the wall, dreaming of hearths and beds and blankets inside. Perhaps even tea.

Molly left the shelter of the porch only long enough to find a large rock. Gritting her teeth and shielding her eyes, she hurled it at the window beside the door. It crashed through the glass, taking out the bottom row of panes. Careful not to cut herself, Molly reached in, unlocked the door and pushed it open.

Chapter Twenty-Four

Molly crept through the dark, silent, wonderfully dry house. It was impossible to see the entire ground floor, but she could just make out the furniture of what appeared be a combined dining area and drawing room. Molly made her way to the fireplace, where she ran her hands along the mantel. To her immense relief, she found a box of matches and a candle.

After lighting the candle, Molly held it up to look around the room. It was rustically furnished, as she would expect of a hunting lodge, but comfortable. A timeworn blue sofa faced the hearth, and just behind it stood an oval dining table and chairs.

The far side of the room was completely shrouded in darkness. Molly would explore more thoroughly in the morning or by the light of a fire. Perhaps there was a doorway to another chamber, or a staircase leading to the upper floors.

There was dry wood beside the hearth and none of the furniture was covered, which led her to wonder if the lodge had been used more recently than Roger knew.

As Molly shivered in her wet habit, a ridiculous yet necessary idea came to her. She sighed. She'd have to. Setting the candle down, she unbuttoned her dripping jacket and draped it over one of the wooden chairs flanking the fireplace. Next, she undressed down to her chemise, which she wouldn't consider taking off even though she was alone. She wrung her clothes out and hung them over the dining chairs.

Molly looked at the ceiling and wondered if there might be clothes upstairs. Men's clothes, perhaps, but dry clothes. If nothing else, she'd give a great deal for a pair of dry woolen socks. Maybe in a little while she'd go explore the upper floor. She knelt beside the fireplace, holding the candle to see. It was clean and looked like it had been recently used. Within moments she had a blazing fire going. Molly pulled a chair closer to the hearth and collapsed into it, dearly wishing she had some tea. Or better yet, whiskey.

She would have to stay here all night, as there was no way to find Waverly Hall in the dark even if she wanted to venture out into the storm. She wondered if anyone would realize she wasn't home. It was possible her absence wouldn't be noticed until morning.

She held her chemise out toward the fire to dry it faster. Once it dried, she'd look around for a bedchamber, find a blanket and settle on the sofa for the night. There must be a kitchen, and if there was a kitchen there had to be tea. Possibly even food? Not that she was hungry, but she might be by morning. Though Molly was safe now, it was unnerving to be out alone in the woods with thunder rumbling and lightning cracking over the house.

Some time later, Molly nearly fell out of her chair when a bang echoed through the lodge. She jumped to her feet, turning this way and that to determine where the sound had come from. A branch hitting the roof wouldn't be that loud, would it? Perhaps a falling tree? She'd just decided it had been a distant lightning strike when she heard it again. Molly gripped the candle, the flickering shadows on the wall mimicking her shaking hand. Against her thundering heart's better judgment, she crept to the far side of the room to where the sound had come from.

Then came a muffled cry. "Molly?"

She could have wept with relief. "Roger!"

"Molly, where are you? Let me in!"

His voice was coming from the other side of the wall. She hurried across the house, candle aloft, and flung the door open. Roger wasn't there. Molly stepped out onto the porch, horizontal rain spattering her clothes and hair. The candle spluttered and went out.

"Roger!" she shouted as loudly as she could.

The sound of squelching footsteps came from around the corner and a moment later he appeared, drenched to the skin, holding a lantern.

Despite the wind and rain, Molly was suddenly warm all over. "Where were you? It sounded like you had a battering ram."

"I was at the back door, but it's boarded up." Roger held up a tankard-sized rock. "My battering ram." He tossed it into a puddle, where it landed with a muddy splash.

Molly held the door open wide. "Come inside."

As Roger started up the steps his eyes popped and Molly realized, too late, that she was wearing only her thin chemise. Blush would not describe what happened to her face, neck, and probably whole body.

"Oh!" Her hands flew to her chest as she took a hasty step back, dropping the candle and knocking over an umbrella stand beside the door. She left it, moving as fast as she could through the lodge. Fortunately, it was too dark for Roger to see her once she'd left the light of his lantern behind. Molly hurriedly dressed and had just pulled her jacket on when she heard the door slam.

"May I come over?" Roger called.

Molly finished buttoning her jacket. "Yes."

Roger's boots echoed loudly as he crossed the house, his lantern's light growing brighter as he neared. When he reached the drawing room he placed the lantern on the table and began unbuttoning his jacket. "How long have you been here?"

"I'm not sure. How did you find me?"

"I saw a light in the window."

Molly had never imagined anyone would search for her tonight, least of all Roger, so it hadn't crossed her mind that light from her fire could act as a beacon. "I'm surprised you saw it, with the rain."

"So am I, but I'm glad I did." Roger removed his jacket and hung it over a chair in front of the fireplace. Water dripped off the sleeves, the drops sizzling on the hot bricks. He tugged at his wet shirt, which clung to his chest. "How are you?"

Molly looked away. She was so many things at once it was hard to decide how to answer. She'd run the gamut of emotions tonight, not to mention being cold and wet. Roger's unexpected arrival only added to her jumbled feelings. Finally she settled on the simplest answer. "Fine."

Roger looked like he didn't believe her, but made no comment. He sat in a chair to remove his boots, glancing up at Molly. "You don't mind, do you?"

"Not at all." She lifted her skirt infinitesimally and wiggled her stockinged toes. He smiled, and Molly realized she hadn't seen his eyes light up like that since the morning after the ball.

Roger sobered almost at once and set his boots in front of the fire to dry, then rose and rubbed his sopping hair. "Why did you come out here, Molly?"

"It wasn't intentional." She took a step closer to the hearth and held her hands out to the flames, flinching when an especially loud thunderclap boomed overhead. "I took a walk and lost my way. It was foolish. I wasn't paying attention to where I was going. I'm lucky I found this place. Otherwise I'd still be out there."

"I'm so glad you're not. I've been terribly worried you were lost or hurt." Roger met her eyes for the first time in days.

Molly thought she saw a shadow of that affection she'd seen once or twice before but shook her head to clear it of fancies. The last few days had made it abundantly clear he didn't think of her that way anymore, if he ever had.

They were both silent, the reason for her running away hanging in the air. He must know it was because of what had happened in the office.

"Do you think we should go back to the house tonight?" Molly asked, though she didn't want to leave the lodge and tramp through the stormy forest.

"No, we'll wait until morning. We're safer here. There are bedchambers upstairs, or we could stay by the fire."

A night alone in the woods with a man? Molly shuddered to think of what Caroline's aunt Hazel would say. And her mother. But there didn't seem to be any other choice. Since Roger's arrival all uneasiness had left her, and the fear she hadn't wanted to acknowledge had disappeared. Perhaps she could sleep upstairs while he stayed down here. Suddenly exhausted, Molly walked to the sofa and collapsed onto it, hugging a pillow to her chest. She ran her fingers over the needlepoint depiction of two deer leaping over a fallen tree.

Roger moved about the room, opening closets and cupboards, pulling out blankets and more lanterns. Once the extra lanterns were lit the room felt like a drawing room back at Waverly Hall. Roger stirred the fire until it blazed, then placed a blanket over Molly's knees and sat at the other end of the sofa. He wrapped a blanket around his shoulders and let out a deep sigh as he relaxed into the cushions.

They sat in silence, watching the flames. Molly wanted to ask why he'd come after her without a hat or overcoat. Or why he'd come after her at all. Perhaps he hadn't followed her but had been caught off guard by the storm as she had. Something about his expression didn't welcome questions, so she kept them to herself.

"I was going to look for the kitchen to make some tea," Molly said after a time.

Roger jerked his head toward the dark hallway on the other side of the house. "It's in the back of the lodge, but I doubt it's stocked."

She pulled the blanket further up on her lap. "There's always tea."

"We don't need to bother with that." Roger slid the blanket off his shoulders and crossed the room to his wet jacket. He pulled a heavy flask out of the inside pocket and held it up for her to see. "I have some."

Molly looked at it in astonishment. "You brought *tea*?"

He pulled the cap off as he walked back to the sofa, his wet socks leaving footprints on the hardwood floor. "I thought you might be thirsty if you'd been walking for a while. It's probably cold."

"I don't mind." Molly set the pillow aside and scooched to the edge of the sofa.

Roger handed her the flask and resumed his seat. "I'm afraid I didn't bring glasses," he said, tugging the blanket around his shoulders like a cloak.

Molly took a sip. It was the best thing she'd ever tasted. "It's lukewarm. Would you like some?"

Roger nodded and she handed him the flask. They sat in silence, sharing tea in front of the fire until their clothes were all but dry.

As the minutes ticked by, tension built in the room. There were things that needed to be said, but was this really the time or place? Molly wanted to ask Roger about the past few days, but maybe that didn't matter anymore. He'd come out in a storm to search for her. That had to mean they were friends. What did it matter, anyway? She was leaving tomorrow.

Molly was about to tell him she thought someone must have used the lodge recently, but Roger spoke before she could.

He cleared his throat and looked down at the floor. "I knew you weren't at the house because I saw you from the attic window. I wanted to talk to you, so I went to the stables. The groom told me you hadn't been there but had walked into the forest. I waited for a long time and when you didn't come back I followed you."

A hint of a smile came to her lips. "With tea and a lantern?"

"It was rainy and dark by then, and I thought you might need…something. Help? Tea? At the very least, light. I stopped at the house for supplies before setting out to find you."

"Why did you want to talk to me?" Molly picked the pillow up and hugged it to her chest as if it might muffle the pounding of her heart.

He stared straight ahead as he spoke. "I'm sorry for the way I've been acting. I don't have the easiest time with women."

Molly wanted to point out that after all they'd been through together she'd hope she was in a different category than just "women." But she didn't. She said the first other thing that came to mind. "Fred said you were jilted."

Roger's shoulders tensed and he leaned forward, elbows resting on his knees. "It wasn't as simple as that."

She said nothing but waited for him to go on, watching his face in the firelight.

"Six months ago I was about to get engaged to a woman named Jane. I bought a ring and was going to propose to her. But then I had my accident. My ankle, remember? I was supposed to go to a ball with Jane that same evening, but I couldn't walk. I told her to go by herself and have a good time." His shoulders drooped. "Jane went to the ball, and she met a man."

Molly gasped and her hands flew to her mouth.

"You've guessed it, haven't you?" Roger asked, looking at her with sad eyes.

She lowered her hands. "I'm sorry. Go on."

He slouched into the sofa, eyes on the ceiling. "Jane and the man fell in love, and they were married within three weeks."

"I'm so sorry," Molly said, fighting the urge to place a hand on his arm.

"Jane was kind about it. I'm not angry with her anymore. Love just happens sometimes, and can't be planned or controlled. But I was devastated when it happened."

A log in the fire cracked, sending sparks into the air and filling the room with a sweet, smoky aroma. Molly had almost forgotten the storm.

She tucked her legs under herself and faced Roger. "Is that why you wanted to be alone all the time and avoided me and Caroline? Because you were unhappy?"

"Partially. At the time I thought women couldn't be trusted."

"That's understandable, after what you'd gone through."

Roger rested his arm on the back of the sofa, shifting toward Molly. "Still, I shouldn't have let my past sorrow taint what I thought of all women."

"What do you think now?"

He looked into her eyes. "Now I know I was being an ass."

They laughed together easily, a sound Molly had heartily missed these last few days.

Molly shook her head. "What a thing to happen."

"That night at the tavern, I'd just sent the ring back to the jeweler. I don't know why I held onto it so long."

"That's why you were melancholy," Molly said. She hadn't noticed she'd inched closer to him until their knees were almost touching. "Is it also why—"

"What?" Roger asked. He stared at her but she couldn't meet his gaze. No more than she could ask him this question.

Molly faced forward and put her feet back on the floor. "Never mind."

"Why what, Molly?" His voice was soft, like that day in the attic.

She gripped her knees, not allowing her eyes to venture anywhere near his. "Is that why you don't want to be my friend?"

Roger instantly closed the gap between them, his leg pressed close against hers. "I do want to be your friend. I like to think I *am* your friend."

Molly didn't want to upset him any more after he'd just told her about his heartbreak, but if they were going to move on from here, she had to say it. "You aren't acting like my friend when you shut me out. I never know from one day to the next how you're going to treat me. I can't even be sure if you like me."

"Oh, Molly. I do like you." The unmistakable tenderness in his voice surprised and thrilled her. "I missed you while I was away. I missed your voice, and your blushes, and the way you twirl your hair around your finger when you're reading. I missed everything about you."

She blushed, of course. "I missed you, too. I waited so long to see you, but when you came back you acted like…like we'd just met." Molly lifted her eyes to his.

"I'm sorry, Molly." Roger's gaze intensified as he reached out a hand to stroke her hair. "The truth is…I tried not to like you, but I can't help it. You're—you're fascinating and kind, and funny and smart. And you're so, so beautiful. It scared me to care so much about someone again. That's why I've pulled away any time I thought we were growing closer. But you're impossible to stay away from. I'm drawn to you—like a hunger, a thirst. Being with you fills me up. You're like a beacon shining from a lighthouse. I feel safe with you."

He tried to take her hand, but she drew it away. Molly rose and walked to the fireplace, her back to Roger so he couldn't see her face. She stood there, heart racing, hardly able to comprehend what was happening. He'd said what she'd dreamed of him saying. But as much as she wanted to believe he meant it, how could she? He'd hurt her before, even if he hadn't realized he was doing it. Did his explanation matter? Did it forgive what he'd done? She turned back to Roger, her arms wrapped around her waist.

"If we decide to be…friends…how do I know you won't turn away again?" Molly's voice was a mix of hope and despair. "I don't want to…to shine for you, and have you disappear again. It hurts too much."

Roger stood up. "But Molly, I wo—"

She held up a hand. If she didn't say this now, she never would. "Roger, I like you. I want to be with you and laugh with you and have your eyes light up when you look at me. But *I* need to feel safe, too. I need to know you won't run away again. Our friendship means so much to me and I never want to give it up. But I will if it means my heart could be broken according to your whims."

Chest heaving, Molly stared at him, waiting for his reply.

Roger's eyes never left hers as he slowly crossed the room. "I won't break your heart, Molly. If I did I'd break mine, too."

Molly swallowed as inch by inch they inexorably moved toward each other, not stopping until she was close enough to feel his sweet breath on her face. An exhilaration she'd never known rushed through her as she rested her hand on Roger's chest, his heartbeat pounding against her palm. Molly wanted to say something—anything—but words failed her.

Roger wrapped his arms around Molly's waist and drew her close. Trembling, she put her hands on his shoulders and closed her eyes as he bent to kiss her.

His lips on hers were like nothing she'd ever felt and all she'd ever wanted. Soft, searching and perfect. Kissing Roger was like something from a dream. Head swimming, Molly allowed herself to be utterly overtaken by these new, incredible sensations. Her knees shook as she pressed herself against Roger, wanting nothing more than to be as close as she could possibly get.

When Molly pulled away to meet his gaze his eyes were molten, unlike anything she'd ever seen, and she wanted more of it. Bringing her mouth back to his, she felt his smile and Molly thought she might swoon—for real, this time—for the first time in her life. Roger must have felt her sag against him, because he stood up tall and wrapped his arms tightly around her. She buried her face in his shoulder as they clung to each other for untold minutes, until their breath steadied and her heart had almost gone back to its normal pace. She wasn't sure it ever would again. When Molly looked into Roger's eyes she could swear there were tears in them, but perhaps it was a trick of the light.

He smiled softly. "You're blushing."

"If I am, it's because of you."

"I will happily take credit for that."

He wrapped an arm around her shoulders and led her to the sofa. As they sat together he stared at her, his eyes shining with love. Had it been there all along? Did hers look the same way? They must, because her heart was full, her soul singing.

Roger kissed her, taking both her hands in his. "I won't shut you out, Molly, not ever again. I'm sorry I didn't talk to you about all of this before, and that it took me so long to understand what a fool I've been. I want to be with you, even if it means I might get hurt some day, because I'd rather open myself up to you than risk losing you. But I don't really believe you'd hurt me. I know who you are, Molly, and I trust you."

Molly put her hand on his cheek. "I won't hurt you." And she knew she wouldn't. She'd heard of falling in love and had imagined it would happen to her one day, but she'd thought she would be aware of it. She hadn't known it would happen almost without her knowing it, until at some moment—this moment—she would realize her heart was no longer her own, and she didn't want it to be.

Feelings Molly had been trying to deny welled up inside. Feelings she no longer needed to hide. Was it too soon to tell him? Looking into Roger's eyes, she knew she could have told him weeks ago and it would have been true. "I love you, Roger."

"Molly Merriwether—" He wrapped his arms around her, holding her so close she felt his heartbeat hammering against her.

Molly could have stayed snug in his arms like this for the rest of her life, but a moment later Roger pulled away and tilted her chin up to look into her eyes. He said in the softest, sweetest voice imaginable, "I love you, Molly."

Chapter Twenty-Five

Molly would never have dreamed the happiest moment of her life would happen in damp clothes, on an old sofa, in the middle of a rainstorm. But it did.

"You love me?" Molly could barely speak through her smile.

Roger pushed a lock of hair behind Molly's ear, looking into her eyes. "You look surprised."

"I am. It's too fantastic to believe."

"I love you." Roger kissed her forehead, her cheek, her lips. "I love you."

Molly shook her head wonderingly, gazing at him. Her insides danced as her mind sought to comprehend this sudden change. Astonishing as it was, she knew without a doubt that Roger meant it. But still...how?

Roger touched her cheek. "What's that look?"

"I'm not sure I can believe this," Molly said with a grin, searching his eyes.

He took her hand and entwined his fingers with hers. "Why not? You're wonderful. Why wouldn't I love you?"

"I've spent almost the entire time we've known each other believing you either didn't notice me or think I'm a pest. I never had the impression you liked me very much, at least not until recently. Even then I thought I was imagining it."

"Perhaps I've hidden my feelings too well. If you

could have read my mind…"

She touched his red cheek. "What's that look?"

Roger laughed. "If you could have read my mind you'd have known how often I thought about you. That day in the attic, when you cried, you would have known I was already in love with you."

Molly's heart could have burst from hearing those words. Recalling the state she'd been in that day, she blushed. "I was such a mess."

"No. You were real, and open, and…and you. I've never met anybody like you before. I would have said something, but I wasn't sure you felt the same way. I did suspect." He arched a brow. "All the blushing."

"That happens if I pick up the wrong fork at a dinner party. But it often gave away my true feelings, it seems. Traitorous cheeks."

Roger leaned in and kissed each cheek. "I love them for it."

Molly pulled back slightly and looked down at her lap. "But if you suspected my feelings, why were you so cold when you came back? I thought something happened while you were away, or I'd offended you somehow. After the ball, I thought things had changed between us. I thought you if not loved at least liked me. But then you barely spoke to me."

His face lost all trace of humor. If anything, Roger looked like he had a sudden headache. "I'm so sorry for that. The day I left, you mentioned you are going to have a Season. I thought that meant you were looking for a suitor, and it would *not* be me. I thought if you liked me you wouldn't be going. It was foolish. I should have told you there and then that I love you."

Molly's eyes snapped back to his. "It didn't mean

that at all! I'm having a Season because my mother insists on it. I don't want it, I never have. I was going to do it next year, but after the unchaperoned debacle, my mother decided I'm too unruly to remain unmarried for much longer. That, and she wants to parade me around in pretty dresses."

Roger wrapped an arm around her shoulders and brought their linked hands to his heart as he stared into her eyes. "You don't need to bother with a Season, Molly. But if your mother insists on you having one, I'll be at every ball and claim every dance."

"Oh, Roger," Molly whispered, eyes glistening with tears. "I'll save them all for you."

Their lips met in a soft, tender promise.

Molly leaned her head against his shoulder. She could barely think. It was the closest Roger could get to a proposal.

Their sweet words echoed in her mind as they sat in silence, listening to the steady rain. He stroked her arm, kissing the top of her head from time to time. Molly kept her hands on Roger simply because she could. His knee, his arm, his chest.

"Are you tired?" Roger asked after a while.

Molly hadn't had time for thoughts of things like fatigue since he'd arrived, but as soon as he mentioned it, she let out a tiny yawn. "Yes. I wonder what time it is."

He glanced at his pocket watch. "Two o'clock."

"Is it? That means we can't go back for hours." Molly stretched her legs out in front of her, pointing her toes.

"Do you want to go to sleep? I could make up a fire in one of the bedchambers."

Kate Ellington

A bed would be most welcome, but did he mean together? Shocked as she should be, Molly liked the idea. Was it really much different than cuddling this close on the sofa? They would be wearing their clothes, and it might be a cozier place to talk more about…everything. "Do you think the beds would be dusty? And are any of them large enough for the two of us?"

Roger looked surprised. "I meant I could settle you in one and I'd stay on the sofa."

"I don't—never mind. I'll stay here with you." Color flooded Molly's cheeks. Oh, what must he think of her? She covered her face with her hands.

Roger pulled them gently away and looked into her eyes, smiling. "If you don't think it's inappropriate, we might get some sleep. There are hours left of the night, and we'd certainly be more comfortable."

"It's not inappropriate. We'll be dressed."

His expression grew serious. "I won't—I mean to say… I'll be a gentleman."

She smiled. "I know that, Roger. I know *you*."

"And I know you, Molly Merriwether."

Molly let out a long, soft sigh. "You have no idea how much I love it when you call me that, do you?"

Roger laughed. "Do you? Remember I said your name sounds like a nursery rhyme character?"

"How could I forget? Wasn't there something about feathers?"

"I also recall it isn't even your real name." He grinned and sat up straighter. "Do I get to hear it now?"

Molly rested a hand on his chest. "Not yet. It might destroy your image of me."

"Nothing could do that. What is it? Miriam? Margaret?" Roger peered at her as though her name would magically appear on her face if only he looked hard enough.

She stood and held out a hand. "Let's find a place to sleep."

"No, you wait here. I'll go start the fire first." He rose and kissed her forehead. "Marie?"

"I'm not telling you tonight," she said, giving him a playful shove.

Roger took a lantern and crossed to a staircase on the far side of the lodge. Halfway up he looked back. "I won't be long."

When he'd gone, Molly slowly paced around the room. Was this really happening? Was it a dream? She ran a finger over her lips, smiling softly as she remembered Roger's kisses. She'd never have guessed, even a few hours ago, that she and Roger would have declared their love to each other tonight. To think she'd planned to leave tomorrow and never see him again!

He'd been so sweet when he shared his feelings, and her heart broke for all he'd suffered with that other woman. Now that Molly understood the circumstances, it was easy to see why he'd been hesitant to let himself care about her. But still, those times he'd ignored her had stung. Hopefully those days were over now. In her heart she believed they were.

Molly found a mirror in the corner of the room. Her blue eyes were shining, her skin luminous in the firelight. Her *hair*, though. She ran her hands over it, trying to smooth it, but it was impossible. She took the pins out and combed it with her fingers, trying to remove the tangles.

She glanced around the room, which wasn't nearly so cozy now that Roger wasn't in it. Rain pummeled the windows and thunder rolled in the distance, but it was some time since she'd seen a lightning flash, although she'd been so distracted it was possible she'd missed a hundred such flashes.

Molly moved to a window and pulled the curtains aside, but the pitch dark made it impossible to see anything. Smiling, she recalled the night Roger had urged her to look out the window at the dull, overcast moon.

"Happy?" Roger asked, coming up behind her.

Molly jumped and spun around. "You gave me a start. You're awfully quiet, aren't you?"

He lifted a trouser leg to reveal his stockinged foot. "No boots. Cold feet, though. I'm surprised you didn't notice my light." He set the lantern on a table.

Molly stepped away from the window, letting the curtain fall back into place. "I was deep in thought, I suppose, and not paying attention."

"May I inquire as to what has you so distracted?" he asked, grinning.

Molly didn't bother trying to hide her cheeks this time. "I believe you already have a good idea," she said, holding her hand out to him.

Roger took her into his arms, holding her as though they'd been apart for days. "I like your hair this way."

"Tangled?"

"Flowing. It suits you."

He kissed her and that molten heat she'd seen in his eyes earlier spread through her body, warming her in unexpected yet tantalizing places. Molly reveled in the feel of Roger's broad chest against hers as she deepened their kiss, and when his hands fell to her hips she lost all track of time. Held in Roger's embrace, immersed in his kisses, Molly felt beloved in a way she'd never dreamed possible. She ran her hands up and down his back, delighted when he shivered at her touch. Finally they pulled away and gazed into each other's eyes, catching their breath.

After a few moments, Molly remembered he'd gone to look for a place to sleep. "What did you find upstairs?"

Roger kept his hands on her waist. "One of the bedchambers looks like it's been used recently, so I built a fire in there. Fred told me this place has been shut up for years, but someone's definitely been here."

"I had the same thought earlier."

"I'll ask Fred about it tomorrow. Are you ready to go up?"

"Yes, after I get my boots." Molly picked her dry boots up and slipped them on. Once Roger had put on his boots also, he reached out a hand.

Molly took it and they climbed the stairs to the second floor. If anyone ever heard of her spending the night here with Roger, even a whisper of it, she would indeed be ruined. But with his strong hand wrapped around hers, her lips still warm from his kisses and his familiar scent now on her clothes and in her hair, it was difficult to worry about the future.

Her skirt trailed along the floor as they walked down a long corridor arm in arm. After passing a number of closed rooms, they came to a door that opened onto a stone staircase. Only a few steps of the winding stair were visible in the lantern's pool of light. Treading carefully, they started up. Narrow slits acted as windows in the dank passage, but heavy clouds and wild skies obscured any hint of moonlight that might have trickled through.

"We're in the turret now," Roger said, his voice echoing off the thick walls.

"I can tell. It's colder." Molly wrinkled her nose at the musty smell.

He put an arm around her waist and pulled her close. "The room will be warm."

They came to a landing, and Roger led Molly through a door that opened onto a round chamber. The centerpiece was an enormous four-poster bed that must have been ten feet wide. Two burgundy, tapestried chairs flanked the fireplace, and a trunk stood at the end of the bed. This room smelled airy, as if the windows had been opened recently. A vaguely familiar floral scent hung in the air.

Molly gasped. "Good gracious! How did they get this bed up here?"

"It must have been built into the room all those years ago." Roger closed the door and set the lantern on one of the bedside tables.

Molly walked over to the fire to warm her hands. Downstairs in the drawing room, the idea of sharing a bed hadn't seemed much different than the sofa. But now that they were here, it was decidedly more intimate.

"Would you like to sit by the fire first, or…?" Roger asked.

"Let's get into bed."

"You're blushing…Maude?"

"You may as well stop trying. You'll never guess. Is it all right with you if I remove my jacket and boots?"

"Yes. I'll do the same, if you don't mind." Roger sounded oddly formal, and Molly suspected she wasn't the only one who was nervous.

Molly hung her jacket on a hook in the wall, then sat

in a chair to remove her boots. When they were both ready, they exchanged a shy look and climbed into opposite sides of the bed.

If Molly hadn't seen Roger get in, she never would have known he was there. It was an ocean of a bed. How many people had once occupied it? The wooden posts and headboard were carved with intricate images of wild animals. None of the sweet ones like rabbits and chipmunks. No, here were boar, elk, wolves. The heavy, green velvet curtains surrounding the bed were held back by thick cords of golden tasseled rope.

Roger's voice floated over from the other side. "Are you warm enough?"

"Yes, I won't even get under the covers." Molly lay flat on her back, hands folded over her stomach. The bed was deep, soft, and unexpectedly fresh, not like a bed that had been unused for years. Only the curtains let off a slight whiff of damp.

"Good," he said.

She turned her head in Roger's direction. All she could see were his feet, which he'd propped up on the footboard. "Are you comfortable?"

"Very."

As Molly let her muscles relax, bumps and bruises from her flight through the forest made themselves known. She started daydreaming about a hot bath at the manor, but then Roger spoke and she knew there was nowhere else on earth she'd rather be.

His voice was soft. "May I come over for a moment?"

"Yes," she said. Molly settled her head on the pillow and watched him crawl over. The sight stirred up curious feelings.

When he reached her, Roger lay down beside her and took her hand. "I wanted to say goodnight."

"Goodnight," she whispered, smiling. She'd have thought being in bed with a man would set her heart thrumming like a wild bird's wings, but it was calm, as if nothing steadied her like Roger's presence. And her heart was right.

They held each other's gaze, then Molly laughed.

"What is it?" he asked.

"Would you ever have imagined this, this time last night?"

"No, but I've certainly dreamt it." He leaned over and gave Molly a sweet, gentle kiss. "Goodnight, Molly." He kissed her once more, then went back to his side of the bed.

As Molly snuggled into the pillow, something hard touched her cheek. She picked it up and held it toward the firelight, then burst out laughing.

"What's funny?" Roger asked.

She held it up for him to see. "This!"

He peered across the bed. "What is it?"

"Caroline's earring."

They both laughed, then settled down to sleep. Molly grinned in the dark. She'd have her own news to share with Caroline when she returned from her honeymoon.

Molly awoke to sunlight flooding in through the open window. Roger was already awake, looking outside.

A soft grin came to her face. "Roger."

"Good morning," he said, turning around. His clothes were wrinkled, his hair messy, and his eyes shining. Molly had never woken up to anything more adorable.

She sat up and shuffled to the edge of the bed, rubbing her eyes. Her feet dangled a good ten inches above the stone floor.

"Did you sleep well?" Roger asked.

"Better than I would have thought. Did you?" Molly rose, shivering in the cool morning air. The fire had gone out and the floor felt like a frozen lake.

"I didn't sleep long, but it was sound. Perhaps it was the company."

She smiled. "Perhaps." Molly was tempted to go straight into his arms, but her cold feet demanded attention. She went to the hearth and pulled her boots on, wondering as she did so if it would be too bold to kiss him first thing in the morning.

Roger turned to a shelf built into the thick stone walls, where a full decanter and clean glasses stood. Another welcome feature of this supposedly abandoned lodge. He poured out two glasses of sherry and handed her one. "I know it's a little early, but we haven't had anything besides tea since last night."

"Thank you." The sherry went down, smooth and warm, to Molly's empty stomach. She drained the glass and set it on the mantel.

Roger came over and offered her his hand. When she took it, she was swept into his embrace. Memories of their words last night swirled inside her head as they stood wrapped in each other's arms. Molly rested her head on Roger's chest, listening to his heartbeat.

He gently massaged her shoulder. "Would you like to go upstairs?"

Molly pulled away to look at him, but the question she was about to ask fled her mind as soon as their eyes met. Without even thinking about it, she put a hand on the back of Roger's head and drew him in for a kiss. A smooth, bubbly sensation rushed through her. Who would have guessed Roger was as intoxicating as champagne?

After a few moments, Molly opened her eyes and looked into his face. "Aren't we already upstairs?"

"What?" Roger blinked as though he, too, had lost all train of thought.

She rested her hands on his waist. "You asked if I want to go upstairs."

"That's right. We can go to the top of the turret. You can see the countryside for miles around—Marion?"

"No." She laughed and took his hand. "Let's go."

After donning their jackets, they left the room, Caroline's earring in Molly's pocket. They followed the spiral staircase to a door that opened onto the top of the crenelated tower. A brisk breeze rushed up to greet them when they stepped outside.

Heavy mist hung over the forest, which had the same disheveled look as Molly and Roger. Branches lay willy-nilly over the ground and trees bent under the weight of rain they'd accumulated the night before. A birch not far from the lodge bore marks of a lightning strike. In the distance, Waverly Hall's windows glinted in the pale morning light.

Molly walked to the edge of the parapet and rested her hands on the rough stone. "It's breathtaking."

"On a clear day you can see even farther." Roger moved to her side, squinting as he looked up into the clouds.

As Roger gazed at the sky, Molly gazed at him. His chestnut hair was tousled and he had a relaxed, easy look about him. A soft smile made him even more handsome. Molly felt she'd learned more about him last night than she would have in years and had a deep understanding of him now.

He turned to face her. "Your eyes look lighter today."

"It must be the sunshine."

"Perhaps." Roger took her by the shoulders and bent to kiss her. His lips were as soft as his smile, and warm and curious. Molly had never kissed a man before last night, but with Roger it felt like she'd been born knowing what to do.

When they broke apart, Roger put an arm around her waist and Molly leaned into him as they looked out over the new day. The new world.

Suddenly Roger stiffened, focusing on something far away. "Oh."

"What is it?" Molly asked, following his gaze.

He pointed to three horses trotting out of Waverly's front gate. Once on the road, they broke into a gallop.

"I wonder who it is?" Molly asked. A group out for a morning ride, or had their absences been noted and the riders formed a search party? Hopefully the former. If anyone saw them coming out of the forest together, Molly didn't even want to consider what would be left of her reputation. Or what her mother would say when she found out.

Roger leaned forward to get a better look. "The front horse looks like Birdie, so that will be Fred. I can't tell who the other two people are. Probably Mr. and Mrs. Clarke."

"We'd better go down," Molly said, heading for the stairs. "Do you think they saw us?"

Roger took her hand. "No, not through the mist. We could only see them because we're so high up."

They went downstairs and tidied as well as they could, then made sure all the fires in the house were out. While Roger put the blankets and lanterns away, Molly went upstairs and tried to make the bed look like they'd never been in it.

When she joined him in the drawing room, Molly looked around, memorizing all the details. She'd never forget last night, or the things she and Roger had shared here.

Roger took her hand and they left the lodge through the door Molly had broken into last night. She cast a regretful glance at the shattered window, making a mental note to tell Benedict about it so he could see that it was repaired.

The forest was still, silent and misty, like something from a fairy tale. But this time Molly knew she wouldn't get lost, because she had Roger to hold onto. They had no problem finding the trail, but had to detour around a number of fallen branches and deep puddles. Trees swayed in the breeze, occasionally sprinkling them with droplets of rain.

They'd almost reached the pond when they heard the sound of approaching horses. Molly turned to Roger. "Am I presentable?"

He stopped and held her arms out wide, looking her over from head to toe. "You're perfect."

Molly flushed. "You're sweet. But do I look like I spent the night in the lodge? Maybe Fred and his parents will think we're just out for a morning stroll. They needn't know we've been out all night."

Roger plucked a crinkled leaf out of her hair and let

it flutter to the ground. "Lovely as you are, I don't think I could say you're presentable. And I assume I'm not, either."

She brushed a patch of mud off the arm of his jacket. "No, but it's all right. We'll just tell them—"

"Molly!"

Molly froze.

Caroline's was the least expected but most welcome voice she could have heard. She was supposed to be on her honeymoon, but at least now Molly needn't worry about any rumors starting. If anyone would keep her secrets, it was Caroline.

Molly watched in disbelief as Benedict helped Caroline off Opal. "What are you doing here? We didn't expect you home for two more days."

"We came home early. It was stormy at the coast." Caroline took a step closer to Molly, her eyes narrowing as they went from Molly's unbound hair, to Roger, to Molly's jacket, which was inside out.

Molly attempted to flatten her hair, but it refused to be tamed. "It was stormy here, too. Did you enjoy yourselves? When did you get back?"

Before Caroline could answer, Benedict came forward and took her hand. "Where have you two been?" he asked, glaring at Roger.

Roger looked at Molly.

Molly looked at Roger.

Fred laughed. "Lost in the woods?"

"Something like that," Roger said.

"Roger wasn't lost, but I was. He came to find me." Molly's tone sounded loving even to her own ears.

Caroline looked like she wanted to grab Molly by the arm, march her into the forest and demand an explanation. Fred was staring at Roger with the exact same expression.

"I'm glad we found you so soon," Benedict said. "We worried you were lost."

"But how did you know we were out here? When did you get back?" Molly asked, ignoring the urge to wrap an arm around Roger's waist.

"We arrived late last night, but nobody realized you were missing until a few hours ago," Caroline said.

Fred all but winked as he looked at Molly. "Kitty said you didn't sleep in your bed last night, and when I went to ask Roger if he knew where you might be… Well, I put two and two together."

"How did you know we were in the woods?" Roger asked.

Benedict's answer sounded like a chastisement. "The groom told us you both took walks and hadn't returned as of nine last night."

"But it would have been better if he'd told us yesterday," Caroline added.

Fred waved his riding gloves in the air. "Oh, it doesn't matter. He probably didn't realize they never came home. It isn't as if he stays up late keeping an eye out for wayward guests."

"So what happened?" Caroline asked.

Molly avoided her eyes. "It's a long story."

"We spent the night in the hunting lodge," Roger said in a would-be nonchalant tone.

"That must have been comfortable." This time Fred really did wink, but Molly had the feeling it had only been intended for Roger.

There was an awkward silence as everyone waited for Molly and Roger to elaborate.

When it became clear they wouldn't, Benedict started toward the horses. "We should get back to the house. Mother and Father don't know you two are missing, and I'd like to keep it that way. We didn't bring extra mounts, but I daresay we can share. Caroline will ride with me, Molly on Pearl, and Roger and Fred can take Birdie."

"We'd be too heavy for him," Fred said as the big horse stomped his enormous hooves. "I'll ride Pearl, and Roger and Molly can take Birdie."

Benedict eyed Birdie. "Too heavy?"

"Yes, darling," Caroline said and kissed his cheek. "Roger had better ride with Molly. Don't you think so?"

Understanding dawned on Benedict's face. "Yes, of course. But they shouldn't ride past the front of the house. Mother and Father might see them."

All the way home, Molly leaned back against Roger, relishing his breath on her hair and the feel of his arms around her as they rode through the awakening forest.

Back at the house, Molly's bath took longer than usual because she needed to wash her hair twice before all the bits of forest came out of it. She'd just wrapped herself in her dressing gown and sat at the vanity when the door flew open.

Caroline marched into the room and plopped down in a chair next to her. "What happened?"

Molly had known it wouldn't take long for Caroline to visit her, but she'd expected at least enough time to finish dressing. She picked up a brush and set it to the worst of her tangles. "We told you. I got lost in the woods and Roger came to find me. We spent the night at the lodge."

"What exactly do you mean by *spent the night*?"

"Nothing happened," Molly said, her eyes on the mirror. "Which is more than I can say for you and Benedict."

"*We* were on our honeymoon."

Molly picked Caroline's earring off the vanity and tossed it to her. "You didn't spend your honeymoon at the lodge."

Red as an apple, Caroline caught it. "Fair enough. Now that it's just the two of us, tell me what really happened."

"Let me finish my hair," Molly said. Only four snarls to go.

Caroline rose and stood behind Molly, holding her hand out for the brush. "Here, let me."

Molly relaxed in her chair, savoring the simple routine they'd done a hundred times before. "Why did you and Benedict come back early? I wouldn't think storms would matter to a honeymooning couple. I assume you didn't spend very much time out of doors."

She gave Molly's hair a light tug. "As a matter of fact, we did spend a good deal of time outside. But a leaky roof puts a damper on certain indoor activities. Not to mention the people who come to repair said roof."

"Oh, how unfortunate."

"Now I'm especially glad we came home early, so I could see you stumble out of the forest with Roger."

Molly's cheeks went pink. "We didn't stumble."

"No, it was more like skipping." Caroline set the brush down and ran a hand over Molly's hair. "Your hair is done, now tell me what happened."

Molly rose, smiling as she tightened the sash of her dressing gown. "I couldn't wait to tell you about it. Let's sit on the sofa." She happily told Caroline every detail—

sharing it made it feel less like an enchanted dream she'd had.

When she finished, Caroline hugged her. "I knew it!"

Molly laughed. "How could you? I didn't."

"Yes, you did. You've liked Roger for ages. You were just too shy to admit it. Or confused? Either way, it's marvelous."

"It is, isn't it?" Molly crossed the room to look through her wardrobe, settling on a simple teal gown.

Caroline went to the vanity and opened Molly's jewelry box. "What happens now? Are you engaged?"

"No," Molly said as she stepped behind the screen to change. "But Roger implied he'd like to be. He knows I'm having a Season."

"You don't need that now."

While she changed, Molly recalled Roger's words last night. Every ball. Every dance. Would he really do that? She had the feeling it wasn't something he would say without meaning it. But how would she explain to her parents? And what of Mr. and Mrs. Bailey? Would they so willingly agree to Roger courting someone they barely knew? Perhaps they had other plans for him.

After dressing, Molly returned to the sofa. "My mother's coming to get me in a few days. Before she left she warned me not to get 'entangled' with anyone."

Caroline sat beside her and handed her a pair of sapphire earrings. "You'll just have to explain to her about Roger. Your mother likes him, doesn't she?"

"She liked him well enough when she met him at Walsingham, but she hasn't been keen on him since your wedding. She was worried he'd get in the way of her plans for the Season, and she was right—he did. You know she has her heart set on going to town."

"Let her. She can take Albert and Tristan."

"I'll think about what to tell her." Molly paused to put her earrings in, then turned to Caroline. "But now, my dear, it's your turn to tell *me* everything. How was the honeymoon?"

"Oh, Molly, I don't know if I can," Caroline said, trying to cover her face.

Molly held her hands so she couldn't hide behind them. "You promised!"

"I know, but— Well, I'll tell you. But it isn't easy to explain."

Molly didn't answer but gestured for her to go on.

"I won't bother telling what exactly happens, physically, because you already know that part. But the feeling." She sighed. "It was like…like being wrapped up in love and kisses, and every good feeling you can think of. Especially toward…toward the end. The feelings take you over, and you almost forget who you are for a moment." Caroline stared off into the distance, smiling.

"Is it…similar to anything?"

Caroline looked up as if she'd forgotten Molly was there. "What?"

"Does it feel like anything else you could describe?" Molly clasped her hands together and placed them in her lap, listening raptly.

Caroline drummed her fingers on her knee for a moment, then looked up at Molly. "You kissed Roger last night?"

There was no use denying it, especially when she knew her face must look like she'd just won grand prize at the village fair. "Yes. More than once."

"You felt something, didn't you? I mean, not only on your lips?"

"I felt something…everywhere. The emotional feelings were almost stronger than the physical ones. Although," she blushed harder, "there were some sensations I've never felt before, ever."

"If you recall those feelings and multiply them by say, one hundred? That's what it's like." She shook her head. "No, really, it's better."

They sat for a moment in silence, the shared secrets casting a warm glow over the room.

Molly sighed and fell back against the sofa, hands behind her head. "I can't wait."

They started laughing and didn't stop for some time.

Chapter Twenty-Six

The next few days were some of the sweetest Molly had ever known. Though she and Roger tried to keep their love a secret, it was probably obvious to anyone who looked at them. There was no doubt Caroline, Fred, and Benedict knew, and Fred had probably told Kitty. Fortunately, it was easy enough to escape the watchful eyes of Mr. and Mrs. Clarke.

The only time Molly wasn't with Roger was when she was asleep. They found plenty to do together, even if it was only sitting together and talking. They rode every day, visited Penny, and spent hours in the attic—not reading. Just last night they'd taken a long walk through the gardens, holding hands and watching the stars until well past midnight.

Now that Roger had confessed his love, he'd apparently decided to open up every corner of himself to Molly. He told her about his childhood, and Molly especially liked the way his face lit up when telling her about his sister's birth. He'd sat outside his mother's room all day and night, even sleeping in the hall and eating his meals there, so he'd be the first to hear the news. Before Penny was an hour old he'd been allowed to hold her.

Besides his past, Roger shared his hopes and plans. He told Molly about the work he did with his father on their estate and the places he'd like to travel. Since she'd longed to travel for years, Molly couldn't help thinking of all the new taverns she'd be able to see if she shared in Roger's adventures. Recalling the smoky Wayside, she turned her thoughts to quaint inns and out-of-the-way museums.

Roger described his plans for expanding the estate and gave her a pointed look when he spoke of the home he wanted to build and the large family he'd always dreamed of. Molly turned away to hide her smile. Nothing could make her happier than to be the mother of those children.

Molly was surprised at how much they had in common, but maybe she shouldn't have been. They both wanted to travel, but most importantly wanted a comfortable home not too far from their families. Molly shared her secret ambition of one day climbing a mountain, and Roger told her he'd always wanted to try his hand at writing a book. Perhaps a mystery.

Without coming right out and saying that it would be *their* home, they both agreed any good house should have a substantial library, many comfortable rooms and extensive grounds for riding—but not hunting.

Molly knew that whatever idea she had or scheme she came up with, Roger would always support her. It was a wonderful feeling and she couldn't wait to do the same for him. They'd be friends and true partners, if what she expected *did* come. It didn't seem presumptuous at this point to expect him to propose. Perhaps in a year or two. He didn't seem like the type of man to hurry into something like marriage. For herself, she was already certain Roger was the one for her.

Roger wanted to know absolutely everything about Molly and never tired of hearing even the most mundane details of her life. He was more wonderful than Molly had imagined and understood her in a way that was astounding considering how long they'd known each other. It was as though he'd always known her, and there was something about him that settled her, fit her like nothing ever had in her life. Roger felt like home.

One afternoon a few days after they returned from the lodge, Molly went to the office. She hadn't seen Roger since breakfast and hoped he'd be there with Penny, but he wasn't. No sign of Penny, either. Assuming Roger had taken her for a walk and would return shortly, Molly settled into his chair to wait. She stared into the empty hearth, recalling the especially lovely time they'd had playing backgammon yesterday afternoon. Molly suspected she was the better player, but Roger distracted her so much with his mere presence she'd only managed to win two of their games so far.

Some time later, it was Fred who strolled into the office.

Molly looked up eagerly when the door opened, and Fred laughed when her smile faded at the first sight of him.

"Ah, the way every man likes to be greeted," he said, placing a hand over his heart.

Molly's face turned pink. "I thought you might be Roger."

"He went into town, but I don't know when he'll be back." Fred crossed the room and stood in front of her chair.

She rose. "I'll go along and see Caroline."

"She's off with Benedict somewhere."

"Then I'll read in the library. Tell Roger when you see him, won't you?"

Molly made to move past Fred but he reached out and touched her elbow. "I'll tell him, but I want to talk to you first."

"All right," Molly said, wondering what this could be about. More details about Roger's past? She couldn't deny she'd welcome it, as the jilting was one subject he had *not* brought up again since that night in the lodge.

Fred made his way to the desk in the corner. "Sit down and I'll pour us some drinks."

Molly resumed her seat, automatically glancing at the door to see if Roger had returned.

Fred came back carrying two glasses of port. He handed one to Molly and touched his glass to hers.

"What did you want to talk to me about?" Molly asked after he'd settled into the chair beside her.

Fred met her curious gaze, unable to hold back a smile. "It's about Kitty. Me and Kitty."

"What happened?"

"What happened is I decided I don't want to be without her. At the ball I told you I was worried our relationship might not succeed, but I realized that's not true. Of course it will. I've known Kitty since we were six years old. I always liked her, and over the years I've never met anyone who understands me the way she does."

"Have you told Kitty all this?"

"Yes. Last night."

"What did she say?"

"Well, you know Kitty. She's practical. She wants to be with me, but not yet. She doesn't want to do anything rash that will upset my parents and suggests we court secretly for a year or so and then tell them. She thinks I can bring them around to the idea slowly."

"Do you agree with her?" Molly finished her port and set her glass on the side table.

Fred rose and leaned against the fireplace, his elbow propped on the mantelpiece. "With the sentiment, yes. If it were up to me, I'd tell them today, but I'll go along with whatever Kitty wants. I don't want to make her uncomfortable."

"That's good of you, Fred, and it will help Kitty understand how much you respect her. All women need that. How will you manage to keep this a secret, though?"

"I'm hoping my new sister-in-law will help me. Benedict says Caroline wants Kitty to be her lady's maid. That will keep Mrs. Lane from bothering her, and she'll have more free time. Really, it couldn't be better." He drained his glass and set it beside Molly's.

"I'm so happy for you both. Speaking of Mrs. Lane, did Benedict ever talk to your parents about her?"

"He did. They reminded him that she's been here since before Father was married, and we need to be understanding of her. They did mention she's already talked to them about moving in with her sister in a year or so. Seems she's ready to retire soon. In the meantime, they've told her she needs to be kinder to Kitty and the other servants."

"I'm glad to hear it. It couldn't have been easy for Kitty—or any of the other maids, for that matter."

Fred glanced at the clock. "Speaking of Kitty, I told her I'd meet her in the gardens."

"I wouldn't want you to keep her waiting," Molly said, standing up. "But do tell Roger I'll be in the library if you happen to see him."

"I will. And I want to thank you again. It was your

scheme with Caroline that got it all started. Well, finished. Kitty and I will always be grateful to you both."

As they started out of the room, Roger walked in. "Molly." He said her name like a sigh.

Fred snickered. "I know when it's time to take my leave."

"Oh, don't leave on my account," Roger said, holding the door open wide.

He arched a brow at Roger. "See you two at tea. Dinner? Tomorrow?"

"Goodbye, Fred," Roger said, making sweeping gestures toward the door.

As soon as the door closed after Fred, Molly wrapped her arms around Roger, burying her face in his chest.

He kissed the top of her head, rubbing her back. "Have you had a nice morning?"

"Nicer now that you're back. Where did you go?"

"I had an errand in town. Would you like to go for a ride…Muriel?"

She pulled away to look into his face. "I'm not telling you yet. My goodness, you're impatient."

"Only when it comes to you."

Molly ran her hand down his arm and entwined her fingers with his. "You wanted to go for a ride?"

"I thought we might go out to the lodge." His eyes, full of secret promise, held hers as he brought her hand to his lips and kissed each fingertip.

Molly shivered at his touch and it was all she could do not to throw herself back into his arms. But she'd been far too careless with these intimate embraces of theirs, and anyone could come to the office at any time. She took a step back, his hands tight in hers.

"I'd like that, but I wanted to see Penny first. Where did you leave her?"

Roger looked over her shoulder to the hearth rug. "Penny isn't here?"

"No, I thought she was with you."

"I haven't seen her all morning." Roger released Molly's hand and went about the room, peeking in all the corners.

Molly glanced out the window to the sunlit garden. "Maybe she went outside. The kennels or the quadrangle?"

Roger frowned. "I didn't see her on my way in."

"That's odd. Let's split up and look for her."

"Will you check the other rooms on this floor? I'll go check outside."

"Of course. Try not to worry, I'm sure we'll find her napping somewhere."

After Roger left, Molly followed the first-floor corridors in each wing of the house, checking every room. She'd hoped to find Penny beside the library fire because she was so often there with Roger, but there was no sign of her. Molly had just searched the parlor when Roger caught up with her. She knew his answer before she even finished asking. "Did you find her?"

"No, she's not in any of her usual places outside."

"I've checked all the rooms on the first floor and she isn't here. Oh! Maybe she went somewhere quiet to have her puppies."

Roger ran a hand over his wrinkled brow. "But where? I hope she didn't wander outside last night after I went to bed."

"I doubt she'd leave the house."

"You're probably right." He took her hand and

started out the door. "Let's keep looking."

Molly pulled him to a stop. "It's a huge house, Roger. We should enlist some help."

"We will if we need it."

They wandered through the manor, looking everywhere they could think of. It was after the seventh room that Molly had an idea. "Roger, what if she's in your bedchamber?"

He glanced skeptically at the staircase at the end of the hall. "I don't think she could have made it up all those stairs."

Molly put a hand on his arm. "She might have tried. Penny feels safe with you."

"I didn't see her when I was upstairs earlier."

"Did you look in your closet? Under your bed?"

"No, I wasn't looking for her. I was anxious to get to town."

"Let's look. If she isn't there, we'll get people to help us."

Roger nodded, his face tight.

"Don't worry, we'll find her," Molly reassured him.

She took his arm as they walked upstairs. Molly had never been in his bedchamber before, and even under the circumstances felt slightly nervous. What if someone saw her go in? Though they spent hours alone together, this felt different; she was entering his sanctuary. She loved that he'd invited her up without a second thought.

"Here it is," Roger said when they reached a room on the third floor. The door was standing ajar.

"Look," Molly said excitedly. "She must be in here."

Roger held the door for Molly, then closed it behind them.

Molly had hoped Penny would be standing there wagging her tail, but the spacious room was empty. Two doors opened off the main chamber—perhaps closets or a dressing room?

Roger got down on his hands and knees to peer under the four-poster bed, then sat back on his heels and ran a hand over his face. "She isn't here."

"Listen." Molly cocked her head and held up a finger. "Do you hear that?"

"What?" Roger asked, rising to his feet.

Molly didn't answer, but followed the sound to a half-open door in the corner of the room. She'd known what she would find when she heard that unique little squeak. Or rather, squeaks.

Roger came up behind her. "Penny!"

Penny lay in the dressing room on top of what looked like all of Roger's blankets and half his wardrobe. Her tail thumped as she looked up at them, a litter of tiny puppies at her side.

"Oh, how sweet!" When Molly bent down to pet Penny, the dog barked happily in greeting.

Roger crouched beside Penny and ran a hand along her back. "Good girl, Penny."

Molly surveyed the puppies. It was hard to tell exactly how many there were, but it seemed more than six. "My goodness! How will you get them all home?"

"We have some time before we need to worry about that." Roger sat on the floor and leaned against the wall, his hand resting on Penny's head. "I'm so relieved. I was worried she got outside last night."

"She was safe and sound."

Roger started to get up. "I'll get her some food and water."

Molly placed a hand on his shoulder to keep him from standing. "You stay here. I'll get it. And tea for us."

"You're so thoughtful. Miranda?"

"No," she said, laughing. On her way through Roger's bedchamber, Molly paused to look around, having been too worried about Penny on the way in to give it much notice.

Despite the high ceiling and elegant furnishings, the room felt cozy. Perhaps because of the clutter. An overflowing bookcase and untidy writing desk stood against the far wall, and Roger's mahogany wardrobe hung open. Various shirts, waistcoats and jackets were strewn across the bed and draped over the backs of chairs. On the dressing table, his brushes and cologne sat among a jumble of handkerchiefs and what looked like bits of paper he'd written on. It reminded Molly of her own bedchamber after trying to decide what to wear to a ball. Two floral armchairs and a drop leaf table stood in front of the open windows, the perfect place to have their tea.

Molly continued on her way, practically skipping downstairs. She wanted to get back to Roger as soon as possible. A part of her had worried that over time he'd go back to his reserved ways, even after the lodge, but he was sweeter than ever.

Only one cloud loomed on Molly's blissful horizon—tomorrow her mother arrived, and Molly would have to tell her she wouldn't be taking part in the Season. She just couldn't go through with it now that she had Roger. Her mother would be angry, but what else could Molly do? Though she might be upset, it wasn't as though Mrs. Merriwether could force her to go to town.

When Molly reached the office, she rang the bell

and ordered a tea tray. When it arrived, she put Penny's water and food dish on the tray and carried it upstairs. She had no hands to knock, so nudged the door with her foot. Roger answered after a few moments and took the tray from her.

"How's Penny?" Molly asked as she followed him into the room. She noticed he'd cleared off his bed and tidied up the scattered clothes.

Roger put the tray on the table in front of the windows, then led the way to the dressing room. "She looks tired, but she's taking good care of the puppies."

Molly rested her hand on the small of his back. "Have you gotten a good look at them yet?"

"They're mostly red, but there are a few brown and white ones. That basset."

"After all your care to keep them apart, too."

"My sister will be happy." Roger placed the food and water close to the drowsy dog.

"Oh! I promised I'd let her know about the puppies. If I write a message now, I can send it in the evening post."

Molly turned to go, but Roger caught her hand and took her into his arms. "The letter can wait a few hours, can't it?" He planted a light kiss on her neck as his hand made its way down her back.

"A few hours won't hurt." Molly's heart hammered in her chest as she threw her arms around Roger's neck and kissed him deeply, with not a thought in the world besides him. He swept her into his arms like he had at the ball and, without breaking their kiss, carried her into the bedchamber. At the foot of his bed he pulled away and gave her a questioning look. In answer she brought her lips back to his.

When he laid her on the bed and slid in beside her, Molly shifted her weight so she was almost underneath him. Roger's eyes were a combination of fiery and tender as he looked down at her. His hand went to her blouse, hovered over the buttons for a moment, then stroked her hair.

Molly kept her eyes on his as she unbuttoned the top three buttons of her blouse, took his hand and rested it on her skin. They both shuddered.

Roger's hand shook as he eased it into her blouse and ran his fingers lightly over her collarbone. He pulled her shirt aside and pressed his lips to the humming skin at the base of her throat, then trailed his lips to the lacy edge of her pink corset. Molly tugged at his shirt, pulling it free so she could rest her hand on his naked back. His skin was smooth, silky and warm.

Her heart thundered as, after another questioning look and her fervent nod, Roger moved on top of her. There was never anything so wondrous as his weight pressing her into the bed. Molly ran her hands over his back, through his hair, clinging to him as he kissed her over and over. She loved Roger. She loved him, and didn't know how she'd gone this long in her life without him. It was odd to think she'd thought him cold when they'd met. He was warm, and funny, and loving. And he loved her. She laughed with pure joy.

Roger looked into her eyes, brushing the hair back from her face. "What?"

"I just—I never knew life could be so incredible and full, and I have the feeling every day after today will be even better. Every day, every year. We'll grow closer, and love each other more, and I want to know everything, just everything, about you. I love hearing your voice and saying your name. Roger. Roger Wolfgang Bailey. It's the perfect name, and you're perfect, and—Am I rambling?"

He smiled. "No, you're reading my mind."

Molly ran a finger over his brow, looking into his eyes.

Roger kissed her softly. "Oh, Molly." He gave her a tight hug, then rolled back onto the bed beside her.

She'd never felt anything so wonderful and overwhelming in her life. She glanced at Roger. Had he? As they lay there in silence, Molly was filled with burning curiosity. She didn't know why it was important, and even had a feeling it was rude to ask, especially at a moment like this. But she had to. "Roger, have you ever been in love before?"

He twirled a lock of her hair around his finger. "No. Have you?"

"No. But what about Jane?" she asked, her throat suddenly dry.

Roger put an arm behind his head and looked up at the ceiling. The other arm held Molly tightly against him. "As I told you, I thought it broke my heart when she left. But even at the time I realized I healed from it faster than I would have thought. Looking back, I think my pride hurt more than my heart."

"Did you know her long?"

"Most of our lives. Our grandparents were friends, and Jane and I both grew up knowing they hoped to unite the families."

Molly fought hard to keep down the jealousy. How could she compete with someone Roger had known, possibly loved, his whole life? He said he was over Jane, but it had been less than a year since he lost her. She let out a low sigh, trying to undo the knot in her stomach.

Roger must have noticed her sudden change of mood, because he turned to look at her. "Is something wrong, Molly?"

"What if you really do love Jane? You hardly know me. What if…what if you change your mind about *me*?"

Roger sat up so fast he almost knocked Molly off the bed. "I do know you. I love you, Molly. The reason I know our love is real, and right, is because I've known that wrong kind of love. Some kind of duty masquerading as love. Jane and I were friends and I loved her more as a cousin or family acquaintance. I was going to propose to her because I was supposed to. It took me some time to understand my feelings, but now it's clear I was never in love with her."

Molly fought back tears as she sat up. "But you thought you were. What if you only think you are with me?"

He gripped her hands. "Molly, I love you. I'm so sure of it that I went to a jeweler in Rochester this morning. But that box can stay in my pocket for a week, or a year, or ten years, if waiting makes you more sure of me. I'm certain of my love for you. I—I *feel* you. In my heart, in my soul, in everything I am. I was drawn to you from the first day we met. These last few months, every day I woke up thinking about you, waiting to see you, listening for your voice in conversations around the house. You know how hard I tried to ignore you, foolishly, but I just couldn't. You were so sweet, from the first day, about my ankle, and Penny, and trying to help Caroline and Benedict get together, and then what you did for Kitty. You're thoughtful and considerate. You sat with a drunk man you hardly knew in a tavern. I

343

fell in love with you long before that day in the attic, but I was too scared to admit it to myself, let alone you. That day at your house, in the willow trees, I could have sung when I saw you. You were more beautiful than I remembered, and it was all I could do not to take you into my arms and kiss you until you were dizzy."

Molly was dizzy *now*. Her mind reeled from his declaration, and from a soul-deep certainty that he meant every word. She gazed into his eyes. "I always thought love would make sense. I thought it was neat, and clean, and easy, and…and pleasant. But it's breathtaking, and mesmerizing, and both a whirlwind that tries to sweep you away and the anchor that holds you down. Love makes no sense at all. I was waiting for you all this time and I didn't even know. Something that was missing settled perfectly into my life the moment we met. Roger, does it make sense if I say I *feel* you, too? That's how I know you're the one for me."

"It does make sense. We belong together." He kissed her, chasing every thought away except for *Roger, Roger, Roger.*

When they broke apart Molly wiped away a tear, smiling. "Roger, there's one more thing I think you should know."

"What's that?" he asked and kissed her cheek.

"My name, and then I'd like a look at what's in the box you bought today."

Chapter Twenty-Seven

Roger's eyes brightened. "I finally get to know your name? Tell me, were my guesses close?"

They sat cross-legged on the bed, knees touching.

"Not remotely," Molly said. "But I need your promise—your solemn oath—that you will never call me by this name."

"Ever?"

"Ever. If you can't promise, I can't tell you." Molly folded her arms in front of her, trying to look stern.

Roger put a hand over his heart. "I promise, by all that I hold dear, I will never call you any name but Molly."

Molly took a deep breath. She'd never told anyone this before, not even Caroline. "My name is Lionel."

"Come now, you said you'd tell me," he said, poking her side gently.

She spread her hands wide. "It *is*. My name is Lionel Molly Merriwether."

"You're serious?" he asked, brows raised.

"Yes."

Roger looked like he was trying hard to hold back a laugh. "May I ask why?"

"After three sons, my parents were convinced they'd never have a girl. So when my grandfather asked my mother to name her next child after him, she agreed. He was on his deathbed, you see, and we all know you can't go back on that."

Roger sat for some minutes, apparently trying to decide if it was a jest or not. Finally, he nodded. "Lionel. So, you're a lion, and I'm a wolf?"

Molly's hands flew to her mouth as she started laughing. "I didn't think of that! See? We *are* meant for each other."

"I already knew that." Keeping his eyes on hers, Roger reached into his jacket pocket.

Molly only saw a corner of the box before he tucked it back in. She got to her knees, waiting eagerly for it to reappear.

Roger sat back on his heels and ran a hand through his hair. "I pictured this moment as being more…romantic."

"You've pictured it?" Molly asked, her hands over her heart.

He smiled softly. "From time to time."

"What could be more romantic than this?"

"I feel I should be sweeping you off your feet or taking you by surprise."

"I *am* surprised! All this time I've been wondering what would happen next. I thought you'd want more time to court me or to think things over, or…or…I don't know. Just, more time."

"All I want is time with you, Molly."

She took his hand. "All my time, forever, is yours."

"But what about sweeping you off your feet?" he asked, giving her that smile that always made her knees weak.

"You've already swept me," Molly said, pointing to her feet on the bed.

Roger took her face in his hands and kissed her. "I

think we should have tea."

"You—What?"

"The tea's getting cold."

She looked at him incredulously. "I don't care about the tea."

"I do," he said, as though it was the most important thing in the world. "You brought it all the way up here."

She'd thought she was about to be offered his hand, a ring, a promise, and he offered...tea. "Are you doing this to vex me?"

Roger smiled. "Just go sit at the table and let me serve you."

She sighed, playing along, and went to the table, where Roger poured out tea for her and offered sandwiches and scones.

"Thank you," she said.

"You're welcome." He moved his chair to the other side of the table so he was facing her while they ate. "How was your day?"

"Roger."

"I'd like to know what you did." He sipped his tea, looking relaxed as if they hadn't just shared their deepest feelings and almost become betrothed.

After eating a cucumber sandwich, Molly described her day—the brief time between when they'd seen each other at breakfast and met in the office. "And what did you do, Roger?"

"I had an errand in town. Are you tired after our moonlight stroll last night?"

"Not really. The past few days I've been too happy to be tired."

Roger took her hand and kissed it. "I'm going to check on Penny. I'll be right back."

Molly started to rise.

"No, you stay here. I'll only be a moment."

"All right." She smiled as she watched him go into the dressing room. Sipping her tea, she wondered if Caroline or anyone else had been looking for her this afternoon. This was definitely the last place anyone would guess they'd find her. Molly glanced out the window, watching fluffy clouds float across the blue sky. She rose and went to look at Roger's bookshelf, where she saw a copy of the novel she'd been reading in the attic.

"Molly."

Roger stood in front of the dressing room door, hands behind his back. He'd changed into a clean suit and brushed his hair.

Molly didn't say anything as he crossed the room, but gasped when he went down on one knee in front of her and took her hand. "Molly, I love you. Will you marry me?"

"Yes! Oh, Roger, I love you." Molly wrapped both her hands around his, tears starting in her eyes.

He stood up, took the ring out of his pocket, and slipped it onto her finger. Set into a gold band was a round, sparkling diamond flanked by two smaller ones on either side.

Molly held it up to the light. "It's perfect."

"Like you," he said, taking her into his arms.

"Roger, I must say, that was very romantic."

"There's only one problem."

"What's that?"

He cradled her cheek in his hand. "I haven't seen you blush in hours."

"Perhaps because I'm so comfortable with you

now."

"Nothing could make me happier than that. Still, I do like those blushes."

"Oh, don't worry, they'll be back."

Roger leaned forward and gently brushed his lips on her neck, his hands moving to her hips. "If you're amendable, I have some ideas that might bring them about."

Molly swallowed, her cheeks glowing with color.

Roger smiled triumphantly.

"I'm quite amenable, and put myself in your capable hands," she said.

"And that's where you'll stay," he said and kissed her gently.

Molly tightened her hold on him. "For the rest of our lives."

Chapter Twenty-Eight

Six months later

Trundling along in the carriage toward Waverly Hall, Molly recalled her arrival all those months ago and marveled at the changes since that day. The circumstances couldn't be more different.

For one thing, it was snowing. She'd been watching flurries through her window since leaving The Blue Swan three hours ago. The sky was dense and gray, somehow lower to the snowdrifts covering the ground.

The second difference was that she was alone. Caroline was already at Waverly—her home now. Molly's family had left the inn before her and had probably arrived an hour ago. Mrs. Merriwether would have gladly ridden with Molly, but she knew this was her only chance to have some time to herself before the wedding.

Which led to the third, most wonderful, most important difference about today's journey. Roger was waiting for her. Molly clasped her hands together, smiling. Roger was waiting.

When Molly told her parents that she and Roger were betrothed, her father congratulated her but her mother was furious and hadn't spoken to Molly for a whole day. Mrs. Merriwether's anger hadn't lasted long, however. She was soon reconciled to the engagement and, to hear her tell it, she'd suspected all along that

Roger would be perfect for Molly. He had many qualities she found most pleasing in a son-in-law, not least of which was that her daughter would live only two hours from home.

One thing Mrs. Merriwether had not been willing to compromise on was the wedding date. She insisted it be put off for a few months. Molly had wanted to argue with her but, as Roger said at the time, since they'd deprived Mrs. Merriwether of a Season they shouldn't also deny her the chance to plan an extravagant wedding. Once she realized just how much planning was involved with the nuptials, she'd put her heart into it and spoken of little besides lace, cakes, gowns, and bouquets for the next six months. Fortunately, she never tried to talk to Molly about the honeymoon.

Molly and Roger chose a wedding date just over ten months from the day they'd met. The time had passed more quickly than Molly would have thought, primarily because she'd spent those months getting to know Roger. There was so much to learn about him, and every day brought a new depth of understanding; more trust, more intimacy and, to Roger's delight, more blushes. He was all a betrothed should be and more, and their bond strengthened with each passing day. While their love had at first felt like a sudden flash of lightning or a storm, it had now mellowed to something like a sunrise. Different every day yet always spectacular, always reliable, always a surprise, something so wonderful it made Molly wake with a smile every morning and fall asleep with a sigh each night.

Oh, why was this carriage so slow? Molly peered out the window, waiting to see Waverly appear in the distance. She tapped her foot impatiently until they finally rounded the bend, and there it was. And there *he* was. Standing in the same spot she'd first seen him, Penny at his side. From the looks of it, at least three puppies scampered around at his feet. But Roger didn't appear to notice them. His eyes were fixed on the carriage.

When Molly pulled up to the front steps, Roger rushed down to meet her, but instead of opening the door for her to get out, he opened the door and climbed in.

She brushed snowflakes off his shoulder, laughing. "Roger, what are you doing?"

"I haven't seen you in so long," he said before kissing her.

Molly leaned against him, her arms around his neck. It was as if she was whole again. "It's only been a week."

"But it felt like a year. I missed you."

"I missed you, too." She kissed his cheek, which was still cold from standing outside in the snow.

Molly hugged him tighter, relishing the feel of him. A week really had been too long.

"We can't stay in here all day," Molly said, nestling into Roger's side.

He wrapped his arms around her, kissing the top of her head. "I'd like to. I wish we were already married."

"So do I. Only one more day. This time tomorrow I'll be Molly Bailey." Her chest swelled at the thought.

"To me you'll always be Molly Merriwether." Roger kissed her long and hard, liquifying her bones, then opened the door as if she should be able to get out and walk on her own after that. Fortunately he kept his arm firmly around her waist as they climbed the stairs.

Waverly Hall was almost as full as it had been for Caroline and Benedict's wedding. After removing their heavy coats, Roger took Molly's arm and they made their way to the parlor, where everyone wanted to say hello and offer congratulations. Everyone except Caroline, who waved from a settee across the room.

As soon as she could, Molly joined her.

"I'd get up, but…" Caroline pointed to her stomach, bigger than Molly had expected. She wondered if twins ran in the Clarke family.

Molly leaned down to kiss her cheek. "Stay right where you are."

"Thank you for having the wedding here instead of Hartford. It was so sweet of you to offer."

"We were happy to. Nobody minded, and I couldn't have gotten married without my maid of honor."

"*Matron* of honor," Caroline said, her eyes welling with tears.

Molly handed her a handkerchief. "What's wrong?"

"Nothing, I seem to cry at everything these days. Especially sweet things."

"I'll have to remember that when my time comes."

"Oh, I hope it's soon! I'd love for our babies to grow up together," Caroline said, foregoing the handkerchief and wiping her eyes on her sleeve.

"What's the matter?" Benedict asked as he approached with a slice of cake.

Caroline just cried harder.

"We were talking about the wedding and babies," Molly said.

Benedict set the cake on a side table and rubbed Caroline's back. She leaned into him, smiling at Molly through her tears.

"I'm all right," Caroline said.

"Are you sure?" Molly asked.

"Yes, it happens all the time." Caroline gave Molly a reassuring smile and reached for the cake.

Leaving Caroline in Benedict's capable hands, Molly stood up. "I'm going to see what Roger's doing."

She found him playing with the puppies in the quadrangle. Wrapping her arms around herself, she shuffled across the courtyard. "It's too cold."

"It's invigorating," he said, rubbing his hands on her arms as snow gently fell around them.

She looked into his eyes, brows raised. "It's freezing."

"Come here." Roger took her into his arms, holding her close. His jacket was cold, but being held like this warmed her anyway. Molly lifted her face to his and he kissed her until they were nearly knocked over by five puppies barreling into their legs. They broke apart, laughing.

"I suppose that's my fault," Molly said. "I interrupted you playing with them."

Roger made a snowball and threw it across the yard, sending the puppies careening after it. "It's time to go in, anyway."

She took his arm as they walked inside. "Dinner isn't for hours."

"No, but we both have things to do this afternoon."

Molly sighed, regretting the long, Roger-less hours ahead. "You're right, but I'd rather be with you."

"You will be. But now our mothers and Caroline, not to mention Penny, have plans for you."

Roger gave her one last kiss, then went to find Fred while Molly made her way to the parlor, where she found her mother, Caroline, Mrs. Darby, Aunt Hazel, Penny, and Mrs. Bailey waiting for her. After a leisurely tea, they spent the afternoon upstairs in Molly's room checking on last-minute wedding details, helping her pack for her honeymoon at the lodge, and chatting about their own weddings.

Penny, the only bridesmaid, modeled her gown and demonstrated the way she'd walk down the aisle. At one point she pulled Molly aside to tell her she considered her a real sister, not a sister-*in-law,* and rattled off a list of activities they'd do when Molly and Roger moved to Concord.

After what felt like hours, they all went to the great hall for dinner, and Molly was finally reunited with Roger. She didn't have much of an appetite. All day her anticipation had been growing, and now her entire body seemed filled not with butterflies, but glowing fireflies.

"You're jittery tonight," Roger whispered in her ear.

She stopped tapping her toes at once. "I'm excited."

"So am I. All my dreams are about to come true."

"Mine, too. I wish we were alone. I want to kiss you."

"I'm done eating, so…" He half rose from his chair.

Molly laughed and took his arm. "We'll have to be patient."

Roger sighed theatrically. "Very well. But after dinner, meet me in the office for that kiss."

Later, Roger made good on his promise with a long kiss goodnight. Afterwards Molly retired to her room with Caroline, where they stayed up late talking.

But that had been hours ago. Now Molly tossed and turned in bed, unable to quiet her mind. Of all nights, tonight she needed to get some rest, but it was impossible. She lay in bed vacillating between daydreaming about tomorrow, trying to sleep, and thinking about Roger. How they'd met, when they'd fallen in love, and how perfect he was. At one o'clock, she gave up.

She climbed out of bed and went to look out the window. The snow had stopped, but rolling white drifts blanketed the grounds. Molly walked over to the wardrobe and ran her hands over her wedding gown. It was ivory-colored with delicate orange blossoms embroidered into the bodice, hem, and wide neckline. The long skirt gathered at the waist and cascaded to the floor. A lace veil would complete the ensemble.

One-thirty.

Molly knew what would help. Hot chocolate or a snack. She'd barely eaten at dinner. After slipping into a dark green dressing gown, she made her way downstairs.

Halfway to the dining room, Molly realized there was no way to get hot chocolate at this hour. Well, at the very least, she could take a glass of wine back to her room.

When she entered the yellow drawing room, the first thing she saw was Penny, the dog, sitting beside Roger's chair.

Roger's hand rested on her head, so intent on his book he didn't notice Molly come in. All the tension left Molly the moment she saw him, and she stood for a moment watching him, then crossed the room. "Good evening."

His eyes still on the book, Molly saw his face break into a grin. "Good evening, Miss Merriwether."

Molly gave Penny a pat and stood in front of Roger. "You can only call me that for a few more hours."

"I know," he said in a very satisfied tone. He set his book aside and wrapped his arms around her waist, pulling her close.

She kissed the top of his head. "How long have you been here?"

"Since midnight. I can't sleep."

"Neither can I. I wish I'd known. I would have come down sooner."

"If I'd known you were awake, I would have come to your bedchamber." He looked up into her face, abashed. "To—to talk. I didn't mean—"

"I know what you meant, Roger. And at this point, even if you'd meant something else?" She shrugged, smiling.

"We agreed months ago to wait until our wedding night. I'd never be so bold as to go back on our pact." His eyes roved over her. "Much as I'd like to."

Molly eased herself onto his lap. "This time tomorrow we'll be at the lodge for our honeymoon and will know what we've been waiting for." She leaned in and gave him a deep kiss that left them both breathless.

"Well." Looking dazed, Roger settled his hands on her hips. "What brings you down here?"

"I was going to have hot chocolate, but then I realized I can't wake anyone just for that. So I thought I'd have some wine."

"That's a nice idea. Why don't you sit on the sofa and I'll get it."

Molly settled on the sofa, enjoying the silence and the flames flickering in the fireplace. She and Roger watched the fire, sipping wine as they talked quietly about their day and what they'd do after they went back to Concord and settled into their home on his estate. Roger ran his hand slowly up and down Molly's arm as she leaned against him. It calmed her as nothing else had all night. Wonderfully drowsy and without even being aware of it, Molly fell asleep on Roger's shoulder.

Standing at the altar the next day, Molly's mind flashed back to the last time she'd been here. She'd had an inkling then that Roger cared for her, but she would never have dreamed that less than a year later she'd be standing here beside him, vowing to love and cherish him forever, and Roger would repeat the same promises with tears in his eyes as they slipped gold bands onto each other's fingers.

After the wedding, everyone went back to Waverly for the reception. Molly didn't let go of Roger's hand as they walked among the guests, accepting congratulations. When it was time to dance, she was glad for the excuse to sink into his arms.

Halfway through their second dance, he whispered in her ear. "I want to take you away from here."

Molly's heart leapt. "I'd like nothing more. But the party will go on for hours."

"We don't need to be here for it. Let's slip out. Nobody will notice." Roger's eyes sparkled as he held her gaze.

She laughed. "Of course they will."

"But we do like to make a spectacle of ourselves at weddings, don't we?"

"We do," she said, beaming. "I'll go upstairs to change, then you can slip out after me. You'll need to change, too."

He took her arm and led her to the empty punch room. "Meet me in the front hall in five minutes."

"Thirty." There was no way she'd be ready in five minutes, not unless she left right now and wore her wedding gown to the lodge.

"Too long. Twenty?" Roger pulled her into his arms and gave her a lingering kiss, his hands caressing her bare shoulders.

She shivered with delight. "Twenty."

Molly managed to get back downstairs in fifteen minutes, where she found Roger pacing in front of the door. Without a word he took her hand and they ran outside.

The forest was dark and quiet, with only the carriage's lanterns to light their way. Snow clinging to tree branches shimmered in the moonlight. Molly and Roger didn't speak but sat close to each other, holding hands under the thick blankets covering their legs.

When they reached the lodge, the driver tipped his hat and went on his way. Molly had expected to find it locked up and dark, but someone had come earlier to light the lamps. Almost every window glowed, giving the lodge a welcoming, homey feel.

Roger offered his arm and they climbed the steps to the door. At the top, he swept her into his arms.

Molly squealed and tightened her arms around his neck. "What are you doing?"

"Carrying you over the threshold, of course." He kissed her as they walked through the door, but didn't put her down once they were inside. "Do you want to go to the drawing room?"

Molly looked around the lodge. Whoever'd been here to light the fires had left champagne, wedding cake, and a picnic basket on the table. Soft blankets waited on the sofa in front of the fire, and a silver tea service stood on a cart beside it. It couldn't have been more welcoming.

But Molly had other plans.

Knowing she was turning pink, Molly looked Roger in the eyes. "I'd like to go upstairs."

"Oh, thank goodness," he said with a tremulous laugh.

Roger set her on her feet, and as they climbed the stairs with their arms around each other, Molly's heart doubled its pace.

The turret was colder than the rest of the lodge, but a crackling fire in the bedchamber hearth chased the chill away. The room looked much different than it had the last time, and Molly detected Caroline's hand in it. The old bed hangings had been replaced with white ones, and a new floral quilt covered the bed. Flowers sat on every available surface, and a bottle of champagne and two glasses stood on the bedside table. With, as Molly noticed with a smile, a small jewelry box sitting beside a note that read, "*For your earrings.*"

"This is lovely," she said, turning to Roger.

He pulled her into his arms. "Not as lovely as you."

"You're so sweet, Roger."

"So are you. I might also add beautiful, perfect and…mine."

"*Yours*. I am, truly. And you're mine."

"I feel like I've always been yours. I was just waiting to find you." He kissed her again, more urgently this time. They broke apart after a long moment and stood gazing into each other's eyes.

Molly took Roger's hand, which was not so stable as usual, and led him to the foot of the bed.

"Turn around, Molly," Roger said, his voice husky.

Normally she might have asked why, but after one look at his smoldering eyes she turned, clasping her hands in front of her. Roger ran his fingers over her shoulders and Molly trembled as one by one he gently removed the pins from her hair. The feel of Roger's hands and the heat of his body against hers filled her with longing. At last he'd removed them all, and Molly's hair cascaded over her shoulders. He wrapped his arms around her from the back and she leaned her head on his shoulder for a few moments until she couldn't bear not seeing his eyes. She twisted in his arms and kissed him deeply, openly, oblivious to all but Roger and the waiting bed.

Now that she was here, Molly wasn't sure if she should undress first, or let him do it, or wait a while. Roger answered for her by lifting her into his arms and placing her on the bed, then climbing in beside her. As they lay holding each other tightly in the middle of the giant bed, Molly's body tingled with anticipation.

"I love you," she whispered.

"Oh, Molly, I love you so much."

The words released the sweet tension and answered all of Molly's questions. Roger crushed his lips to hers as they began tugging at each other's clothes, which were gone in the blink of an eye. Passion coursed through Molly at Roger's first touch, and she could hardly fathom the wonder that was his glorious, naked body against hers. She'd never imagined his muscles would be so beautiful or so marvelous to caress.

Roger's smooth, sweet-smelling skin was a miracle she'd never expected, and touching him was the most natural thing in the world. She was amazed at how perfect he felt, and how she didn't feel in the least bit shy. Molly held her breath as his lips trailed down her throat, over her collarbone, to her heart. He soothed her soul but set her body on fire.

"Roger," she sighed.

His name on her lips unleashed a new passion, and when Roger moved on top of her, Molly's whole world opened wide.

Afterward, as they lay entwined in each other's arms, Molly marveled at the feelings she'd never known existed and at the impossibly deep love she had for Roger.

He gazed at her in wonder. "I had no idea anything could feel as incredible as this."

"Neither did I. We should have married months ago," Molly said, resting her hand over his heart.

Roger laughed and brushed a hair off her shining face. "I agree. Just think, from now on we'll go to bed together every night."

"And wake in each other's arms every morning." She nestled into his chest, her fingers stroking his shoulder.

"Our life will be wonderful, and it's all thanks to you."

Molly kissed his chin. "And you."

"You helped me open my heart again, Molly, and now it's yours."

"You supported me when I needed it most, you trusted me and let me be my true self around you. I'm so glad I fell into that pond and got lost in the woods."

Roger laughed. "And hid in the attic?"

Molly smiled, recalling that day. They'd been so close when she'd stood in his arms, and now she knew he'd already been in love with her. The thought pulsed through her like rays of sunshine. "I loved those afternoons because they brought us closer, and you were so sweet when I was upset about Caroline."

A light tone crept into his voice. "I must admit the second day I knew you'd be up there. Well, I hoped."

She raised her head to look at him. "And I foolishly believed your little ruse about needing a quiet place to finish your book."

"It was the best excuse I could come up with. I knew you wouldn't turn me away, and I'd have said just about anything to spend time alone with you."

"Now you can be alone with me as often as you like." She leaned in to kiss him. "I love you, Roger."

"I love you, too." Roger's hand caressed her hip. "Are you tired?"

"Not in the least," she said. Her hands had begun to wander of their own accord.

Roger looked into her eyes. "We have all night."

The tenderness had been replaced with a sultry look that sent Molly's pulse off at a gallop. "If we stay up long enough, we'll be able to watch the sunrise," she said, pressing herself against him.

"Our first sunrise as husband and wife—we don't want to miss it." Roger's leg hooked around hers as he drew her closer.

Molly would have answered, but his kisses kept her distracted for quite some time.

The next morning, they stood on the top turret as the sun peeked over the trees and cast a dazzling light over the snowy forest. Molly's arms were wrapped around Roger, who held a blanket around them both.

"This was worth staying up for," Molly said.

Roger put a hand on the back of her neck and drew her in for a long, soft kiss. "Watching the night fade to dawn while I held you in my arms was worth staying up for. I don't think I slept at all."

"Neither did I, but somehow I'm not very tired."

He touched her cheek. "We still have a week here."

"I could do with two more, at least." She tightened her arms around him. "But now I think it's time for tea. I'm so hungry. Aren't you?"

"I haven't thought of anything besides you since we arrived. But I suppose breakfast would be welcome."

"We'll eat, and then do whatever strikes our fancy for the rest of the day."

Molly was well aware of what they'd be doing all day and couldn't be happier. In fact, nothing on earth could make her happier than Roger did, no matter what they were doing. The joy she'd found with him was strong, solid, and eternal. Molly felt like happiness itself and the feeling was hers forever, because Roger was hers forever. Looking into his eyes, the world disappeared. There was no yesterday, no tomorrow; only today, only now. Only their love, and the knowledge that their fates were entwined, and they'd be together for the rest of their lives. Smiling, Molly took Roger's hand and led him downstairs for tea.

Epilogue

Almost a year to the day after their wedding, Lionel Wolfgang Bailey was born, much to the delight of his parents. Before long he was joined by Roger, Victoria, Eliza, and Basil. Their home was full of love, laughter and, naturally with five children, noise.

Over the years, Molly often marveled at the quirk of fate that had brought her and Roger together. She'd gone to Waverly Hall for Caroline to find love, not herself. Sometimes she wondered what would have happened if she hadn't gone out in the rain that night, or if either one of them had let their fear stand in the way of telling the other how they felt. What if, that day in the attic, Roger had left her alone and they'd never grown closer? But somehow Molly knew, even if she hadn't gone to Rochester, they would have found each other. Maybe she would have been at a ball in town, and he would have asked her to dance. Perhaps she would have finally convinced her brothers to take her to a tavern and she'd have spied a handsome man across a smoke-filled room, reading a book. Unlikely, but possible, because without a doubt fate would have brought them together.

Now, years later, Molly's heart still leapt when Roger unexpectedly walked into the room or came up and wrapped his arms around her. She loved nothing more than the simple pleasures they shared—taking walks, reading together, watching the children play, riding out into the forest or lying in each other's arms at the end of the day, talking about anything and everything.

As for Roger, he never shut Molly out again. He remained open and honest for the rest of their lives and supported her in all of her endeavors. With Molly by his side, his plans were fulfilled and dreams became realities. Through the years, Roger continued to delight in her blushes, probably because he was so adept at causing them.

Every day together brought new joy and understanding and, though she could never tell Caroline, Roger eventually became Molly's best friend. In tender moments she always knew he would call her Molly Merriwether and for the rest of their lives, if ever Roger piqued her, he once more became *Mr.* Bailey.

A word about the author...

Kate Ellington grew up in a small, woodsy town not far from the New England seacoast. She read her first historical romance at age eleven when a teacher challenged her to find a book in the library written by an author she'd never heard of. Thus began a lifelong love of love stories.

She currently resides in the Pacific Northwest with her delightful family and three cats. When not writing she can be found reading, baking, traveling and spending time outdoors.

Thank you for purchasing
this publication of The Wild Rose Press, Inc.

For questions or more information
contact us at
info@thewildrosepress.com.

The Wild Rose Press, Inc.